Where the hell was the airfield?

The desert was unrolling ahead of me, the air currents were throwing me around, and so far as I could judge I was only just going to miss the edge of the storm.

Where was the bloody airfield?

I flipped the landing-light switch, both to arm the fuse on one tank and illuminate the lamp on the other, and in the same instant caught sight of the parked Boeing. I checked its appearance and saw the PIA lettering, knew there was no mistake. I was there.

I swept out of the turn and into a steep dive, pressed down on the firing button then hauled back on the stick, gave her full throttle and soared upward. At three thousand feet I rolled over on to my back, turned to survey the scene below.

I wasn't leaving until I knew if I had scored . . .

"The continent-hopping pace is swift, plot intricasies delightfully eye-popping, and technical detail solidy convincing . . . a top-notch thriller."

— *Publishers Weekly*

"A novel that crackles with international excitement. Ground Zero is great entertainment."

— *Press Register*
Mobile, Alabama

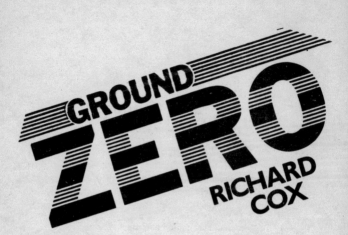

GROUND ZERO

RICHARD COX

BERKLEY BOOKS, NEW YORK

GROUND ZERO

A Berkley Book / published by arrangement with
Stein and Day, In˙.

PRINTING HISTORY
Stein and Day edition published 1985
Berkley edition / July 1987

ISBN: 0-425-10010-3

A BERKLEY BOOK ˙ TM 757,375
Berkley Books are published by The Berkley Publishing Group,
200 Madison Avenue, New York, NY 10016.
The name "BERKLEY" and the "B" logo
are trademarks belonging to Berkley Publishing Corporation.

PRINTED IN THE UNITED STATES OF AMERICA

10   9   8   7   6   5   4   3   2   1

Acknowledgments

I owe a debt of gratitude to many people who assisted with this book, especially Colonel Don McBride, a former Sabre pilot; Mr. Peter Barclay, who generously lent me working space; my wife Francesca who both helped clarify my thoughts and typed the manuscript; and, last but not least, Mr. Peter Grose, who long encouraged me to write this particular story.

I SHOULD HAVE smelled a rat from the start. But the Savoy Hotel is no bad address. Why shouldn't an international oil company be interviewing job applicants there? Besides, if you were a pilot who'd been without regular flying for nine months and was worried about keeping his licenses in date, would you start asking why an American firm that had a London office wasn't using it? For sure I wasn't going to. I was as happy as Larry to be interviewed at all. Having only heard about the advertisement several days after it appeared, I reckoned a hundred others might have applied ahead of me. Airlines have been shedding flight crews like autumn leaves these last couple of years. Someone else was bound to have got in first. I didn't realize they'd allowed for that until much later.

"COMPANY PILOT SOUGHT BY INTERNATIONAL OIL CONSORTIUM," the advertisement had run. "MINIMUM 2,000 HOURS COMMAND TIME ON JETS. G3 RATING DESIRABLE. BASED EUROPE. REPLY BOX 25302."

All very straightforward. The G3—the Grumman

Gulfstream Mark 3, to give it the full name—is a marvelous aircraft too. A company jet that's as sleek and fast as a dream. True, I'd never flown one. But I did have twice the flying hours they wanted. That must have counted, I decided, when a man with a New York accent phoned and asked me to be at the Savoy at 3:00 P.M. I didn't argue: simply canceled my afternoon stint at the car showroom, polished my shoes, and took a bus to the Strand. The man had said they'd pay travel expenses, but I wasn't chancing cash on taxi fares, not on my present income.

Some people are born salesmen. Without question I'd rather be what I am, which is a natural-born pilot and a pretty professional one at that. Flying is my business, not selling, and this showroom job was a last resort. Probably the fact that I'm in my late thirties, keep my hair cut short, and look tolerably honest was my problem. Selling secondhand cars is a rogue's game, and people expect to buy from someone twice as smooth as butter. Anyway, whatever the reason, my honest-Injun patter had sold very few. I was expecting the sack any moment.

In case you don't know the Savoy Hotel, it lies in the heart of London between the Strand and the river. From the Strand side you enter a vast reception lobby, with armchairs and sofas to the left and a range of reception and porters' desks to the right. The whole area is heavily policed by flunkeys in pearl gray uniforms. I mention this because the Continental and Oriental Oil Corporation had evidently been taking care of the staff. The suites are only identified by room numbers, yet when I asked for their number, the response was slavishly cordial.

"Captain Lloyd? Yes, sir, you are expected, sir." The receptionist was obsequious. He lifted a house phone and announced my arrival, though I noticed his eyes flick over me appraisingly. I suppose hotel clerks develop the same instincts as customs men, always looking for giveaways. Even if this one didn't like my squadron tie—and I don't go much for the ex-service image myself—he wasn't revealing any distaste. "The page will show you up at once, sir."

A little runt in a dwarf's version of the gray unifom led me to the lift and then along deep-pile-carpeted passages for what seemed like a half a mile until he knocked on a door and ushered me into the suite.

The room was elegant enough, but I hardly noticed the furnishings. What dominated the scene was the man who welcomed me. It was not his physical size, because he wasn't tall or hefty, it was plain physical presence. The first thing that struck me was a villainously hooked nose and heavy-lidded eyes, set in what police descriptions call a swarthy complexion. Yet it was a thin, keenly edged face, and when he moved forward I realized that under the conventional blue suit his whole body was as lean as a long-distance runner's. His thick black hair was cut short in the French style, *en brosse*, which looked incongruous on an Arab—I assumed he was an Arab—though it did fit the athleticism. Nor did the sharp New York accent seem right.

"Glad to meet you, Captain Lloyd. My name's Arain," he said, gripping my hand firmly and smiling. The smile did something to soften the image. "Meet Captain Newland, CONOIL's chief pilot."

I shook hands dutifully with the other man, who seemed a completely conventional aviation type: broad face, crinkles around the eyes, the steady look of a pilot who's watched thousands of miles of tarmac runway coming up at him and knows he'll see many thousands more before he's through. The kind who isn't going to let girls or gambling get between flying and his judgment. He was the man I would be directly answerable to if I got the job, though I knew the decision would be the Arab's.

"You brought your license and logbooks?"

I approved of the question. Those blue-bound log-

books recorded every minute I had spent at the controls
of an aircraft. They might look uninspiring to an out-
sider, but to a professional they were the documentary
proof of wide experience as a jet fighter pilot and an
airline captain. They said a lot more about my abilities
than a series of puffed-up job titles ever could.

Newland seemed happy. He flipped through the
pages, scrutinizing occasional entries, then gave the
books back. "You have the kind of background we
need. Only thing we would have liked is a G3 endorse-
ment." He glanced at the Arab. "Have you any questions, Mr. Arain?"

"What went wrong in Dubai, Captain Lloyd? Why
was your contract terminated?" Arain was holding the
CV I had sent. "You have any kind of reference from
them?"

"I didn't ask for one." Hell, if he'd guessed that
much what did he expect me to say? In my book an
Arab is an Arab is an Arab, which means Arabs can be
the biggest bastards in the world. Lawrence of Arabia
admired the noble Bedu, but he didn't know them after
they found oil. The most charitable explanation was
that wealth had undermined their characters. I looked at
the man confronting me, at the dark eyes gazing back.
Maybe he was Americanized enough to understand.
"My contract was terminated for personal reasons," I
conceded.

Arain just went on staring at me, waiting.

"I was taxiing a 727. There'd been a sandstorm
earlier, there was a lot still on the tarmac. Some blew up
over the sheikh. I was fired."

"And deported?"

"They didn't give me long to pack." I still felt angry
at the memory. They had put me on the next plane to
London, and I never got a penny compensation. I'd
been warned that was the kind of chance you took if you
worked in the Gulf and I hadn't really believed it.

"So it was no reflection on your flying ability?" Arain was still pressing.

"Emphatically not." The question was an insult. I had been rated "above average" from flying school onward, which was a classification the RAF did not award lightly.

"Cool it, Captain," Newland interrupted. "Now, let's just go back over your career again. You had twelve years in the RAF, right?"

"Flying Hunters, Phantoms, and, later, Nimrods. That's how I got the civil license." The Nimrod was a maritime reconnaissance development of the old Comet airliner, and captaining one had gained me my airline transport pilot's ticket.

"Then you joined Laker, but three years later Laker folded?"

"Correct." I bit back a different set of feelings this time. I had admired Freddie Laker. It had been a bad time for others too. Continental had shed two hundred pilots. Braniff had gone under.

"OK, so that was the recession," Newland said, reading my thoughts. "After that you flew for an air-taxi service, then you had this contract with the Dubai government's air wing . . .?"

"And now?" Arain asked, none too softly. I reckon he hadn't liked my attitude.

"I'm working as a car salesman," I admitted. It hurt.

"We all have to live." Newland was more sympathetic. "You're supporting your ex-wife?"

"So far as I can."

"Join the club." Newland grinned. He was definitely the prisoner's friend. "Well, Captain Lloyd, we're still seeing people, but you have the qualifications. We'll be in touch. I mean that. Either way, we'll let you know."

As a matter of fact I would have trusted him to do that anyhow. When we shook hands I reckoned that I was in with more than just a chance. What surprised me more was Arain's conciliatory farewell.

"Don't judge all Arabs by a single experience," he said. "They have good and bad, like anyone else."

I didn't agree, and I'm sure he knew it.

I left the Savoy, declining the top-hatted doorman's offer to hail a taxi, and walked briskly out into the Strand again. A fresh May wind was gusting along the street, and I was glad to jump on a bus at the traffic lights. It was already four and I saw little point in returning to the car showroom.

The bus took me near where I lived in what real estate agents euphemistically called the "Chelsea-Fulham" borders of southwest London, where newly arrived middle-class residents believe they're creating an alternative Sloane Ranger stamping ground among the endless drab Victorian terraces. I had bought an apartment there after my divorce for different reasons: it was cheap and I could manage without a mortgage.

Maybe if I had the correct public-school background and hadn't depended on scholarships and grants to get a science degree, I would be less apprehensive about long-term debt. Maybe when I'm fifty I'll be more status-conscious where housing is concerned. As things were, or rather had been, I had scraped through with the remains of my RAF gratuity and a bank loan that I paid off month by month from my Laker salary. It hadn't been easy, what with the maintenance for my ex-wife, Mary Anne, having first call on my income. But now I was immensely glad I had made the effort. Having a home of my own had saved my bacon, even if it was only the ground floor of a converted house near Fulham Broadway. Furthermore, the couple upstairs were as decent, honest, working-class Londoners as you could hope to meet, which was a huge bonus when I was away, as good as having resident caretakers in fact.

Flying was what had broken my marriage, ironically, given that in retrospect I'm sure Mary Anne had only accepted me because of the uniform. She was dead set on being a wing commander's wife, and as I discovered what promotion meant I became equally determined not to wind up piloting a desk. She had the nerve once to suggest that if I'd been properly educated I would appreciate the importance of rank. No one was particularly surprised that she departed in the proverbial cloud of dust when I announced my resignation, though it was more than the statutory two years before we got divorced.

In character I admit to being as amenable as a mule on occasion, and flying was my life, the thing I was best at, an occupation that gave me incomparable satisfaction. I could stagger back into the crewroom, bleary-eyed after a nine-hour patrol in the Nimrod, and feel no greater ambition than to fly again tomorrow. As for the Phantoms, those had stretched my faculties exhilaratingly further. But one must be a realist. The fighter jock's career is over in his mid-thirties, when experience ceases to compensate sufficiently for slowed reactions. So I had said good-bye to Mary Anne, half-expecting her to come back, and opted for commercial flying, which would keep me in the air, and well paid, until I was fifty-five. Except that the recession had intervened.

The silver lining to the recession had been called Susie Winter, and you'd have to go a long way to find someone with a less appropriate nametag. She was a beauty, Susie, and far from cold. Tall, with long brown hair that she pinned up when she was going on duty, a welcoming smile, and a kind of sexy warmth in her voice. She was an air hostess with Gulf Air, and we had met at Dubai airport when we were both waiting for crew transport that was late. Mine came first so I gave her a lift to the Hilton, and we wound up having dinner together.

Now, a year and a half later, Susie had been the instrument of my introduction to CONOIL, and that in spite of our having broken up four months ago.

By all the laws of nature the evening at the Hilton

should have been the beginning and end of the affair. I never knew where the ruler or his family would want to be flown next, and she wasn't even based in the Middle East. Susie was one of only a few European stewardesses on Gulf Air's international routes, basically employed to keep Western passengers happy, but she had such problems fending off amorous Arabs that Gulf eventually agreed to her living in London. Air hostesses tend to go one of two ways in the Gulf, and I admired Susie for turning down the more profitable direction. More than that, when chance deposited us both in the same place a number of times, culminating in a week when the ruler was in London, I fell in love with her. She moved into the Fulham apartment and naturally was there a lot more often than me until we lost our jobs, both for roughly similar reasons. She had some kind of quarrel with the management. I never discovered the details, though I imagined that a sheikh she had refused to shack up with was the ultimate cause. I was wrong, as it turned out. In fact, I misunderstood what made Susie tick in a lot of ways.

The first was in supposing that knowing as much as she did about the job hazards of commercial flying, she would sympathize indefinitely with my being down on my luck.

When the crunch had come and we were back in London scouring the "Situations Vacant" columns in aviation journals, Susie had simply barreled along to British Caledonian at Gatwick and a week later had been treading the skies again in that neat tartan uniform of theirs. Meanwhile, I had to go after what freelance air-taxi work I could get. Though I tried to fit in with her roster, I was invariably offered jobs at short notice, and we saw less of each other than when I was in the Gulf. Within months of my leaving Dubai she had melted out of my life. Until she rang and told me about the CON-OIL advertisement.

"Is that you, Tom?" she had asked, as nervously as

if we had met accidentally in the street. "How are things?"

"So, so," I had replied. I didn't want to mention that I had been forced to take the job at the car showroom. "And with you?"

For a minute or so we had shadowboxed, keeping emotion at bay, and I was wondering why she had phoned at all, when she abruptly came to the point.

"Listen, Tom. Did you see last week's *Economist*? There's an ad for a company pilot." Then her confidence had tailed off, and she had added lamely, "I was afraid you might have missed it."

"Last week's?" I had asked, thinking fast. She was damn right. *The Economist* hadn't occurred to me as a placed to look. Come to think of it, I was astonished that Susie read the magazine. "Did you take the address?"

She had spelled it out and rung off, leaving everything in the air with a vague, "Take care of yourself, sweetheart." Perhaps she had guessed I was too broke to ask her out for dinner.

Yet the fact remained that Susie had surfaced and tried to help. I made myself some coffee in the galley kitchen and attempted for the hundredth time to puzzle out what had really gone adrift in our relationship.

One day I had found a list written in her large, rounded handwriting on the back of an envelope lying on the counter in the kitchen. She'd obviously been distracted and forgotten it. "Omelette pan," it began, "paring knife, herb jars . . ." I had assumed it was a shopping list until I read "apron." Hell, the apron was hanging behind the door as usual, shiny and printed all over with a huge Union Jack. Suddenly I had realized. She was moving out. Those were all the things she'd brought to the apartment. I don't think I'll ever forget the moment I realized exactly what that list meant. There had been nothing I could do about it, either. She was en route to Lusaka, six thousand miles away in

Africa, and before she was due back I would be off on a
three-day stint flying a businessman around Scotland.
In the end I had just left a huge bunch of red roses with
a note saying, "I love you, Tom," and put the list near
it. Maybe she would change her mind.

Two days later when I returned to the apartment the
herb jars were gone. Propped in their place was a long
and emotional letter that told me the future was "just
too uncertain." She had been crying her heart out but
"Please don't write or phone, darling. That would only
make things worse."

A lot can happen in fifteen weeks. Jesus, a lot had
happened. Susie was gone. The air-taxi firm had gone
under, and here I was on my tod, trying to sell cars and
answering magazine advertisements like a newly qualified twenty-year-old. Unemployment does things to
one. I had all this skill, all this experience, and no one
wanted it. Except perhaps CONOIL. I could only hope
Newland had liked me.

The interview at the Savoy had been on Thursday.
When I went back to the car showroom on Friday morning no one seemed to have been worried by my absence.
Then, after lunch, the manager called me in. Jack Morgan was one of those outwardly jovial sporting types,
who wore a handlebar mustache and a blue blazer and
pretended the mechanics were "blinding him with science." Altogether he behaved as if he didn't know a
control from a condom. Underneath he was as sharp as
they come, and he didn't bother with inviting me to sit
down.

"Tom," he said, glancing up from a wide desk ornamented with racing-car models. "Your heart's not in
this trade, is it?" I knew the Christian name bit was due
to my being a pilot. Secretly all garage owners want to
be aces. But there was a nasty edge to his bonhomie.
"We like our sales staff to show willing, right? That
could include being here. What the hell were you up to
yesterday afternoon?"

"I went for an interview." There was no point in arguing. It would only be demeaning and he knew my background.

"And never bloody warned anyone you had a buyer for the Merc?"

"What buyer?"

"What buyer, he asks!" Morgan indulged his Welsh ancestry in a moment of dynamics. "Jesus wept! You have an American here who's leaving tomorrow. He wants the car. You promise him the service history, and when he calls no one knows what he's talking about!" His face was flushed with genuine anger now. "Well, he's gone forever and you can bloody follow him. Don't you even think of your own commission on twenty-seven grand?" Morgan buzzed his secretary. "Mary, get Mr. Lloyd's cards out will you. He's leaving us." He clicked the intercom switch back and glared at me.

"Listen, Mr. Morgan." I kept my cool. "No American asked me for anything yesterday." It was the truth.

"Are you calling me a liar?" Morgan stood up his full five foot seven. "You promised this Yank the details. He was livid. I spoke to him myself." His fury suddenly collapsed, as if he knew he was pursuing a hopeless cause. "You're fired Lloyd. And don't expect me to fly your next airline. If you find one."

There was no point in protesting. I left, wondering why I'd been set up, and by whom. It crossed my mind that the mysterious American could have been Arain or Newland, except that there was no reason for them to put me out of work. Morgan was devious enough to have invented the whole saga. Only one thing was certain: I needed the CONOIL job more than ever.

Thank God, I wasn't kept in suspense long. The phone rang at breakfast time on Saturday.

"Captain Lloyd. This is Newland here. We have a proposition for you, but we're leaving pretty soon. Can you come to the Savoy right now?" I said I could. "Great." Newland paused, hesitating apparently. "Just so there's no misunderstanding. We found a guy with a G3 rating. That vacancy's filled. This is something different, kind of unusual, but it could fit your experience.''

"What is it?''

"We'll explain. I just didn't want you having any wrong expectations.''

"So long as it's flying,'' I said.

"It's flying, OK,'' Newland assured me. "And the pay's high.'' He rang off.

This time I didn't quibble about taxi fares, and I was in the Savoy Hotel twenty-five minutes later.

Two suitcases stood in the tiny vestibule of the suite, a beige Burberry lying across them. Newland's departure was obviously imminent.

"Come on in,'' he called.

Arain and he were seated on either side of a low gilt table with a tray and cups on it. The sun was shining in through the windows, and this time I noticed that there was a view of the Thames beyond the trees outside.

"Take a seat, Captain.'' Newland indicated an elegantly upright armchair. "I'm glad we found you home. Coffee?''

He went on talking as he poured me a cup. "Like I told you, the Gulfstream slot has been filled. However, Mr. Arain and I were impressed by your military experience. Highly impressed.''

"Thank you,'' I murmured, taking the coffee and wondering where this was leading.

"I guess if you've been in the Gulf,'' Newland continued, "you know how much military flying is done under contract. Uncle Sam has pilots in Saudi. The Russians have them all over the goddam place. Sometimes there's no secret about the fact, sometimes there is.''

I nodded. He was perfectly right. Whether you called them officers on secondment, or contract officers, or simply mercenaries, the Middle East was crawling with expatriate pilots doing the high-performance combat flying that the Arabs could pay for but not yet do satisfactorily themselves. At one end of the scale you had a few ex-RAF officers instructing for the Sultan of Oman; at the other there was the Libyan Air Force with hundreds of Russians, East Germans, North Koreans, and Pakistanis, not to mention a few Americans. What I had been doing in the Dubai Air Wing was only a civilianized version of the same principle. Even the air traffic control in the Emirates was solidly expatriate.

But in what way could an oil company be involved?

"Would you have any scruples about that kind of flying?" Arain asked, his eyes locking on to mine like a rangefinder, and in the same instant I knew he had set me up at the showroom. Therefore he must want my services, or the services of someone with my skills, extremely badly. The flying was not likely to be legal either, which suggested a string of corollaries more connected with cash than morals.

"If I do have scruples," I said curtly, staring straight back at him, "they won't be altered by selling or not selling a secondhand Mercedes. Why don't you lay your cards on the table, Mr. Arain?"

"Maybe we should explain the background, huh?" Newland suggested, fixing my estimate of him as conclusively as film developer fixes a negative. He was the soft touch and Arain was the hard guy. It's an old, old trick and I knew all about it from the course in resisting interrogation. The two pretend to be in dispute, so that you start trusting the friendly one.

"OK," Arain said, as if giving way reluctantly. "Let's put our problem in context." He vouchsafed me a quick, sharp smile, the sort that cuts ten percent off a contract in as many seconds.

"We do have a problem, Captain Lloyd, and you could help us solve it."

"In the Gulf?"

"In Libya. To be exact, with Libya's ruler, Colonel Muammar Qaddafi. Are you familiar with the action he

took against American oil companies there a few years
back? I'll remind you. In November 1981 Exxon was
forced out. In March 1982 President Reagan imposed
the oil embargo. That July, Mobil ceased operations. In
October we had to quit ourselves. The Libyan National
Oil Company gained control of most of the output. You
with me?''

I was, though baffled as to how I fitted into the picture.

"Right," Arain continued. "Qaddafi led OPEC into
the 1973 oil price hike that triggered the recession. Having gotten control of Libya's oil he'd have liked a repeat
of 1973, but with the slump in demand there's been no
way he could fix it. Now he's short of cash. He hates the
United States for everything from the Sixth Fleet being
off the Gulf of Sirte to Reagan throwing out Libyan
students. He hates the Israelis even more. He also hates
the Saudis, the Sudanese, King Hussein of Jordan, and
the Egyptians, who all have American alliances. What if
at one stroke he could simultaneously boost the oil price
and cripple his enemies—Arab, Jew, and American
alike?''

Because Arain had something of the performer in
him, he left the question hanging. The answer was so
obvious that I threw it away.

"Qaddafi's been trying to spark off a Middle East
war for years," I said dismissively. "But he won't succeed, even with Iraq fighting Iran and Lebanon in
chaos." Qaddafi set off plots at the rate Catholics light
candles. In the Gulf he was regarded as something of a
buffoon, albeit a dangerous and charismatic one.

"You don't think so, Captain?" Newland intervened.
"He's been financing terrorism most any place you care
to name—Northern Ireland, London, Germany, Sardinia, Morocco, Kenya. Who tried to have the U.S. am-
bassador in Paris murdered? Who's been infiltrating
saboteurs into Sudan? You believe he invaded Chad for
anything else than its uranium?''

"He hasn't the clout to start a full-scale war," I insisted.

"You're wrong, Lloyd," Arain said quietly. "This autumn he'll have the bomb."

That did make me sit up: metaphorically and physically. In my book it won't be the superpowers who ignite the nuclear holocaust: in the final analysis their heads of state are aware of what mutual destruction means. It's in the Third World that the bomb will be let off by a leader so fanatically determined to cripple some age-old enemy that he neither assesses, nor even cares, whether his own country can escape retribution. And what if his own country is predominantly desert and its wealth is underground?

"How do you know Qaddafi has it?" I asked, though the concept of an Islamic bomb had been public property since a BBC television program revealed a few years ago that Qaddafi was paying Pakistan to construct a nuclear weapon.

"We built up quite a network of contacts in Libya over the years. Oil companies have to. Oil always gets mixed up with politics. We didn't drop our informants when we had to go. The company just opened some new Swiss bank accounts. Word about the bomb began leaking out a couple of months ago. Last week we heard the delivery date. It's September 1, Libya's National Day."

"You're certain?" I struggled to recall the Islamic bomb story. Qaddafi had come to an arrangement with President Bhutto of Pakistan sometime in the early seventies. Alongside their peaceful nuclear-power projects, Pakistani engineers had begun assembling a plant for enriching uranium, and so creating weapons-grade material, thanks to extremely astute equipment purchases in Europe. But Bhutto had been overthrown, and in 1979 he was hanged in Rawalpindi jail.

"Didn't that alliance die with Bhutto?" I queried.

"No, sir," Newland chipped in emphatically. "It did not."

"Sure, it soured relations for a while," Arain conceded. "Qaddafi had paid Pakistan upward of five hundred million dollars, and although no one knows how much had stuck to Bhutto's fingers, the Libyans weren't writing off that kind of investment. Not when neither the Kahuta nor the Sihala plants were controlled by international nonproliferation agreements. Qaddafi could put the screws on the Pakistani experts employed in Libya, too." Arain allowed himself a gesture of distaste. "Personally, I imagine any Pakistani government would have continued with the bomb, if only to retain a balance of power with India. And now General Zia is turning the country into a Fundamentalist Muslim state."

I needed no further convincing. You can't work in an Arab country without appreciating the stern, inflexible, almost mindless devotion of the fanatical Muslim to his creed. The two most extreme of the day's Islamic leaders were the Ayatollah Khomeini in Iran and Colonel Qaddafi in Libya. Both, though from different angles because Khomeini was a Shia Muslim, were committed to holy wars, not only to destroy Israel and recover Jerusalem, but equally—as Arain had pointed out—to destroy the Saudi monarchy and liberate Islam's most holy place of all, Mecca.

To understand the mentality you have to go back a century to the Mahdi's hordes, high on drugs, sweeping like fire through the Sudan and killing Gordon at Khartoum. Losses do not count in the equation.

"We have to stop those weapons reaching Qaddafi," Newland cut in. "Otherwise we'll all be out of business. Arabia will go up in smoke. The Saudi monarchy will be overthrown. No oil will get out through the Straits of Hormuz. Iraq and Syria will close ranks with Libya, if the Russians don't take them over first—1973 will look like it was a kid's baseball game. This time the whole economic structure of the West will collapse."

"Would you feel any scruple about helping prevent

that?" Arain demanded, and went on before I could answer. "We would not." His harsh accent had mellowed into an impressively deliberate way of speaking. "When this information came into our hands, we knew we had to act on it."

"How about the Israelis?" I demanded. "They destroyed the Osirak reactor in Iraq fast enough. What are they doing about this?"

"That we don't know," Newland commented, wryly. "They're none too communicative with strangers and we have no interests in Israel. But Osirak was within the range of their air force and Tripoli isn't."

"They could shoot down the plane transporting the bomb," I argued.

"Not when it's a scheduled civil flight with half a load of passengers. That would be inviting reprisals against El Al. The only government that would take the risk is the Soviet Union, and they're interested in destabilizing the Middle East, not calming it down."

So that was it. Newland had at last put their cards on the table himself. They wanted me to shoot down the plane. "You say it will be a scheduled flight?" I asked.

"Yes. In effect." Newland bent over the map, tracing a route. "We're told that a combination Boeing, its freight already loaded, will be substituted at the last moment for a regular PIA service from Karachi to London, flying the usual route via Dubai until it makes an unscheduled landing at Rome. There they'll off-load the passengers and head south to Tripoli." He straightened up. "A fighter based in Malta or Sicily could bring it down over the sea."

"A handful of Pakistanis would lose their lives," Arain said dispassionately. "Millions in the Middle East would survive. So would our company."

I had to admire the way he still made no mention of money, even though if I accepted I would be a mercenary pure and simple. He had stuck to the political justification as a worthier motive, and it was a potent

one. The only snag I could see was that the scheme was
totally unworkable. Outside of a James Bond movie,
that was.

"I'm sorry," I said, "but it can't be done."

"You know how much CONOIL's daily take is?"
Arain replied, and the tautness was back in his tone. He
clearly didn't like having ideas rejected. "Our output from Libyan wells alone ran neck and neck with
Mobil's. Sixteen thousand barrels of oil a day. At
twenty-seven dollars a barrel. Figure it out and you have
more than a hundred and fifty-seven million dollars a
year. That's what we lost in one country. Overall, our
Middle Eastern production is worth ten times as much.
You think we wouldn't spend a few weeks' profit to
safeguard it?"

"Why not buy the Italian Air Force then?" I wanted
to jolt him and I succeeded. He turned as near purple as
an Arab can. But before he could get a word out I explained. "An interception needs backup. Even if no one
asked questions about my taking off from Malta or Sicily with guided missiles mounted on a civil jet, I
couldn't just hang around the sky waiting for the PIA
Boeing to come past. Not only would I have the Italian
Air Force investigating me, I'd never find the airliner
itself without directions from the ground. You think I
could buzz every plane on an international air route
until the right one came along?" I didn't elaborate further. I was too amazed at Newland not having thought
this through. "Why don't you station someone outside
the perimeter of Fiumicino Airport with a missile to
shoot the plane down as it leaves."

"That occurred to us," Arain snapped angrily. "It
offers no guarantee of the bomb on board being eliminated. At the other extreme, if it were to detonate,
Rome Airport itself would be destroyed."

I was about to remark that if the airport in question
were Tripoli everyone would be happy to induce a
ground-zero explosion, as the experts refer to a nuclear

weapon going off at ground-level, when I realized that there might be another way of tackling their problem.

"The shooting-down scenario's out of court," I said. "But suppose I could blow the plane up on its arrival in Libya?"

"How?" Newland challenged.

"By attacking from the air immediately after it's landed."

He looked at me with disbelief. "Now you're being crazy," he said. "Qaddafi has one of the best-equipped air forces in the area. He has Russians flying his MiG-25's. You'd never get within fifty miles of Tripoli."

"But if I could?" A plan was rapidly forming in my mind, though not a detailed one.

"We'd put you on the payroll with a hundred thousand dollar bonus on completion," Newland said calmly, though I knew I had stirred his hopes. Even so, the money was hardly a fortune in the terms Arain was talking about a moment ago, and the risk was colossal.

"I'd like to sleep on the whole idea," I said. "Why did you pick on me anyhow?"

"The other guy had a G3 rating, you had a lot of experience on Phantoms. We couldn't exactly advertise the second job." Newland made it sound absurdly logical. "We'd pay the G3 salary, plus the bonus."

Arain swung to his feet. I will say one thing: he could move as fast as a cat. He handed me a business card, printed in traditional script with the words "Continental and Oriental Oil Corporation, 245 Park Avenue, New York, NY 10167." Alongside he had written a number with a 212 area code.

"Call me collect tomorrow," he said, then pulled a wallet from his hip pocket, and thumbed out a couple of $100 notes with the dexterity of a card sharp. "For the cab fares," he said. "Don't forget to call."

As I left the Savoy I wondered what Susie would think of the job she had introduced me to, though having done her good deed it was a hundred to one that she would vanish again. I remembered my lost job at the showroom. Arain was a tricky bastard, not to mention an unusual character. He must be CONOIL's number one Middle Eastern troubleshooter. It takes an Arab to match an Arab. The question was, quite apart from the risk and the money, did I want to work for a man like that? On the other hand, did I want to be on social security?

That evening I spent the first $80 taking a new girl-friend out to dinner. If I was going to sleep on the proposition, at least I didn't have to sleep alone.

→ TWO →

OUTSIDE A SPARROW chirped. I was suddenly awake, the craziness of a dream still vivid, yet tensely aware of something else. It was not the sparrow that had awakened me. A door clicked shut. The living room door. I knew that sound exactly. What was the girl doing? Searching the place? I sat up in bed, listening. Then the last fuzziness of sleep disappeared, and I remembered. That had been the night before last. So who the hell was in the apartment? I swung out of bed, pulled on a bathrobe, and shot through into the hall. A noise came from the kitchen. The door was ajar and I kicked it open hard, then paused a fraction to force the intruder into a move. But the intruder had the advantage even so. She stood there in that familiar tartan uniform, slightly startled but still more composed than I was, the kettle in her hand. The intruder was Susie.

"I didn't want to disturb you," she said coolly. "Just in case you had company."

For a moment I was dumbfounded. Slightly shaken, delighted she had come back, amazed at her sheer bloody nerve. I felt like saying, "And what if there had been someone here?" But that kind of challenge never works. At least not with a girl like Susie. Anyway, I was too relieved to make an issue of it.

"I'd forgotten you still had a key," I said, hoping that my emotions weren't written all over my face. The emotions weren't made any less conflicting by a vivid memory of her having left the key in the kitchen, along with her farewell note.

"I'm always losing keys. I'd had a spare one cut. I only found it the other day." She put down the kettle, moved a step closer, and said, "Well, are you glad to see me or not?"

There was only one answer. I took her in my arms and hugged her, and the natural place to go then was back to bed.

"So," she asked afterward, half-lying across me, propped on one elbow, her breasts soft on my chest, "who was the champagne for? You really shouldn't leave empty bottles around, you know."

Women do have this unblushing capacity for digging their nails into potential rivals. A fly on the wall might have thought it was I who had deserted Susie.

"I had a small celebration," I admitted. "If you'll tell me how long you're here for," I kissed her cheek, "maybe I'll tell you what I'm doing."

She pushed herself up on both elbows, her long hair falling around her face, and looked down at me.

"I didn't plan to come in at all. I just meant to drop the key off on the way home. I don't trust keys in the post."

"Which means?" I tried not to let the catch in my throat be audible.

"I'm on a charter to Pakistan tomorrow. I'm not sure I can even stay tonight."

"Do you want to keep the key?"

"Yes, darling I do." She gave me a hug. "And now tell me, what was it you were celebrating?"

"I've been offered a job flying for an oil company." I began relating a version of the last few days' events that made it sound as though I would be joining CONOIL for three months as a stand-in for one of their regular pilots who'd become sick. I was definitely not about to tell Susie the truth, but being in the business she would spot anything that didn't add up. "There's no future in it," I concluded, with more irony than I intended. "But it would be well paid while it lasts. I'm still not one hundred percent sure." The truth was that I wanted my plan to be foolproof before accepting.

"Take it, for goodness's sake," she said firmly, sitting up beside me. "At least it's flying, and that's what you live for isn't it? Now I'm going to make some breakfast. If there's anything in the bachelor's paradise to make it with."

Despite her cynicism, there were eggs and bacon and while we ate she made it clear that she thought I would be insane to refuse Arain's offer. I supposed that in the terms I'd described the job, I would have been.

"For God's sake, grab it. A lot can change in three months."

By the time she had commandeered my bed to sleep off her overnight flight, I had decided to call Arain and accept provisionally. Even if she didn't know the true facts, she was right about one thing. Quite apart from the cash, which was an inspiration in itself, what I needed as much as anything was to get back in the air. Furthermore, the dream she had jerked me out of had taken the idea a stage further. In the dream I had been flying a Korean War vintage Sabre jet in hot pursuit of a North Korean MiG-15. Pure Walter Mitty stuff, given that I'd never flown a Sabre. Yet I'd felt the G-forces as I tried to turn inside the MiG, my cheeks sagging within the oxygen mask, my stomach sucked down into the sea, the whole ship vibrating as I pressed the firing button and the guns streamed lead.

I never saw the MiG go down because that was when I

woke. But it left me with one compelling thought: given the right plane I could outwit the Libyan Air Force, earn Arain's $100,000 bonus, and survive to spend the money. The right plane, furthermore, had to be a jet fighter, but I reckoned I knew where to find one.

My enthusiasm must have been evident on the phone, because when I finally did speak to Arain, he scented it at once.

"So, you came around to our way of thinking?"

"Pretty much. I have the basis of a plan. It won't come cheap, but it should work."

"Tell me."

"On an open line? Thank you, no." Having made the decision. I was determined to keep the initiative and hold it. Also, never to reveal more than I had to, which would be essential for my own safety. Of one thing I was completely sure: once I had done the job, CONOIL would have very little concern for my well-being.

"Well," Arain was temporizing. "I'd appreciate some indication."

"The whole operation shouldn't cost you more than half a million dollars, and its origin will be untraceable."

"Sounds OK." He was being carefully noncommittal, and I could imagine the concentration on that olive-skinned face as he listened. For all his American veneer, Arain needed to see, feel, and smell the people he was negotiating with. Underneath, he was Arab all the way.

"Why not come across? Fill us in with the details."

"I need to complete some documentation first."

"Documentation?" His voice sharpened. "What documentation?"

"Licenses and so on." Surely he could guess that I was not going to fly a mission like this under my own name?

"I guess a little groundwork would do no harm," Arain conceded. "What's the tab?"

"Five thousand dollars would see me through." I kept my tone as level as possible, thanked the Almighty that the television phone wasn't available yet, then waited. Five thousand was far more than I needed. The point was to get him putting cash on the line without knowing precisely what it was for. Once he had done that, he would have admitted that basically I could play this my way, and if I could not do that I wasn't going to play at all: the risks were too great.

"We don't ordinarily make advances of that size without a specified reason."

"Are you proposing to put our contract in writing, Mr. Arain? Because if so you can count me out."

"No," he agreed, a touch wearily I thought, given that he could have only just got up. It was breakfast time in New York. "Where do you want the money?"

"American Express in the Haymarket will do." Their main London office was big and anonymous, and for his part he would get a receipt. Later I would have to evolve less traceable ways of being paid. For the moment it satisfied me, and it evidently satisfied him. I heard his grunt down the phone, and he wound up by ordering me to come to New York in a week. "I'd like a progress report at that time. A full one."

"I'll call you," I said. "But what I have in mind my take longer." I didn't want too many misunderstandings at this stage. Happily he accepted that and rang off.

There's a moment anyone who has ever raced knows, whether its running in a school Sports Day or screaming past the pits in a grand prix: the moment after the start when all the tension of waiting explodes into action. That was how I felt when I put the phone down. I knew exactly how to get onto the inside track in this race and I knew too that one hell of a lot of effort was going to be needed to make it: effort and luck. Nor did I intend to rely too much on the latter. If anything did go wrong, I could think of a large number of people with whom I was going to be very unpopular. Qaddafi being the first.

A fanatic who financed terrorism all over the world was not going to waste any time adding my name to his hit list at Friday prayers. The sooner I built up a new identity, the better.

"Building up," I realized, was the phrase. Obtaining a forged passport, or better still a genuine document with a false name on it, was the one thing. I knew there were ways of getting passports. But if I was going to buy a jet fighter and fly it half-way around the world, I needed a complete fictitious flying career, with all the documents than an experienced pilot would have acquired over many years. True, I could fly on an ordinary private pilot's ticket, just as test pilots used to do, because I would not be carrying passengers. But even a PPL contains a variety of certificates, like ratings for night flying and instrument flying and a medical one from a doctor. The British license requires a certificate of experience stamped in the pilot's logbook. That logbook would have to date back some years, and if I carried through the plan forming in my mind, it and my license were liable to be scrutinized far more closely by officials than my passport. The question was how to get genuine ones.

I still hadn't even thought through this problem when Susie appeared from the bedroom, wrapped in a bathtowel, her brown hair falling over her naked shoulders. Her skin was nicely tanned, and the white towel set it off beautifully. Life, I reflected, was being unexpectedly kind.

"Hi, sweetheart," she said, then came across and kissed my forehead. "You look worried. What's the problem?"

"Nothing heavy. I was thinking about the licenses." What exactly prompted me to come so close to the truth, I don't know.

"I suppose you'll need an American one," she shrugged her shoulders delicately, not quite enough to dislodge the towel from around her breasts. "I always thought that was easy."

"It is," I admitted, then suddenly realized the significance. She was damn right. All I would need was someone else's British license for long enough to take it to a Federal Aviation Authority office. Then I could have an American one in that other person's name: a genuine document around which to start building a new identity. My mind circled the idea. There must be flaws. There always were.

"Have you gone into orbit or something?" Susie demanded. She liked to feel she was being paid attention to, who doesn't? "Well, if you haven't, be an angel and go and get some bread, bacon, eggs, and milk. Your kitchen is as bare as Mother Hubbard's. And yogurt." She stepped into the kitchenette and came out with a discarded envelope. "Oh yes, and salt for God's sake." Susie lived on lists. She must have made this one before she went to sleep. I didn't mind at all. The implication was that, even if she left today, she would be coming back.

On the way to the minimarket I stopped at a newsstand and bought a copy of *Flight*. One quick way to lay my hands on someone else's license might be to advertise.

But while Susie cooked up her own version of the late late breakfast show—a sight considerably more amusing that the real thing, given what she was wearing—I had a better thought. Advertising to find a man who had given up flying would be slow and would also mean putting an address in print. Far better to go through every flying school listed in *Flight* and ask them direct. But if I began doing so straightaway, Susie would certainly smell a rat. By the time she changed back into her uniform in midafternoon and began making obvious preparations to leave, I was anxious enough to get to work myself.

"Well, sweetheart," she said simply, looking as demure as they come with her hair up and the ever-welcoming "fly me" expression already slipping into place under her tartan beret, "Time to go." She kissed me affectionately, though without risking her makeup.

"Do you know when you'll be back?" The question forced itself out, against prudence. Susie's sense of commitment always had been erratic.

"No, darling," she paused in the doorway. "But I promise I will be."

When she had gone, and I had stopped wondering why I should have fallen for a born wanderer, I began telephoning flying clubs. I felt a slight quiver of unease at using a false name for the first time. But the quiver didn't last long. I knew what I wanted, I knew what I was talking about, and on the third call I hit pay dirt. The people I had rung were at Biggin Hill Airfield in Kent, a famous wartime fighter station and nowadays the venue of a big annual airshow. Biggin was home to a number of clubs and groups and busy enough for strangers not to be objects of curiosity, as they might be at Redhill or Denham. I asked if they knew anyone who was giving up flying and possibly selling a plane.

"There's a small flying group that uses our facilities," the man who answered told me in a friendly voice. "One of their members is pulling out and offering his quarter share in their Cherokee 180."

"Sounds interesting." The hell I wanted twenty-five percent of one engine and a fixed undercarriage. But I might want the owner.

"It's due for a C of A soon. He's only asking a couple of thousand."

I took down the details, thanked him warmly, and five minutes later was talking to a young-sounding insurance broker named James Hall who, when I explained I was a writer, asked me to lunch with him the next day.

"By the way," I added, "if you can bring your logbook and license along, I'd be most interested to see them. The more detailed the background the better."

That evening I stayed in and polished up my ideas of what an author writing a book on the problems of the private pilot would want to know. If I was going to succeed in borrowing this man Hall's identity for a week I would need a solidly convincing story: not the sort that would send him leaping off to the nearest police station afterward. I half-hoped Susie would turn up, too, but the phone didn't even ring. She was her own girl, Susie, very definitely.

Next day I took the subway to Piccadilly and walked the couple of hundred yards down to St. James's Square. A student of sociology could have derived good source material from the institutions that faced each other across the square gardens and their closely planted parking meters. There was the Royal Institution of International Affairs scrutinizing the world from the Earl of Chatham's old house on the north side, less than a pistol shot from the former Libyan embassy: not that the firing that started the 1984 seige was from a pistol. The Libyan "diplomats" shot a policewoman in the back with a submachine gun, the bastards. They had to be among the world's least-loved nations. Then on the opposite corner of the square was the home away from home for pongos and crabs in the shape of the Army and Navy Club and on the west side the London Library tucked away, ready to meet book-lending demands from Buckingham Palace. Next to it stood the high-ceilinged gloom of the curiously named East India and Sports Club, which was where I had been invited.

Hall himself matched the surroundings impeccably. He was in his early thirties, tall, slightly balding, and dressed in an unobtrusive pinstripe suit. Not the usual flying type at all. He greeted me in the lobby with a firm handshake.

"Good of you to ask me here." I let myself lapse into the appropriately clipped, slightly stilted language of the services. "Should be me entertaining you."

Hall promptly asserted that it was his pleasure, adding, "Strictly speaking I belong to the Public Schools Club. We moved in here a few years ago." He looked around as though worried at the place's resemblance to a mausoleum. "Still, it's convenient. Care for a drink before we eat?"

However, he was confident enough once we were seated in the long bar downstairs, and I soon found myself being interrogated.

"What exactly is this book you're writing?" he demanded.

"Basically it's an analysis of how private flying has been treated by successive governments since the war." I smiled, persuasively I hoped. "That means how life's been made more difficult for pilots. I plan to quote as many individual case histories as possible—with photographs of course."

"Do much writing, Mr. Smith?"

I sensed danger and backed off. "Frankly, this is my first book. I fly for a living."

"Ah," said Hall. "That explains it. I rang a friend from *Flight* who said he'd never heard of you. Whom do you fly for?" This man was a persistent inquirer.

"Just completed a contract doing survey work in the Gulf." I kept to an area I knew. "They don't want me back for three months. I'm hoping the Aircraft Owners and Pilots Association may sponsor the book, or the FAI."

"Really?" I had caught Hall's interest, and his guard went down a little. "I still belong to AOPA myself." He launched into a long account of how he'd learned to fly, problems with one particular instructor, and how he'd bought a share in the Cherokee in the hope that he would be able to use it on business trips to the Continent. That was seven years ago. Then came the recession, while marriage had been the final straw. "She pretends not to be frightened in the air, but she is. And

scared stiff that I'll have an accident, even though I've
had nothing worse than a heavy landing in over four
hundred hours," he explained, adding lamely, "You
know how it is! Anyway, now our baby's on the way
there are more important things to spend money on."

As he led me upstairs to lunch I could hardly believe
my luck. Here was the ideal candidate. What with having kept fit and stayed off the booze, I look a lot less
than thirty-eight and he was only a few years younger
than me. Private licenses don't need a photograph and I
was confident I could impersonate him. He'd done a
reasonable amount of flying, not like those idiots who
keep up their licenses on the minimum five hours a year,
so his logbook would look plausible in my hands. If I
was going to be taking a flying test in his name, I didn't
want to arouse suspicions by inadvertently being too
professional. Flying instructors sense what sort of experience they're dealing with very quickly. The only
problem might be persuading Hall to part with his documents for a few days. I worked on it hard over a lunch
that was an agreeable improvement on the club's decor,
interspersing mouthfuls of excellent game pie with soft-
soap questions about the difficulties he himself had en-
countered.

"You don't mind, I hope," I said politely, as I scribbled occasional notes. "Of course I won't quote anything without your permission."

He waved a hand dismissively. "My dear chap. Anything I can do to help."

"This is all extremely useful," I said, kneading his
ego some more. "But I'm also keen to get a photo taken
of everything a private pilot needs: you know, maps,
protractor, stopwatch, navigational computer, right
down to pencil and rubber, and of course the logbook
and license."

"Well," he said roundly, his perspective on life evidently relaxed by the club claret we had been drinking.
"You're welcome to see mine. The logbook's in my

briefcase. Here's the license." He reached into his pocket and laid a small transparent plastic folder on the table. "Medical's expired, of course. God in heaven, even that cost sixty-one quid the last time. Belinda absolutely blew her top."

I picked up the familiar folder, undid the press stud and let it open like a concertina, wondering yet again how any civil servant could have been dumb enough to design it. Each pocket was so small that the relevant certificate could only fit in by being doubled over. The folder dated back from the early days of the nonexpiring license and, sure enough, the brown piece of paper giving details of the basic license had been issued on 3.5.77. It was headed:

United Kingdom Civil Aviation Authority
PRIVATE PILOT'S LICENSE—AIRPLANES.

It authorized James Hall to "exercise its privileges" in landplanes of Group A, and also in self-launching motor gliders. "Group A" meant single-engined aircraft of up to 7,500 kilograms total weight, which I already knew was no obstacle, because the plane I had in mind weighed more, the FAA would give an extension.

"A friend of mine runs a photographic studio in South Kensington," I explained. "Could I possibly borrow this and your logbook for a few days so that I can get him to do what's needed?"

Hall looked doubtful, his geniality fading.

"The firm's called Studio Ten. I promise they'll take the greatest care. Naturally, I'll give you a receipt." I paused a fraction. "I'd use my own, but it's a commercial."

"All right," Hall capitulated. "But I must have a receipt, and I'd like them back as soon as possible." He smiled thinly, the way insurance adjusters do when they see a loophole in a claim. "I may never use them again.

On the other hand, a logbook's part of one's life in a way."

"Absolutely," I agreed, kicking myself for imagining that anyone in the insurance business would be a walk-over. I got up, muttering excuses, went across to a writing table and sat down briefly to write on a sheet of headed paper. "Received from Mr. James Hall one license and one logbook," signed it George Smith, added the date and put "RAF Club, Piccadilly" beneath. The real George Smith was flying helicopters in the Gulf on a one-year contract.

"I'm not staying at the club," I explained. "But I go there most days and it's my long-term address."

The explanation seemed to satisfy him. When we had finished the coffee he led me out into the somber hall, extracted a well-kept blue logbook from his briefcase, and shook hands cordially.

"I'll be in touch," I said. "Thanks again. If necessary could I leave the things here for you?"

"So long as you let me know."

I didn't exactly dance out into St. James's Square, but I did feel pretty good. The sun had come out. London has a certain exhilaration in early summer, and I knew where I was going. Meanwhile, the first essential was to book a genuine photographic session at Studio Ten. I wanted that out of the way because time was rapidly going to run short.

In order of priority, I needed a new medical certificate for Hall's license and then the five hours' flying that would justify an examiner stamping the certificate of experience in the logbook. The book itself revealed that he had never flown from Kidlington, where the Oxford School of Air Training operates Cherokees, so he was unlikely to be a known there. I collected the $5,000 from the American Express office, banked most of it, then spent the rest of the afternoon having the still-life photograph taken of a pilot's equipment, using my own

maps and equipment in order to keep Hall happy.
Before dinner I drove down to Oxford and took a room
at the Randolph. If Arain was paying for me to risk my
neck, he could pay for reasonable comfort en route.
Before going to bed I devoted half an hour to practicing
Hall's signature.

The first priority next morning was the medical.
There was a CAA-approved doctor in Oxford and I was
lucky: he ran the next best thing to a production line.
You filled the application form in yourself, were shown
by a nurse to a lavatory to leave your urine sample, had
your eyes tested and height and weight checked by another, and only wound up with the medico himself for
the blood pressure and stethoscope routine. As Hall had
never been there, they had no previous records to check
against. I emerged three-quarters of an hour later with a
Class 3 certificate valid two years, a receipted bill for
£40 and reasonable confidence that the examination
report would not be checked by the CAA either, unless I
had a crash. All they normally cared about was the doctor's signature.

However, the chief flying instructor out of Oxford
airport near Kidlington was a different kettle of fish.
He had to be. Neatly parked outside the buildings was
the line up of white-and-orange-liveried Cherokees on
which the school trained would-be airline and service
pilots from all over the Third World. Africans, Arabs,
and Asians came to Kidlington, and he had necessarily
become wary of their credentials.

"So you haven't flown for two and a bit years, Mr.
Hall?" he inquired, in a grating northern accent. He
was a wiry man, with short, graying hair and a sharp expression. I knew he had a reputation for taking no
nonsense from anyone, whatever their rank. "May I see
your license?" He scrutinized it and then went through
the logbook, page by page, suddenly glancing keenly at
me, his eyes narrowing. "I see Geoff Warren instructed
you at Biggin. How is he?"

It was a loaded question and I knew it. What I did not know was the correct answer. What the hell kind of an incident was it Hall had glossed over at lunch in that perfect public-school voice of his?

"I haven't seen Geoff for a long time," I replied warily.

"Had a crash with a pupil didn't he? Nearly lost his instructor's rating. Not to mention his life." The CFI had his teeth into me and wasn't letting go. But had Hall admitted to an accident? Not in so many words. Then I remembered his mentioning the "sticky patch" he had had with his instructor as being peanuts to the problem of a fellow pupil who had nearly been killed. There had been nothing worse than a heavy landing recorded on his own logbook. I took a chance.

"That wasn't me," I said firmly. "I won't say it was all plain sailing, but we parted friends."

The CFI grunted. "Not the easiest of men," he conceded, to my relief. "Though that's no excuse for bad landings." He handed me the documents, "Well, Hall, you'll be wanting to knock up just the statutory five hours I suppose. We'll give you a flying test and if that's satisfactory you can do an hour in the circuit and then a three hour cross-country. Keith Edmonds will take you." He picked up the phone and spoke briefly. "You'll have to sit for the aviation law paper as well. How long can you stay?"

"Three days maximum. I'd prefer to do the lot before the weekend."

"Maybe you would," he replied dourly. "Let's see what Edmonds thinks."

Edmonds proved to be at least ten years younger than me and a competent instructor. Since I had never flown a Cherokee, and handling a jet airliner is a whole different world from a light aircraft, I assumed there would be no need to feign amateurishness. I was right. On the first takeoff I did a nice, clean rotation as we reached flying speed, only to be caught by a gust of wind and have the Cherokee stagger into the air, stall-warning blaring, and sink back to touch its wheels on the tarmac again before we finally did get airborne. By that time Edmonds had taken over control.

"Easy does it," he remarked cheerfully as we climbed away. "This thing isn't rocket assisted, you know. How long is it since you last flew?"

By the end of the hour he was in no doubt of my competence, though he insisted on another hour of solo circuits and bumps: altogether I did ten takeoffs and landings before he was satisfied.

The next day was mercifully fine and I spent the morning on a triangular cross-country, landing at Weston-super-Mare and Shoreham. Homing in again on the Oxford beacon, with the cement-factory-chimney they called "Smokey Joe" and its trail of smoke giving a visual confirmation that I guessed students were glad of, I felt tolerably satisfied. James Hall's license was back in service.

After lunch I took the aviation law examination. Then Edmonds took me through to the CFI to have the new entries in the logbook signed. I had started these on a fresh page so that it could be removed later, and had also made out a "Certified Extract": a summary of all Hall's flying, solo and dual, plus my own five hours. With the Certified Extract I could start a new and legally acceptable logbook. Meanwhile I hoped my imitation of Hall's spiky and precise handwriting would satisfy the CFI.

"Keith tells me you had a shaky start," he remarked, giving me more of a gimlet stare than I welcomed, "but considers you're a reasonably professional pilot."

"Thank you," I muttered noncommittally, wishing I could give young Keith a kick where it hurt, the patronizing runt.

"Very competent indeed," the CFI went on. Suddenly it crossed my mind that he might have been talking to someone at Biggin and discovered that the real

Hall was mediocre. I stayed silent, praying he hadn't, as he checked the new page.

"If the people down there had any sense," he went on severely, "they'd have put you through an instrument-rating course." He paused. "Though I say it myself, ours is the best in the country."

I could have burst out laughing. All the old bastard was after was trying to sell me more flying.

"I'll come back for that," I said, "when I can afford it."

"It's not a luxury, Hall." He didn't even smile. "It's a bloody necessity in our weather." He surveyed the logbook, carefully impressed his examiner's stamp for the Certificate of Experience, signed it, then picked up the other sheet. "Frightened you might lose the book, eh?"

"I did once," I lied, watching as he stamped and signed the all-important Certified Extract.

"Come back any time," he said, with the first trace of warmth he had betrayed. "And keep your hours up, eh? Don't let them lapse again."

I settled the account and drove straight back down the M40 to London, arriving in the early evening traffic and wondering as I crawled along if I would find Susie at home. I didn't. Instead there was a note in the kitchen. "Talk about *my* being in and out. When are you ever here!!! Love, Sue," and then some signs for kisses she had invented, consisting of crosses inside circles. But no phone number. In emergency I could have left a message with British Caledonian's crew-rostering office at Gatwick. I debated that and then decided just to leave a note in the kitchen myself when I went to New York, which at the latest would not be until the weekend. I guessed Arain would put the pressure on now, and I welcomed it. Once I have the bit between my teeth I like to get going.

Sure enough, when I called Arain he was blunt and to the point.

"Listen, Lloyd," he said brusquely, "it's time you came across with some concrete ideas. How much longer is this damn documentation of yours going to take?"

"A few days. Can you suggest a hotel?"

"Yeah." He paused. "On West Forty-fourth. Hell, what is the name? Right across from the Algonquin. You'll find it. There'll be a reservation made beginning Monday night. Call me when you get there. We'll have a breakfast meeting Tuesday. I want this show on the road."

"So do I." Cutting back a less polite reply, I rang off. Arain was like every Arab businessman—once he'd made a decision he wanted the goods delivered yesterday. There would be no merit in undercharging for my services because he would be just as impossible if the price was low or high. You only had to have worked in the Gulf for a week to understand the syndrome.

I spent Friday tidying up the loose ends of business, like visiting the studio to see how the photographs had come out. They were fine and I paid for three full-plate prints, asking the firm to mail one directly to Hall. I wanted to reassure him, yet without making any direct contact until I was through with his license. True, it was only three days since I had borrowed it, but the protective attitude he had taken gave me a gut feeling that I ought to be seen to be using his possessions for genuine purposes.

There were other things on my mind too: foremost the need to forge a second Certificate Extract, this time relating to a mythical RAF career. If the new James Hall was going to fly a jet half-way around the world, he would need jet experience. He would get it from one of the RAF squadrons I had served in myself. That way, if I was ever questioned, my background knowledge would be right, though of course it was unlikely to stand up to official inquiries. But those would only come after the raid on Tripoli, if they came at all, and the new logbook would be destroyed by then.

Fortunately, I still had a few sheets of headed squadron paper from the old days. Unfortunately, no one who had seen the squadron adjutant's clerk at work was likely to forget the decrepit Imperial typewriter he was required to use. I suppose the top brass in the procurement executive of those days thought that if they skimped on office equipment they'd get more planes. It had all changed now and the clerks are women. But the Certified Extract had to look right and I needed an old Imperial. By a stroke of luck I found one in a junk shop in Fulham Road, took the thing home in a taxi, and duly accredited Flight Lieutenant Hall with 2,128 hours of RAF jet experience—roughly similar to my own—a night rating, and an RAF "green card" instrument rating. I signed it with the real adjutant's name, folded and creased the sheet of paper enough to substantiate the date, then went out and sold the typewriter to another shop for £3. I also rented a post office box at the Fulham post office, using Hall's license as proof of identity. On Sunday I caught Pan Am's last flight to New York from Heathrow, the much advertised 103, traveling on my own passport. I needed a working day there before I met Arain.

Although I hold a multiple reentry visa for the United States, fate and flying have always taken me east rather than west. So this was only my third visit to America, and I was perfectly prepared to love New York in June—this being June 3—except that the hotel Arain had nominated was all too obviously his little way of keeping the expenses down. In spite of taking a taxi from Kennedy Airport, it was midnight when I confronted a desk clerk whose ambitions were concentrated on slumber. Luckily there was a spare room, and he woke up just enough to hand over the key but left me to carry my case up myself in the elevator. The room overlooked the well behind the building and had last been refurbished around the time Al Capone hit the

deck. The furnishings smelled of dust and the carpet
was threadbare. I was too tired to argue. I just locked
the door and fell asleep, vowing to move into the Algonquin as soon as possible. I didn't aspire to the Waldorf-
Astoria, but I did want some kind of comfort during the
run-up to a mission as dicey as this.

Nonetheless, first things had to come first, and top of
the agenda was acquiring an American pilot's license. A
friend told me that all I had to do was take a short ride
on the Long Island Railroad from Penn Station and I
would be within walking distance of the FAA's local office. Taking the train made me understand why most
people prefer to drive out to Long Island. However, it
was only a twenty-five minute ride to Valley Stream.
Following instructions, I descended to street level,
crossed the highway at the lights, and easily located the
insurance company building where the Federal Aviation
Administration has an office.

My reception was as friendly as I had been told it
would be. I was interviewed by a genial man in his for-
ties called Neilson, who sat me down in a small conference room and after a few questions gave me the
forms.

"Fill these in," he said, "I'll be right back"—which
suited me because this was one occasion when I had to
get Hall's signature right and I preferred to practice a
few more times in private. For the address I gave the
Fulham post office box number.

I left the FAA with a Permit to Fly to tide me over
until the proper license arrived by mail, which would be
six to eight weeks. That could be the end of July. I had
certainly not started my preparations any too soon, and
I went straight on with them now. Neilson had given me
the name of a shop in the city that sold aviation accesso-
ries. I spent the afternoon buying various items, including a logbook. Back at the hotel I attached the two
Certified Extracts inside it and filled in the pages headed
"Previous Experience." I then made a long distance call

to Canada and finally rang Arain at home, who asked me to come in the evening. Either way I was ready for business. It's an aviation joke that "There are old pilots and bold pilots, but no old and bold pilots." In fact it's the bold ones who don't do their homework who get killed. My homework was going to be unbeatable.

THE BUILDING WHERE Arain lived was a long way up-market of the hotel he had chosen for me. A green uniformed hall porter checked on a house phone that I was expected, while another stood by. The elevator went directly into the apartment, though its occupant could not open the door without a key. Arain himself let me in.

"Good security you have here," I commented.

"It's necessary in this city," he said curtly, leading me through and asking petulantly, "Where were you yesterday? I've been calling you in London. Some lady said she didn't know where you were."

It could have been the cleaning woman or Susie. "Who was she?" I asked, disregarding his question.

"How should I know. Sounded young." He was more concerned with other things. "I wanted you to bring a package. We managed to lay our hands on a film made of Qaddafi's September 1 parade last year. It's coming by courier now."

"Should be useful." I had no reason to feel apologetic, and perhaps it got through to him because he suddenly became more hospitable and offered me a drink, going across to a small bar built into the corner of the living room.

While he poured the whiskey I surveyed the room. The discreet security fitted Arain's style, but the apartment itself revealed little to nothing about his character. The furnishings were blandly luxurious, and I guessed the only things he had added to the interior designer's choices were a photograph of his family in a silver frame, several Persian rugs, and an antique wooden

Koran-holder, which stood on a sidetable with a copy of the holy book displayed on it.

"I don't drink myself," he said, handing me a heavy cut-glass tumbler, "but I see no reason to inflict my beliefs on my guests."

He spoke with the suavity of a ritual, one that had become smooth with much use, but quickly reverted to his normal interrogative style. "Now. You say you have a plan. Let's have it." He waved me to sit on a sofa, and subsided into a deep armchair himself, watching me minutely.

I detailed how I expected to deceive the Libyans with an aircraft similar to one already in Qaddafi's inventory.

"Are you serious?" Arain exclaimed. "I told you before what the man has. Six hundred combat aircraft! From old Russian MiG-15s and -17s to French Mirages, Russian MiG-21s, -23s and -25s. Three hundred and forty-one of those are dedicated to Libya's air defense."

He rose briefly to hand me a typed analysis of the Libyan Air Force's equipment. The figures didn't impress me because I knew the basics already.

"You think you can go in single-handed against a force like that?" he demanded.

I leaned forward and slid the list toward him across the low glass-topped table that separated us. "There are a few things that inventory fails to mention. True, Qaddafi has six hundred combat aircraft. But he only has a hundred trained Libyan pilots and only thirty of those are up to international standards. All the rest of the aircrew are expatriates. Look what happened when he had that brush with the Sixth Fleet in 1981. Two American Tomcats shot down two of his Su-20s in under sixty seconds."

"OK," Arain temporized. "How do we know those pilots were Libyan nationals?"

"We don't," I said. "But if they were North Koreans, Syrians, East Germans, Cubans, or Pakistanis, that doesn't say much for their standards either, does it? What I will agree is that they were unlikely to be Russians. I don't believe the Soviets would let Russian pilots be pitched against the Sixth Fleet. It could be too damned embarrassing."

"I repeat," Arain asked, "what makes you think you can go in single-handed, whether the other side are Cubans, Koreans, or Libyans?"

"If I can cause enough confusion, I can," I said. "They won't speak any better Arabic than I do. The main thing is to have the right aircraft. This is the jet I want." I pulled a magazine out of my briefcase, got up and gave it to him. "I've ringed the entry."

The journal in question was called *Trade-a-Plane*. Printed on cheap yellow paper, it contained nothing but advertisements from cover to cover. *Trade-a-Plane* was unique in world aviation and it only appeared three weeks out of four, reputedly because the brothers who ran it liked time off now and then. Through it you could buy anything from a piston ring to a World War II bomber or a jumbo jet.

"Are you mad?" Arain asked, quoted from the ad. " 'Finished in Day-Glo yellow and orange. This has to be the finest of its kind anyplace.' You want we should pay a quarter of a million bucks for this?"

"Short of stealing a Russian MiG," I said. "It's the only plane. Cheap at the price. Unless you have a Spitfire to trade for it."

I had to admit that the exchange suggested in the ad would have been stretching most dealers' resources. The owner had sounded pretty unconventional too, at least on the phone.

"Mr. Arain," I said. "The only reason this aircraft hasn't sold since that ad appeared a month ago is the fuel consumption. The cost of gas is why the owner's giving her up. I didn't imagine that would worry an oil company."

Arain didn't even smile. "We'll consider the idea,"

he said. "What did you tell the guy?"

"That I'm well enough off to like air racing and thought I might break a few speed records. I made an offer this afternoon, subject to an engineer's inspection and test flight. The plane's in Canada at the moment." I allowed him time to think. "A chance like this might not come again in years. I accepted your deal because I knew this particular plane was available. But if you don't want to go ahead, I'm pulling out." I shifted on the sofa, preparing to leave.

For a while Arain just sat, saying nothing, his heavy-lidded eyes half-closed.

"Are you certain it can do the job?" he asked eventually.

"By the time I've finished with her, she'll be able to."

"All right, Lloyd. Let me know who you want the money paid to. What's the resale value?"

"Before September 1, or after?" His question made me wonder to whom he was accountable. "After the first the plane will disappear." As would "Hall."

"OK," he conceded. "We'll expect to write the investment off."

"During my preparations she'll be registered in the sporting pilot's name," I said evenly. I didn't want them changing their minds and ditching me.

Arain looked at me, his dark eyes curiously menacing. "Your racing pilot isn't called Smith is he?"

"No." I didn't like his question. I didn't like it at all. "Why?"

"The lady I spoke to at your apartment said some fellow had phoned asking for a pilot called Smith, threatening to call the police. She told him no one of that name lived there, but said that she thought he might be a friend of yours."

"Well," I kept my voice carefully under control, knowing how easily Arain would sense any trace of emotion. "It must be a mistake. Smith is the commonest name in Britain. Even the Royal Family has relations called Smith."

"Is that so?" he asked unpleasantly. "Maybe it was some prince. On the other hand, maybe you should check it out. We don't want the cops sniffing around you, do we?"

"No," I agreed, and stood up. "We don't." This time I did leave.

→THREE→

THERE IS A lot to be said for a fighter pilot's training. Apart from anything else, you learn to think fast when things go wrong. It wasn't just the embarrassment that had caused me to back out of Arain's sheikhly presence so quickly, it was the fact that I had come to certain conclusions while he was talking and I didn't want to waste any time before acting on them.

Going down in the elevator, I began putting them in order. Conclusion numero uno was that I must, without question, return the logbook and license to Hall in person, find out what had caused him to panic and calm him down. The last thing I wanted stored in Scotland Yard's computer was a complaint about possible misuse of Hall's license. The next thing would be a cross-check with the Civil Aviation Authority revealing the renewals, and the moment I used the name Hall to fly a plane in Britain I'd risk being blown, even on the American license. I had been confident I could keep Smith untraceable, but I should never have yielded to the photographic studio's demand for a contact phone number.

Therefore, it was imperative to see Hall myself in London, and I knew without needing a timetable that I couldn't catch tonight's last Pan Am or British Airways flights across the pond. Then I remembered about Kuwait Airways. Today was still Tuesday, even if it felt as if the day had lasted forever. On Tuesdays, Kuwait Airways had a jumbo going from New York to the Gulf via London and it left two hours later than anyone else, at a quarter-past ten. I could just about catch it.

I was lucky. A yellow cab cruised past as one of the doormen went to find one. He seemed gratified at the five dollars I gave him, which may have been a reflection on my conventionally English tweed jacket—I imagine I didn't look as affluent as the apartment block's normal visitors. During the short ride I asked the driver if he could wait fifteen minutes at my hotel, then take me to Kennedy, and he replied "If you say so Bud," without any of the aggression some New York cabdrivers display. That did a little to soften the blow, as did my second conclusion, namely that Susie had evidently reacted to Hall's fuss with considerable presence of mind. The next thing was to talk to her: if I could find her.

I knew there would not be enough time to call London while I packed, but my luck continued to hold. The desk clerk had not fallen asleep yet and another five-dollar bill persuaded him to phone Kuwait Airways while I was packing. When I came down again he had the elated look of a man who's beaten the panel in a quiz game.

"I got it," he exclaimed, his voice full of wonder. "Yes, sir, I got that reservation for you." He was a young man, and I began to feel I had misjudged him before. "Say," he went on, "is that Kuwait some kind of an Arab place?"

"On the Gulf," I explained, adding hurriedly, "not the Gulf of Mexico, the Arab one." I didn't want to get involved, but possibly he could be trusted to perform one more service after I had gone. "Could you call this number for me?" I copied it down from my diary. "Tell Mr. Harragin there I can't come to Ottawa tomorrow, but I'll be in touch with him during the afternoon without fail. OK?" I produced a twenty-dollar bill. "Would that cover it?"

"It sure would Mr. Hall!" I never expected the boy to be so alert. "And thanks. I'm going to make that call right now."

"Be seeing you," I said, untruthfully, grabbed my bag, and sprinted for the cab.

Out at the airport I had time to try the number of my flat in London, aware that it was coming up to two-thirty in the morning there and not seriously expecting a reply. I let the phone ring in its distinctive uneven, hiccuping way, six, seven, eight times. Then, as I was about to give up, Susie's voice answered, drowsy and annoyed.

"Yes, sweetheart," she said caustically. "I know it's you. Do you realize what time it is, for heaven's sake? All right, I'll stay here until you arrive. Not that you deserve it." She rang off, leaving me uncertain what she meant. With Susie one always had to expect the unexpected.

During the flight I sketched out the next day's plan of action and came to a conclusion I ought to have reached the moment Arain originally made the proposition: I would need false documents. I should have asked Rajni Patel for advice. Rajni was in the business. The only reason I hadn't thought of him before was that I hadn't seen him for a couple of years.

Rajni was an Asian who had been expelled from Uganda by Amin back in 1973 and had come to Britain, setting himself up as a travel agent. I met him a lot later when he was flying to New York on the Skytrain: one of the stewardesses brought up his visiting card with a re-

quest to see the flight deck. It was always Laker's policy
to keep good relations with the travel trade, so I agreed
and she escorted him up front. He was a small man running to fat, and his suit was creased from the cramped
seating: it was also company policy to load the DC-10s
close to capacity. Rajni had rather sly dark eyes and a
Hindu caste mark between them on his forehead. He
had watched the instrument panels for a minute or two,
listening in polite bewilderment to my explanations,
then grasped my hand in a tight squeeze and thanked me
with unnecessary warmth.

"It is too kind of you," he murmured only just
audibly. "For me this is making a completely new experience, top-hole experience, eh? I am being greatly
privileged, Captain." He produced another card. "You
are wanting anything," he continued in that heavily accented, not quite grammatical language Asians use,
"your friends are wanting anything, tickets, visas,
things like that. I can arrange, no problem."

Frankly, when you're turning around to talk to
someone in the confined space of a flight deck, you
don't always catch every word. There's too much going
on. But I caught the inflexion in Rajni's voice, all right.
The way he said, "You are wanting anything," and the
way he concluded "For me, this is most auspicious
day," left me in no doubt. He didn't give a damn how
the plane worked, he was seizing the chance to meet
crew members, and I knew immediately what he was
after: a little help on the side.

Travel agents like Rajni, selling discounted airline
tickets at prices to make IATA officials weep, can never
have too many contacts in the business. In due course
we came to an arrangement. As I said before, I was able
to buy the flat on money I had saved while flying for
Laker, both legally and through Rajni. Even a lowly
pilot has his chances, and Rajni really did believe the
date, day, and hour of our meeting had been "very

good" for him. In fact, it was why he had booked that flight. Our collaboration had only ended when Laker folded. Now it was time to renew the friendship.

On arrival, I rang Rajni from a phone booth at Heathrow. He sounded delighted to hear from me again and not in the least surprised when I mentioned documentation. We fixed a meeting for midday, which gave me just over two hours to get home, change, and arrange to see Hall. My life suddenly seemed to have become dominated by the telephone and by rushed appointments. It was going to be a relief when my alter ego was fully established and I was in control of him, instead of the other way around. Meanwhile, there was Susie. How much had she guessed? How much could I risk telling her?

I caught the aroma of fresh coffee before I had even opened my front door and, sure enough, Susie emerged from the kitchen as I entered. She had appropriated a short, silk bathrobe of mine, which I kept for hot climates. It was cream colored and she looked as sexy as hell in it, with the belt tight so that very little of her shape was hidden. The sight of her would have made a saint feel randy.

"Hi, sweetheart. Welcome home!" She put her arms around my neck and gave me a hug, multiplying the randiness factor by about a hundred as I held her close and kissed her. But after a few seconds she slipped away. "You need a bath, and a shave," she said firmly. "And unless I'm mistaken you have other things to do today. Anyway, I have to be at Gatwick by one. Coffee?"

As she poured it I stroked my chin and discreetly smelled my breath against the palm of my hand. Holy cow, she might just as well have been kissing a camel! Even my clothes stank of stale cigarette smoke.

"Come and talk to me in the tub," I suggested. "Tell me what you've been up to while I scrub off the jetlag."

"It would be more to the point," she said, when she

had come through and begun methodically brushing her long hair in front of the bathroom mirror, glancing at me as she spoke, "for you to tell me who George Smith is."

"Just an old friend," I assured her. "He asked me to ring this character, but I forgot until the last moment. What exactly was the man so upset about?" I soaped myself vigorously, but couldn't avoid catching her eye because she came and sat on the edge of the bath, amusement flickering across her generous mouth. She suppressed the smile, but it stayed around her eyes. She was unquestionably laughing at me.

"The man, as you call him, seemed extremely anxious to get his logbook back. Not to mention his license."

"Can't imagine what old George would want them for," I said bluffly, sitting up in the warm water. "Anyway, I hope you calmed the guy down. I mean, George was relying on me."

"He was?" Susie's voice and eyes remained mocking. "Well, I think I succeeded. I promised he'd have them back by the end of the week. Otherwise he was threatening to go to the police."

"Good girl!" She was a cool lady, Susie, very cool. Jesus, if Hall had trooped off to the fuzz there could have been real trouble. I clambered out of the bath and sat beside her on the edge. If only I could have explained why I was so pleased. "Thanks, darling," I said, and kissed her, water dripping on the floor and over the bathrobe, but to hell with it.

"That's better," she murmured. "At least you smell decent." We kissed some more and I felt her hand begin to caress my groin. Then, unexpectedly, she took her mouth from mine and gazed at me.

"So who is George Smith?" she asked. "Seriously."

I tried to resume the kiss, but she avoided me, though her hand didn't relax its grip and I was becoming intensely aroused. "He's a chopper pilot who sometimes hangs out here when he's in London." I wished to God she would leave off the questions and get on with the sex.

"Not at the RAF Club?"

"How should I know?" I held her closer. "Let's go to bed, for God's sake."

"George Smith is in the Gulf." She eased herself away from me a little. "And has been for six months according to the man who phoned. I'm glad you're not as bad a pilot as you are a liar."

She stood up, the sodden silk clinging to her breasts. "You are an idiot," she said, stripping off and starting to dry herself. For the life of me I didn't know if she meant I was an idiot to make the gown wet or to pretend about George Smith.

"Listen, sweetheart," she went on. "I like you very, very much, and I don't mind if you don't want me to know things, but the next time give me a little better briefing will you? I might make a boo-boo."

"I can't imagine that," I insisted. In the circumstances loyalty seemed the best policy, and anyway I felt it. She had defused a potential catastrophe. I would have liked to reveal the whole story, but what isn't known can't be told.

"When are you off?" she asked, as I started to shave.

"Tomorrow, probably."

Now she was talking from the bedroom as she dressed, a disembodied voice. "You mean I have to come to New York to see you?"

That caught me in the gullet, just those few words said it all. I finished shaving, wiped my face and went through. She was half-dressed, with her tartan skirt on and a black lace bra. I put my arms around her and hugged her. "I love you," I said. "I'll be back again as soon as I can."

She kissed the top of my nose. "We might even meet here then. Would you like me to move in properly?"

Strictly speaking, I needed notice of that question, given the next few months' projected activity. Fifteen

seconds' consideration told me that, of course, I would
never be here in the guise of Hall. Never. But that was
fourteen seconds too long.

"Never mind, sweetheart," Susie said coldly. "I
shouldn't have asked. Send me a postcard sometime
when no one else is around. I might be free."

I had blown it, and if I tried to argue she would simply shoot me down. Besides, I had compelling work to
do and it was already half-past eleven. So I dressed,
assembled my papers, including Hall's lousy logbook,
and went back to the bedroom to say goodbye.

"That was quick," she commented. "Maybe you
don't need a nursemaid after all."

"I love you," I said, holding out my arms and feeling
about as relaxed as a tailor's dummy.

"When it's convenient, I'm sure you do." She looked
at me tenderly, kissed me quickly on the mouth, and
said, "Off you go then." As I had assumed, there was
no point in arguing.

On the way to see Rajni, I stopped at a public telephone booth to ring Hall. The inside of the red-painted
booth stank of urine, the floor was littered with cigarette butts, and the instrument itself was decorated with
call-girls' numbers in heavy black graffiti. In other
words, it was a typical London telephone, its only un-
typical quality being that the coin slot wasn't jammed.
For obvious reasons I had not wanted to call from the
flat. Now, having only two coins, I found myself up
against a difficult secretary.

"Mr. Hall is in a meeting," she snapped.

"It's fairly urgent. I'm only here for a day."

"Mr. Hall is extremely busy."

"So am I, as it happens." I'd had enough of this
make-believe. "Tell him Captain Smith is on the line."

I suppose the title did the trick. "I'll see if he is
available," she conceded, and just as I put in the second
coin Hall came on.

"I've been trying to find you." His voice trembled slightly, and I wasn't sure if he was angry or frightened.

"Oh?" I wasn't going to apologize. "I had to go out of town. Would you like the documents dropped at your club?"

"I'm terribly tied up." Hall certainly sounded under pressure. He wavered. "I suppose I could meet you around six-thirty."

"Fine," I confirmed breezily. "At your club then." I rang off before the money could run out again, feeling pleased. He had left me the whole afternoon free for Rajni.

The travel business had expanded since I last went there. It now occupied two adjacent shops, one full of airline showcards under the sign "R.P. Tours and Travel," the other a real estate agency. But Rajni himself had not changed. He was still as effusive as ever, though visibly more prosperous: he now sported a gold Rolex wristwatch, and when he led me through to the back room that served as his private office, I couldn't fail to notice a bulky gold cigarette lighter, shaped like a globe, standing on a wide desk. It was meant to be seen, because Rajni himself was a nonsmoker.

Apart from this one display of ostentation, the furniture was as it had been. There was the same plush sofa, the color of pink coconut ice, and an ornately carved, teak coffee table with plastic lace mats on it. On the wall hung a garishly bright picture of Lakshmi, the goddess of fortune, standing barefoot on a lotus flower.

At Rajni's invitation I sat down on the pink sofa and made the necesary polite inquiries about his family until another door opened discreetly and his eleven-year-old daughter appeared, carrying two cups of coffee and a plate of samosas on a tin tray. She was in her blue school uniform, her long dark hair tied in pigtails, and she had obviously been taken out of class for the occasion. She put the tray down, then curtsied self-consciously and after a few words of greeting left us again.

"You are honored guest," Rajni explained proudly. "She is happy for meeting you."

"She's growing into a lovely girl," I complimented him, realizing I must have done more for the family than I knew. We sipped the coffee and nibbled at the spicy, hot samosas.

"Now, my good friend," Rajni broached the subject with expansive goodwill. "With what can I be helping?"

I took Hall's license from my pocket. "I need a copy of each of these certificates, except the medical one."

Delicately, touching them only with his fingernails, he drew each one out and then, in turn, gripping them in a corner of a spotless handkerchief, held them up to the light. He was a cautious man, Rajni.

"Without watermark," he commented. "Ordinary paper. Printing is litho. But the typing is by different machines." He examined the small rectangular Civil Aviation Authority imprint that had been rubber-stamped on each certificate. "The stamp is no problem. An easy pie. How long can I keep?"

"Only this afternoon, I'm afraid."

"No problem. I myself will find suitable paper today. When do you need finished product?"

"A couple of weeks."

Again he insisted it was no problem, and for safety he would do the job personally. "You can be picking up passport same time," he said cheerfully.

I almost spilled my coffee, then collected myself and grinned. "You're a mind reader, Rajni."

"Only a realistic man, my friend." He rolled the word "realistic," as if he was especially fond of it. "In our community we are having always to be realistic. How otherwise can we survive? You have the photographs?" He took the two passport photos I had ready and then started making notes. "It is British subject, isn't it? Citizen of the United Kingdom and colonies? Residence UK?" Each time I nodded. "With right of abode in UK?" He smiled. "Without that it is nothing, isn't it? Useless, eh?"

He was dead correct. My impersonation of Hall would look more than odd without the all-important right to live in the United Kingdom.

When he had the necessary details, Rajni became unexpectedly apologetic. "The license, please accept as gift. But for passport work I must pay others. Paper and things like that." His hands fluttered and the gold Rolex flashed like a huge jewel above his cuff. "One thousand pounds is OK? I am making no profit."

"That's OK, Rajni," I confirmed. "I assume you'd like it in notes."

He inclined his head in graceful acceptance. "Cash is convenient."

Not a bad motto, I thought. I ought to try the idea on Arain. I thanked him and was making farewell noises when he caught me completely unawares.

"My friend," he cut in. "Perhaps this is not for me to say, but I want only to assist. You must have this day of birth, this ninth of October? I do not think it was a good day." He bent down, pulled open a drawer in the desk and lifted out a large file. "When you are choosing day for important things, you must be careful." He began flipping through the papers. "For myself, I am always consulting my guru before big decisions." He nodded toward a framed photograph on the wall of a gray-bearded man in voluminous robes and a white turban. "Always I am consulting. God is reincarnated through him. He knows. He is never wrong." As he spoke, Rajni found what he wanted. It was some kind of chart printed on yellow paper. "I was remembering. In October that year only the sixteenth was good. Why not change, please?"

"No dice, I'm afraid." I grinned. If Hall had been

born with bad luck, I should just have to live with it.
Then I thought, hell, Rajni's being serious, I should pretend to be. "Tell me, how about September first?" I inquired. "This year. Would that be good?"

"For marriage, business, what thing?"

"Business." Even as I named the day I had one of
those funny inner qualms you can't avoid at a fortune-
teller's. You may think the whole performance is crap,
the tea leaves, the cards, the crystal ball, whatever. And
yet. Suddenly I regretted asking. One shouldn't mess
about with fate. What if the day of Qaddafi's parade
was one hundred percent inauspicious?

"September first, that is Saturday." Rajni traced the
way around what I could just see were segmented half-
circles on the chart. "For business purposes," he said,
evidently relieved, "the day is OK, but up to midday
that period is not to your benefit. From one-thirty is
better. The actual very good starts at three in afternoon.
If you like I am writing to my guru?"

"Don't worry," I assured him. "Things could
change." I wondered if the parade would be in the afternoon. Sadat had been assassinated at an afternoon
parade by extremists encouraged by Qaddafi. Then I
pulled myself together. I wasn't in the game of either
fate or poetic justice. I thanked Rajni with a suitable
display of enthusiasm and departed to find a decent,
down-to-earth, pub lunch with no date on the menu.

That evening, what with retrieving the license from
Rajni and devoting a few careful minutes to exercising
the two pages I had used in the logbook, together with
their pairs on the other side of the stitched binding, I
was late arriving at Hall's club. He was standing waiting
in the cavernous lobby, obviously in an emotional state.

"You've caused me a lot of worry," he burst out, not
even shaking hands. "Your club told me you were
abroad. I didn't know how on earth to find you." He
faced me, his cheeks flushed, puffing with outrage. He
looked absurd.

"I was abroad," I answered bluntly. "I had to leave on short notice."

"They said they hadn't seen you in months!"

"Then they're bloody well blind." I laid my briefcase on a table and gave him the logbook and license. "Here you are," I said. "Now would you mind giving me the receipt back?" I didn't want him retaining a specimen of my handwriting, and I reckoned that if he'd forgotten it he would collapse like the proverbial pricked balloon.

"Oh." He retreated a step, almost as if I had threatened him. Being in the insurance game, receipts probably meant more to him than holy writ. "Oh, yes," he muttered, and started digging into his own briefcase like a pig after truffles. Eventually he found the piece of headed notepaper I had written on. "Here you are." He stood up again and handed it over, the color slowly subsiding in his face.

"Well, old chap," I said, dropping into a friendlier tone. "You might tell me what the panic was all about." I needed to know for safety's sake, what with that threat about the fuzz, but he caught me on the hop with his answer. Badly on the hop.

"I'm being transferred to Hong Kong," he said. "Next week. I'll be able to start flying again."

"Jolly good show!" I tried to sound enthusiastic in the best Biggles tradition, while wishing the floor would open and take him down under by the direct route. He could fly in the crown colony on a British license and in no time the CAA would start wondering why he was indulging in two medicals in two months, instead of two years.

"I hope so," he said. "There's a flying club apparently, though that may have to wait until we're settled in."

I remembered his wife and blessed her heartily for being pregnant. From what he'd told me before, she'd be in a permanent state of nerves in case he accidentally flew into Chinese airspace and got himself shot down.

"When's the happy event?" I asked. All I needed was three months' grace.

"Late September. The great thing is Belinda can have an ayah. Isn't that what they're called?"

"That's right," I confirmed, and decided to take a chance. "Maybe for her sake you ought to delay flying again until after the baby's born. You know how women are about these things."

I couldn't have touched a more appropriate nerve. "I expect you're right," he agreed wistfully. Then, obviously deciding he'd been betraying the "old pals act" with someone as concerned as me, he began apologizing for the panic. "I just had sudden visions . . . I say, I never offered you a drink."

"Jolly decent of you," I said, almost puking at my own language. "Actually I'm a bit pressed," I smiled cautiously. "But the best of luck for the future. When the book comes out I'll send you a copy." I shook hands firmly and made off, the incriminating receipt safely in my pocket. All in all, the outcome could hardly have been more satisfactory. He was going to be on the opposite side of the world and deeply preoccupied throughout the time I would be using his identity. The only residual danger would lie in his reading about his own supposed activities in the aviation press. But that was unlikely in Hong Kong.

In fact, now that things were beginning to move, I had to double check every aspect of my own security. I took this thought to a pub near St. James's Square and pondered it over a pint of bitter in a quiet corner. Normally I've never been a beer-swiller, even at those parties they occasionally had in the mess. All alcohol does is destroy one's powers of concentration. Even so, sometimes a drink seems to help one think around problems, and I had plenty to consider now.

Instinctively, I play situations by ear. In the past this has both got me into trouble and got me out of it. In fact, my critics would say I was a touch too much of an opportunist and my friends would answer—at least I hoped they would—that a fighter pilot was no damn good unless he was one. Either way, if I was going to carry off leading two lives for the next three months, I would have to calculate the farthest effects of every action I took, like a chess player. The tactics and the planning for this operation had to be impeccable, and I forced myself to admit that I had made mistakes already.

Looking back on it, I should never have phoned Hall or Arain from my flat. The cut off that the mythical Smith provided between myself and Hall had been good, but not total. Dialed phone calls can be traced, and even though I had no reason to think my phone was being tapped, all my calls should be made from other locations. So the next bout of telephoning would be best done from the international lines at the post office near Trafalgar Square. After coming to a few conclusions about my relationship with Arain as well, I walked up there and made the necessary contacts with New York and Canada.

Finally I took the subway to Fulham, thankful that the British Airways schedule to Ottawa did not leave until lunchtime next day and I would be in the Canadian capital in time for dinner. It had been a long day and, for all my experience, I still get mentally disoriented by transatlantic time changes. So I hit the sack as soon as I got home, noticing with gratitude that Susie had made the bed before she left. But as I subsided on to the pillow, there was a curious crunching sound. I rolled over, ferreted around and retrieved a piece of paper. On it was written, in Susie's big handwriting, "Take care, sweetheart, and don't let him into places I wouldn't approve of." A dozen of her circle-and-cross kisses followed.

Jesus, I thought, just the kind of message a bachelor needs in his bed! I suppose it was her way of telling me not to abandon hope. I was going to have to rethink my relationship with Susie too: should I confide in her, or cut her out? Next day, I thought about it all the way to Canada, on and off.

Ottawa was a new experience. The short Canadian summer had just begun: the cabdriver who drove me in from the international airport said it had been snowing only three weeks ago. I checked into the Four Seasons Hotel and was allotted a comfortable room with a picture window looking toward the Parliament buildings, their Gothic architecture and dark stone reminiscent of Westminster, while the famous Château Laurier framed the right-hand side of the view. The scene sparked my imagination. Life was showing its kind side for a change. For much of the next twelve weeks, assuming CONOIL paid up, this was how I was going to live, like something of a rich playboy. It would be a touch different to the flat in Fulham, or indeed the air-conditioned bachelor quarters in Dubai, with their prospect of other houses' walls and sand. It wasn't going to be too hard adapting.

I was taking a shower when the phone buzzed from between the twin beds. Wondering who it could possibly be, I grabbed a towel and took the call.

"How's tricks?" inquired a deep, gravely American voice. "Care for a drink?"

For a few seconds I thought it must be some kind of practical joke. "Who is that?" I demanded cautiously.

"Bob Newland. I'm in three two zero. Come on down."

There was no refusing. Arain must have sent him here to check my purchase. That was fair enough, except that I hadn't told anyone where I would be staying, for the good reason that I didn't want Arain booking me into another fleapit for the sake of economy, and I had wanted to spend the evening rehearsing my role for tomorrow. Cursing them both mildly, I dressed and took the elevator down.

Newland let me in, then returned to the icebox where he had been fixing himself a scotch on the rocks with one of those damned stupid miniature bottles that hotel minibars always have and that cost about the same as half a liter in the duty free. I asked for a Coke. Newland might have appeared a more sympathetic character than Arain when we originally met in London, but I knew there was nothing social about this encounter and I was going to need my wits about me.

"Guess you weren't expecting callers," Newland said, grinning as he passed me the glass. "Have a seat." His relaxed friendliness hadn't changed. "We decided we'd like to see what you're buying. A quarter of a million bucks is a quarter of a million bucks, even to an oil company. Fill me in, will you?"

Newland had come to the point in exactly the straightforward way I would have expected. No dirty cracks about expensive hotels or problems locating me, and none of Arain's deviousness, but that didn't make the crunch any the less explosive. The time had arrived when they were going to have to trust me, because I sure as hell wasn't going to trust them, at least not with any detailed plans.

"The owner of the plane is from California," I said. "He has come up here to fly in a display at the weekend." Newland was obviously going to have to meet him. "As far as he's concerned my name is James Hall —'Hawker' Hall to my friends—and I'm a vintage-aircraft buff with enough cash to fool around a bit."

"So?"

I shrugged my shoulders. "Do you need to know more than that?" I laid a lot of emphasis on the word "need."

Newland drank a little of his scotch—I noticed he wasn't really a drinker either—savored it reflectively and chuckled.

"Only about a hundred other things I need to know, Lloyd," he said lazily, "like, if we approve the buy, how precisely are you going to use this ship to destroy Qaddafi's bomb? Where are you going to base yourself? How come the Libyan Air Force won't shoot you down first? How are you going to arm yourself anyhow? You can hardly fly around in civil markings with missiles hanging under the wings. What's the plan?"

I noticed he failed to raise the query most likely to concern me, namely how was I going to get out alive at the end.

"I'm glad you asked those questions, Captain Newland," I replied evenly, giving the traditional politician's opener to a nonanswer. "I'm glad you asked them before spending the money because, as I told Mr. Arain before, how I put paid to the Islamic bomb is my affair. All I promise is to fix it. If you want to back out, now is the time."

I will say one thing for Newland, he took it on the chin. He just sipped his drink again and laughed. "I wouldn't go that far," he said genially. "But there is one thing we have to clarify. By the time the manufacturers had finished modifying this type of airplane in the 1950s it could carry almost any kind of load, from a Sidewinder to an atomic weapon. I'd like to be sure the one you choose is going to work."

"It will." I could say that with conviction. Still, the request was reasonable, and I explained more precisely what I had in mind.

Newland nodded a few times as he listened. "OK, Lloyd," he said finally, "you have got yourself a deal." He seemed to forget he'd said the same thing ten days ago. "Would you care for something stronger now?"

"A scotch would be fine." I paused a moment. "However, there is a further point."

"Which is?"

"How do we communicate? How do I receive the final go-ahead come the end of August?"

"Now you want to know *our* plans, huh?" He straightened up and handed me the glass. The ice in it cracked and tinkled as I added water. "I'll give you the instructions tomorrow. With twenty thousand dollars expenses in advance. Half the hundred thousand bonus will go to your bank, like we said. That satisfy you?"

"I'll drink to it."

We both raised our glasses, toasting what amounted to mutual satisfaction with each other's mutual wariness.

"You most likely won't be seeing me again after tomorrow," Newland said. "Though you'll be speaking to Mr. Arain. But we won't be far off and if anything goes wrong, which we sure hope it won't, we'll be expecting both the plane and the fifty thousand back. The salary and expenses you'll keep. Is that clear?"

"Like crystal," I replied, unnecessarily. "Incidentally, did you have any trouble finding me here."

"Not so as you'd notice," he said calmly. "We're starting as we intend to continue, staying behind you all the way."

There was no real answer to that, so I didn't attempt one. I simply said I would see him in the morning and went down to the restaurant for dinner and a spot more thinking.

UPLANDS AIRPORT IS a twenty-five-minute drive from downtown Ottawa through prosperous looking suburbs. My rendezvous on Friday morning was at the offices of an aviation company called Innotech, which specialized in handling private jets and occupied a low building to one side of the main terminal. I walked in with Newland a step behind. We made our way to the reception area and the first thing we saw through the window, standing outside on the tarmac next to a Learjet and gleaming like a Day-Glo yellow dream, was the "civilianized" fighter I had come all this way to buy.

Newland whistled involuntarily. No pilot with an ounce of imagination in him could have reacted otherwise. "For crying out loud," he exclaimed. "If that isn't the damnedest ship I've ever seen."

"Only claimed it was the most beautiful F-86 in the world," cut in a drawling voice behind us.

I spun around and found myself facing a lanky man of around thirty in an old-style U.S. Air Force flying suit, with a badge-emblazoned white flying helmet secured under one arm. He had a crew cut and a short, neat mustache, and I knew at once the breed of man he was: namely, one of those cool-as-a-thousand-dollar-bill fanatics who fly in the Confederate Air Force in the South, consider mint juleps to be the only serious restorative, and run an annual airshow that is practically a war in itself.

"You must be Harragin!" I pumped his free hand enthusiastically. "I'm Hall. My friends call me Hawker. This is a friend from New York, Bob Newland."

"Glad to meet you." Harragin eyed my tweed coat suspiciously. "Bring your flying gear?"

I held up the flight bag I had with me. "Not the bonedome, though. Might not have the right jack connections." Usually protective flying helmets have the earphones and cables for the radio built into them.

"Guess not." Harragin spoke in very clipped sentences. "Come and have a look at her." He led the way out again through another door to the airfield. It was only then, as we walked across the tarmac, that a full appreciation of what he had for sale came home to me.

The Sabre, or F-86, was the pursuit plane I had been flying in my dream that morning when Susie woke me, and the dream must have derived from reading Harragin's ad a few weeks earlier. The F-86 was the West's first swept-wing jet fighter and was still reckoned one of the finest aircraft ever designed, a classic that had been manufactured in many variants as the design had developed. Of the 6,233 built in the United States and Canada up to 1958, very few had survived, and most of those were in museums. This one had been superbly restored. I didn't personally care for the yellow color, but the fuselage was silky sleek, the air intake in the nose giving it a hungry look, the bubble of perspex that enclosed the lone pilot glittering. Harragin's advertisement had called it "spectacular" and it assuredly was.

"Nicest piece of airplane I ever strapped to my ass," he observed laconically.

"Who did the restoration work?" Newland asked. He was clearly impressed.

"Fighter Imports out of Chino." Harragin gazed at his steed proudly. "New wiring, new hydraulics, UHF and VHF radios, transponder, glideslope indicator —you name it." He smiled quizzically. "You want to say good-bye in a hurry, she has a rocket seat."

I nodded. The ejection seat was a near-essential part of my plan. "You have any spare drop tanks?" I asked. Only with additional fuel could she be ferried across the Atlantic, or could I fly my mission for that matter. It would be useful to have spares.

"Back home I have a couple." He indicated the side of the nose, which was flush along where in her fighting days there had been channels for the machine-gun ports. "I have those panels too. Kept them in case some buff wanted her back military again. No gunsight though."

Harragin spent a few more minutes explaining her history, how she was one of the Mark 6s manufactured by Canadair in Montreal for the Royal Canadian Air Force and still had the original Orenda engine. That was why he'd been invited up here to show her off in a veteran aircraft display.

"You flown one before?" he queried.

I shook my head. "Hunters and Phantoms. Sabres were before my time."

"Maybe you should take a little groundschool first."

I could visualize what was going through his mind. The F-86 being a single-seat job, your first flight was your first solo. The insurance was likely to be very restrictive.

"Be glad to give you a coupla days' instruction if you

buy her. I've time on my hands right now. Show her
paces myself if you want."

That was evidently as near as we were going to get to a
flight test, so Newland and I gave her a thorough visual
inspection and then watched as Harragin taxied her out,
the low whine of the Orenda bringing several heads to
the Innotech windows. One of the staff came and joined
us, a middle-aged man in a dark-blue baseball cap.

"Haven't heard one of those flying in Canada for a
long while," he commented reflectively after the noise
had subsided. "Last one I knew of crashed into a store
and killed two kids. After that they went around all the
ones on display as memorials and cut the wing spars
through, made sure they couldn't fly."

"This one was safe in California," Newland said.
"Could your boys do a technical check for us?"

The man pondered briefly, rubbing his chin. "I
believe they have a Sabre 6 and all the manuals over at
Rockcliffe," he said. "They have pretty well everything
that ever flew in Canada there. Yep, with some help
from the National Aeronautical Collection, we could do
it."

"Could you find out?" Newland asked.

As the man retired again to the offices we heard the
far-off crescendo of noise as Harragin began his take
off run. A moment later the Sabre came into sight,
gathering speed until it lifted off and roared away into
the distance in a gentle climbing turn.

Harragin might talk like a cowboy, but he certainly
knew how to fly. He must have fixed things with the Air
Traffic Control too, because he next came past like a
searing yellow flash at about 100 feet and 500 knots,
pulling up over the airfield into a faultless series of near
vertical eight-point rolls until at around 5,000 feet he
came out on his back, flipped level and passed overhead
again, a crisply defined arrow in the pale blue sky.

"OK," Newland said. "If you'll buy her, we will."
He gave me a sharp glance. "You know something, that

silhouette is damn much like a MiG-15.''

"The similarity had occurred to me," I admitted. "Our friend still has a few."

He roared with laughter and slapped me on the back convivially. "Great minds think alike." He reached into his inside pocket and produced a thick manilla envelope. "Here's the dough and the briefing. Call Mr. Arain when you have the bank draft details for Harragin and Innotech has given its report."

"Thanks," I said. I liked Newland, even though he worked a double act with Arain.

"I'll take a cab downtown." He shook hands. "Good luck. Now all you have to do is turn her back into a warplane." He made it sound a lot simpler than it was going to be.

→FOUR→

THE REALITY OF the Sabre turned out different from the dream. Harragin had spent the rest of Friday morning with me, going over the controls and instruments, when he suddenly said, as if regretting his earlier hesitation. "Shit, man. You've flown Phantoms, you take her." Even so, he made it sound as though he was offering me his kid sister for a night out. Reluctantly.

I climbed into the black-painted cockpit, which Harragin found cramped, being so tall, but that for me had everything neatly to hand, started her up, waved away the power trolley, and taxied cautiously out.

I can never step into a plane I haven't flown before without a tingling of apprehension in the gut. Everyone claimed the Sabre "had no vices at all" and she'd responded like a prima ballerina to the way Harragin had treated her, but when they were in service Sabres had created their quota of widows and I wasn't taking any chances.

However, as I released the brakes to let her roll for the take off, and the Orenda's power punched me in the

71

back, all the old exhilaration returned. I pulled the nose
up at ninety-five knots and had to keep on pulling to get
her airborne, but after that it was fine. The wheels and
flaps came up at 150 and seconds later I was at circuit
height, a few of Harragin's injunctions ringing in my
ears. "Shoot the circuit at eight hundred feet," he had
counseled. "Take it wide." I did just that and was delighted to realize what a magnificent field of view the
bubble canopy gave. "You can see your six o'clock
easy," he had assured me, and sure enough in straight
and level flight I could scan the suburbs vertically below
if I leant slightly to one side. Coming around the circuit
I lowered the gear again, flipped the airbrakes switch on
top of the throttle, and settled at 170 for the final turn,
keeping a margin well above the minimum, not trying to
impress anyone. There was no need for that excessively
nose-high attitude the Phantom demanded, which so
curtailed one's forward vision, and I made a nice, easy
approach, flaring out over the threshold and, as Harragin put it, "chopping the throttle on the button." We
rejoined Mother Tarmac with a slight bump and an obe-
dient rumble from the tires.

After three more circuits I was as happy as Larry and
decided to taxi in. So far as her handling and conditions
were concerned, the reality had proved one whole lot
better than the dream. What I was acquiring was a piece
of aviation legend, as much a part of history as the Spitfire Harragin had wanted in exchange. That would only
have been a burden if she had not been in first-class
shape. There was no time in my schedule for refurbish-
ing or anything more than the essential modifications.
But because she was such a beautifully kept classic I
knew that my plan for reforging her as a warplane could
hardly fail. In principle.

There was one immediate snag. The whole armament
control panel had been removed. Originally it would
have been straight ahead of me below the main instruments. Now, where formerly there had been switches

and levers for activating guns, rockets, and bombs, some of the new radio gear had been installed. True, the bomb-release button was still on the stick, where you could press it with your right thumb, though Harragin had told me it was not wired up. That would have to be reconnected, because although you could drop a bomb by using the jettison button, to do so involved taking your left hand off the throttle, which would be less than desirable in a live attack. True, also, I wasn't planning to reinstall guns anyway, and as Newland had observed, I could hardly fly across Europe with rockets dangling under the wings. But I was going to need the aiming devices that enable you to hit a target with a bomb. In fighting terms, the Sabre was comparable to a rifle with a trigger but no sights or firing pin, or a computer without a program. I had forgotten how heavily I used to rely on electronic aids in the Phantom. By comparison this plane was a beautiful body with no brain. Except my own. I wondered how far I dared try to reinstate her killing capacity here and now. I hardly wanted to provoke awkward questions when, not having collected Hawker Hall's passport, I was checked in at the Four Seasons in my real name.

"Looked OK to me," Harragin commented as I swung my left leg over the side and clambered down, scrabbling for the steps inset into the fuselage.

"She's fine. Could we run over a few details?" I would start with the more innocent requests first.

We went inside and the Innotech engineer joined us, introducing himself as Jim Grainger. It rapidly emerged that Harragin had been meticulous in obtaining as much equipment for the Sabre as any sporting ace could reasonably require. He had all the service manuals. Back in California he had the tools and spares of all kinds, cannibalized from a wrecked Sabre he had located in a junkyard. He had a back parachute he could sell me, and the seat pack I had strapped to my backside during the flight was authentic, containing all the necessities for survival on land, like rations, matches, and mosquito netting. That made a good starting point.

"The net might not be too good in the Atlantic," I joked. "I'm going to need the maritime pack with a dinghy."

Grainger grunted. "You have a problem. We can find you a dinghy, but not in a seat pack. What else?"

"Well," I chose my words carefully, "I'm expecting to hangar her in Britain at a field belonging to our Imperial War Museum. They have a whole galaxy of historic aircraft. It may be one of the conditions that I repaint her in service colors."

"That's OK if you tell us the paint scheme," Grainger assured me.

"Could we also lay hands on any of the old equipment that would interest visitors there?" I edged closer to my real needs. "I'm not with you," Grainger said. "What do you mean?"

"Well, Mr. Harragin here has the original gunport panels. There's no need to have the guns themselves, but the gun-and bombsights would look good in the cockpit."

Harragin shook his head. "I guess those went before she was restored. The military would have kept that kind of thing."

"Hey," Grainger interrupted. "Like I told you before, why don't you go across to Rockcliffe? The National Aeronautical Collection there has two hangars just full of planes and gear. If it's for your War Museum, they might help." He reached for a slip of paper and scribbled a name. "Ask for Luke. He's an engineer too. I'll call him if you like." He got up and went along to his office.

"Say," Harragin asked as soon as Grainger was gone. "What else you planning on having?"

"I could use a Collins HF radio." I didn't specify the 68,000-channel set with a worldwide voice capability. Even so, he stared at me in such surprise that I felt compelled to explain. "With an HF set I could call the office from pretty well anywhere."

"Holy smoke. Where you planning on going?"

"Around Europe. I like to keep in touch." That was the understatement of the year. The orders Newland had handed over included a day and night phone number and I had a more than strong feeling that the moment would come on this operation when it might not be convenient to land the Sabre at the nearest airfield and go to a coinbox. With the military version of the Collins I had once heard a Navy pilot talk from a helicopter flying around Hong Kong harbor to Lossiemouth in Scotland, clear as a bell. The Dubai Air Wing used the civil version to communicate direct with their Boeings as they left Heathrow or Kennedy so as to know exactly when this or that sheikh would be arriving. Better still, provided you had an American Express card number to quote, you could call Stockholm Radio and they would patch you through to any telephone number in the world—at least any number that could be dialed—in little more than thirty seconds. It was all a far cry from the graffiti and jammed slots of the Fulham phone booths. More importantly, I could afford it. Or rather, Hawker Hall could.

"I guess it'd be possible," Harragin said reflectively. "We used some of the ammunition bay for the transponder, but there's plenty of space left." He seemed embarrassed for a moment, which was unlike him, then went on abruptly. "Listen, man, have it done at Chino, right. Those guys know more about this ship than anyone. Do a good paint job, too, if you have to change."

For Harragin this was a pretty long speech and I could hear the regret in the last sentence. He clearly preferred the Sabre being colored like a hallucinating canary.

I was just thinking that Chino, which is a suburb of Los Angeles, must be almost as far from Ottawa as Ottawa is from London and that it was diametrically in the wrong direction, when another consideration struck me. When Harragin added that he'd be glad to fly the Sabre down for me if I needed to get back home, I agreed. It wasn't as though Los Angeles was inaccessible, and flying myself back from there would be a useful way of familiarizing myself with the plane's capabilities before the long ferry flight. One thing stuck out like a mourner at a wedding in the pilot's notes: you had to know the Sabre to extract the maximum performance from her. There was no point in forging a weapon unless I learned how to use it.

The decision delighted Harragin. He was indeed only selling the plane because of rising fuel prices—she drank 4,100 pounds an hour at low level—and underneath his brusque, cowboyish exterior he was heavily sentimental about her. I could understand why my shopping list had confused him. I was about to change the character of his baby. In one direction I was trying to make her into a museum piece; in another to install state-of-the-art communications equipment. Since there was no possibility of explaining this paradox, I contented myself with concluding the financial arrangements, subject to Innotech's check report.

As soon as was possible I took a cab to the National Aeronautical Collection, vowing not to make so many demands on one person again. My plan rested on conditioning people to see the Sabre in the light I wanted it seen, and I was going to have to keep that conditioning process simple. I should only have bothered Harragin and Innotech with questions affecting the ferry flight, like the liferaft. The Aeronautical Collection would be the place to discuss restoring the plane's appearance to a fighter. When it came to acquiring bombs: well, that was another ball game altogether, and for the moment it would have to wait.

Rockcliffe turned out to be a sprawling, largely disused airfield and the cabdriver had difficulty finding the isolated hangars that housed the National Collection.

He refused to wait and left me to wander around until I
found a small side-door leading into some workshops.
The security was not exactly tight. I asked for Luke and
eventually a young, bearded man in white overalls appeared and introduced himself. From then on it was
plain sailing.

Luke, who looked about twenty-eight but must have
been older, quickly revealed himself as an enthusiast
who had quit working as a licensed engineer for an
airline to come here because he was mad about restoration. He obviously loved the place. By the time he had
shown me only part of the collection I appreciated why.
The two vast hangars were an Aladdin's cave spanning
at least sixty years of aviation history, everything from
Northwest pioneers' floatplanes to jets.

"Trouble is, we haven't the staff or the funds to fix
them all," he said, eyeing a prewar Messerschmitt built
in Spain. "But we do have a beautiful Sabre 6." Then
he couldn't hold back his curiosity any longer. "Say, is
it true you just bought one? That really is something.
Gee, I'd sure like to see it."

In that instant I knew I had him hooked. He was
going to see my plane the way I wanted him to, and
when he left me alone to inspect their Sabre at leisure I
kept my sticky fingers off its equipment. In almost any
other circumstances I would have been a trifle unscru-
pulous as far as stores were concerned: "Who needs,
takes" was my motto. But I reckoned Luke would be
too good value as a friend to risk it. So I examined the
gunsight, the armament panel, the drop tanks, and a lot
of other detail and contented myself with making careful notes.

My seriousness paid off. When I told Luke about the
Imperial War Museum's array of aircraft at Duxford,
he fully understood.

"I expect to be flying her there at open days," I said,
lying in my teeth, "and of course the gunsight and the
head-up display aren't essential for that. But if she's

going to be in service colors again—Royal Canadian Air
Force colors—I'd like to have the equipment right. Visitors feel cheated if it's missing. A lot of specialists go
there for research work too."

That was laying it on thick enough, I thought, and I
cut myself short.

"I'm sure the director will want to help," Luke assured me, "especially since she's a Canadian aircraft. I
know we have a spare gun-bomb-rocket sight stored
away. Would you want the radar?"

"Well . . ." I stalled because he had gone much further than I dared hope. The radar, from what I'd read,
was basically for tracking enemy aircraft, rather than
low-level bombing.

"They had a lot of trouble with the radar," Luke
went on, helping me decide. "That AN/APG 30 was a
bastard. You could spend a fortune making it work.
And it's not visible."

"Let's forget it." I was happy not to sound eager all
the time. "What happened when it went unservice-
able?"

"There was a manually operated backup system."

"Using the Mark I human eyeball?"

"You said it," Luke laughed. "So what else can we
help with?"

I told him a few more things. He promised to do what
he could and asked when I would be back. I hazarded a
fortnight and then he suggested that for items like the
seat pack I ought to try a government agency called
the Crown Assets Disposal Corporation. He was sure
the seat pack was the same as the one used in the T-33
jet trainer, so there ought to be some around still.

"They're right here in Ottawa," he explained. "On
Rideau Street."

In the end he called them on my behalf, made an immediate appointment, and then, as he wasn't too busy,
offered me a lift there. At the Crown Assets offices, I

put in formal requests to buy the maritime environment seat pack plus two 167-gallon and two 100-gallon drop tanks. They weren't as bushy-tailed about the idea as Luke, but after all they were strictly in business, selling government surplus, and there's nothing romantic about that. Nonetheless, I caught the London flight on Friday evening well satisfied.

Back at the flat in Fulham, which I reached after breakfast the next morning, there were the usual brown envelopes of bills lying on the carpet in the hall: evidently the cleaning woman hadn't come. Nor could Susie have done, or she would have picked them up. I suddenly felt more alone than I had for a long time. It's always liable to be a bad moment, returning to an empty home, and I was so tired that my joints ached. This is going to get worse, I told myself firmly, and it has to be faced. The closer September 1 gets, the more acute the moments of stress will become and the worse the feeling of isolation will be. I made some coffee, ran a bath, and tried to concentrate on the positive aspects, like the mechanics of the flying and the pot of gold at the end of the rainbow. But all the bath achieved was to bring back memories of Susie caressing me last week, and it took all my self-discipline to go to bed afterward for a few hours of what the services used to call "enforced rest."

The phone woke me with Rajni's soft sibilant voice on the line, asking if it would be convenient for me to come over for coffee. My immediate thought was that he must have hit a snag with the documents, though he didn't say so. In fact he didn't even say his name. He was a model of discretion, Rajni. I forced myself fully awake, feeling half-drugged from the interrupted sleep, dressed and walked over, taking a couple of thousand dollars with me as a precaution. I also pocketed my own passport in case I wanted to make comparisons.

Rajni welcomed me with his customary unctuousness and led the way to the back office, where, after the routine of serving coffee, he fished out a thick envelope from his desk and gently slid the contents onto the heavily ornamented teak table.

"That was quick!" I complimented him, carefully picking up the various certificates comprising Hawker Hall's flying license. At first glance they appeared perfect.

"You must sign," Rajni insisted. He produced a gold pen and I put Hall's signature on each of the three pieces of paper in turn. "I am not finding plastic cover," he went on apologetically.

"No sweat." I explained that I could get one easily enough from the CAA myself.

He seemed relieved by the news, but obviously had something else on his mind, though it took a few minutes to bring it to the surface.

"With passport I am making one mistake," he finally admitted. "Very stupid mistake."

Praying his contacts hadn't done something really damnfool, like trying to con the passport office, I told him not to worry.

"We are dating this passport last year, isn't it?"

"It would look better."

"Then if it is not being new and you are with profession 'businessman' we must be putting stamps in that document. Foreign stamps." He reached out his right fist and thumped the table, miming an immigration official. "What countries you like to be visiting?"

The point was a good one and I should have thought of it myself. I took out my own passport, grateful for the premonition that had made me bring it along, and suggested he should copy a few entry and exit markings, particularly this week's Ottawa ones. Luckily, British citizens don't need a visa for Canada and the entry stamp had been a simple red rectangle, with "Canada Customs" at the top in both English and French.

"Easy pie," Rajni declared happily. "No problem. We are having ready Monday evening."

"Fantastic. Can I give you some money now?" Frankly, I hated carrying all this cash around. When Newland gave me the $45,000, $25,000 had been in a draft made to bearer that I had banked immediately in my Geneva account. But Hawker had to be established with solid banking credit of his own in London and the other twenty could not be deposited until I had proof of his identity available.

Rajni made a short and unconvincing show of not being in a hurry for the cash, then accepted $1,400 as a rough equivalent of the £1,000. It seemed a sensible moment to raise the question of my future requirements.

"Could you do a Malta entry stamp for this passport?" I asked. "In a couple of months."

He laughed and slapped me on the shoulder. I guessed the small sheaf of banknotes had a faintly intoxicating effect on him, while as for the goddess of fortune up on the wall, I could have sworn she was smiling.

"My friend," he assured me, pure joy in his eyes, "you could not be coming to a better person. I am sending tours to Malta every week. You like to vacation there, I am giving you best possible discount! I am arranging top-hole package vacation half-price special for you. Vacation with very select group."

I stared at him, a new idea dawning in spite of the fatigue. In outline, my plan was complete, but flexibility is the hallmark of good planning. Malta was conveniently close to Libya and if I had to go there, a package tour might not be a bad way. This was early days though, so I merely thanked him and filed the possibility away in my memory. There were more immediate matters to attend to over the next four weeks.

I walked back to the apartment. It was a glorious summer afternoon, the kind of day when you ought to be by a river with a picnic hamper, a bottle of wine, and your favorite girlfriend. Inevitably, by the time I was home the urge to call Susie was well-nigh unbearable. There was no answer at her old number, and I left a message with the British Caledonian rostering office at Gatwick, resigning myself to the possibility of her not getting it for several days. Even so, the thought of going through the routine of ringing around to find someone else to take out failed to appeal. When this was all finished, I told myself, I ought to think seriously about Susie.

In fact it was over a week before the message elicited a reply, and the days between passed with a reassuring lack of drama, given that I spent them building up Hawker Hall's background step by step, always half-afraid someone would question the forged passport.

Hawker, as I trained myself to think of my alter ego, acquired deposit and current accounts at Lloyds Bank in Pall Mall, a traditional bank for service officers to use, and with these he obtained an access card. Next, this card plus bank references enabled him to rent a serviced apartment in a well-run building in Sloane Avenue in Chelsea. The building specialized in business visitors and had a switchboard to take messages.

So far so good. But Hawker could not survive in America without a driving license. Here my heart sank. In its wisdom the British bureaucracy ran a computer center in Wales for all road licensing, which had acquired a reputation second to none for incompetence. If there was ever a place where computerization had reduced the ordinary citizen's efforts to a meaningless struggle, the Vehicle Licensing Center was it. Their computer needed a minimum of a month to spew out a license after receiving the driving-test examiner's certificate. I had to find another way, and while I searched for it I decided to put the new passport over its first major hurdle by applying for an American visa.

The consular department of the United States embassy has a side entrance in the Grosvenor Square building. I went up the stone steps, submitted to having my briefcase searched, and was let through to a large, marble-floored hall principally occupied by a waiting congregation of young travelers. They sat on benches around the side, the men in jeans with long unkempt hair and knapsacks, the girls looking much the same, though with an occasional flowering of ethnic dresses. At the far end was a line of inquiry counters staffed by officials behind protective grilles. I completed the long form, handed it in, and found a seat alongside a traveling couple, who eyed my short hair and lightweight gray suit with extreme suspicion. They even shifted away a little. I suppose I must have looked like a CIA stooge to them.

However, I was at least looking like a stooge in the right place. I had hardly been there fifteen minutes before my name was called.

"I'm buying an aircraft in California," I explained to the lady officer behind the grille. "I'd like to go across next week."

"I'm sure there'll be no difficulty, sir." With a faint inclination of her head she indicated "youth on the march" behind me. "Those are the ones we worry about. All pretending they won't be living off the land. Who do they think they're kidding? How long would you be staying?"

"Two weeks or so."

"I'll mark it for multiple reentry." She smiled graciously. "California's a great state. You might like to return." She glanced at my passport, filled in a receipt, and pushed it gently across to me. "Come back tomorrow afternoon, sir."

I thanked her warmly and retreated, the couple I had sat next to eyeing me morosely as though there was no justice in this world. Nonetheless I still feared the embassy might put Hawker's passport through some kind of X-ray examination that would show it up. However, when I returned next day there was no fuss and one page of the document was occupied by a blue-and-

red visa with the space under "Valid Until" marked
"Indefinitely" in capitals. I felt like giving Rajni a tes-
timonial.

Furthermore, my luck continued to hold. Pursuing
the driving license problem, I visited the Automobile
Association where a friendly official tipped me the wink
that there was one perfectly legal method of obtaining a
license in a hurry, though it would cost the price of an
airfare and an hotel room.

In consequence, the next three days saw the Channel
Islands tourist figures boosted by one late booking. I
checked into the Old Government House Hotel overlooking St. Peter Port in Guernsey on Wednesday and
was the possessor of an old-fashioned, very definitely
noncomputerized, provisional license the same afternoon. An obliging local garage proprietor, who doubled
as an examiner, rented me a Ford the next morning and
took me on a test drive around the narrow lanes of the
island and through the confusing one-way streets of the
old town. He also gave me a lecture on bad habits, like
the way I held the steering wheel, and then asked tautly
how long I had been driving. However, a story about
mislaying my original Canadian license satisfied him
and by the following morning I had a brand-new full
license, issued by the States of the Bailiwick of Guernsey.

"Remember you can't drive on this in Britain forever," the girl cautioned me when I gave the Fulham
box-number address. "But you can get a UK one with
our test certificate."

"A year'll see me through," I said cheerfully. "And I
promise I'll come back here for my next holiday."

"Take care," she said, and smiled shyly as I left. All
in all it had been a good week for lady officials.

By the time I was flying back to London I felt a small
celebration was due, because Hawker Hall was now furnished with virtually all the documentary accoutrements

a respectable man of the world required, apart from an unpaid tailor's bill. Which was a point. His wardrobe ought to be a trifle flashier than mine, and he would have to keep clothes of his own in his new apartment or the management would become suspicious. I was still cogitating on this when the taxi dropped me outside my own apartment and I walked in to find Susie there.

"Hi, sweetheart," she said equably, kissing my cheek with unusual restraint. "That was nicely timed." She was out of uniform for a change, greeting the summer warmth in tight-fitting white slacks and a scarlet silk shirt, and looking delightfully unlike "youth on the march." "I only got your message this morning. Where have you been?"

"To Guernsey for an interview." One thing I'd learned about deception during my brief married life was that one should stick as close to the truth as is feasible, especially with regard to places. If I'd said Paris, for example, there would sure as hell have been a strike at Charles de Gaulle, or fog, or both. "There's a local airline down there I might get a job with," I elaborated.

"So what's wrong with CONOIL?"

"No future." I made a gesture indicating futility, put the briefcase with Hawker's papers safely under the hall table, and gave her a spiel about being kept on standby all the time and never actually flying. "I'm not even keeping my hours up." Jesus, that was true too. At this rate a large chunk of my bonus was going to have to disappear straight into my own logbook, unless I risked logging the ferry flight across the Atlantic.

"That's bad." She looked quite troubled. "Have a drink?"

"Coffee would be better." I went through to the kitchen and switched on the kettle myself, thinking that I could now afford to get myself a decent coffee percolator. "Anyway," I asked, "where have you been? Pakiland again?" It struck me as quite a funny coin-

cidence that she kept going to the one place I would like
to have had a snoop around, Pakistan being the home
of the Islamic bomb.

"That's next week's delight." She laughed. "If one
happens to like Karachi. All I ever do is lie by the pool
at the Holiday Inn, watching the hawks circle over the
kitchens and wishing they served something stronger
than orange juice in the evenings." As a description of
how flight crews spend their stopovers in Muslim countries it could hardly be faulted. I laughed with her until
she abruptly shifted to the attack. "And how's the
famous Mr. Smith? Still around?"

"He's gone back to the Gulf," I replied warily, getting a glance of the plainest disbelief in return.

"Hence the message."

"You might say so. Also I was missing you."

"It's nice to know when one's wanted," she said sardonically, promptly changing her tune again, coming
into the kitchen and giving me a warm hug. "You are an
idiot. Why do I like you so much?" She stamped her
foot in pretended indignation. "Why *do* I?" She tossed
her head, then kissed me again. "Anyway, since I do,
let's go and have a super dinner somewhere."

So I had my celebration, though Susie never knew the
true reason, and the next morning, after a long and
tender lie-in, she wanted to go to the country for a long
weekend. It was almost the first time that one of us had
not had to rush off on duty. The weather was glorious.
So I suggested Cambridge, which would enable us to
stop at Duxford en route and see the collection of aircraft there. One of the less attractive aspects of my
character is that I seldom do anything without an ul-
terior motive. However, she didn't seem to mind.

"You really do think, sleep, and dream airplanes,
don't you, sweetheart?" she remarked, half-approv-
ingly.

Duxford is maybe ten miles south of Cambridge and
was originally constructed in 1917, later serving the U.S.

Eighth Air Force as one of the many World War II air-fields scattered around the flat, low-lying East Anglian countryside. Under the aegis of the Imperial War Museum it had achieved a rebirth and there were scores of visitors gawping at the line of planes on parade in front of the hangars. However, once Susie had peeked inside the first Concorde airliner and commented rather tartly on the smallness of the galley, her interest became less than total. When I wanted to talk history to one of the staff she retired to sit in the sun, which suited me very well.

The man I had accosted was the English equivalent of Luke and equally helpful. To my surprise he told me there had been a former RCAF test pilot who had kept a number of aircraft here.

"She was Ormond's," he said, pointing to a Sea Fury parked on display. "And he had two T-33s. And an Anson. And a Harvard. He recruited a whole team of volunteers from the Aviation Society to service them. Everyone had white overalls with 'The Black Knight' printed on their backs. That was what he called himself —The Black Knight. He was a character, Ormond."

"What happened?" This man sounded as though he had done exactly what I had in mind for Hawker, only more so.

"No one knows for sure. He was flying a Mustang in the circuit and plowed."

"Poor bastard." A crash on the airfield was not the end I had in mind for either Hawker or myself. However, there did seem to be a precedent for the earlier stages of my scenario. "As it happens," I said, "I've just bought a Sabre in the States and I want to bring her to England. D'you think they'd let me hangar her here?"

"Don't see why not." The man considered the idea. "You'd be welcome, I reckon, so long as it was available on open days. You'd have to ask the director though and he's not here."

He gave me the name and telephone number and I departed to rejoin Susie, well content. With space available here, and the well-known firm of Marshalls in Cambridge nearby to service her, my mount would be well stabled.

The rest of the weekend passed enjoyably enough and, not wishing to spoil things, I left it until we were back in London to tell Susie that I would be away for the next two months, though if there was any chance of meeting I would cable her. "I have to work out the contract," I explained, pretty unconvincingly I thought, "even if I do spend all the time sitting on my backside waiting."

She accepted it philosophically: Susie was the least predictable girl I've ever known. But she could read my mind, read it straight through. As we hugged goodbye she said, "I tell you what, sweetheart. If there's the slightest chance, let's sneak off abroad for a holiday. It doesn't matter where, so long as it's warm."

As I say, she was a mind reader because it had already occurred to me that a tender loving companion, capable of providing an alibi, might be very useful in the final days of the operation. She need not even know what was actually happening until it was over. If I could trust her afterward, that was. I let the idea ride, just promising to do my best. Afterward, it occurred to me, was going to be the rest of my life.

The next week brought one bonus I had been anticipating. The first batch of mail-order junk from America landed in the Fulham post office box. That meant the American pilot's license was on its way. There's a not-so-subtle difference between the British and American systems in this regard. Whereas the British do not record an address on a private license, the FAA goes to the other extreme and passes one's details on to various companies that consider pilots creditworthy, though God knows why. The item I wanted was an American Express gold card to supplement the Ac-

cess one. Sure enough, the application form was there
and I lost no time in completing it with Hawker's new
bank references. I also alloted him £70,000 in assorted
industrial shares and a £180,000 house in Kensington,
which was rented to an oil company, this explaining why
he himself lived in a Sloane Avenue apartment. I
doubted if they'd check any of it. All in all, their faith in
the natural-born solvency of the flying fraternity was
touching.

I flew back to Ottawa, spent four days assembling
stores for the Sabre, and continued via New York to Los
Angeles. The time had come for a major step in reforging the aircraft into a weapon.

If California is not the most aviation-minded state in
the union, it must come a close second to whichever is.
Quite apart from testing spacecraft and building airliners, the neighborhood of Los Angeles is home to
dozens of airfields, large and small. Chino was situated
near Highway 10, which threads east through the San
Jacinto mountains to Palm Springs and Arizona. Like
any field, Chino had its complement of Cessnas, Pipers,
and the other breeds of light plane that held keep
Californians air-mobile. It also had the added glamour
of aircraft Fighter Imports had restored, and I soon
learned that the Sabre had attracted its quota of ad-
mirers. At the moment, however, she was in a hangar
while mechanics tinkered with her wiring. Although
Harragin was away, he had done me a good turn: he had
brought the bombsight with him and it was already
being fitted.

"We had a problem with that gizmo," one of the
managers explained. "Needed a single-phase inverter."
He was a short man, wearing a T-shirt under a lightweight windbreaker, and his fleshy, cheerful face was
topped out with a blue baseball cap on which were em-
broidered wings and his name, Lewis. Another badge on
the hat announced him as one of the "Warbirds of
America."

"That head-up display was awkward too," he continued. "Come take a look."

There was a ladder against the Sabre and I climbed up, clutching a copy of the Pilot's Notes, to see if everything appeared correct. It did. The head-up display consisted of a small glass reflector panel mounted inside the windshield onto which the gunsight threw an illuminated image of a dot in the center of a circle of dots. When flying the plane, the pilot could line up these dots with his target without having to look down. Hence the name "head-up." The way the dots were projected onto the glass could be adjusted to allow for the trajectory of either machine-gun fire, rockets, or bombs.

"Without the radar," Lewis observed, stating the blindingly obvious, "it won't be automatic."

"No sweat," I assured him. "I only need to be able to work it manually. So long as I can demonstrate the principle on display days, that'll be fine." In fact, I thought happily, you might even term September 1 a display day. "Could I fly her tomorrow?"

"She'd be ready."

"Then if you could fill the drop tanks . . ." I saw the surprise on his face and hastened to reassure him. "Don't worry, I'm not leaving without paying or anything. I just want to get the feel of her fully loaded." I was not about to tell him my plans for tomorrow.

The desert, as Californians collectively refer to everything east of the Sierra Nevada mountains, is the size of Connecticut, more than twenty thousand square miles. Out there, in a parched and searingly hot landscape, are the Mojave and Colorado deserts; the dry lakes like Rogers, where astronauts bring the space shuttle to earth; the buttes and mountains that have featured in a thousand Westerns; and vast tracts of barren real estate belonging to the Naval Weapons Test Center, the air force and the military. With all that space I could surely do my own weapons test without anyone noticing. I'd forgotten the old Gulf joke about how, if you stop your vehicle where the population is two to the square mile, those two Bedu will immediately pop up from behind the nearest rock.

So next morning, with the sky showing blue above the Los Angeles smog, I eased the Sabre off the runway and headed east, having told the tower I would be doing a few high-speed low-level runs out of everybody's way. The air there was crystal clear and 120 miles out I crossed the Twenty-Nine Palms beacon, avoiding the restricted area of the Marine Corps base, and swung north at 8,000 feet, scanning the ground for an isolated, abandoned building and feeling conscious of the rate the Orenda was gulping fuel at this low altitude.

I had been told that there were ghost towns in the Mojave, though a mere shack would serve as an aiming point. Near a soda lake, its surface dirty white, I flew over a chemical plant, shining silver in the wilderness like a science-fiction project on the moon, with ranges of jumbled, blackened rock in the distance. At last, close by a dirt track, I noticed what appeared to be a hut, so I let down to 1,000 feet and made a run along the line of the track, peeling off in a screaming turn to observe the hut. Its roof had caved in and there was what might have been rusted mining machinery alongside it, but not a car or human being in sight. I had found my target.

Pulling up again, I marked the spot as accurately as possible on the map. Appropriately enough, it was in an area called "The Devil's Playground," at least twenty miles wide and enclosed by a rough horseshoe of mountains. I went methodically through the drills, setting the sight manually for a bombing height of 1,500 feet, then descended and came past at a comfortably slow 250 knots for a preliminary run. That was how I planned to overfly Qaddafi's parade: with no rush, taking it easy on a straight-in approach. Until I hit the button, that is, after which I should get the hell out, leaving behind a big bang and a high degree of chaos. The scenario de-

pended on very accurate flying, the newly fitted bombsight, and today's practice.

Immediately there was a snag. As I flew toward the
hut it became hidden by the Sabre's nose. Normally one
would be making a straight-in attack at only 500 feet or
lower, as close to the deck as possible, and then there
would be no forward-vision problem. However, it
would be futile practicing at anything except the altitude
that circumstances would force me to be at on September 1, so I circled, looking for a feature short of the
hut that was approximately the distance between the
boundary fence of Tripoli airfield and the terminal
building. I found it in the shape of a slight bend in the
track and made a second dummy run.

This time I pushed her into a dive over the bend and
the hut came close to the circle of dots on the head-up
display. I went around yet again, checking that there
was still no sign of life below, and allowing a long run-in
for what might be the only "live" practice attack I
would be able to make before September. The drop
tanks were streamlined and fitted with fins, so they
should arc down like bombs, though until the bomb-
release was reconnected I could only let them go by
pressing the jettison button. The wind, so far as I could
judge from the shadow of a solitary puff of cloud, was
about ten knots toward me, the usual southwesterly
desert breeze. At five miles out from the hut I settled her
down straight and level along the line of the track.

For all that this was a practice and against no opposi-
tion, I felt my stomach muscles tighten. Glancing down,
I could see the Sabre's shadow streaking across the
stony ground. Suddenly I was over the curve, pushing
the nose down, focusing on the hut. It came in the center of the dots, I pressed the jettison with my left thumb,
the Sabre bucked as the tanks fell away, and when the
hut flashed past underneath I crammed on the power
and banked into a tight left turn, craning sideways to
observe the result.

The hut was untouched. Fifty yards short of it a small cloud of dust, and dark stains on the sand, showed where the tanks had hit. I continued circling, fixing the relative position of the track, the hut, and the impact firmly in my mind. The tanks must have split open. They lay some ten yards apart. I had a pad strapped to my leg and noted it all down because I should have to recalibrate the sight and try again. Then, as I made the last circuit, I saw a pickup coming along the track. It was moving fast, a long plume of dust billowing behind.

The only thing to do was to run. I piled on the power and climbed away at the Sabre's full 11,000 feet a minute toward LA, wishing to hell the plane wasn't still painted that vivid, Day-Glo yellow. As a precaution, I called the nearest airfield, Daggett, on the radio and reported the accidental jettisoning of two drop tanks over the desert. The controller simply asked me to file a routine explanation with the tower at Chino. I didn't yet know there would be far worse news waiting for me when I got back there.

====→ FIVE ====>

AFTER LANDING AT Chino, I put on my best imitation of an aging student who has just made a total fool of himself.

"Hear you lost something," Lewis commented succintly, tugging the peak of his much-decorated baseball cap a shade lower over his eyes as he squinted at the Sabre's wings.

"Hit some turbulence during a low run," I said, with what I hoped was the right mix of self-assurance and apology. Everything I said and did from now on would be building an image of Hawker's character, so that the end I was intending for him would cause no surprise. "She went nose down, and I thought I'd better get rid of those tanks." I grinned as if I was pleased to be alive. "Anyway, it cured the problem."

"Guess so," Lewis conceded. "Lucky Harragin had a spare couple of them." He scratched his chin, as though trying to visualize my emergency, then shrugged his shoulders. "Anyway, Harragin'll be here pretty soon."

So I walked across to the tower and said my piece

95

there. As a matter of fact, it wasn't a bad invention, as stories go. When I was in flying training school, my instructor told me he used to fly Sabres and he'd once lost control after passing over a strong up-current. He said he porpoised along for a minute or two, first up, then down, and found when he landed that the meter showed he'd pulled 8G.

"Could have happened to anyone," the Chino controller remarked equably. "But we just had a complaint from the state troopers at Barstow. Seems some crazy prospector out there claims you tried to kill him."

"That's nonsense," I protested. "There was no one for miles."

The controller shrugged his shoulders and passed me a slip of paper with a number on it. "You'll have to call them."

He was right of course. The most annoying thing being that I had planned to drive out to the Devil's Playground and pick up the pieces. I needed to know exactly how the tanks had struck the ground and to measure their precise distance from the hut. That old phrase about "a near miss" is just face-saving. A bomb either hits or it doesn't. What I would need on September 1 was a hit. The sight would have to be accurately calibrated, prospector or no prospector, although I was far from certain how to calm down a man who sounded as overexcited as this one. He did have to be off his head too because, as the controller explained, serious prospecting there died out around the same period as the mule teams stopped hauling borax in from Death Valley. "The proving ground for hell" is how he described the Mojave.

However, I did telephone the police, and the officer, for all that he adopted a more relaxed attitude when he heard I had reported the incident by radio, nonetheless demanded a written statement in view of the complaint. Since I wanted the file closed, I agreed to drive out in the next couple of days. Of course, I could have given a statement in Los Angeles, but I hoped the trooper might escort me to recover the drop tanks.

Harragin's arrival distracted me from fruitless speculation about how I could have avoided being caught out and, since I reckoned I owed him a lunch for bringing the bombsight from Ottawa, I offered whatever the diner on the airfield could provide.

We settled down to steaks, french fries, and a side salad served by a blonde waitress who I swear had one blue eye and one brown. Harragin commented on her being the place's main attraction, then remarked, "Hear you nearly bought the ranch."

"That's a slight exaggeration," I explained, thinking that by tomorrow rumor would probably have me dead.

"Speaking personally," he said thoughtfully, "I never met with any pitch-oscillation problem. Guess the best way out could be just to let go of everything and she'd come out flying straight and level."

"You think so?" To my mind letting go the controls at a few hundred feet and several hundred knots would require a positively yogalike detachment from one's own wellbeing, though he could be right. I made a mental note of the theory and then changed the subject, asking how his flight from Ottawa had gone.

"Fine."

That was what he said, but a sudden hardness in his voice and the way he looked at me belied it.

"Did you fix the seat so it wouldn't go down?"

"Do what?" The accusation jerked me out of the playboy role with a jolt. As with a car, the Sabre's seat was adjustable. However, beyond that the comparison ended, because the aircraft's ejection system could punch you out like a steam hammer in an emergency and be lethal if it didn't function properly.

"Being so tall," he said, "I have to put that seat right down. But the damn thing was jammed. Had one of the worst rides I've ever had."

I looked at Harragin mystified, yet with an increasingly chilly feeling taking possession of my gut. I don't like planes I fly being tampered with. "How was it during your display?" I asked.

"Fine." Suddenly he realized what he was acknowledging. "Guess you couldn't have fixed it," he admitted slowly. "Don't make no difference who did though, that seat being stuck could make ejecting mighty dangerous."

"I know," I said curtly. "I've read the Notes."

The Pilot's Notes, which were produced originally by the air force, were not intended to dampen enthusiasm. They shrouded the ejection seat's possibilities in neat language.

"Should the canopy fail to jettison . . . it is possible to eject the seat through the canopy . . . it is important to first lower the seat fully, to permit the top of the seat rails to strike the canopy and thereby shatter the plexiglass."

Translated, what this meant was that if the seat was not lowered, the item of equipment that shattered the canopy was the pilot's head. Exit one dead pilot dangling on a parachute. Assuming that the device that removed the canopy was not working.

"Well," said Harragin, whose speed of reaction did not include jumping to conclusions. "If you didn't fix that seat, what did happen?"

The question was unanswerable. In fact, as I watched Harragin knife into his ribeye, I began wondering if some tool used by a mechanic had not been dropped and forgotten, ending up obstructing the seat. Hundreds of air crashes, thousands maybe, have been caused by screwdrivers and wrenches being left behind in cockpits and subsequently jamming the controls. What made me queasy was the importance of the rocket seat for my escape after the mission. Although the meal was on me—or to be more exact on Arain—Harragin did not get the enjoyment he deserved. He was an observant man under his cowboy hide and he finished his steak quickly.

"OK," he suggested. "Let's go find out."

With Lewis directing a mechanic, I began our investigation, making sure the locking pins were installed so the seat could not be sent skyward accidentally. With proper tools and a torch it took only ten minutes to discover the obstruction to the seat's movement. Right out of sight, hammered in under the frame, was a narrow wedge of aluminum. In shape it was like a roughly trimmed doorstop, and there was an indentation where it had been forced into place.

"Shit," Harragin said in perplexity. "It don't figure."

Unfortunately, so far as I was concerned, it was starting to. The next step was to find out whether the canopy jettison device had been put out of action. Half an hour later, we knew that it had. The wiring to the detonators had been disconnected.

"Still don't make any sense," Harragin insisted. "You could open the canopy the normal way."

Technically he was correct. It would still be possible to open the canopy electrically, or by pulling physically, provided the speed was below 215 knots, though if you were out of control or on fire there might not be time. When things go wrong in a jet fighter, they usually go wrong fast. In my plan they were going to happen very fast and I was virtually certain to eject at over 215 knots. Ergo, if I had not found the wedge, I could have ended up dead. However, Harragin couldn't know that, and two brains are always better than one, so I didn't stop him thinking things through further.

"Listen, Hawker," he said eventually. "You might never eject at all, OK? So anyone aiming to hurt you, they'd have to build in another fault, kind of thing would create an emergency, right? Force you to go."

"I don't see it either," I maintained, though the

whole equation was rapidly becoming clearer. Two possible situations would force me to eject. First, my own escape as planned, which would not allow time for slowing down and struggling with the canopy. Second, if the Libyan Air Force was on my tail. I considered both. The second was unpredictable. But the first was certain, which opened a disturbing possibility.

"Who had access to the Sabre before you left Ottawa?" I asked.

"Oh man!" Harragin reacted with the evident realization that his security had been lax. "Mechanics were all over her. That guy from the National Collection came. Your pal Newland likewise. She was on ground display one whole day during the airshow. People were pawing her like a pet dog."

"Newland?" I queried. He had told me he was returning to New York.

"Yeah. He came back after you'd gone. On Monday. Wanted to take some photographs."

There are moments of truth in one's life, thank God not many, when everything stands still, a kind of mental equivalent to the split second between the symbols lining up on a fruit machine and the jackpot jangling out. Suddenly everything connects. This was one of those moments. Up to now the dangers of this operation had been implicit yet remote. Flying missions are always like that, a different world from briefings and preparations on the ground. I assumed I would survive because I was entirely confident in my ability to outwit the Libyan Air Force. Even the idea that Qaddafi's agents might pursue me afterward seemed an abstraction. But this attempted sabotage wasn't abstract at all. It was real and it begged a major question.

"Did Newland spend much time with the plane?" I asked.

Harragin considered this. "Couple of hours."

Who else could have done it? Newland must have

found plausible reasons for instructing a mechanic to disconnect the jettison device, which required technical expertise, though he would have had to jam the wedge in position himself, since to do that would have been manifestly dangerous. A conversation with Arain came back to me, when he had asked about the resale value of the Sabre. I had remarked that after September 1 it would be irrecoverable and later I had told Newland this was because I imagined the mission would end with my ejecting. Beyond that, I had been unspecific, and he had said that how I organized my escape was my affair. Nonetheless, he knew the guts of my plan and the conclusion was inescapable. CONOIL had arranged for me to kill myself. That was going to be their subsidiary jackpot: saving $50,000 and losing an employee who, once the mission was over, was a potential embarrassment if he was not silenced.

"You think he did this?" Harragin wasn't slow.

"Good God, no!" I retreated hastily into the too-British-for-words act. "He's a good friend. I merely thought he might have noticed what the mechanics were up to. Didn't they go over her on Monday as well?"

"That's true," Harragin grunted and hitched up his jeans, tightening his broad buckled belt a notch and making it clear he was fed up with my problems. "Well," he said. "No one got hurt and she's your baby now. But in your shoes I'd have her checked out real good while she's here."

He was about to go when I stopped him. "Could you do me a favor?"

He looked at me as if to say that I should damn well learn to wipe my own backside.

"Keep this under your hat, would you? I'll be meeting those people in Ottawa again, and I don't want a lot of ugly rumors floating around. Only creates bad blood and there might yet be an innocent explanation."

"OK." He shook hands a shade more warmly than I

expected, said "Be seeing you," and walked off, leaving me weighing the aluminum wedge in my hand. I was about to chuck it away when I realized how crucially important it still was. That chunk of metal ought to be put in place under the seat every time I parked the Sabre, just in case Newland sent anyone nosing around to check. It wasn't only Qaddafi's men whom I had to outsmart from now on. The thought made me cold and angry.

Feeling that further trouble could wait for me, rather than my seeking it out, I delayed driving to Barstow until I had made a few other arrangements. Mainly these consisted of a few days' stay north of Santa Monica, where the flight school at Van Nuys airfield could put me through the instrument-rating tests that Hawker Hall would have to pass on his U.S. license if he was to ferry the Sabre back to Europe. Of course I was fully qualified to do the trip, but "Hawker" needed the official documentation too.

I believe there was once an American railway company that used to advertise "Scenery is on the ground." Whether the argument kept any passengers off the airlines, I don't know, but it was valid enough. Two days later when I drove in a rented pickup through the coastal range to the Mojave I found the landscape vastly more dramatic than it had seemed from the air. The mountains came into their true daunting perspective and the desert beyond seemed to stretch to infinity.

Barstow itself had been on the old stagecoach routes, or so a state trooper told me as I waited at the police building. He added proudly that today California had the highest ratio of automobiles to population in the U.S. of A., and therefore, presumably, in the world. A fair sample of them passed by while I was there. When it came to the interview, the sergeant was no less informative about the numerous laws I had broken by jettisoning the drop tanks. I ought to know that, he said, though what with my service background, being a visitor, and various other factors—like it was an emergency—he was not going to take the matter further.

I thanked him wholeheartedly and explained that I had brought a pickup truck so that I could salvage the junk. Would this prospector object?

"You could always take a sheriff and a posse with you." The sergeant laughed as though this was one of the wildest ideas he'd ever heard. "The guy goes bananas if anyone so much as looks at his concession. I'd make sure he was away if I was you." He chuckled. "Not that there's any gold there. Guess he's a wetback, or his pa was. They get kind of excitable when they've been out in the sun too long."

Clearly he wasn't going to send a trooper along with me and I could hardly blame him, since it would be an eighty-mile drive. So I set off, mindful of their directions. I had to take the dirt road around the back of Old Dad mountain, and if I turned right near a clump of Washington palms and after that left by a Joshua tree and right again by a big rock, then in due time I'd see a post with a steer's skull on top and that marked the track. They said I couldn't miss it because out there steers' horns were as rare as the gold the prospector was digging for. All in all it sounded about as simple as crossing the Sahara, and twice as inviting, what with a demented Mexican waiting at the end of the trail.

The country was rugged, a stony wilderness on which the sun now beat with high-noon intensity. The pickup had no air conditioning and opening the windows merely let in a dusty furnace blast, though it was better than having them shut. The area certainly deserved to be called the Devil's Playground. I was half-fried by the time I found the steer's skull. However, it did lead to the bend in the track and a mile or so further on I saw the hut, shimmering like a mirage. I continued cautiously, stopping at intervals to take stock, until I spotted one of the crushed and dented drop tanks to the right. Then I turned the pickup around—just in case I had to leave in a hurry—switched off the ignition, and got out.

The silence was tangible, broken only by the faint rustle of the desert breeze and metallic ticking noises from the engine as it cooled, if anything could in this heat. The hut, seen close, was roughly constructed of timber and stones, while a few yards away were some diggings and a rusting bulldozer. The whole place seemed as devoid of life as it had from the air. I walked over to the nearest of the two tanks, noting the marks on the ground where it had tumbled and skidded before coming to rest. The original impact had been some fifteen yards further away from the hut. There was still an odor of kerosene and the tank was in a sorry condition, with the nose caved in and the underside crumpled and ruptured. But so far as I could tell the nose had hit the ground first, which was what mattered, because that meant its trajectory had been like a bomb's. I made some notes, and was about to pace out the exact distance to the hut when prudence guided me against the idea and I made a mental assessment instead. Then I squatted, eased my arms under one battered tank and staggered with it to the pickup. As I deposited it with a thud in the back the first shot cracked past overhead.

The pongos always claim they have a monopoly of knowing how to react under fire. Believe me, they don't. No soldier could have moved faster than I did, not even one as scared as me. I raced around the side of the truck and was crouching by the door several seconds ahead of the next bullet, which whammed into metal somewhere at the back. Squinting beneath the chassis, I could see a rifle barrel with a dark face tucked behind it at the corner of a window in the hut. The muzzle shifted and I guessed he was trying to locate me before firing again. Jesus, I thought, it doesn't matter if he's a wetback or a deserter from the Marine Corps, those bastard troopers could have warned me he was armed. Still keeping my head well down, I reached up and opened the door very slowly, wishing to hell I'd left the engine running.

As the door swung outward I realized I was on the wrong side: this was a left-hand-drive vehicle. However, the instinctive error proved an advantage. I was able to snake my way in across the floor, turn on the ignition, and start the motor without raising my head above the level of the bench seat. My friend down the track heard the noise, though, and loosed off another round, which shattered the rear window and went out the front, spattering me with glass where I crouched and leaving the windscreen totally crazed. There was only one solution. I foraged hastily for a handkerchief in my jeans, wrapped it around the knuckles of my right hand, scrambled up and punched a hole in the windshield, sending glass tinkling all over the hood. Then, as another shot banged into the rear, I slammed her into gear and gunned the engine. But in my haste my foot slipped on the clutch pedal so that she shot forward, the wheels spinning and dust enveloping the cab.

The dust saved me. Glancing in the mirror as the pickup gathered speed all I could see was a cloud of it obscuring everything. Equally it must have hidden the pickup, because a couple more bullets sang past wide, and after that I was out of range. Nonetheless I kept going hard, bumping and swaying down the track, though the hole in the windshield gave me artificial tunnel vision. In fact it was so bad that by the steer's skull I risked stopping long enough to jump out, find a large stone and hammer away some more of the glass. My hand was cut and bleeding. I paused to suck away some of the blood, looked back across the bend to the distant hut and saw that there was a new dust cloud rising there. Not content with behaving like Custer's last stand, he was coming after me. I took the pickup off like a bronco, the hot wind tearing at my eyes and making them water so much that it was no better than the restricted vision before. But at least I was sure of one

thing: with the dust trail I was raising he'd have one hell
of a job getting close, let alone overtaking, even if his
car was faster.

Unfortunately, I was underestimating the man's determination. When I reached the junction by the palms
and had to slow down for the turn, he must have been
very close behind because he cut straight across the corner to head me off. I saw him clearly for the first time
then. He had grizzled hair and a mustache and he was
driving an old Ford Mustang, its faded red paint
scratched and dented. He was only twenty yards to my
left and gaining rapidly, churning up grit and stones,
when the Mustang suddenly slewed around, out of control. He must have hit a rock or burst a tire. I wasn't
stopping to find out precisely. As I accelerated away a
final shot ricocheted past. He was a tryer, that man, if
nothing else.

It was only when I reached Highway 15 near Baker
that I began to relax. For a few miles I pottered along at
around thirty-five miles an hour, so as to reduce the
blast of air coming in, and did some mental summing-
up. Hugely different though the sophisticated sabotage
of the ejector seat was from the prospector's trigger-
happiness, the fact was that this had been the second attempt to kill me in two weeks. It was one thing for
Hawker Hall to acquire a reputation for getting into
awkward situations. That would be an advantage. Indeed I could use this shooting incident coupled with the
loss of the drop tanks to build up the idea that he was
accident-prone. I knew I had more than enough professionalism in the air to make him appear a hairy pilot
without incurring any actual risk. But real accidents
were emphatically not part of the plan. It was going to
be enough trouble keeping a step ahead of Newland and
Arain all the time without creating problems for myself.
Absurdly, an idea began to grow in my mind as I drove
toward Los Angeles. It was that in some inexplicable

way this character Hawker Hall, in spite of being my own creation, would prove accident-prone in his own right.

I had just about persuaded myself that this theory was undiluted crap, when I realized that the drivers overtaking me not only had scant regard for the fifty-five mile an hour limit, but they invariably gave me very curious glances as they passed. The bullet holes in the back of the pickup must have been more conspicuous than I realized. The next thing would be that someone would alert the highway patrol. I decided I ought to stop and have the windshield replaced at the nearest town: that, of course, was Barstow.

The attendant at the first service station directed me to the local Ford dealer, who said he could fix both the windscreen and the rear window. I assured him I was not on the run from a bank robbery, but had simply trespassed on private land by mistake and been shot at. Then I went to find a beer and a hamburger. However, when I returned there was a highway patrol car parked alongside and the same sergeant I had met before was standing there with notebook in hand.

"Looks like you've been in trouble," he said in a less than friendly voice. "You carrying a gun, sir?"

"Definitely not, officer." I began laying on the pompous British accent. "As I explained earlier today, I'm only a visitor."

"You're telling me you didn't fire back?"

"Absolutely not."

"You don't have a gun, sir? Is that correct?" There was a degree of incredulity mixed with the mistrust now. I didn't like the way his earlier dismissive attitude had vanished.

"One hundred percent, officer. I went and collected the drop tank, as I said I would, and when I was some way off the windshield shattered. Then I realized I was being shot at." I grinned stupidly. "So I just went hell-for-leather away from there."

"Well, sir, I guess you'd better come along to the office."

"What for? I don't want to lay any charges. You warned me off and I should have known better. Anyway, I've got what I wanted." I jerked a thumb at the battered metal lying in the back. "I have no complaints, officer. If you don't mind, I'd rather like to drive on back to Los Angeles."

The sergeant's leathery face flushed and he confronted me, his fists on his hips.

"I don't know what all this is about," he said curtly. "But I don't like it and I'm filing a report. You planning to stay long in California?"

"A couple of weeks."

"Let me give you some advice, sir. Cut it short. Something tells me you're the kind of visitor we don't want."

With that he strode back to his patrol car and drove off, leaving me to wonder if I would find the FBI waiting at Chino.

Happily, they were not. In any case, by the time I reached the airfield I had decided to capitalize on the adventure to boost Hawker's aura of eccentricity. Lewis appeared impressed in spite of himself. After we had unloaded the tank, he found a shot hole in it and poked his finger around the neat puncture.

"That guy could have opened up when you were flying overhead too," he suggested, shaking his head in wonderment. "Guess you had a lucky escape. Sure are some crazy fools around."

Tactfully taking the last remark not to mean me, I cracked a joke about life being here to be lived, and after we had agreed that the tank was beyond repair, we got down to settling the camouflage scheme in which the Sabre would be repainted. I wanted her in the usual irregular brown and green patterns that most air forces

use. Her appearance would change radically from the
flashy orange and yellow.

"As this was a Canadian aircraft," I added, "she
should have blue and white roundels with the maple leaf
in red in the center.

"If you say so," Lewis agreed. "We could put the
civilian numbers on the tail fin. Some people do that."
Although it was common practice to decorate restored
warbirds in air force colors, often with veteran squadron insignia, international law still required them to
carry a civilian registration. The Sabre's was American,
of course. "D'you want your name underneath the
cockpit?" he asked.

That was a good point. United States pilots invariably
have their own and their crew chief's names emblazoned
below the canopy. Old-time Canadian Air Force pilots
were more reticent. What would Hawker do?

"Why not!" I said enthusiastically. "Give her a bit of
class won't it? Look nice in the photos too." Hawker
was definitely fond of showing off.

So we settled the final stage of the Sabre's reforging
and Lewis assured me she would be ready in a week. As
I was walking away I overheard him speaking in an
aside to one of the mechanics.

"Might as well paint that guy's name straight onto a
coffin," he remarked. "I'll bet fifty bucks to a . . ."

The rest of the sentence was lost to me, but I hardly
thought he was laying odds on Hawker dying of old age,
which was excellent. The more the buzz among aviation
circles predicted an interesting future for my alter ego,
rather than a long one, the better. Besides, the British
like and respect well-heeled, slightly mad amateurs, so
long as what they're doing is connected with sport.
Hawker would be a blood brother to gentlemen jockeys
in the racing world. He would receive sympathy and
help, but probably few headlines, which would be just
as well.

   Meanwhile, an instrument rating was a necessity. The great thing about flying schools in California is that they like to get pilots qualified quickly, and the weather normally helps them. The days I spent up at Van Nuys were highly organized and in consequence successful. If fog hadn't rolled in off the Pacific just when my flight test was due, I would have finished in four days. As it was, the ground school and the minimal flying took five. The instructors were complimentary about my professionalism and I was about theirs. Everyone was happy. I decided to keep things as uneventful as possible from here on to crossing the Atlantic.

   Even so, by the time I flew the Sabre to Ottawa the following week, Hawker's fame had arrived ahead of us. In fact, as I taxied in at Uplands on the afternoon of July 17 I found a small reception committee to greet me consisting of Luke, a friend of his from the national collection, plus a Canadian Air Force colonel named Collins, who explained that he had flown Sabres in the 1960s.

   In view of the RCAF markings on the plane, I could only welcome all concerned, but Collins seemed a touch too well-informed. Although he made all the appropriate enthusiastic noises as he looked over the plane, it struck me that he was only likely to be out here on a working day if he was on business. He had a strong, intelligent face and more medal ribbons on his dark green tunic than normal, given that the Canadians are almost as conservative as the British in the matter of handing out decorations. When he mentioned that he had served as air attaché in London and was currently on the staff in Ottawa, though fed up with "flying a desk," I was certain Colonel Collins had come to inspect Hawker Hall, not the Sabre.

   Sure enough, after we had adjourned to the Innotech reception for coffee, Collins launched into a series of penetrating questions, asking what exactly had gone wrong over the Mojave Desert.

"Well, colonel," I insisted, "I was always taught to ditch the external stores in an emergency. Maybe I shouldn't have obeyed the book." I paused, as if going over the memory, and added provocatively, "Certainly caused enough trouble afterward." I wanted to know if he had been reading the police report.

"Is that so?"

He hadn't risen to my bait, so I was forced to explain.

"Guess we all make mistakes," he replied in a tone implying that only fools did. "But let me be frank with you, Mr. Hall. We're none too keen on having our air force colors involved in any kind of incident." He gave me a pretty cold glance. "I'm sure you understand what I mean."

The colonel must have learned this oblique language when he was a diplomat. He probably didn't know what he meant himself, and I wasn't about to fall into the trap.

"She's in RCAF colors for the benefit of the Imperial War Museum," I answered blandly. "And she's too expensive a toy to make any more mistakes with."

He appeared to accept that. At all events, when I threw the ball into his court by asking for assistance from the RCAF during the ferry flight, he became almost friendly and promised it would be forthcoming, suggesting I stage at Goose Bay.

"That's the route I was planning," I told him. "Via Goose Bay, Greenland, and Iceland. I believe it's the way the RAF took their Sabre deliveries across in the 1950s. Do you have any special advice?"

"Wait for a good met forecast," he replied immediately. "Don't challenge the weather. Take it easy. You'll find her deicing equipment is good." He glanced at me quizzically. "Nothing much else you shouldn't know already. I'll inform Goose you're coming." He stood up to leave. "Well, nice meeting you, Mr. Hall. Have a safe flight."

On balance I reckoned I had come out of that en-

counter on the credit side. Almost anyone is flattered by
being asked for counsel. However, the next thing was
far more important, namely to pump Luke on the subject of Newland's activity.

"How do you think she looks?" I asked, to set the
conversation going.

"Great." Luke was a natural enthusiast, thank
Heaven. "Only point I'd make is that the underside's
wrong. We have our Sabre 6 duck-egg blue under the
fuselage and wings. I think you'll find that's correct."

"I suppose it was in those days," I admitted warily.
The idea of the blue was so that the plane would merge
into the sky when seen from beneath. However, my
Sabre was dark in accordance with a different concept
and it wasn't one I could explain. Happily Luke shifted
the subject, producing a folder of snapshots.

"Thought you might like one or two of these," he
suggested. "I took them after you left."

Expecting routine color prints, I began examining
them politely and very nearly flipped. In several pictures
two men were standing by the Sabre, one of whom was
Newland.

"Who was that?" I asked, leaning across and pointing out the other fellow.

"They didn't introduce me. I wanted them to move,
but they were pretty busy checking things." Luke smiled
sheepishly. "I guess professional photographers are
tougher when they find a good subject."

I went on sifting through the pack of thirty-six prints.
There was one taken from straight ahead of the plane's
nose, which showed this other man clearly. He was
standing up in the cockpit, only his head and shoulders
visible. He was swarthy, with thick black hair and for a
crazy moment I wondered if he could be a Libyan. But
whatever his origin I knew I was looking at the man who
had interfered with the canopy jettison system. I had
doubted if Newland had sufficient technical expertise
for the sabotage, unless he'd been masking it very as-

tutely. Here was the explanation. Not wanting to arouse
Luke's curiosity, I continued sorting the photos, eventually choosing three, including the important one.

"Could you spare these?" I asked. "Pity that man's
in the picture, but still. Was he there long?"

"All the time I was. Mr. Grainger wasn't too happy
about him either."

I let that comment ride, because I suddenly had a better idea. "Listen Luke," I said enthusiastically, "I'd
very much like to have a couple of these blown up. You
know, to frame and hang on the wall. Could I borrow
the negatives while I'm here?"

"Sure thing. Aren't you flying out tomorrow,
though?"

"What's a couple of days? I'm in no hurry and, you
know something, I've just realized that I haven't a
single photograph of the Sabre as she was before. I completely failed to take any."

He grinned sympathetically. "It's the easiest thing. I
clean forgot to do the same with an old Tiger Moth I
rebuilt." He handed across the wallet with the film.
"D'you need a lift downtown?"

"If you don't mind waiting ten minutes."

I needed to talk to Grainger before leaving, both
to give instructions and to ask about Newland. But I
learned nothing more than that Newland had insisted he
had authority to check out some of the equipment on
my behalf and they hadn't felt they could argue. "He
had that letter from you," Grainger said, reaching
across his desk for the Sabre's servicing file and showed
me a sheet of paper. On it was typed: "Kindly give Captain Newland access to the Sabre if he requires."

The name "Hawker Hall" was in capitals below, with
a scrawled "H.H." in ink. The scrawl bore little relationship to the usual carefully practiced signature I
executed for Hall, but then the way people initial a
document often does differ in style from the way they
sign their name in full and, at second glance, the first

"H" wasn't so bad. Jesus, Newland was sharp. He must have memorized the shape of that initial from my signature in the flight authorization book.

"Stupid of me," I said, "I'll forget my own name next. Of course I gave it to him."

Grainger looked relieved. His firm had a reputation to maintain. He turned quickly to the question of preparation for the ferry flight. Quite apart from checking the plane, there would be a pile of flight-planning documentation to do. Eventually we settled on the next Monday as a suitable departure date.

Luke dropped me off near a photography store and I ordered the enlargements: one side-view of the plane and another of the head and shoulders of the saboteur. The shop assistant warned that the latter might come out slightly blurred. What was being blown up to half-plate size was only a tiny fraction of a thirty-five millimeter negative. No matter, I assured him, and in fact when I collected the prints next day the result was tolerable.

Back at my hotel—not the Four Seasons this time since I was traveling on Hall's passport—I sat and studied the face, memorizing its salient features. Their owner was a man in his late twenties, with a slightly hooked nose and fleshy cheeks. His chin bore a dark five-o'clock shadow and I now saw that his hair curled down over his ears, with long, thick sideburns. Another of Luke's pictures showed him as short and stocky in build. All in all, he was a type you can find anywhere around the Mediterranean from Cyprus to Spain, one man in ten, or twenty or maybe fifty million. He could be anything from a fisherman to a politician. But it didn't throw me, because he had one distinctive characteristic: a thin hard mouth, which gave an oddly prissy twist to otherwise sensual features. I figured I would be able to recognize him anywhere. In fact, it felt good to be able to put a face on the immediate enemy, even if he did represent a mind-blowing doublecross. If he interfered with the Sabre again, he'd regret it.

Dealing with Arain, I had to admit, was a different question. Arain wasn't going to expose himself to physical danger and I suppose at this stage I should have phoned him, told him he could do what he bloody well liked with the plane, and quit, keeping the first fifty thousand dollars and the expenses. I doubt he would have argued the toss; that kind of money was peanuts to CONOIL. However, I'm an obstinate bastard myself and having got this far my inclination was to play for the jackpot, particularly as I was convinced I could win. So I did not back off, as a wiser man would have done. But then a wiser man wouldn't have taken this job in the first place. What I did decide was to demand the second fifty thousand dollars in advance as well. So I sat for a while on the side of the hotel bed, sipping a self-indulgent bourbon on the rocks and pondering possible moves in what had become as much a chess game as an air strike, and it occurred to me that the ferry flight might provide a chance to force Arain's hand. If I could bluff better than he could.

The long-range met forecast showed a low over Labrador drifting southeast, which would be replaced by an area of high pressure at the weekend between Labrador and Greenland. That would give my route clear weather while I would have the usual westerly wind helping me along at high altitude. Since the weekend might also be better for talking to Arain, I speeded up my departure, and after three days of organizing diplomatic clearances and sending telegrams, was set to go. Harragin's smaller drop tanks were crated and consigned to London, along with another pair from the Crown Assets Disposal, and replaced by the 167-gallon ones from the same source. The Sabre was fueled, loaded, and given a final check. I squeezed my canvas travel bag behind the seat—she was no touring aircraft —and stowed the carefully rolled maps for the first two stages in the leg pocket of my flying suit. At eight o'clock on Saturday morning, with the ever-enthusiastic Luke waving farewell, I taxied out.

The takeoff had to be at a higher speed with such a load, so I rotated at 125 knots and delayed a little over raising the flaps. But even with the extra weight the Sabre's urge to climb was undimmed. I had to plead with air traffic control to allocate me higher and higher levels, because the economical way to fly her for range was to go straight up to forty thousand feet, and at one hundred percent power she could get there in six minutes. Old though she was, they couldn't easily accommodate that kind of performance within a civilian airway.

Fuel is always a worry on a ferry trip. Theoretically, with the larger drop tanks the Sabre carried enough for over 1,200 miles, and since no leg was more than 950 miles, there should have been no problem, especially with a tail wind. But a jet fighter drinks at a rate even patrons of the Munich Oktoberfest might envy. Once I started calculating, the 691 gallons, or 5,389 pounds of Jet A1 I had on board seemed frugal. Cruising at forty thousand feet and a speed over the ground of 570 miles per hour, the Orenda engine gulped 1,950 pounds an hour, just about twice the consumption of a modern twin-engine executive jet. When you added in the allowances for climb, descent and landing, the maximum margin on any leg of the trip would be around 1,500 pounds, or twenty-two minutes flying at sea level. Twenty-two minutes represents a lot of mileage in America or Europe, where airfields are as plentiful as currants on a cake. Over Greenland and the North Atlantic it could be eliminated as a safety factor by a single storm. I knew I would have one eye on the fuel flowmeter throughout this trip.

Happily, the promised clear weather bathed the wastes of the Labrador landscape in summer sun and I could have located Goose Bay without any navigational aids. My actual groundspeed had been 584 miles per hour and I touched down with all the safety margins comfortably intact at 9:43 A.M. When the RCAF personnel there began bustling around, proving that Colonel Collins had been as good as his word, I felt confident of making Iceland on schedule in the late afternoon: late afternoon eastern standard time, that is. At Keflavik it would be evening, though still completely light in those arctic circle latitudes. There I could find a hotel, and continue to Scotland next morning. When an air force captain at Goose Bay offered me a second breakfast, I accepted gratefully.

"You may not find too much at Sondrestrom," the captain advised, as he guided me to the officers' mess. "I should eat while you can." He had also obtained an updated route forecast for me and warned, "You could run into some weather east of Iceland." In return I expected to answer a few probing questions. However, the only clue he let slip to having been briefed by Collins was a reference to the Imperial War Museum and a suggestion that I ought to change the Sabre's markings to those of the RCAF's 439 Squadron that had been stationed at North Luffenham, not so far from Duxford. He also told me that there was still one groundstaff member at Goose Bay who could recall the RAF's ferry operation all those years ago. By the time I was clambering back into the Sabre an hour later, I had concluded that if the Canadians were keeping watch on my activity, they were doing so in a pretty low-key manner.

Crossing the rocky Labrador coast and heading further north over a sullen gray sea changed my mood. Before long I began noticing the jagged white blobs of icebergs below. The forbidding immensity of this arctic ocean made me feel detached and lonely in the warm cocoon of the cockpit, despite the reassuring steadiness of the dials and gauges on the instrument panel. Most pilots experience a moment of panic some time or other. I wouldn't say that I felt that, but I did suddenly feel in a very fragile relationship to the world outside. I fought it off by doing routine checks, like whether the engine revs were correct for maximum range, adjusting the trim, and so on. Then, confident I was on track, I fell to considering how to handle Arain.

The considerations were complex. For a start, everything hinged on Arain believing the sabotage had gone undetected. So long as he expected me to kill myself, he could afford to be generous. Conversely, so long as he wanted Qaddafi's bomb put into balk, I could make demands. It also occurred to me that CONOIL's profit and loss equation might include taking out hefty insurance on Hawker Hall's life, or on the aircraft; the irony of this being that I saw no way of collecting on the aircraft policy myself after the attack because Hawker Hall was going to have to disappear. But of course Hawker could collect on an accident now.

I switched on the Collins HF radio, consulted the frequency diagram, called Stockholm on 17.916 MHz, giving my approximate position, and asked to be patched through to the Swiss telephone number. It worked like a dream. I barely had time to wonder whether Arain would have rented an office or an apartment in Geneva before the Stockholm operator came back on the air.

"November Four Sierra," she abbreviated my callsign, "go ahead."

The line was as clear as if I had been in Europe myself. I asked for Arain.

"Mr. Arain is not available. Who is speaking please?" The voice was a woman's, mature, slightly accented. I presumed she was Swiss. I told her I was Hawker. There was a moment's silence, then, "Please wait. I will try to find him."

Five minutes later—an extremely long five minutes during which I traveled forty-nine miles closer to Greenland, and the Stockholm operator twice asked if I was still speaking—Arain's voice came over the radio. He sounded annoyed.

"What's the problem, Hall?"

I dropped the idea of getting into the subject by telling him the Sabre's reequipment was complete and came straight to the point. "Someone tried to shoot me in California."

"Did what?"

"A half-crazy character who didn't like my low-flying practice. Luckily he missed." I called it "low flying" instead of "bombing" because the Stockholm operator could be listening.

"So why are you telling me? You want to quit or something?"

"No." I had to balance my words carefully. "But there are more risks in this than I reckoned." Before he could make the obvious retort, I pressed on. "Some I knew about. If anything went wrong now, for instance, and I had to ditch the plane, the insurance would pay out and we'd all get our money back."

That caught Arain's attention all right. "Where the hell are you?" he demanded.

"At forty thousand feet over the Davis Strait," I replied equably.

The unspoken implication was that if I ditched the Sabre and the air-sea rescue system worked, I could walk away with a quarter of a million dollars' insurance money. Not that I was going to be stupid enough to say that. Not that anyone but an idiot would want to do it in a plane with such poor ditching characteristics. What I wanted was to set him thinking, and I succeeded. He might be an Arab, but his mind analyzed information faster than a computer.

"We'd be sorry if anything went wrong at this stage, even though we're insured," he said smoothly.

"The flying won't go wrong," I assured him. "Barring unforeseen accidents. What bothers me is getting hurt on the ground. Someone might try again and succeed. Just in case they do, I'd like the second half of the bonus in advance. Also, another ten thousand expenses. The fuel is costing a fortune." That was true. I could

have run my car for two years on the quantity the Sabre
was burning to cross the Atlantic.

"I'll consider it," he offered.

"I want a decision, Mr. Arain." The moment had
come for the bluff. I'd thrown in enough factors for
him to consider, and the ferry trip wasn't going to last
for ever. "If you can't make one I'm leaving the plane
in Iceland. You can have a ferry pilot fetch her."

For the first time in this conversation, Arain paused.
"Is there some way I can call you back?" he asked eventually.

"Through Stockholm Radio. Make it at twenty hundred GMT." By then I would be halfway between
Greenland and Iceland and not too busy with other
radio contacts.

Arain agreed, sounding reluctant, and I switched off
the HF set not feeling entirely certain that I had played
my hand well. He was a very tricky character, Arain.
But there had to be others senior to him in CONOIL
and they wouldn't want the project aborted now. With
only six weeks to go they'd be stretched to find another
pilot, except maybe a Japanese kamikaze. I put it out of
my mind and began checking my position.

Sondre Stromfjord, to give the airfield its full name,
is right on the arctic circle and scenically spectacular, if
you like snow-covered mountains. But its east-west runway is in a valley and no place to be uncertain of one's
position because the mountains blind the radar in certain sectors. However, with the good weather holding, I
settled the Sabre down with the usual slight bump and
clatter, ten minutes ahead of schedule thanks to a high-
altitude tailwind. But while she was being refueled I
learned that the met service telex was on the blink, and
although the last report received from Keflavik had
given two miles visibility and five-eighths of cloud at fifteen hundred feet, a deterioration was anticipated later
due to the low over the eastern Atlantic. In other words,
there was an all-too-familiar situation of uncertainty.

Bearing in mind the excellent navigational aids at the other end—Keflavik is a joint civilian and U.S. Air Force field with a precision approach radar, which the international airport at Reykjavik lacks—I decided to press on, rather than risk being grounded in Greenland for several days. The ground crew turned the plane around commendably fast and I took off again at 6:32 P.M. GMT, drinks time in London. I suppose it was one way to spend the happy hour.

This leg was just over nine hundred miles, and it was not until long after the fjords of the eastern Greenland coast had slipped beneath the Sabre's nose and I was halfway across the Denmark Strait that the horizon became rimmed with white haze. I was still in beautiful conditions at thirty seven thousand feet, with the sun glinting on the wing if I glanced back and the air so clear that I felt I ought to be able to see the North Pole. But there was no mistaking the import of that fudge of cloud ahead. I called Keflavik and could get no answer.

It was 7:49 P.M. and I had just begun to receive signals from the VOR on the airfield beacon, showing one hundred twenty miles to run, when I finally raised Keflavik. The air traffic control there told me visibility was down to five hundred yards and worsening, with a three-hundred-foot cloudbase. They advised me to divert either to Prestwick in Scotland or Bergen in Norway. I reminded them curtly of the endurance stated on my flight plan and said I would start my descent in one minute. Could they give me a precision approach straight in to the airfield?

"Affirmative. Precision approach radar available. Squawk four three four two," came the answer.

That was good. Going straight in would save the time normally spent in going over the beacon and then descending in an instrument approach pattern to the airfield. "Squawk" referred to the transponder, an instrument that enabled them to identify which blip was mine on their radar screen. A moment later they announced that I was positively identified and at one hundred ten miles out I began my descent, cutting the throttle back to as near idling as would maintain the necessary jet-pipe temperatures. The outside air was at minus sixty degrees Celsius.

There are a lot of maneuvres a jet fighter can make that an airliner cannot, at least not safely. The Sabre could be dived down at a rate of twenty seven thousand feet a minute in an emergency. But there was no point in doing that here. The aim was to cover distance with the minimum of consumption of fuel. So I had used the old rule-of-thumb arithmetic of multiplying the altitude in thousands by three to obtain the letdown commencement in nautical miles, which had meant starting one hundred ten miles out. Descending at a relaxed two thousand feet a minute should bring me over the instrument landing system outer marker at the correct altitude.

I should then have 1,350 pounds of fuel in hand. Enough to overshoot if I missed the runway in the murk, and come around again on instruments. Enough to try once more. Not enough to settle for anything after that except abandoning the aircraft by courtesy of the rocket seat and praying I parachuted onto something soft. Parachuting in fog is a mug's game.

Keflavik monitored the descent with quick, precise orders, giving me occasional changes of heading toward runway eleven. There was virtually no wind down there.

When I was sixty miles out the sea below became gradually obscured, as if it were slipping under frosted glass. By forty miles the mist had thickened into an undulating layer, as featureless as cotton. Then that layer became hidden by cloud in the same insidious way. Approaching five thousand feet I cut back the speed to 185 knots, put on some flap and soon began clipping the top of the cloud, shreds of it flashing past the wings and making the navigation lights glow back at me.

"Heading one zero five. Descend to four thousand

feet. Ten miles to run," came Keflavik's instruction.

As I ploughed down into the cloud a light began blinking on the radio panel, and a tone sounded in my earphones telling me I was being called on the HF set. Thanks to the Secal system, Stockholm could alert me that I was wanted without my having to keep a listening watch. I swore. With an emergency on my hands I had completely forgotten Arain, and to speak to him would mean interrupting my communications with Keflavik in the last crucial moments of the approach. But I had little alternative.

SIX

THE SNAG ABOUT the radios in the Sabre was that having only one headset I had to receive all transmissions through the same earphones. Equally, when I spoke it was into a microphone inside my oxygen mask. So either I had to talk to Stockholm or to Keflavik, though when not transmitting myself I could hear both if I wanted. The cloud was as thick as anything I had ever flown through, seeming to cling to the canopy, becoming grayer by the second as I went down further, shutting me into the tiny enclosed world of the cockpit. I was low on fuel and there were mountains in the vicinity. Suddenly money had a very low priority in my scale of values. I was about to tell Stockholm to get off the air when Keflavik called.

"Heading one zero eight. Descend to three thousand feet. Eight miles to run." I acknowledged and eased the throttle back a touch more, bringing the nose up to give myself 170 knots. The outer marker was five miles off, or a minute and a half. I reckoned I could spare Arain thirty seconds, selected the HF and asked Stockholm to come in, praying Keflavik would not give further instructions while I was talking.

Arain sounded aggressive and unpleasant. "We've considered your request," he snapped. "It is not, repeat not, acceptable without guarantees."

"They can wait. I'm busy."

Arain might just as well not have heard. "First," he continued in the tone of an ultimatum, "we want . . ."

"Stockholm I have an emergency. Wait one," I said. The operator would understand and react.

"Are you trying to force my hand?" Arain interrupted.

At that moment Keflavik came on over his voice.

"Stockholm out to you," I said crisply. "Keflavik go ahead." I switched off the HF completely, imagining Arain's fury, and was rewarded with more bad news. Visibility at Keflavik was down to two hundred yards and the cloudbase to one hundred feet. Landing must be at my own risk. I could hardly blame them. The altitude at which one was officially supposed to break off an attempt to land there was one hundred eighty feet.

"Heading one ten. Descend to two thousand feet. Four miles to run." The controller was keeping his cool too, as calm as ice, ready to give me the kind of second-by-second talkdown that can jockey a fighter pilot down to five feet above the runway centerline, though he would expect a civilian aircraft to use the instrument landing system with its marker beacons.

Lights flashed on the instrument panel, and a bleep sounded in the headphones. I was over the outer marker of the ILS. I disregarded it, concentrating on keeping the instrument needles centered, bringing the speed back further and letting the undercarriage down with a comforting clunk that the indicator lights to my left confirmed.

"November Four Sierra, you're on the glidepath. Two miles to touchdown. Clear to land at your discretion. Wind calm."

The inner marker lights flashed. Half a mile to go and
I knew I must be over water, because the runway was
beside a fjord. At three hundred feet I began looking out in spite of knowing I would see nothing. Two
hundred feet. Still nothing. I was sweating, my neck
clammy. The cloud hung to the canopy, unbroken and
shapeless. One hundred feet. Jesus, by now I should
have abandoned the attempt. This was crazy.

"November Four Sierra. Touchdown three hundred
yards."

Peering down I glimpsed a different dullness: the cold
gray of arctic water. Then at eighty feet, as if revealed
by steam slowly clearing off the windscreen, two yellow
lights appeared, then a few more, stretching ahead into
the murk. A stony shoreline flashed below. I pushed the
nose down for fear of losing contact, jinking to line up
between the lights, cut the throttle, floated a second and
bumped down, going fast, the wheels rumbling. I let the
nosewheel touch and charged on into the fog, lights
flashing past, braking hard, then relaxing the pressure
to avoid skidding, braking again, gradually bringing the
Sabre to a halt.

"Hold position," came the controller's order.
"We're sending a truck."

"Thanks for your help," I said. I meant it too. The
controller's last transmission telling me the runway was
straight ahead had been psychologically crucial. Without it the only sensible action would have been to overshoot, climb away and eject. The fog was so thick that
the small pickup truck with an illuminated "Follow
me" sign on its roof had to guide me the whole way to
the buildings. There were 1,100 pounds of fuel remaining. But having enough to have gone around again was
irrelevant. When I climbed out the visibility was barely
thirty yards. Keflavik was fogged in as tight as a clam
and no one could have landed now, except maybe the
angel Gabriel.

However, this was at least a hospitable place to be

grounded. Once I had cleared customs, an obliging American arranged a hotel room for me and ordered a taxi. It is extraordinary how drained a long flight can leave one, especially if it ends by calling on all one's reserves of nerve. The take off from Ottawa in the morning seemed light years ago. I needed a bath and a drink, needed them badly. Arain could wait. Besides, I wanted time to think. He had mentioned guarantees and I couldn't imagine any that I was in a position to give.

During the long taxi ride into Reykjavik, I pondered further and still came up with a blank. The only weapon in my armory was threatening to quit. But threats are a wasting asset and by the time I rang Arain from the hotel I had determined to avoid repeating myself. He would remember well enough.

"Listen, Hall!" Arain practically exploded when the Swiss woman connected me. "Let's get one thing straight. You don't put the goddam phone down on me, right? I give orders, you take them, right? Is that clear? Where the hell are you now?"

I told him, keeping my tone as cold as fjord water and adding that the Sabre was safely parked at the airfield.

"It is?" he queried and I knew he hadn't forgotten the threat.

"Undamaged. Only needs refueling." In other words, flyable. By someone else if necessary. I didn't think he would take the implication kindly and he didn't.

"Then why'd you try to screw me with all that crap about emergencies?" he almost screamed. "We don't like blackmail, Hall. We don't like it at all."

"And I don't like being shouted at," I said. "Not when I've just saved your investment the hard way."

"What d'you mean?"

I told him. Strictly factually. Mentioning that the airfield had closed ten minutes after I landed.

That silenced him for a good three-quarters of a minute, and it occurred to me that Newland might be with him, giving an opinion. If so, the advice must have been favorable, because his tone became less hostile, though the next question he put was neatly double-edged.

"Why didn't you eject?" he asked. Cunning bastard. There would never be a more appropriate moment to find out how much I had discovered.

I thought for a few seconds and decided the truth might carry conviction. "Some part of me just didn't want to give up," I said, then half-joked, "Anyway, the water here's too cold."

"Warmer further south, huh?"

Again I had to admire the speed of Arain's reactions, but the way he followed up betrayed him. He wanted reassuring that I would eject eventually and I realized that I could now give him the best guarantee of all without arousing any suspicion.

"Too right," I said. "I'm saving the pleasure. If I do go further south."

"OK," he dropped the banter instantly. "You will be going. I guess the way you've handled today is enough for us. You can have the second half on September first."

"Morning, not afternoon. I might be shot down."

"After you take off."

"Before. I'm going to be busy after. I'll want some confirmation from my bank before." Jesus, Arain would have gone around the world to save ten cents. "Even if our mutual friends do get me, I still have dependents."

I was trying to think who they might be apart from my ex-wife when, to my surprise, he helped me out.

"Your aged mother?" he suggested in a deadpan voice.

"She's a cripple," I agreed. Well, she had been, poor dear. I sensed that beneath his restrained sarcasm lay a need to justify agreement to his superiors.

"We wouldn't want her to suffer," he said. "You have yourself a deal. Now, there's that video I want you to watch. Where can we send it?''

I reminded him obliquely of the service apartment in
Sloane Avenue.

"Call me after you've run it. Call me Sunday,'' he
ordered.

When he had rung off I was almost as perplexed as I
was pleased. Arain's character was incredibly con-
voluted. For a time I had thought Newland might have
sabotaged the rocket seat without his knowledge. But
this conversation had led to a diametrically different
conclusion. Namely, that Arain might have organized
something further, something more subtle, a fail-safe
device as it were, though since it was in his interest to
keep both me and the Sabre in good order until after the
mission, it was hard to imagine what the device could
be. The thought that I was secure until September 1 gave
me some consolation, but not enough.

In the end I stayed two nights in Reykjavik, waiting
for clear weather, and flew to Prestwick in Scotland on
Monday, continuing to Duxford in the afternoon. The
staff there was expecting me and the Sabre elicited a
gratifying amount of interest and admiration. Capitalizing on this, I asked if some small modifications could be
made to her and was introduced to a young member of
the Aviation Society called Ted, who had come out
from Cambridge especially to watch my arrival.

Ted's appearance was deceptive. He had a fresh face,
with tousled brown hair blowing across his forehead,
and being dressed in jeans and an old leather jacket
looked more like a sixth-grade student than the full-time
engineer at an electronics factory that he was. But when
I explained that the Sabre's existing landing lights were
not adequate for operating out of international airports
and I wanted, if possible, to fix additional ones in the
tip of each drop tank, he absorbed the essentials in
seconds.

"There must have been several electrical circuits
through the wings and down to the wing pylons,'' he

mused, "otherwise how could the bombs be fused or the rockets fired?"

"The jettison mechanism is electrical too," I prompted.

But prompting was hardly necessary. He was down under the wing examining the attachment of one tank to its streamlined aluminum-sheathed pylon before I'd finished speaking.

"Leave it with me, and I'll see what I can do at the weekend," he said. "Will you be down then?"

"I'll make sure I am."

"Well," he grinned, "we'll have a crack at it."

The upshot was that after I'd completed a few formalities, he drove me into Cambridge to catch a train to London. In effect he had appointed himself as the Sabre's unpaid crew chief, and I knew I had found the ideal collaborator. Given encouragement, I felt sure he would work wonders. Provided, of course, that I could keep him so occupied with the mechanics of modifications that he did not question their practical advantages too much. Happily, he seemed to accept that the Sabre's one landing light was inadequate by present-day standards. So that was a start. Far from continuing to be accident-prone, Hawker Hall had hit a lucky streak.

By the time I was ensconced in the Sloane Avenue apartment, it was too late to rent a video cassette-player that day. So although the uniformed hall porter had Arain's package waiting for me, there was nothing I could do with the unlabeled tape inside beyond gaze at it and speculate, which was a decidedly unprofitable way of spending the evening. Being back in London also produced a near-irresistible urge to ring Susie. I fought it down. For the next week I had to be Hall and no one else. After that, when everything was set up, perhaps I could allow myself a weekend in my own flat. So I treated myself to a solitary dinner in a small Italian restaurant down the road, making a rough checklist of what remained to be done as I ate.

Today was July twenty-third and five and a half weeks was adequate for the one major aspect of my planning which remained to be tied up. Otherwise it was all a matter of fine tuning. But bringing the preparations so much closer to Libya had created a tension in my gut that no amount of Italian or any other cooking was likely to soothe. I badly needed briefing on the target. It was one thing to know, in principle, that Qaddafi would be out at Tripoli International Airport to greet the crew of a Pakistan Airlines Boeing carrying the bomb: quite another to relate my own split-second attack to the airliner, the buildings, the reception committee and the air force flypast that Arain said would take place. I could only hope the videotape held some clues.

Next morning I rented a video machine from a shop in the King's Road, lugged it back to the apartment, and settled down with all the documentation I had gathered. The documentation did not amount to much. The Libyan Jamahiriya News Agency in London distributed various newspapers and journals, but they were amazingly short on photographs of Libya. Plenty of column inches on Qaddafi's thoughts, on the *Green Book* and his Third Universal Theory. Plenty of attacks on other nations, from "Israel's Apartheid Connection" and "Terrorism American-style" to "Saudi Violations of Islam." Damn all about Libya itself. In fact, the only solidly useful items I had obtained were the approach and landing charts of Tripoli airport in the Jeppesen international aviation manual, which showed the relationship of the runways to the terminal. With those in front of me, I switched on the video.

If Libyan security was tight, Arain's was a match for it. The tape revealed no origin, though the first twenty minutes was evidently an edited recording of a Libyan English-language television program. Since Arain did nothing without a reason, I knew he must have left in sequences of the announcer deliberately. The announcer was a light-skinned Arab with short hair, an attractively

weatherbeaten face and a relaxed manner, accentuated
by his wearing an open-neck shirt under a light pullover.
He sat at a green baize table, the microphone un-
ashamedly prominent on it.

"In the name of God, the most gracious, the most
merciful—" He repeated the formula with conviction,
then tackled what was evidently the main news item.
"Today the Leader reviewed the forces of the People's
Jamahiriya celebrating the glorious anniversary of the
revolution." The screen filled with women soldiers
marching, followed by three columns of Russian T-62
tanks, dust swirling behind him. Next the camera
searched skyward and caught a flypast of aircraft. I
pressed the control that froze the picture and started
making notes, letting the film advance frame by frame.
This was worth more than a thousand blackboard briefings.

The aircraft were Russian MiG-23s, their sharply
pointed noses and swept-back wings dark against the
bright sky. They were in a series of wide V formations,
and I guessed the pilots were unwilling to converge any
closer to each other even for Qaddafi's sake. Their
height above ground was about a thousand feet, though
when the top of a minaret showed briefly I revised my
opinion to make the level between twelve and fifteen
hundred. The flypast continued for six or seven
minutes, and most of Libya's known inventory of
planes were represented, including the Mirages Qaddafi
had purchased from France. The last to go over were the
oldest, three MiG-17s with a single MiG-15 taking the
box position within the V.

I stopped the video again and examined the last frame
carefully. Even though it was in color, the glaring sun
made the precise colors of the camouflage undetectable.
The salient feature of each plane was its silhouette. For
a moment I indulged myself in the exultation one enjoys
after backing a winner at a hundred to one. Despite
what military reference books stated, there was still at

least one MiG-15 in the Libyan inventory, and seen
from below the Sabre would be indistinguishable from
it. I had been right to paint the underside dark. Finally,
which was a bonus, the MiG-15 came last in the loosely
disciplined procession. If I could join on the end I
would be in business with a vengeance. If.

"If" has always been the largest small word in the
dictionary. Tagging on to the end of Qaddafi's September first flypast was going to demand knowing a lot
more than just the height the aircraft would be flying at.
I had to discover where they would take off from, and
where planes from different airfields would join up to
form the procession. I had to know their route and the
radio frequency their pilots would be using. In short, I
needed the Libyan Air Force's Operation Order, which
was asking for the moon. Even if I had it, and even
though I spoke enough Arabic to understand the formation leader's commands, the timing would still be split
second. I started the video going again, in the hope that
the rest would be more revealing.

The second half was astounding. My respect for
Arain's organizational ability rocketed. Photographing
airports is forbidden in most Third World countries. In
Libya it's an invitation to immediate imprisonment on
charges of espionage, plus extremely rough treatment.
Qaddafi's constant support of terrorism in other countries has made Libyans paranoid about their own security. So how Arain had obtained the photographic
coverage in the video beat me. Obviously it had been
difficult, because all the pictures were stills, some
shadowed by whatever disguise had concealed the
camera. Typically of the man, he had turned the lack of
moving footage to advantage. What I watched on the
television screen was more like a videograph presenta-
tion to a salesmen's conference than a film, and it had
the same terse, well-explained impact. I recognized the
unseen narrator's voice at once. He was Newland and he
was talking exclusively to me.

"Tripoli International is situated nineteen miles directly inland to the south of the city that is on the Mediterranean shore," Newland began, as an overall aerial view of the airport came on the screen. "It was originally constructed there to be out of range of naval gunfire. The prevailing wind is southwesterly and on past occasions flypasts have flown into wind over the city, approaching from the east. It is anticipated the aircraft will fly parallel to runway two seven. The runway elevation is two hundred and sixty-three feet above sea level."

A small pointer of light indicated the runway on the photograph. "The following shots were taken on the approach," Newland continued, as color pictures came on of small square fields, mostly looking sandy, with occasional palm trees and olives at their corners. "At the end of August the landscape is dry and brown. At midday you can expect low-level turbulence."

He went on describing the airport, referring to its recent expansion and ending with a close-up black-and-white photograph of the terminal buildings. The main block was concrete, long and white, while at the far end was an elegant circular edifice with an array of high white flagpoles in front of it.

"That is the VIP building. Unfortunately, this shot is taken from the opposite direction to your approach. Initially your view may be obstructed by the new control tower. The VIP building stands two thousand feet to the north of runway two seven and will be on your right. The Pakistan Airlines Boeing will be parked in front of the flagstaffs, where Qaddafi will stand on a dais." The camera zoomed in to enlarge the area of the flagstaffs, then reverted to the larger aerial view. "Be warned of the 150-foot pylon north of the terminal building, which presents a hazard when pulling out of a low-level attack."

Decent of him, I thought cynically, to point that out when he was planning to kill me off fifteen minutes

later. Presumably Arain didn't want a crash on Libyan
soil, in case I fell into Libyan hands alive, and I was
with him all the way on that score.

Newland's briefing ran on another twelve minutes,
with descriptions of how previous flypasts had been
organized. The former American airbase of Wheelus,
now called Okba Ben Nafi, on the eastern outskirts of
the city, was certain to be utilized as a rendezvous point,
and he even mentioned a couple of features on the
coastline that would help me find it at low level, in addi-
tion to the radio beacon. I imagined he had obtained
this information in Washington. Overall, the material
was a masterpiece, while the end incorporated a nicely
twisted touch of humor. There was a cut back to moving
film, showing a female Arab announcer.

"We hope that our program for today has proved interesting," she intoned, smiling sweetly, "and we will
now have a reading from the Holy Koran. In the name
of God, the most gracious, the most merciful—"

I made some coffee, then sat down with my maps
spread out on the table and went through the briefing
again, stopping the video frequently to absorb details.
They were enough to send Qaddafi berserk. Newland
had even specified the UHF frequency on which the
flypast commander would be operating. The only
reason the whole thing left a slightly sour taste in my
mouth was that it underlined by inference how professional Arain was likely to be in arranging my own disap-
pearance afterward. He must indeed have something
more subtle than the ejection seat up his sleeve, and it
worried me that there was no way of locking the Sabre's
cockpit against intruders.

Putting aside these apprehensions, I hired a car on
Thursday, drove to Leicester, and spent the entire after-
noon at the offices of the Royal Aero Club in Vaughan
Way. Although the club is sadly reduced from the days
when it occupied a handsome residential building in
London's Piccadilly, it remains the umbrella organiza-

tion for almost all sporting flying associations in Britain, and represents British interests at the Fédération Aéronautical Internationale. The staff are appropriately enthusiastic about every form of aerial locomotion from hang gliders to formula racing, and the attractive brunette I spoke to was unsurprised to find that Hawker Hall's burning ambition was to break the existing speed record from London to Nice, Nice to Malta and Malta to Cairo.

"I'd have liked to try Cairo to Khartoum and Khartoum to Nairobi," I explained jovially, "but frankly that would be stretching the Sabre's range."

"I wouldn't take any jet fighter through the Middle East just now either, even an old one," she advised, hazel eyes smiling at me. "Your motives could be misunderstood. Cairo may be tricky. You'll have to get your own clearances. But the Maltese are dead keen to show willing. When did you plan to go?"

"Around the end of August. Thought I might do Nice and Malta on the thirty-first, overnight in Malta and continue to Cairo on the first. Maybe Cairo-Athens as well."

"Then you'd better get moving on the paperwork," she advised briskly. "You'll need a competition license from us and photos of the plane. We organize the timekeepers, pay the fees, send the telegrams claiming a record to the FAI and prove all your time and distance calculations to them." She smiled again. "It's going to cost you, I'm afraid. There's a separate set of fees for each attempt."

"I can afford it," I said blithely. "Sabres held the world speed record from 1948 to 1953. I'd like to put a Sabre in the books again."

"Shouldn't be difficult," she remarked lightly, "given that no one's ever established a record on any of those routes in the C-1-F class. But don't expect a lot of publicity. That's one thing we can't guarantee. The newspapers aren't much interested these days."

"Unless you're a woman?" I teased her with deliberate intent.

"Even if you are." She looked at me scornfully. "Women don't have the sort of money you're going to spend. Sheila Scott was always short of sponsors: and she broke more records than you'd believe." She cut herself short. "Sorry, Mr. Hall, but you asked for that."

"My fault," I grinned sheepishly. "I suppose I am a bit of a chauvinist."

She shot me a glance that said plainly that she thought me half-witted, and when we settled down to the documentation I tried to reinforce the impression of having more money than sense. To help me along she gave the relevant city-center coordinates of latitude and longitude and advised me to lay hands on a computer for calculating the exact Great Circle distances. Nonetheless, by the time I left I had submitted four entry forms for record attempts, paid the relevant non-refundable fees, promised to abide by the sporting code of the FAI and undertaken not to publish any results myself without the words "subject to official confirmation."

"Don't worry," I assured her. "I won't go jumping around pretending to be a hero without permission."

"It's surprising how often people do. Success goes to their heads."

She obviously thought it would go to mine, and I left Kimberley House well-content with the image I had created. When Hawker Hall vanished she would assure everyone concerned that he'd been a nutter from the start.

After spending the night in Leicester I drove east across the country via Stamford to Peterborough, King's Lynn and that curious rectangular indentation in the east coast, the Wash. I remembered vaguely from my schooldays that King John had lost the crown jewels in the quicksands there. They might be a suitable place to lose another pair of drop tanks. It's not easy to find a stretch of Britain's coast that's free of holidaymakers in late July. With the aid of the ordnance survey map and half a day's walking I located a suitably deserted few miles of short along Holbeach Marsh, where the skeleton of an old fishing boat lay exposed on the mud at low tide. I also plotted reference points that would lead me to it from the air. Then I drove south again to Cambridge and treated my new crew chief to one of the better dinners of his life.

He was a good lad, Ted, and his enthusiasm deserved more solid material rewards than the ethics of the Aviation Society allowed. He had brought a number of technical drawings with him to the restaurant, all meticulously done and annotated in his small neat handwriting.

"Molding Plexiglas covers for the landing lights is a specialist job,' he said apologetically, as he explained how he would fit a reflector and bulb into the nose of each one-hundred-gallon drop tank. The tanks themselves were streamlined, like long silver fish with two fins at the tail end. "I can cut the tip off and fit a leak-proof bulkhead behind the light. The wiring ought to run inside pipes. But I can't do the Plexiglas."

"Doesn't need to be particularly strong," I remarked. In fact the more fragile it was, the better. "How long will it all take?"

"Three weeks. Less if I'm lucky."

Today was July twenty-seventh. That would take us through to August seventeenth. I told him I was planing a series of record attempts at the end of the month.

"Don't forget the Open Day on the Bank Holiday."

I glanced at him with a sudden premonition and reached into my pocket for my diary to conceal my concern. "I've been abroad so much I tend to be out of touch with public holidays," I said, flipping the pages.

"August twenty-seventh," he prompted. "Late summer holiday. It's one of our biggest days. Thousands of people turn up. Everything we have goes on show. We must have the Sabre there.''

"Then she will be," I promised. The twenty-seventh was a Monday. It wouldn't affect the timing of my departure for Nice, but it did mean I shouldn't have to be at Duxford keeping a hawk eye on my property. Dismissing sabotage from my mind, I spent the rest of the meal discussing some other modifications to the Sabre's systems, notably to enable the drop tanks to feed fuel separately, instead of together.

The next day, I found to my relief that the four one-hundred-gallon tanks airfreighted from Ottawa to Gatwick had been delivered to the airfield. Equally importantly, the maintenance manuals had arrived by post: they had been too heavy to stow on board the Sabre during the ferry flight. Ted was delighted, not least because the spare tanks had been completely cleaned out and dried for their transportation and he could start cutting their metal without fear of an accidental spark igniting residual kerosene vapor inside. That alone put him ahead of the game by several days, and, as I gently reminded him, we would soon be counting in days rather than weeks.

"As you've got the tanks to get on with," I announced over our mid-morning cups of coffee, "I think I'll take her out over the sea for a few high-speed runs this afternoon. Just as well to do them when there's no military activity."

On weekdays East Anglia can be extremely active, aeronautically speaking, what with the U.S. Air Force operating from Lakenheath, Mildenhall, and Woodbridge, while in spite of defense cuts there are still quite a number of RAF stations. But Friday night is leg-over night, as we used to say in the squadron, and nowadays service pilots are more likely to be alongside their wives in the local supermarkets on Saturdays than breaking the sound barrier. Nor was the Wash in any civil air traffic control zone, either. So, the day being near perfect, with a light easterly breeze and only scattered clouds, I had decided to conclude the bombing tests.

We spent the rest of the morning fitting on one pair of the one-hundred-gallon tanks, doing routine checks on the Sabre, and curing a small hydraulic leak. After lunch I phoned the duty officer at Marham, the RAF station nearest where I would be flying. Marham used to be a master diversion airfield for emergencies, with radar operating twenty-four hours a day. It wasn't any more, and the duty officer told me politely that his lack of interest in my flying was total, since they were only open Monday to Friday. Napoleon called us a "nation of shopkeepers" and I guess he was right.

The fifty miles to King's Lynn took me six minutes, as against an hour and a half in the car. As I swung west over the Fens at three thousand feet I could see the high stone tower of Boston Church in the distance, the famous "Boston Stump" that guided so many bomber crews home to Lincolnshire during World War II. The Wash itself lay spread out like a lightly rippled blue carpet, the marsh forming a crescent along the southwestern side. I made a slow pass above the shore, picking up the reference points off the map and recognizing the insignificant carcass of the stranded fishing boat. Turning short of Boston, I then began another run back at fifteen hundred feet scanning the area for signs of life. There were none, apart from two white-sailed yachts much farther out at sea.

At five miles out everything was so well in hand that I elected to make this the only run. There was a long drainage ditch that I had chosen to represent the Tripoli Airfield boundary. As I crossed it at two hundred knots, making a track to the left of my target, the boat came into view nice and early because it was to one side, not straight in front. I banked and eased the nose down to center the sight, held it on the weathered wooden skeleton for a second, then pressed the button on the stick. The Sabre jolted upward as the weight of the

tanks fell away and I pulled her into a steep turn, the
G-suit clamping my legs and stomach, my head craned
around to observe the result.

A shower of mud and sand had enveloped the wreck.
I relaxed the turn, flipped her level, flew out to sea some
distance and came back very low with the air brakes out
and the speed right down to take a closer look.

There was no chance of doing better. One tank was
embedded in the boat's ribs; the tail fins of the other
were projecting from the mud some four yards to the
side. I had scored a bull's-eye. I piled on the power and
took the Sabre up to five thousand feet, then headed
south, scribbling notes on my knee-pad. The sight had
been calibrated for a 750 pound bomb under each wing.
A one-hundred-gallon tank laden with fuel weighed
only slightly more. Although drop tanks invariably
tumbled on release, it appeared that these full ones had
followed much the same trajectory as the kind of bomb
I had in mind, both here and in the Mojave. All I needed
now were the bombs themselves, and I had known precisely where they were coming from since the day I accepted Arain's offer.

BACK AT DUXFORD, I was able to spin a fractionally more convincing tale of excuse than had been available in California, though I tried to spice up the telling in case it sounded second hand. Possibly I overdid things.

"Damn silly, really," I told Ted, "though I believe it used to happen quite often when Sabres were in squadron service. Meant to adjust the trim on a low-level run over the Wash and bingo, the tanks were gone."

He looked at me with something close to disbelief and I began to worry. No one likes to be crew chief to an idiot.

"Hop up and take a gander," I said. "The bomb-release is hardly an inch from the trim button. See what I mean," I went on as he climbed into the cockpit. "They're both on top of the stick."

The control column was a thick, black-finished "stick" of the old-fashioned kind, surmounted by a handgrip. Holding this grip with the right hand a number of switches could conveniently be operated by one's thumb. In action it was vital to be able to drop

bombs or fire rockets without shifting either hand off
the controls, and I'd had the proper bomb-release
reconnected while the Sabre was being worked on at
Chino. Not that I intended revealing the fact to Ted.

"Were the tanks still full?" he asked, still obviously
horrified.

"Thank God, no," I lied, realizing with embarrassment that a man who was giving his weekend for free
was unlikely to be amused at such waste—those two
hundred gallons represented two or three weeks' pay to
him. "No," I emphasized. "I'd been using the fuel in
them first."

"That was a bit of luck," he conceded, then after a
moment's thought suggested, "Do you think we ought
to disconnect that bomb-release?"

"Oh, I don't think so. Won't happen again." I eased
him off the subject by turning the conversation onto
other questions, including the need for the plane to be
kept locked inside a hangar at all times when he wasn't
around.

"Don't want anyone mucking about with her," he
agreed. "Not when she has to be in tip-top shape for
those records."

I left it at that, not wanting to go so far as to suggest
that she might be interfered with and experiencing a
twinge of conscience at how let-down Ted was going to
feel in a month's time. However, he wasn't the one who
was taking chances. He stood no risk of getting hurt.

Before leaving I also wrote a brief letter to the police
at King's Lynn, reporting the incident and stating that
so far as I was aware no damage had been caused. Then
they'd have something on the file if anyone did complain, though I doubted if the wrecked boat's owner
would get as worked up as the prospector in the Mojave
had. People are more placid in Norfolk.

Saturday evening was bad: bad for my morale on several counts and due to get worse, as I rapidly discovered.

The urge to see Susie again became something approaching a compulsion. Not unendurable, because you have to be seriously lacking in self-control if you let a woman get between you and your work at crucial moments, but extremely strong. Before he went into battle, Napoleon may have been wishing he had Josephine with him—on occasions when he didn't, that is—but I'm damned certain he forgot her once the action started. The same principle had worked well enough for me in California. There had been no question of asking Susie across, so I had contented myself with sending her a couple of postcards and in all other respects following the RAF jungle-survival pamphlet's advice on how to avoid trouble, namely by keeping one's hands off the local ladies, though I have to admit the one with different colored eyes in the Chino diner had posed a temptation.

The truth was that I knew Hawker Hall's limitations. He had been accepted in the flying fraternity everywhere because the ownership of the Sabres were both a glamorous introduction and a guarantee of wealth. But women always ask one question too many, and Hawker's roots emphatically did not go deep enough to survive female curiosity. Nor had being alone bothered me. Most of my friendships have tended to be the "out of sight, out of mind" sort. When you fly for a living the way I do, you tend to exist for the place and the moment.

However, I discovered during those weeks that Susie had changed my attitudes. She was in my thoughts far too often for complacency, and as I drove back to London on Saturday evening it hit me that since the groundwork for the raid was virtually complete I could now afford to hang up Hawker Hall's identity in the Sloane Avenue apartment for a day or two. Nor was there any reason why Captain Lloyd should not escape from CONOIL for a weekend.

I rang Susie almost as soon as I got inside the door of

the apartment. There was no answer. Having become
thoroughly steamed-up by now, I rang again at intervals
for nearly an hour, always with the same result. Then, it
occurred to me that she might have left a message at the
apartment in Fulham, as she sometimes used to. I
crammed a few clothes into a bag, locked Hawker's
documents away in the miniature safe and left to hail a
taxi in the King's Road: the rented car would look odd
when I had my own MGB garaged down there. I had
become very conscious of details since that business
with the wedge.

The twilight was fading and the streetlights had come
on when I paid off the taxi. A few drunks were singing
outside the pub on the corner and a warm wind blew
scraps of paper across the pavement. The city seemed to
be breathing again after an oppressively hot day. There
was no sign of life at the apartment. Presumably my
neighbors had gone away for the weekend. I let myself
through the outer door, snapped the hall light on, and
hit a problem. The key to the flat did not fit. My first
reaction was that I had used the outer key again by
mistake. But I hadn't. Then I noticed the brassy new-
ness of the Yale lock. It had been changed and I was
shut out.

Mystified, I stood back considering whether to break
in, then went upstairs and knocked on the neighbors'
door. The reply was complete silence, until a tiny noise
from below made me spin around and look down. My
own door had opened and now stood ajar, with only
darkness beyond.

"Who is it?" asked a voice. A soft, cautious woman's
voice. Susie's voice.

I ran down the stairs calling out, "It's me you idiot,"
pushed at the door, and was rewarded by its swinging
straight back in my face.

"Wait till I undo the chain," she said more calmly.
"Don't be so impatient."

There was a sliding, grating sound and then Susie was

standing there in a nightdress. She was panting slightly
and her breasts heaved under the flimsy nylon. She had
obviously been asleep and I had given her a fright. I
stepped inside and she fell into my arms.

"I thought someone was trying to get in. Darling, I'm
so glad you're back. I didn't know where to find you."
Her voice dissolved and she burst into tears.

I kicked the door shut with my foot, guided her into
the living room and sat her down on the sofa. The story,
as it emerged with the help of a lot of comforting, was
both simple and disturbing. She had moved in ten days
ago, when the girl whose room she was occupying
elsewhere had returned unexpectedly from Australia.
She had phoned my New York number and the man
who answered had promised to let me know. He hadn't
done so, of course, because the "number" was only an
answering service.

Then last Saturday she had returned from doing some
shopping to discover a break-in. The thief had evidently
entered through the garden window and ransacked the
place, though nothing of obvious value had been stolen.

"Your desk had been turned out, there were papers
all over the floor, and every single drawer and cupboard
was open." She was as distressed as if it had happened
an hour ago, so I simply held her tight and let her go on.
"But the TV was OK, and your camera. He didn't seem
to have taken anything."

"He?" I asked gently.

"There was a man leaving by the front door as I came
back down the street. I'd only been out for less than an
hour, I hadn't even meant to be as long as that."

"What did he look like?" If my tone was a shade
sharper, it was because Susie was normally more
switched-on than this. She wasn't the weepy type.

"I hardly saw." She made an effort and shook her
head in aggravation. "Short, dark-haired, a bit flashy.
He had very tight yellow trousers."

Hardly a description to launch Interpol into ecstasy,

but it caught my attention all right. Could it be the same
man who had interfered with the Sabre? The idea
tripped a sequence of speculation. On Saturday I had
ferried a Sabre across. On Saturday I had made those
demands of Arain.

"What time was it?"

"About five-thirty?" She took a deep breath. "I was
only going out for a few minutes. I completely forgot
about the window. Darling, will you ever forgive me?"

The answer was naturally "yes." I kissed her and she
clung to me and we would have gone straight on from
there if my brain hadn't been working overtime in other
directions. Was it conceivable that Arain had organized
a search of the apartment between my ultimatum in the
morning and his replying in the evening? I dismissed the
possibility. The timings would have been far too tight.
If I went on like this, I told myself, I'd soon be the
equivalent of a hypochondriac about the saboteur. But
what had the burglar been after? I disentangled myself
from Susie's embrace sufficiently to ask.

"He took the spare keys I'd had cut. That's why
there's a new lock."

I disentangled myself some more and stood up. The
inference could only be that he intended to return. It
was imperative to check on what he had—or had not—
found. I began systematically sorting through the desk,
while Susie gave advice.

"Everything's bound to be in the wrong place," she
apologized. "I couldn't just leave it until you came
back."

"Did you call the police?"

"No, sweetheart, I didn't." Her voice was a lot
firmer now that she'd admitted her guilt, so to speak. "I
was due at Gatwick in two hours and anyway I had no
idea what had been stolen. The people upstairs
promised to fit a new lock. They were angelic. I just had
time to ring you again. Where have you been?"

"California," I said over my shoulder. "I did write to your old address." Then I changed the subject because I had made a discovery and an extremely unwelcome one at that. "You didn't see a little key anywhere? Smaller than a doorkey. Silver colored."

"No. I looked under the furniture for things. Was it important?"

"A safe-deposit key," I lied. "I'll phone the bank first thing in the morning. Luckily it wasn't labeled."

In fact, the key was the spare to Hall's Fulham post office box, which was the address given on his American license, on all the Sabre's documentation, on his driving license and on the credit-card applications, which should have been answered by now. I swore silently. If the thief was the man from Ottawa, then the lack of a label was not likely to impede him. Newland must have seen the post office box number. Could the key be all they had wanted? And why? I continued searching for clues until Susie wearily suggested we go to bed, but found nothing. My only firm conclusion was that this crime ought to remain unreported.

Next morning I crawled out relatively early, leaving Susie fast asleep. She had needed an early night originally because she had been flying all the previous one. Now she had three days off, which was perfect, except that I had a few things to do on Hall's behalf.

The first was to check the post office box, since I had the other key with me. I walked briskly up to the post office, and found the expected American Express hold card safely there among numerous mail-order letters and leaflets. Much more important, Hawker's American pilot's license had arrived, so I no longer needed the Permit to Fly. Nothing that was due was missing. I opened all the envelopes carefully, finding no immediate sign of their having been tampered with. It would be a waste of time having them tested for fingerprints. What I could do was leave a trap. The most re-

cent letter was one from Guernsey. Fortunately the flap
had been well gummed. I plucked a hair from my head
and, placing an inch of it in the closure, resealed the
envelope. If the letter was opened again the hair would
fall out. Hardly a new idea, but better than nothing.

From the post office I strolled in a leisurely way to
Rajni's travel agency, crossing the road occasionally
and glancing at reflections in shop windows to make
sure I was not being followed. I wasn't, though I had an
increasing suspicion that Arain had me under some
form of surveillance.

As I had anticipated, Rajni was in his office, Sunday
or not. If you want to know why Asian immigrants
make a success where native-born British go bankrupt,
that's the reason. They slave away for about sixteen
hours out of every twenty-four, seven days a week. As
usual, Rajni ushered me into the back room, and
beneath the discreet gaze of the goddess I explained
what was required next, at the same time handing over
Hall's new passport.

Rajni flipped through the pages, examining the
legitimate U.S. visa and the various immigration stamps
with evident pleasure.

"What was I telling you," he breathed. "This is top
drawer, very best class document."

"Certainly is," I assured him. "Why not put the new
stamp on a page that's been partly used? Wouldn't it be
less obtrusive?"

"I am not agreeing," he reflected after a pause.
"Those wogs, they are all being same, liking to use new
page for their conceit." He laughed and closed the
passport with a snap. "And tickets? You are wanting
one or two?" He winked with surprising lasciviousness.
"No vacation is a pleasure without, isn't it? They are
having only double rooms, private bath or shower, all
complete. Why not take advantage?"

The idea had not occurred to me. "Can I let you

know in a week?" I temporized. "My girlfriend might
be able to come."

"No hurry, no rushing at all. Next week is OK. I am
holding seats for you."

I left Rajni with a variation on my plan rapidly acquiring credence. This part of the scenario called for
behaving and looking as normal and middle-class as
possible. The normal thirty-eight-year-old on vacation
has a wife or girlfriend in tow. The question was how
far I could trust Susie: or else how far I could keep her
in ignorance. I turned the possibilities over in my mind
on the way to Sloane Avenue for the second part of the
morning's mission.

The elderly hall porter in Sloane Avenue knew me by
sight and name already: it's amazing how quickly these
people latch on to potential sources of revenue.

"I believe there is a message for you, Mr. Hall, sir,"
he intoned, moving off to fetch it and then pocketing
my loose change with the smoothness of a conjurer. The
message was from Ted at Duxford. It said the police had
been inquiring about the activities of an aircraft over the
Wash on Saturday. What should he say?

From the apartment I called Duxford and explained
that I had already sent a written statement about the incident to the police. That satisfied the controller, and I
settled down to the serious task of speaking to Arain.

The Swiss woman spent several minutes locating him,
and when he answered he was not as brisk as I would
have expected at midday.

"The video was excellent," I said warmly. "Couldn't
have been better."

"Oh yeah. Good." He muttered something, then
said, "Hang on a moment, will you." There was a
pause, and I realized he was talking to someone else
with his hand cupped over the instrument because I
distinctly heard the word "coffee." Then he came back
on. "Right. Are you set to go?"

"Just about."

"I want you in position and ready on the night of the thirtieth."

"Is there a change?"

"The date might be brought forward." He offered no reason.

"I'd like to know," I insisted, cursing because there was scarcely time to alter the record schedules this week, let alone later.

"You'll know as soon as we do," Arain snapped. "There are unexpected factors." He did not explain further. "I have to be away for some time. You're to call this number routinely once a week, understand?"

So that was all. Arain hadn't told me much and certainly nothing that would make sense to an eavesdropper. Except for one slip. He wasn't in Geneva. He was either in New York or some other place where it was early enough in the morning for him to be sleepy and wanting a first cup of coffee. The Swiss number must be no more than a form of telephone exchange, patching calls through to wherever he was, on the same principle as Stockholm Radio had patched me through from the aircraft. In security terms it made sense. It also made me feel more than ever that it was essential to have someone I could trust on my own side. For all her emotion, Susie had displayed plenty of common sense over the break-in. I was going to have to get her involved. All I needed was to have someone providing a cover for my activity.

When I got back home to Fulham, Susie was in the living room, swathed in my bathrobe and sipping a Bloody Mary. She looked marvelous and I raised the subject there and then.

"How would you like a holiday, sweetheart?" I suggested. "The sunny Mediterranean."

"I think I'd like it very much. When?"

"Last two weeks of this month."

"Wait a minute." She rose elegantly from the sofa and disappeared into the bedroom, returning with a

sheet of paper. "They gave me the August roster yesterday," she explained, tracing the columns with her
finger. "The third week I could change, but I have a
Karachi charter on the twenty-seventh and no one ever
wants to do a swap on those. Could I come for the first
half?"

"That would be wonderful." I swept her up, whirled
her around and kissed her happily.

"You haven't even told me where it is yet!" she protested.

"Malta," I said.

"Malta?" She sounded less than enthralled. "Is there
anything to do there?"

"More than you'd think," I promised. "I spent a
year or so there in the RAF. I'll tell you if you come to
the country."

In fact it was hardly necessary, because the next two
days were such an unqualified success.

We took the MGB down to Wiltshire and stayed in an
attractive old inn by a trout stream; lay on the bank in
the sun holding hands and watching the fish in the cool
shallows; drove through the lush countryside, heavy
with summer, looking half-enviously at idyllic thatched
cottages; drank good wine with dinner and stayed in bed
late the next morning to make love again with a more
relaxed and understanding sensuality than we had ever
enjoyed before.

"This is so beautiful," Susie said at one moment. "I
don't want it ever to end."

When it had to, and I departed "for Heathrow" on
Tuesday evening, going to Malta together seemed the
most natural thing in the world to plan for. In fact,
Susie was becoming quite possessive about my
whereabouts, and it was a relief to be able to make firm
arrangements. Marriage is a formality I've tended to
sidestep ever since Mary Anne took off. Once is enough.
Yet I was still brooding over the idea to such an extent
after we had said goodbye that I nearly forgot to tell the

taxi driver to turn around and go back to Sloane Avenue instead of the airport.

The next morning, far from breakfasting in the Big Apple, I drove down to Wiltshire again to visit a pyrotechnics factory, where an old RAF friend of mine had a retirement job. It proved to be a day that acted itself out with all the sharply etched clarity of a cameo scene in a play.

The factory was among cornfields on the edge of the army's Salisbury Plain training area. Basically it occupied part of a former camp, with old World War II Nissen huts, plus a few newer brick buildings. In the distance an observation tower faced over the gunnery ranges. Except for the high security fences and guard-dog warning notices, the whole establishment was straight out of a Nevil Shute novel. It looked the epitome of the traditional British way of achieving scientific miracles with two men, a dog, and a box of discarded cotton reels. As I signed the visitors' book at the gate office I reflected that it was the sort of place old Moon had always been destined for.

Flight Lieutenant "Moon" Watson had been the armaments officer on the RAF station where I first flew Phantoms twelve years ago. The nickname was absurdly inappropriate. He had risen from the ranks and still sported the magnificent tawny-colored handlebar mustache that had been part of his persona as a warrant officer. We young pilots had all stood in awe of him. Even now, if he felt so inclined, I felt sure he could give me more guidance in an hour than reference books would in a month. Like bombs, pyrotechnics usually go off with a bang, and bangs had always been Moon's passion, the bigger the better.

When he appeared I hardly recognized him. The great mustache had gone, and without it Moon looked both less authoritative and less jovial. His face seemed thinner and more lined. Only the very pale blue eyes were the same, regarding me quizzically in the way I remembered so well.

"Sorry to keep you, Tom," he said, shaking my hand warmly. "Have to check people in, you know. Wouldn't want the IRA observing our little secrets, would we?"

He led me along tarmacked paths to his office, a sparsely furnished room, where the available space was mostly taken up by a table spread with blueprint drawings, sections of fractured metal, fuses, and other impedimenta connected with making things go in directions God never intended. I noticed a couple of small puttylike lumps of plastic explosive and guessed he was experimenting outside the factory's normal field.

"So we want to brush up on a few technicalities, do we?" The famous lecture-room style had not deserted him. "May I offer congratulations on this prospective appointment. Assistant Commandant, eh?" He looked half-pleased and half-regretful. "A pity you ever left the service, a pilot as above average as you were."

"That was a few years ago, Moon. One forgets. As I said on the phone, the general running this Middle Eastern Air Force Academy—I can't reveal which until the appointment's confirmed—assumes I know all about ground-attack weaponry. Well," I smiled confidently, "no one needs to teach me about tactical flying. But I'm a bit rusty on how the weapons themselves function." I cracked a joke, wanting to put him at ease. "You always did say short-service officers don't know their ears from their assholes."

"Did I, indeed?" Moon affected surprise. "A little wet behind the ears some of us may have been, on occasions, I admit. What kind of weapons are we talking about today?"

"Rockets, cannon, bombs, napalm—"

"Napalm, eh? Chemical weapons too, I suppose? They're a nasty lot. Always were. Wouldn't trust them with our grandmothers, would we?'' Suddenly he remembered that my prospective employers were Arabs. ''Beg your pardon, Tom, but you know what I mean. They've been using those sorts of things in the Gulf I've heard. Well, now, where would we like to start?''

''The construction of a typical bomb.''

Moon cleared the papers on his desk into a neat pile, reached for the large pad and began making sketches to illustrate his explanations.

''The casing of the bomb contains the high explosive that may be detonated by an impact fuse, a timed fuse, or—if we desire an airburst—by a proximity fuse. This fuse will be fitted to the nose of the weapon.'' He went on drawing as he talked. ''It will be activated by an electrical circuit switched on by the pilot.''

''In the case of napalm?'' I prompted.

''Ah,'' he exclaimed, as if to say ''I told you so,'' raised his fingers to his mustache, remembered it was no longer there to be stroked and hastily brought his hand down again. He always used to make that gesture when considering a tricky point. ''Now with napalm, or jellified petroleum, we are considering a most unpleasant weapon, are we not? Easily manufactured also, since we only have to add the jellifying agent to normal fuel. Yes,'' he continued, ''the ball of fire that napalm creates is a most effective weapon against troops in the open, vehicles, or other exposed targets. If, for example, we drop two five-hundred-pound napalm canisters they will burst upon impact and throw the bulk of their contents forward a considerable distance.'' Moon traced two elongated oval shapes that overlapped each other at the sides. ''The length of the dispersion will be at least a hundred feet and the width fifty feet.''

I nodded, trying to imagine the inferno of flame that those two oval areas represented.

''The chance of human survival in the impact area will be minimal,'' Moon commented. ''We will find soft-skinned vehicles totally destroyed, will we not, while the crews of armored ones will be suffocated even if they survive the heat."

That was it, I recalled. If you weren't roasted, you were asphyxiated because the flames consumed all the available oxygen.

"The only risk we take with the napalm bomb is that if the fuse detonates too early, the requisite ball of fire might not be created."

"It has an impact fuse?"

Moon glanced at me. "It uses a fuse a twelve-year-old could make. All we require is a battery, two leads, and a trembler spring that will complete the circuit when the weapon hits the ground. The resultant spark will ignite the petroleum jelly." He drew a diagram.

"And if you added explosive, would it be more effective?"

"Possibly." Moon pointed at the lumps of plastic on the table. "If we utilized those, for example, we would be overcooking the goose, would we not? A tenth of that amount of plastic in a letter bomb could blow out the wall of this room."

"You're joking!" I said, visualizing precisely how to employ the stuff.

Moon rose to his feet, went to the table, separated a small segment from one of the lumps, popped it inside an empty matchbox and handed it to me.

"If we take that to a piece of wasteland and detonate it with great care, we will know what we are talking about. But we will not reveal its origin, will we?"

"We will not," I assured him. "And now, remind me what happens when a nuclear bomb detonates at ground-level?"

"Ah," Moon's interest was aroused to such an extent that he completely dropped his lecturing voice. "D'you reckon they've got the Bomb?"

"Probably." I traded on my self-awarded status. "The Iraqis are working on it, so are others. Whether my people are, I'm not sure. I doubt if they'd tell a foreigner. But they're interested in low-level delivery systems.''

"Well, as to delivering nuclear weapons in the ground-attack role,'' Moon reverted to his usual manner, "there's no secret about the damage ground-zero explosions cause and we need no reminding of the dangers, do we?''

"We do not, Moon,'' I agreed emphatically. The snag about dropping a nuclear weapon from low level is that the blast of the explosion travels so fast it can catch you up. Poetic justice, the CND supporters would call it, but they're prejudiced.

Moon continued his explanations until lunchtime, when I invited him down to a pub in the valley for a bite and some beer. It had been a most successful morning.

Of course, I had known all along that the Sabre's drop tanks could be converted into napalm bombs that would completely incinerate the airliner bringing Qaddafi his nuclear weapons and probably the Leader himself, depending how far away his saluting base was. Now Moon had indirectly confirmed the validity of using the new landing lights as fuses. The only remaining question was whether the intense heat generated by the napalm would cause the nuclear bomb to detonate in turn. I had always supposed it would not, but there's no point in going to the oracle if you don't ask for advice. Over lunch I phrased the question in the context of an accident.

"Difficult to be certain,'' Moon observed, spearing a chunk of chicken pie with his fork. "We have the example of that American Air Force crash in Spain, when fire damage affected the nuclear bomb less than was feared. Some leakage of radioactivity would be inevitable. As we know, kerosene burns at three hundred eighty degrees centigrade, or eight hundred fahrenheit. Much would depend upon the construction of the device itself.''

It was hardly either a conclusive or comforting answer. If the Islamic bomb was made to the usual Pakistani standards it would melt down in seconds. I had once seen a Pak Air Force Hercules refitted locally . . . but that's another story.

"This one would be of local manufacture?" Moon asked, neatly reading my mind.

"You could assume that."

"Well, Tom," his face creased into a smile and he took a long pull from his tankard, "if I were faced with such an eventuality, I would advise discovering urgent business elsewhere. We should encourage those Arabs to sort out their own problems sometimes, should we not?"

So the answer was that there was no answer, at least not without more technical detail than I was likely to obtain. The Islamic bomb might go off on September first and fry me in the process. Or it might not. There was no point in pressing Moon further. After lunch I drove him back and promised to let him know the outcome of my interviews. None of our few mutual acquaintances would be surprised to hear that Tom Lloyd had been considering another job in the Gulf, and I reckoned he had rather enjoyed his morning, like a schoolmaster being consulted by a successful old boy. As for myself, I could now carry on with a test explosion.

Up at Duxford, the modifications Ted was making were completed nine days later. He rang and told me he had fitted a standard General Electric landing light into the nose of each drop tank and had also bought two spare ones on my instructions. They were the type used on most American executive planes: a lot smaller than car headlights, the glass being barely four inches in diameter, but giving a strong beam thanks to being sealed units filled with halogen gas. Not that I gave a damn about the light. The important aspect of their design was that the whole lamp was effectively a bulb, with the filament projecting on two strong supports from the center of the lamp's reflector. This filament could easily be converted into a "trembler" such as Moon had described, which would complete a circuit and spark if anything pushed it backward, such as impact with the ground.

Ted had done a beautiful job of fitting the lights, and I thanked him warmly when we met on the evening of Friday the tenth of August. The only things missing were the plexiglass covers, which would maintain the aerodynamic shape of the tanks, but he was expecting those to be completed any day. We spent an hour in the early evening discussing various aspects of the Sabre's maintenance vis-á-vis the record attempts. He was worried about the routine servicing and suggested flying out to Malta separately to help.

"I'd pay your fare, of course," I insisted with Hawker's habitual generosity, "and it's extremely decent of you to offer. But I really don't feel it's necessary. There will only be ten hours flying in the whole round trip." And less than half that to complete the mission, I thought. Jesus, the last thing I wanted was young Ted watching my preparations for leaving Malta. Even he would smell a rat.

"Well," he said, accepting the put-down reluctantly, "if you do change your mind, you can count on me. I could get the Friday afternoon off." Obviously he had worked it all out. Reluctantly, I had to kill the idea.

"I'm flying the first two legs earlier anyway," I explained. "Leaving on Thursday the thirtieth. But I will be here for the Open Day on the twenty-seventh."

That mollified his disappointment somewhat and he readily agreed to my using his workbench for an hour or so after he had gone.

The hardest part of converting one of the spare lamps into an explosive fuse was opening the sealed casing. From there on it was simple. Following Moon's description, all I needed was a battery-powered circuit that would detonate enough plastic explosive to ignite the tank when it hit the ground. The elements in this circuit were a small, high-power battery; a solenoid switch to connect it to the lamp filament; and the filament itself. Come September 1 the filament would be severed to form a trembler. Today, because I could not simulate the impact without blowing myself up in the process, the circuit would be completed by the solenoid.

Using metal-bonding fixative I attached the battery and the solenoid to the outside casing of the lamp and joined the lamp leads to the battery. With extreme care I molded the ball of innocent-looking plastic around one filament support. Then I taped the glass back on. The whole unit was now a miniature bomb in its own right, ready to go off the instant the current passed through it.

The next step was to warn the nightwatchman that I was making an experiment. I placed the converted lamp in the car, together with a four-gallon can of kerosene, and drove to the main gate. He was ensconced in his hut, brewing up tea.

"Listen," I said. "Would it worry you if I tested a fire extinguisher in the corner of the airfield?"

"I don't suppose it would, sir," he said warily, looking at me with suspicion born of experience. He was middle-aged and wore an overcoat in spite of this being a warm summer evening. "What did you have in mind, sir?"

"Setting a can of kerosene on fire." I held up the car's fire extinguisher. "If I can't douse the flames with this, then I'll need a better make for the plane."

He squinted at the canister and grunted assent. "You know there's no fire trucks at nights and the grass is like tinder?"

"There are plenty of old dispersal areas," I reminded him. "I'll take care. And by the way, don't worry if you hear a bit of bang when it ignites. I'm trying to simulate an emergency."

I returned to the car and drove around the perimeter track until I found a circle of disused hardstanding

dating from World War II, its concrete cracked and
grown with weeds. The declining sun was casting long
shadows from the hedges, and for a moment I imagined
the Flying Fortresses that might have stood on this same
patch all those years ago, while the crew clambered on
board for a night raid over Germany. There's always a
certain sad mystique about old airfields, and a lot of
men had gone to their deaths from this one. I dismissed
any thought of joining them in Valhalla yet awhile and
began setting up my test.

For this evening's purpose the car represented the
Sabre, while the can of kerosene was the drop tank. I
stood the can in the middle of the hardstanding and
taped the lamp to its side. Then I ran a long cable from
the solenoid switch to where I had parked the car, a safe
fifty yards away.

The result when I connected the cable to the car battery was a vivid lightning flash, followed instantly by a
deafening explosion. Things whistled past me despite
the distance and I felt a surge of heat as flame erupted
from the can and cascaded over the concrete. Five
seconds later it was a mini inferno with thick smoke
belching into the twilight.

For a couple of minutes I let the kerosene burn,
reckoning it was way beyond the extinguisher's capacity
to put out. But rivulets of fire were running along the
cracks of the concrete, making torches of the weeds. At
any second the surrounding grass would catch fire. I ran
forward, the heat searing my face, and began spraying
foam on the blaze. Gradually the flames were
smothered and died. A twisted outline of metal became
visible: all that was left of the can. I was just wondering
whether I would find any recognizable fragments of the
lamp when I heard a car engine revving behind me. The
watchman had arrived in an old Ford.

"You all right, sir?" he asked nervously, peering at
me in the fading light.

I wiped the sweat off my forehead, discovering that

my hands were filthy and my trousers and shoes spattered with foam.

"Well," I said, trying to sound as triumphant as a schoolboy. "It worked."

He looked at me, at the extinguisher and at the foam subsiding all around.

"Don't think I'd try it again though, sir, if I were you."

"No need to," I remarked. "Hope I haven't caused you any trouble." I fumbled in my hip pocket for a five-pound note. "Here, buy yourself a pint on me. I'm going back to the hangar to clean up. I'll call at the gate before I go."

I didn't appreciate the full wisdom of telling him what I was doing and the generous tip until later. I merely thought that when the man gossiped about my experiment, as he was bound to, the story would confirm the reckless character of Hawker Hall. Who, except a complete idiot, would nearly immolate himself testing an extinguisher?

However, what occupied my mind immediately was my success. The napalm in one drop tank would be twenty-five times the quantity of the kerosene in the can. If 100 gallons of the stuff did not emulsify an airliner and its cargo, nothing would. Nor did I feel much sympathy for any Libyans or Pakistani officials who might be burned with it. The fireball from the nuclear weapon they were delivering could obliterate an entire city center.

What was starting to worry me more was the chance of their bomb going off before I could fly clear. The Sabres that were specially modified to deliver nuclear loads did the job by a "toss-bombing" technique, letting the thing go when they were halfway through a loop and then rolling off the top to get the hell out of the area. That option was not open to me, not if I wanted to hit a pinpoint target. I had to hope Moon's gloomy assessment was wrong.

I drove back to the hangar, parked the car by the side door, and after washing up, devoted half an hour to modifying the other spare lamp. This time I cut away the extremity of one of the filament supports and soldered a tiny flange to it, so that the springlike filament would be sure to make contact when the tank hit the ground. I then packed the lamp away again in its box. The battery and the solenoid could be attached in Malta before the final run. My preparations were complete.

The next morning I ferried the Sabre the few miles to Cambridge airport for a complete check by Marshalls. I was going to fly the record attempts for real in three weeks' time and both they and the attack on Tripoli would stretch the plane's performance to the limit.

RAJNI'S IDEA OF a vacation flight was not mine. I had never imagined it would be. The charter from Gatwick deposited us at Luqa Airport at ten-thirty on the evening of August eighteenth and we resignedly joined a long line for immigration formalities. The airport buildings were not air-conditioned and the atmosphere inside was a sweaty mixture of stale air, humidity, cigarette smoke, and kerosene fumes from aircraft outside. Shuffling inch by inch toward the immigration desk, clutching hand baggage and forms, we listened to the patient wisecracks of other people on the package tour.

"Never mind, Fred, think of the beach tomorrow," a woman said.

"I don't want a beach tomorrow, love, I want a beer now."

I squeezed Susie's hand affectionately. "It's all right, sweetheart," I whispered. "We're in a decent hotel." Although I had to be on a package, I had refused to accept Rajni's standard seafront accommodation.

At last we came face to face with the immigration officer, a typically swarthy Maltese in a short-sleeved white shirt. He was keeping cool, if no one else was.

"Business or vacation?" he demanded.

"Two weeks' vacation."

"Your address in Malta?"

I pointed to the form where I had written "Phoenicia Hotel." He made a petulant display of adding "Floriana," stamped the passports, and then suddenly asked, "You are not a reporter? All press require visas."

"Airline pilot," I said firmly, and he let us through.

Twenty minutes later, after the usual hassle with the baggage, we emerged into the fresh night air outside the terminal and I knew that the island hadn't really changed. There were the same cheerfully wheedling taxi drivers, the same friendly confusion, the same distant stone churches illuminated by floodlights, the same brilliant stars above. I breathed it all in, feeling as though I had rediscovered a forgotten lover, and reluctantly turned my attention to a woman courier who was rallying our group from among the crush of other tourists.

"Melita Sunshine Tour, Coach Zero Eight please," she was calling. She spotted our baggage tags. "Melita Sunshine Tour, over there please, your coach is waiting." She half-waved, half-pushed us toward a bright yellow single-decker bus of ancient vintage parked among others opposite. I picked up our cases and we went across. The windshield was plastered with stickers: "Arsenal FC. The Gunners," "No smoking on the coach please," "Melita Sightseeing," "See the Blue Grotto," and others. We mounted. Inside, a gaudily painted statuette of a saint was perched above the driving mirror. The driver himself, a peaked hat squashed almost flat on his head, gestured us down the aisle.

After another fifteen minutes everyone was aboard and the courier began calling our names, distributing large brown envelopes to each passenger in turn with a synthetic smile. At last she had us all ticked off her list and the bus lurched into motion, while she gave a running commentary of advice over a loudspeaker about the program of excursions and entertainments to be found in the envelopes.

Eventually, long after midnight, the bus reached the high stone edifice of the Phoenicia, rumbled up the short drive and stopped with a jerk under the portico. We descended, the only couple to do so; a brown-uniformed hall porter appeared and we and our luggage were whisked indoors.

"I am coming tomorrow," shrilled the courier. "You will see on the notice board. I will be happy to help."

I waved back, thinking she was unlikely to forget us, which was the aim of the exercise. We checked in, surrendering our passports and not eliciting a flicker of surprise from the receptionist at having different names. The Phoenicia always has operated with admirable smoothness, and when we were shown our room it was everything I had promised Susie it would be: spacious, recently redecorated, and with a balcony overlooking Marsamxett harbor, though it had twin beds instead of a double.

"Never mind," she commented, folding her arms around my neck and nuzzling close. "Let's be thankful for other mercies. And now, sweetheart, why don't you tell me what this is all about?"

"What do you mean, 'about'?" I asked, kissing her cheek, while I did some rapid thinking.

It was no part of my plan to have her asking awkward questions this early. Later, when we'd settled down to soaking up some sun and I could judge how well my essential preparations were developing, then I would slip a hint or two that might—or might not—prompt her to lend a helping hand in connection with a quite different operation that I had invented for the occasion.

"This is a vacation, for heaven's sake," I insisted. "A chance to get away from it all."

"In CONOIL's time." She leaned her head back and looked me straight in the eyes. "They must be very generous employers."

"They were." I emphasized the past tense as a preliminary to edging into an explanation. "They've paid me off from the end of this month. Luckily they honor vacation commitments."

"How nice of them." The way she said it was half-sarcastic, half-vengeful. I was surprised until I remembered that she had urged me to take the CONOIL job in the first place, so she could reasonably be bitter on my behalf. Maybe it was a sign of genuine attachment, too.

"So they gave you two weeks vacation after only three months? Why not pull the other one, Tom?"

She had the bit between her teeth all right, even after an exhausting journey. Reluctantly I decided to let her pry out the rest of the story I'd prepared. It wasn't as though she would be involved in any danger, either in the fictional scenario or the real one.

"Their letting me come here wasn't entirely altruistic," I admitted cautiously. "They needed a courier to bring back some offshore drilling samples, 'core samples' they're called. There's some dispute between Libya and Malta over territorial limits." I kissed her lightly. "Frankly sweetheart, the politics are beyond me. I'm happy enough to have the vacation."

"I see!" She pushed me away from her, eyes blazing. "So they send you out to do some dirty work with your dolly bird as an alibi and no one's supposed to dream what you're really up to. Thank you for nothing, Tom Lloyd. I've half a mind to leave again tomorrow."

"Do as you like." I feigned anger and stepped back myself. If this was going to be her attitude, she'd be a liability all along the line, which I could not afford. My anger was rapidly becoming real too, except that it was directed at myself. How had I ever been fool enough to imagine Susie would not mind being used, even for such innocuous purposes as I had set out? She was still her own woman and no one else's, and being in love with her did nothing to improve matters.

"As it happens," I went on hotly, "CONOIL asked me to bring back the samples after I'd booked the package, not as a condition of it, and you will have left by the time they're ready." That was equally true of the real plan. She would be on the charter to Pakistan while I was flying Hawker's record attempt and attacking Tripoli.

She looked at me with a mixture of yearning and resentment, then said in a small voice, "I wish I could believe that."

"What you believe is up to you."

There was no possibility of revealing the truth. Not yet. When this is all over, I thought, we'll get our act together properly. I wish I could have explained that to Susie now as she sat on the edge of one of the beds, looking wide-awake and furious, despite the time.

"Listen, darling," I said, reaching for her hand, which she promptly snatched away. "If you want to fly home again tomorrow, that's fine. If not, that's better. Either way, we can't do a damn thing about it until the morning, so let's at least get some sleep."

The twin beds saved the day, so to speak. Without a word she disappeared into the bathroom, came back ten minutes later with a nightdress on, and threw back the sheets of the bed away from the door.

"Captain Lloyd," she said, as she made a show of turning her back on me, "you are the original male chauvinist pig. Goodnight."

She could hardly have expected me to agree, and when I had undressed myself and turned the light out I found sleep unattainable and lay awake, listening to the quiet hum of the air conditioning, and tracing through the past few weeks' events in my mind.

We were now in the early hours of August nineteenth. Every detail of my preparations was complete, except the part that could only be done here in Malta. The hell Susie was going to stand in its way. With that thought I must at last have fallen asleep.

An insistent buzzing from the telephone between the beds woke me. I tried to take no notice. My head felt as withered as a crab apple in autumn. Who on earth could be wanting us?

"For God's sake answer it!" Susie moaned.

Reluctantly, I reached out and took the receiver.

"Mr. Lloyd?" a voice demanded. "Mr. Lloyd are you there?" It was the woman courier of last night, speaking with the distinctively accented and grammatically precise diction of the educated Maltese. "Mr. Lloyd, today we are going by boat to the Blue Lagoon. The bus will be calling past your hotel at eleven. Will you please confirm you are coming."

"Hold on," I said. "We haven't had breakfast yet."

"Mr. Lloyd, the time is already ten-fifteen." She sounded scandalized. I suppose she made her money off tour-operator's commissions. "We have special bookings with Captain Morgan's cruise. The buffet lunch on board is famous. Have you not read the brochures?"

"What is going on?" Susie muttered.

I told her and she sat up, sweeping her long hair back from her eyes. "I'd like to go on a cruise," she said firmly.

"Not back to London?" I had to settle that point.

"Stuff you, Tom Lloyd. Tell the woman yes before I throw something."

Since she had obviously decided she could adapt to the situation, I told the impatient courier we would take a taxi direct to Sliema Strand. Last night's bus journey had not been an experience to repeat. Then I ordered breakfast and drew back the heavy curtains before taking a shower. Light flooded in. It was a glorious day, the sun already beating down on the blue water of the creek and the pale yellow limestone fortifications of Manoel Island, beyond which lay Sliema. I had no objection to a cruise. Quite the reverse. One of the people down there was bound to know where I could hire a fast boat for deep-sea fishing, and that was my first priority.

When I emerged from the bathroom the breakfast had arrived and Susie was sitting in her usual toweling gown, pouring coffee.

"White with sugar?" she asked equably.

"Two spoonfuls." Maltese coffee never escapes the brackish taste of the island's water.

"You were very fond of this place, weren't you?" she remarked.

"Pretty fond," I admitted, surprised at her perception. "I flew Nimrods here for a year and a half before the base closed. You either like it or you don't."

That was a serious understatement, I thought, as I sipped the coffee. If you wanted things to run like clockwork, Malta was a place to avoid. Island people enjoy living slowly, and the Maltese were no exception. Their character was an extraordinary mix of lethargy at work and wild enthusiasm for football or firework displays; of commercial acumen and selfless generosity; of intense individuality and voting socialist. The blood of Phoenician traders, Arab corsairs, Italian cooks, and British sailors ran in their veins. They ate pasta and drank beer. Most Maltese would cheerfully kick an enemy when he was down, yet do anything for a friend. I had always found them easy to get on with and I certainly knew my way around their islands, which constituted two good reasons for being here rather than in Sicily, Sardinia, or anywhere else within reasonable range of Libya. If things came to a crunch I would stand a chance in Malta, though I could hardly explain that to Susie.

"I hope you'll like it as much as I do," I said, leaving the whole lot unspoken.

"So do I." She held out her hands appealingly. "I'm sorry about last night. You do whatever you have to while we're here. I'll keep out of the way if you want."

The volte-face surprised me, but was no less welcome for being sudden. I took her hands, pulled her gently to her feet and gave her a long hug.

"You're a pretty unpredictable lady," I said, kissing her. "Very pretty and very unpredictable." That was putting it mildly.

"And how else would you want me, sweetheart?" she challenged and returned my kiss, tenderly at first, then more and more passionately so that I lifted her onto the bed and we made up the brief quarrel in the most natural way.

The result, of course, was that we caught the boat with only seconds to spare, the taxi bumping and sliding on the greasy tarmac of the waterfront road as if we were the driver's last fare before eternity. The courier lady scolded us politely on the quayside, and we settled down on the open deck to enjoy the voyage around the island.

The Blue Lagoon is an almost totally enclosed bay on the little island of Comino, between Malta and the other principal island, Gozo. The water there is limpidly clear, undisturbed by waves, and the sandy seabed creates its pure azure color. We swam, had lunch and swam again, while the day stoked up to full summer heat, making the whole rocky island shimmer. I noticed the haze along the horizon and recalled that when the sand-laden sirocco blew from North Africa the visibility became quite poor. Meteorologically speaking, Malta sits in an extension of the Azores high from April onward, ensuring good weather until the autumn thunderstorms develop. I could have used bad weather on September first, but I was unlikely to get any so early.

While Susie was sunbathing I chatted to the captain about hiring boats. What I wanted, I explained, was to go after the fighting fish that frequent the deeper waters of the Mediterranean. Did he know anyone who could organize big-game fishing?

"The lampuki season has started," he suggested, sounding mystified. "Some people are rigging boats for lampuki still."

"Surely," I insisted, "you served swordfish in the buffet today. Who catches them? And who brings in the tunny?"

"Oh," he answered with a "why didn't you say so before?" expression on his swarthy face. "That is commercial fishing. The boats for that sail from Marsaxlokk."

"Never for pleasure?" It seemed extraordinary, given that the Manoel Island marina was lined with expensive craft, though many were little more than floating gin palaces.

The captain considered this. "There was an Englishman at Marsaxlokk last year. He used to take people fishing. Something went wrong, and he was deported. The boat is still there, I think."

"What happened?" I asked.

He gave me a sideways glance. "We have strict regulations these days. People can no longer anchor for the night where they like. All foreign boats must be in either Valletta or Marsaxlokk or Mgarr before sunset, and may not leave until dawn."

That was a minor jolt to my planning. In the old days one of our favorite excursions had been to sail around to Gozo for the weekend, slipping anchor in the picturesque bay at Xlendi. I thanked him, not wishing to appear overinquisitive, and rejoined Susie, who was half-asleep on the sand.

"Would you mind going for a drive when we get back?" I asked. "I'd like to see a man about a boat."

"You would?" Susie inquired, opening her eyes and looking up at me with lazy curiosity, like a cat. She made an effort and propped herself on one elbow. "What's this all about? A new side to your character?"

"Just an idea," I temporized, introducing it gently. "I thought we might organize our own cruise one afternoon."

She glanced around the recumbent tourists near us, two fat women grotesque in bikinis prominent among them. "Perhaps you have a point there," she conceded, and firmly returned to her sun worship.

That evening we came rattling down the hill to Marsaxlokk in a rented car just as the fishing boats were returning. The village was essentially two streets of stone houses, some painted in faded colors, which stretched around one inlet of a vast bay and were now gilded in late sunlight. I remembered there had once been plans to establish an international freeport here. They must have collapsed because Marsaxlokk seemed as quiet and sleepy as ever. That might be either good or bad from my point of view. I couldn't be sure yet.

However, there was no mistaking the boat I had come to see. Traditional Maltese craft, from rowing boats to ocean-going *luzzus,* are made of wood and strikingly painted in bright blues, yellows, and reds. They usually have the Eye of Osiris carved in deep relief on either side of their high prows. The cabin cruiser stood out among them like the intruder it was. It lay moored a short distance out, swinging gently on the tide, and a fisherman patiently mending his nets on the quayside told me I could find out about her at a bar further along.

The bar was appropriately unpretentious. A weathered sign above the door announced its name as the Saint George. We pushed aside the beaded fly-curtain and found ourselves in a small room furnished with scrubbed wooden tables. A Maltese of about fifty was sitting at one, a half-empty glass in front of him. The bar occupied the far wall. I asked the bartender about the cabin cruiser and he nodded at his only customer.

"Paul can tell you," he said. "He is looking after her."

He called out something in Maltese and the man looked around and gestured us to join him. He had a wrinkled, nut-brown face and short, graying hair and was dressed in an old brown sweater and once-blue trousers. When he stood up I noticed that the trousers were rolled above the ankles, and he was barefoot. I guessed he wasn't making a fortune out of the boat, although maybe he wasn't the kind to change his style even if he had been. He shook hands and I ordered wine, the rough-tasting local stuff that I suspected contained more chemicals than grapes.

"I understand," he said, when I had finished explaining. "You would like to go tomorrow?"

"Tomorrow would be fine."

"I like you see the ship first. I will take you now. She is called *Wanderer*." He spoke with a strong, slow, confident accent and I felt his concern to have a satisfied client was a good omen. We drained the wine and he led us along the quay, stopping where a *luzzu* was tying up.

"That one has been out for tunny," he said. "If you are interested in big fish you should look."

Lying in a row across the aft deck were five large tunny, their bellies shining dull silver; alongside were two swordfish, with bladed snouts a good foot and a half long.

"That's what I want to go after," I commented enthusiastically. "Only bigger. Tunny or broadbill."

"I never knew you were keen on fishing," Susie cut in. "What happened to the cruising scheme? This afternoon's one. Remember?"

"That tunny must weigh five hundred pounds," I

said. "It would be worth being out all day." I was addressing myself as much to Paul as to Susie. She looked incredulous, but kept quiet while he indicated the *luzzu's* forward deck, where a jumble of large triangular floats lay piled, each with a hook beneath.

"Our way is to bait the hooks with mackerel," he explained. "We put paraffin lamps on the floats. The fish come to the light and take the mackerel. We always fish at night."

"But you have sporting tackle on *Wanderer*?" That was vital.

"Tony left everything." Paul's weatherbeaten face crinkled with a not unkindly smile. "He had to go in great hurry."

We walked further along to a smaller boat, a *dghaisa,* with a diesel engine mounted under a wooden cover in the center, and were soon chugging out to *Wanderer*. Paul scrambled up her side with great agility, clutching a rope, then fitted a short ladder over the stern for us. I went first and gave Susie a hand up after me. The boat rocked gently. I stood in the stern, in what I think they call the "cockpit," and surveyed her, while Paul unfastened coverings and opened the cabin.

"She is a Fairey Huntsman," he said proudly. "Tony always say she have the finest sea-keeping hull for her size."

Wanderer was certainly sleek, though not as well kept as she must have been in her prime. She had a fighting chair in the cockpit, and a door for dragging heavy fish aboard. Outriggers curved out high over each side. The solidly built steering shelter was as roomy as a cabin and led to a forward compartment with a tiny galley, an electrically operated toilet, four bunks, and a table. I examined the controls. She was fitted with Seascan radar: the make meant little to me, but I could see at a glance that it operated at ranges of up to sixteen miles.

"How fast does she go?" I asked.

"Thirty knots. But that is expensive for fuel." He opened a mahogany cupboard and produced a dog-eared brochure.

"She is for sale if anyone want."

I sat down in the captain's chair and studied the technicalities. *Wanderer* was powered by two turbocharged Perkins diesels, each developing 185 horsepower, carried ninety gallons, and driven at a respectably fast twenty-three knots had nine hours' endurance. In other words she could beat a swift path halfway to Libya and back and still have a reserve in hand.

"Would you be interested in a two-week charter?" I asked.

"Are you serious?" Susie almost shrieked. She had watched with diminishing patience as Paul showed me around *Wanderer*. "You mean you want to spend this whole vacation fishing?"

"On and off, darling," I acknowledged, trying to catch Paul's eye and reassure him that he wasn't about to lose the biggest break of his season.

"Then don't complain if I stay by the hotel pool." Susie brushed her long hair away from her face angrily and glared at me. "A cruise around the coast you said. One. *Uno. Un seul.* In the singular not the plural. Whose vacation is this anyway?"

I had seldom seen her throw such a tantrum.

"All right," I conceded. "We can simply cruise, swim off the boat, picnic where no one else goes. Malta's a whole different world with your own boat."

Moreover, it would be far easier to reconnoiter the cliffs and inlets of the rocky southern coast from the sea than the land. Hiring *Wanderer* was strictly business.

I tried throwing out a mild challenge to disarm her perversity. "If you don't like the fishing idea, that can wait until you've gone."

In fact it absolutely could not. Tom Lloyd had to be established as an amateur sportsman this week. There would not be time later. Sure enough, Susie did a complete about-face, though if I had known what was going to result I would have kept my mouth shut.

"No," she said abruptly. "I think I'd like to try fishing once. But not tomorrow. The day after."

She knew she was being as contrary as they come and smoothed it over with a seductive smile at Paul. "I think *Wanderer's* lovely. You must show me over her properly when we go. It's just that I'd rather not have two days at sea in a row."

Poor old Paul was in no position to argue. He looked at me for guidance, I nodded, and he told Susie he could be available whenever she wished. A brief huddle ensued to agree on a retainer, and I gave him £100 Maltese in advance and he ferried us back to shore in the *dghaisa*. The more I saw of his calm, philosophical behavior, the more I liked him.

So we spent Monday sightseeing and shopping in Valletta's narrow streets, indulged in the ever-persistent courier's evening tour, and on Tuesday morning drove down to Marsaxlokk bright and early.

Paul was waiting on the quayside, looking visibly smarter. He had on newer trousers and was wearing plimsolls, though his old flat cap remained pulled down squarely over his eyes. As we boarded *Wanderer* I realized that the boat was a lot cleaner too, except for a slimy growth of algae at the waterline and streamers of kelp showing below. However, I did not care to point them out when he had made such efforts in other directions. He had even loaded a cold box with beer, lemonade, and mixers. What with the packed lunch and the bottle of gin we had brought, we were well set up for the day.

The diesels fired immediately and ran with a steady, confident beat as we gathered speed, passed the handsome stone tower of Saint Lucian built by the Knights of Malta on the point, and headed south across the main expanse of the bay. Further out, the water was a dark, dull blue and choppy waves slapped against *Wanderer's* sides.

"See the wind is gathering. With a south wind there is always a swell." Paul began a running commentary. "HMS *Breconshire* was sunk here in the war. See there." He gestured to the right where a concrete slipway was visible with large sheds beyond. "That was for flying boats. The air force had a camp behind a Kalafrana. My father worked there and I also."

"I was in the RAF," I said.

"You were, sir?" Increased respect sounded in his voice.

"Not during the war, of course."

That set him off on a tide of reminiscence that lasted us until the coast was well astern. As he talked, I tested the radar. The constantly circling arm of yellow light on the screen was still giving an accurate picture of Marsaxlokk Bay at five miles distance, despite a backwash of clutter from the swell, and other ships were clearly defined. The radar was going to be one hell of a bonus.

"Does it work enough?" Paul asked with sudden concern. "Tony does not send money for repairs."

I assured him everything was fine and unobtrusively observed how he handled the controls, which proved to be very competently, although sitting on the upright black-upholstered chair behind the wheel he looked somehow out of place, in spite of no longer being barefoot, as if he had been suddenly promoted from deckhand to captain: that must have been exactly what happened when the fellow Tony was deported. Paul was as powerfully built as any deckhand, too. His grizzled head hunched into his shoulders, his body was thickset and he had rolled the sleeves of his blue shirt to the elbow as a first concession to the day's warmth, revealing well-muscled forearms. I needed a strong man. What with his loyalty to the RAF he was ideal for the job, if he would agree to do it, which was a subject to be broached when I knew him better and Susie was not around.

Meanwhile, we couldn't gossip forever and I asked him to put *Wanderer* through her paces. He nodded, grunting assent, and confidently eased the two chromium throttle levers fully forward.

Wanderer's bow rose as the two turbocharged diesels wound up to twenty-four hundred rpm. She began forging ahead, her wake churning white in two great crisscrossing Vs behind us, spray flying.

Susie stood in the stern, her hair blowing in the wind, her face glowing with pleasure as the boat roared through the water.

"How fast are we going?" she shouted, not waiting for an answer, but coming into the shelter and standing beside me as I checked the gauges.

"Twenty-seven knots. Not quite what the book says."

"You mean all that weed stuff is holding her back?" Susie said.

She was one hundred percent correct and Paul glanced around at us, embarrassment in every line of his expression. "I will start cleaning tomorrow, sir."

"How long could you keep up this speed?" she asked, as *Wanderer* hit a trough in the swell, bounced and came down on the next wave with a jarring crash.

"If the sea is too rough I slow down."

"Let's try cruising speed anyway." I suggested, wanting to assess the whole range of her performance. Sure enough, at two thousand rpm the diesels were only extracting twenty knots from her instead of twenty-three. That might sound a fleabite's difference, but it could matter a lot if we were being pursued by another ship. The hull would definitely have to be cleaned. I made a few mental notes and turned to the subject of fishing.

We spent the next three hours idling along with two

rods set in their holders in the stern, the lines splayed
clear of the boat by the outriggers. Periodically one or
the other rod would jerk, Paul would rush to secure it,
and Susie or I would jump into the fighting chair ready
to play the big catch. But every time it was either a false
alarm or a small lampuki. By lunchtime I was becoming
worried. I was hardly going to establish a reputation in
Marsaxlokk as a big-game fisherman if we returned
empty-handed.

Knowing nothing about the sport didn't help either,
though Paul had some advice to offer about watching
for shoals of small fish that would attract the big ones,
and equally watching for terns swooping down on those
shoals. He apologized that his own experience was
mainly of inshore fishing with nets. Tony had been the
expert.

Sitting drinking cool beer and devouring the lunch
boxes, I raised another subject as casually as I could.
Did Libyan ships come up here much? I meant the
Libyan Navy, but I didn't want to spell that out. The reaction my question produced was vehement.

"Those are not friends of mine." Paul glanced at me
with real anger in his eyes. "They stop Tony and me
once. They say they open fire if we do not go back.
Then they search the boat."

"International waters don't mean much to them?"

"Nothing, sir. They are barbarians." He swore ob-
scurely in a most uncharacteristic way. I was about to
question him further when one of the rods jerked as if a
demon had seized it, the outrigger clip snapped free and
the rod bent double as the line screamed out. Paul leapt
to save it.

"You go," Susie called out impulsively, which was
nice of her, so I shot into the chair and strapped the
harness on.

The fish, whatever it was, did not appreciate being
hooked. It raced away, taking line off the reel at a rate I

was unable to control. The one time I tried to stop the run the rod immediately flexed almost double again and I had to give way. Then, just as suddenly, the line went slack.

"Reel in, sir. Reel in," Paul shouted. "She's a big one. Very big."

I turned the handle furiously. The fish must have doubled back toward us and I realized how easily it could snap the line by turning away again and bringing it taut. I was still reeling in like a madman when a flash of silver gray broke the surface and a magnificent broadbill rose in the air, crashing down into the sea with a great splash. Within seconds the rod was bending again and I dropped the tip forward in the nick of time to prevent it breaking as the line shrieked out.

That was the way the fight ran for one hour, then two, and still the huge fish seemed tireless. My wrists began to ache despite the harness holding the rod, and my spine felt ready to crack. But I had begun to learn how to let the fish run when I had to, yet take in line whenever it pushed back toward us.

"It is a swordfish," Paul confirmed enthusiastically, as he coached me. "You're in luck, sir."

Then it took me unawares. At its seventh leap it came up alongside the boat like a submarine missile, its long sword cutting the air and its forked tail thrashing the water white as it splashed down again to dive right beneath *Wanderer*. But it was tiring. For maybe ten seconds it surfaced beside us and in those moments Paul grabbed the trace and gaffed it, leaning out over the side so perilously that Susie seized his ankles. He finished it off with the heavy wooden baulk he called a "priest," and we combined to haul it aboard through the transom door.

Seen at close quarters the fish was huge. It completely occupied the cockpit as it lay twitching and jerking on the floor, its glistening colors rapidly turning a dull gray. It was at least ten feet long from the tip of its tail to the end of its long black bill, far larger than the ones I had seen on the quay in Marsaxlokk.

"Two hundred and fifty pounds weight, sir. At least." Paul was still panting from his exertion, but exultant.

For myself I felt completely drained and found my hands shaking.

"Are you all right, sweetheart?" Susie asked, noticing.

"Fine. Nothing a cold beer won't cure." I flexed my wrists and arms, knowing how stiff they would be tomorrow, then looked down at the fish. I'd read that swordfish stay in the Mediterranean around Sicily until September and go up to one thousand pounds. This one had put up a hell of a fight and I felt almost sorry. But I could hardly present better credentials for the quayside gossips back at Marsaxlokk.

Sure enough, a small crowd soon gathered when we tied up there an hour and a half later to take the big fish and the few lampuki ashore. As we were hoisting them out of the boat a man in khaki uniform, thin and slightly stoop-shouldered, strolled across and inquired where we had been. At first I took him for a policeman, until Paul introduced him as the harbor's customs officer. He wore dark glasses, which did not conceal a cadaverous and pallid face: pallid by Maltese standards, that was. Overall he reminded me of a tired vulture.

"This is my English client," Paul explained with pride. I supposed he had picked the word up from the late-lamented Tony.

The customs officer grunted amiably, gazing down at our catch, and remarked that swordfish steak was his favorite, better even than lampuki. Grilled in butter with a slice of lemon . . .

"Can we cut it up?" I asked. "Or must the fish market have the fish whole?"

There was a ripple of laughter from the onlookers. Legally, the whole catch had to go to Valletta, though of course the law was often dishonored, and I had put the official politely on the hook, I now took him off again.

"Our only transport is my car," I said to Paul. "I think we shall have to cut it up here."

So the customs officer was given his delicacy, shook hands warmly and wished us "even more success." I then arranged to see Paul the next evening, when as well as making a final agreement, I would provide him with an additional radio.

"You've made a few friends there, my sweet." Susie observed as we drove away, tactfully leaving the lampuki behind. "Next thing they'll vote you tourist of the year."

I laughed and made no comment. I did indeed think I had established a satisfactory relationship with Marsaxlokk, and it was nice to know that the authorites weren't overzealous.

During the remainder of the week we utilized *Wanderer* twice. The first time to explore the otherwise inaccessible cliff-guarded inlets of the southern coast; the second on the Saturday to visit Xlendi, in Gozo. On the way to Xlendi Susie wanted to handle the boat herself and made an excellent job of it, even keeping our course steady at full power. When she wasn't feeling fey she could be extremely competent.

"I didn't know you were an expert," I said jokingly as she maneuvered past the headland. "You should be giving us lessons."

She glanced back at me from the wheel. "That's your modern air hostess for you. A Jill of all trades." She dropped the banter and added in genuine admiration, "What a super place."

"Your last-day treat," I said.

"It really is something else."

I wasn't going to dispute that. Xlendi is at the end of a fjordlike inlet of crystal clear sea, with a waterfront of color-washed houses set as if posed for a tourist poster. Susie had to leave on the first flight the following day, and since nostalgia was certain to creep up on us, I had chosen the most romantic place I knew to help it along.

"Hard to believe you'll be in Karachi on Monday," I said, holding her hand across the table in the restaurant of the little Saint Patrick Hotel. "Is it the Holiday Inn again?"

"That's where they book us," she agreed, sighing. "But this time I'm going to break loose. Some friends have a beach house."

"At Sandspit?"

Her hand trembled and slid out of mine, while something very like alarm flickered across her face. "You know Sandspit?"

"Who doesn't?" I reacted without any logical process of thought, aware only that I had accidentally triggered a fear about which I wanted to learn more. "Friends of mine have a house there too. A Dutch family. They work for the UN." I tried to think of a convincing Dutch name.

"How extraordinary, darling!" Susie was recovering herself fast, but her exclamation rang as true as a plastic dollar. "What a small world it is!"

We both fell silent. For myself, I was remembering Sandspit two years ago. My real-life acquaintance there was a Pakistani pilot. He had driven me out through the shacks of Karachi's suburbs, past creeks with buffaloes wallowing in putrid water, out into sudden semidesert, where the last village looked as Bedouin as Asian, and on through a military area until we reached the barrier of windblown dunes that separated a lagoon from the Indian Ocean and was called Sandspit.

A line of beach houses stretched along this finger of land, some no more than dilapidated wooden bunga-

lows, some two-story concrete affairs. Amir's villa had
tiled floors and a proper bathroom. We had sat on the
verandah in the breeze, drinking orange juice laced with
illicit vodka, and watched a party of white-cowled nuns
paddling in the sea, decorously lifting their habits above
their ankles. He had told me how easily girls could be
lured out to Sandspit at weekends, simply by the promise of an escape from the unendurably humid heat of the
city. Only European girls, of course. Correctly
brought-up Muslims would never be seduced so crudely.

"August," Amir had told me, his sensual mouth
crinkling into a smile beneath his stiff mustache.
"August is the best month for girls. August is too
damned hot, I can tell you." He was a good enough
looking man and I didn't doubt him.

Now Susie was staying in Sandspit in August. I gazed
at her across the table. She was completely composed
again and smiling at me in a detached sort of way, as if
she too had been momentarily engrossed in memories. I
told myself not to be absurd. The likelihood of her
knowing Amir was negligible. And yet.

"My friends were the Zwagers," I said, snatching a
name from the past. "There was an airline pilot who
had a house there too."

Worry showed again in her eyes.

"Bloke called Amir," I added, dropping the name
like a stone in a pond.

She relaxed instantly. "I must look out for him," she
said lightly. But she didn't ask his other names. So all I
could guess was that she did have a boyfriend in Karachi
and he was probably another pilot. There was little
point in pursuing it further.

However, Susie herself did, albeit obliquely.

That night she made love with an intensity eclipsing
anything before, almost as if this were the last time we
would be together.

"I shall miss you, darling," she murmured when it

was over, lying in the crook of my arm. "I shall miss you a lot."

"It's only for a week." I stroked her hair. "We have a date in London next Sunday, remember?" Then the new life began. With one hundred thousand in the Swiss bank account.

"Yes," she said in a curiously flat way, again as though the past few days had prompted her to end our relationship, yet she wasn't willing to say so. She became so tense that I touched her cheek to feel if she was crying. She wasn't, and eventually she reached up, kissed me fondly and said goodnight with the firmness of a decision.

The next morning I drove her to Luqa Airport to check in for the British Airways scheduled flight to London. Being aircrew herself she got on for ten percent of the fare, while I kept her charter ticket just in case she came back. When her turn came in the passport line she gave me a big, affectionate hug that was much more like her usual self.

"Thank you for a lovely vacation," she said, kissing me and sounding every bit as though she meant it.

"See you next Sunday."

"If they don't change the roster again." She darted a final kiss at my cheek, turned away and passed out of my life. At least I assumed that was what she was doing.

As I returned to the hotel I wondered what could have gone wrong, but I hadn't time to brood. There was too much to do before Hall's flight left in the afternoon.

I told the Phoenicia that since Susie had been recalled to her job I was going to spend a few days in Gozo, left the bulk of my luggage in the room, and made it to the Marfa ferry in a thirty-five minute dash, only to find a typical peak season line of cars and trucks trailing back from the quay. The scene I created by driving to the front and insisting on being loaded caused a lot of acrimony: memorably so, I hoped.

Two hours later I was back at Gozo's Mgarr harbor, waiting for a return sailing as a foot passenger and being determinedly patient and unobtrusive. Once on the Malta side I boarded a local bus with a gaggle of village women clutching baskets of vegetables and talkative German tourists in lederhosen, laden with rucksacks.

"The light here is so plastic, no?" a heavy blonde squashed next to me remarked by way of introduction. "It is wunderbar for artists, no?" Her thick fleshy thighs pressed against mine and I muttered agreement, wondering if Rajni's artistry with the Malta entry stamp was going to pass muster at the airport. Unaccountably, I was worried.

The foreboding proved justified. The flight was hideously overbooked and I had to change to first class, using Hall's new credit card, in order to get a seat at all. As for the boarding and passport checks, they were repeated three times by different officials. Inevitably the moment came when my one-way ticket was queried.

"You arrived only eight days ago, but with no return?" the immigration officer observed, scrutinizing the black rectangular stamp inserted by Rajni in the passport, as though it could speak to him. Which in a sense it could, because it incorporated a number, presumably of an official. Rajni had used "24." I wasn't sweating from the heat alone. Was it possible that "24" was this man's number and he had not been on duty that day? He picked up my exit card.

"You have been on vacation?" he demanded.

"That's right." I could hardly say otherwise, having written "vacation" on the form.

"With a single ticket."

"Some friends were taking me to Italy on their yacht," I explained. "They never turned up."

With great slowness, as if he could break my story by delay, he examined every page of the document. The woman immediately behind me in the long line pushed impatiently, and I could feel her breath on my cheek. It was stiflingly hot. From further back an angry British voice announced loudly, "I'm never bloody coming here again." A general mutter of protest followed and people began to push forward.

Reluctantly, the official acknowledged the line, raised his rubber stamp and pressed it down beside Rajni's forgery. I moved on and the others shuffled forward a step. When I was through into the departure lounge, I looked at the passport. The new imprint read "BY AIR—25" with the date August twenty-sixth.

The near-miss quality of this encounter was still on my mind five hours later when I paid off a taxi outside the apartment block in Sloane Avenue, and walked straight into a load of further trouble.

THE ELDERLY HALL porter at the Sloane Avenue apartment block was doing an evening shift. As I walked up the steps I saw him through the glass doors, hovering like a gray-faced sentinel of the Styx by the reception desk. But the instant he saw me he jerked into puppet-like animation, as if anxious to prove that the dead can rise.

"Ah, Mr. Hall, sir," he exclaimed, as I emerged from the swing doors into the lobby. "We've been worrying about how to find your, sir. Allow me, sir." He spotted my bag and made an octagenarian version of a sprint to assist me. "It's a relief to see you, sir."

"What's happened?" The worst I could imagine was a call from the local cop shop on behalf of the Norfolk police.

"There are several telegrams, sir." He hovered uncertainly in front of the reception desk, then went around and handed them over, remaining lugubriously poised behind the teak counter, as though needing its protection. "I'm exceedingly sorry to tell you, sir, that your apartment has been broken into.''

"When?''

He recoiled as though I was about to hit him. "The cleaners discovered it yesterday, sir.''

"You'd better follow me up.'' I made for the elevator. There was one thing I wanted to check before he got there.

The apartment door was on a long, drab passage, a gift to thieves, and bore no signs of forcible entry. Inside, things were different. Unlike Susie after the Fulham burglary, the cleaners had left the chaos as they found it. The video machine had gone, every one of the few drawers and cupboards had been turned inside out. Stepping over Hawker's spare shirts and socks jumbled on the floor I went straight to the minisafe built into the wardrobe's back wall. The metal door was closed but unlocked. I flicked it open, thankful for having taken Hall's driving license and credit cards with me to Malta. Arain's videotape was still there: the Sabre's insurance policy and £200 in notes were not.

"We have informed the police, sir.'' The porter's voice made me swing around. He was standing nervously in the doorway. "They sent an officer around. But we were unable to say what was missing.''

"I'll make a list.'' I doled out a fiver for his pension fund and began piling clothes on the bed.

"Thank you very much, sir. The Chelsea Police Station is just around the back, sir.'' He retreated again.

When he had closed the door I opened the mail, telegrams first. The porter had exaggerated their quantity. Nonetheless it was quite a postbag for an identity only three months old.

The first cable I opened was from Switzerland and demanded "Call Geneva office urgently.'' The second had come via Western Union from Ottawa and read simply, "Contact me soonest, Luke.''

An express letter from the Royal Aero Club in Leicester enclosed a telex from Cairo regretting that the last leg of Hall's record attempt from Malta was no longer acceptable due to the international situation. The club asked for further instructions. I decided on Heraklion in Crete instead.

The fourth item was a summons ordering "Hall" to appear at King's Lynn magistrates court on October second to answer a charge of unauthorized low flying in contravention of the Air Navigation Acts. If I wished to enter a plea of guilty, etc., etc. That at least was good for a laugh.

By any standard, Arain had to be dealt with first. I righted an upturned chair and settled by the phone, which curiously had not been disturbed: perhaps the burglar had been using it.

Arain answered himself, which meant he must be in Geneva, ready for the countdown. "I've been waiting for your call," he said in a more restrained tone than usual and leaving plenty unspoken.

"The arrangement was once a week," I reminded him, coolly. "I rang last weekend."

"As of now it's daily. Take note of a new frequency. Two three one decimal seven five. Call sign 'Jalloud.' OK?"

The reference must be to the September first flypast. Major Jalloud was Libya's foreign minister, and presumably the new callsign was a tribute to him. But how did CONOIL's informant in Tripoli have access to Libyan Air Force orders? Whoever it was must be exceptionally well-placed. Not for the first time I wondered if my mission might be part of a larger coup against Qaddafi. Not that it made much difference. I was interested in the pay, not the politics.

"Are the timings the same?" I asked.

"No change."

"Confirmation?"

"When we're good and ready." The old Arain arrogance flashed briefly. "You have your instructions."

"Of course." I was nettled. Did he think I was some

kind of amateur? Newland had provided a list of code-
words back in Ottawa, which I had memorized and
destroyed. They were good ones, easy to remember and
unmistakable. The go-ahead was JOHN and the cancel-
lation COLETTE, for example.

"Any problems?" Arain asked in a more conciliatory
way.

"Some insurance papers were stolen, but that won't
affect the trip." Ninety-to-one he had the policy with
him by now, although I was not sure the burglary had
been as odd as the one in Fulham. Either way, I wanted
him to know I didn't care. He'd discover why the moment he made a claim: after finding the wedge I had obtained a refund by deleting the cover of air racing of all
kinds.

"Call me tomorrow then," he ordered, without further comment.

"It may be late," I warned. Tomorrow was the Open
Day at Duxford.

"I'll be here," he said evenly and rang off.

He was very cool, Arain, and I found it hard to believe he would bother with the insurance money. On the
other hand, who else would want the policy? Who else
would have known about the post office box key? I decided to go down to Fulham and check the trap I had
set, though first I had to contact Luke at home in Ottawa.

"I'm sure glad you rang," he said, sounding as
though he really meant it. "Listen, Hawker, we had a
break-in at the national collection Monday night." He
paused just long enough for me to reflect that there were
enough robberies going on to last me a lifetime. "Our
security guard saw the guy's face. The description
sounded like the man who worked on your Sabre at Uplands. I brought those photos in and the guard identified him."

"Are you certain?" I asked cautiously. Why should a

saboteur infiltrate a place where most of the aircraft never flew?

"One hundred percent. That's why I sent the cable."

"What did he do?"

"Since you ask, he lifted the whole IFF system out of our Sabre." There was an edge of hostility in Luke's voice, as though he suspected me of being involved.

"He what!" If I had been mystified at first, now I was totally foxed. "IFF" stands for "identification friend or foe." Basically it's a radar that operates automatically, responding to interrogation signals from air defenses on the ground and enabling them to tell instantly whether a plane is one of their own or not. Nowadays it's a lot more sophisticated than it used to be. What would anyone want a twenty-five-year-old set for?

"I don't understand any more than you do," I said. "My Sabre still has the IFF, though it's inoperative. Harragin left it in, the same as he left the UHF radio."

"But that guy did work for you."

"For Newland. Not for me. I don't even know his name."

"Are you telling me you don't know who he is?" Luke's voice deepened to an uncharacteristic growl. "Listen here. We did all we could to help you and we did it for free. Would you mind coming clean with us?" His anger was unmistakable. There wasn't much option but to reveal part of the truth. Otherwise he'd be on to the Imperial War Museum creating hell, and I couldn't say I would have blamed him.

"He interfered with my Sabre too," I said, and was gratified to hear a whistle down the line that wasn't transatlantic atmospherics. "He disconnected the canopy-ejection detonators. I tackled Newland, we had a blazing quarrel, and I haven't seen either of them since." That was near enough correct, though it didn't lessen my ambition to lay my hands on the bastard in the future. Then I had an idea that should have occurred to me weeks ago. "Hey, Luke," I went on. "Innotech could have made him sign in that day at Uplands. Why not ask them?"

With reluctance Luke agreed and said he would call me straight back. When he did, he was an ally once more.

"You were right Hawker. Grainger remembered. He wanted proof of identity before they touched your plane. Newland showed an American passport. His sidekick had a Maltese driver's license. The name was Micallef." He spelled it out. "Joseph Micallef."

That shook me, though not for reasons I could explain. I suggested Luke should tell the police and said goodbye with real regret, sorry that I should never be able to meet him again. He was a thoroughly decent man, and it gave me a queer feeling to realize that I now had to start discarding the acquaintanceships I had so assiduously built up for Hawker Hall.

Meanwhile, there was the newly identified Micallef. He wouldn't be so easy to dispose of.

The name Micallef is as common in Malta as Jones is in England, and I kicked myself for not having recognized him as Maltese from the photos. It needed no imagination to guess that Joe Micallef would be around at Luqa Airport before I took off for Tripoli. But for what possible reason had he wanted an IFF?

The question troubled me all the way down to Fulham, where I found the post office box crammed with flyers. The hair was missing from the flap of the Guernsey letter, which confirmed that Hawker's mail was being opened, though that no longer worried me. If Arain wanted to try an insurance claim after Saturday, he was welcome. I was far more concerned to establish the significance of the theft in Canada. My approach to Tripoli would be too low to be picked up by radar, so the IFF was all but irrelevant, and although I had not told Newland, he would surely have figured that out for himself.

On the way back I concluded that the theft must be a blind. Micallef must have been after something different, something that could induce a disaster after I had completed the attack, forcing me to eject in a hurry, though what it could be I could still not imagine.

Then I remembered that Qaddifi's agents sometimes used Maltese credentials, which it had been easy for them to obtain before the two governments fell out over the undersea oil exploration. That precipitated a whole train of further speculation along the lines of my being part of a political coup, none of it pleasant, and the proverbial final straw came when I decided to glance at the Sunday paper before going to bed.

When I was back at the apartment block the hall porter, no doubt inspired by a desire to mend his fences vis-à-vis the burglary, had offered me a paper. For some reason there had not been any newspapers available on the plane and I was glad to catch up with events after a week's absence: glad that is until I got beyond the main headline report about a maniac rapist in Scotland. Rape is always a better story than war, especially if, as in this case, the maniac has the bizarre habit of forcing his victims to eat cheese-and-pickle sandwiches before assaulting them. Nonetheless, potential conflict still has a place on the front page, and when I read the subsidiary lead it knocked everything else straight out of my mind.

"LIBYA ACCUSES UNITED STATES," the headline screamed, and went on from there with the bad news.

"This week a third American nuclear-powered aircraft carrier, the USS *Forrestal*, joins the U.S. Sixth Fleet in the central Mediterranean despite reprisal threats by Libya's Colonel Qaddafi. In Washington, Defense Department officials stated the reinforcement was a 'routine' preliminary to annual Fleet exercises.

"Accusing the United States of planning to invade Libya, Colonel Qaddafi said he would not hesitate to attack NATO bases in southern Europe as well as the Sixth Fleet itself and called America's policy 'nuclear terrorism against all Arab countries.' "

It sounded a typical Qaddafi outburst. I read on, half-amused until the sting in the tail caught me.

"Meanwhile, diplomatic sources discounted reports that Qaddafi is about to take delivery of the long-awaited 'Islamic' nuclear bomb."

In other words, the United States knew damn well Qaddafi was about to get the bomb, and the exercises were as much routine as my Methodist great aunt drinking whiskey. I didn't like the implications of those denials at all.

The reported followed up with an analysis of the forces that would now be eyeball-to-eyeball in the Mediterranean. They totaled more than nine hundred combat aircraft, plus ships ranging from the three American carriers to Libyan corvettes and fast patrol craft. Not counting such fringe spectators as the Soviet Mediterranean Fleet and Air Force, the Italian armed forces and a few of our own British destroyers.

The central Mediterranean east of Malta was going to be a hornet's nest. If the Libyans didn't zap me, the Americans probably would.

Studying the map printed in the newspaper, I realized there might yet be a saving grace to the situation. The Gulf of Sirte appeared to be the flashpoint as before, and it was a full two hundred miles to the east of my own projected route. Could I slip past to the West while the Yanks and the Libyans distracted each other?

I had poured myself a whiskey and considered the question with the aid of a map for almost half an hour before the corollary of this idea struck me so forcibly that I spilt the drink. Old tricks are often the best. There was one way I could almost certainly get American aircraft into the sky over waters that the Libyans claimed as theirs, with the precise result I wanted. Furthermore, doing so would involve only a minimal variation in my plan.

This tactic was still refining itself in my mind when I went to bed: Qaddafi or no Qaddafi, I needed some sleep before the Duxford Open Day tomorrow.

The Open Day, originally an event that fitted into my schedule without too much trouble, had become an incubus. It meant driving at the crack of dawn to Cambridge, settling up with Marshalls, who fortunately were willing to send staff despite the public holiday, and flying the Sabre across to Duxford before the crowds arrived.

By the time I landed I was thoroughly impatient with the whole make-believe. However, Ted's enthusiasm softened me up. He was waiting on the tarmac along with a squad from the Aviation Society, all in clean white overalls and ready to position the Sabre in the lineup of historic aircraft. They had prepared a descriptive board, giving her technical details, and a stepladder so that visitors could peer inside the cockpit. We maneuvered her between a Spitfire and a Sea Fury, and I forced myself to put on a cheerful face for the benefit of the hundreds of schoolboys who were expected. One thing I could not afford was to leave the plane unattended.

In fact, the genial atmosphere was infectious and I enjoyed explaining points about the Sabre. But in the early afternoon, when the crowd must have numbered several thousand, it began to rain. The flypast had to be partially canceled and people began to drift away. By six everything was over, except clearing up the litter.

Ted had undertaken to change around the drop tanks after the show, fitting on the ones with the landing lights, rather than leaving them until Tuesday evening. While I was in Malta the perspex covers had arrived and the modifications were complete. So we pushed the Sabre back into her hangar and began the work. He had done the conversion beautifully and after a couple of hours the job was complete. The new lights operated off the main landing- and taxi-lamp switch in front of the throttle box, conveniently close to my left hand when flying.

"Did you have problems with the wiring?" I asked sympathetically.

"Well," he admitted, wiping his hands on a rag. "That part wasn't so easy. Connecting it up I mean. I had to go out to Marshalls one evening to finish it." He grinned. "Don't worry. Shouldn't have said I'd do it if I wasn't prepared to." He rubbed his hands down the backside of his jeans and flexed his shoulders, as if weary. "Anyway, it's done. By the way, I found something in the cockpit that ought not to be there." He reached down into his engineer's toolbox. "Here. Could have jammed the controls." He was holding up the aluminum wedge.

"Good God!" I feigned surprise and took it from him. "When did you find this?"

"The night at Marshalls."

"One of the mechanics must have dropped it," I said. "Bloody careless." I could hardly replace it under the Sabre's seat, so I stuck it into a pocket, and changed the subject. "Would you care for a meal? You've certainly earned one."

We locked the hangar and left in Ted's old rattlebox van, nonetheless rating a salute from the watchman, who recognized me. Since I wanted to return afterward and was dependent on Ted for transport back to Cambridge, we chose a pub not far away. This being a holiday, the place was full. We ordered steak and chips and waited. And waited. And waited.

Certain minor occurrences can affect one out of all proportion to their immediate significance. The slow service at the pub was one such. In the end it saved my life.

We did not get back to the airfield until ten, when it

was completely dark. If we had been in less of a hurry I might have paid more attention to a saloon car parked on the roadside a hundred yards short of the gate, which was caught by the van's inadequate headlamps as we passed. As it was, my mind was on other things.

The airfield was ghostly and largely unlit at night, though the entrance was illuminated. As my watchman friend raised the barrier I told him we would only be a few minutes.

A number of hangars loomed up, high and forbidding, as we drove around. There was a glow from the windows in the Sabre's hangar, which I thought for a moment was a reflection of the headlamps. Then I realized it could not be.

"Would any of your group have come back?" I inquired.

"Don't think so." Ted evidently shared my apprehension because he eased the van quietly to a halt beside a nearer building. "We were the last to leave."

I felt in my pockets. Apart from the wedge, I was completely unarmed. "Have you got anything heavy?" I asked.

He fumbled for a flashlight, shone it briefly around the vehicle's littered interior and handed me a short iron bar. For a moment the beam flickered across his face and I saw his concern. The Aviation Society was a law-abiding bunch.

"Just in case," I said. "It's probably nothing." But I knew instinctively that it wasn't.

We walked to the hangar's side door and I tried the handle gently. It was unlocked. I opened it very slowly, flashlight in hand, and Ted followed me inside.

By day, with the huge sliding doors open along its entire frontage, the hangar always seemed light and airy despite its bulk. At night, with those doors closed and a solitary naked bulb switched on near the side entrance, the place was a dark cavern in which the planes created a labyrinth of wings and fuselages, casting grotesque shadows on the floor and walls, while the roof girders were a dimly perceived network above.

I guided Ted away from the pool of light by the door and stood listening. A rat scurried away, scrabbling across the concrete. Nothing else stirred. Until a faint metallic noise echoed from somewhere out of sight beyond the gaunt shape of the World War II Blenheim bomber standing nearest us. I froze. An indistinct scraping sound followed, then was stilled. Someone was moving extremely cautiously in the center area of the hangar: the area where the Sabre was.

"Stay here," I whispered to Ted, wanting him to guard the only exit, and very slowly eased myself down on to my knees to scan the hangar at floor level.

Beyond the Blenheim's undercarriage struts I could see the wheels of another aircraft, and dimly recognizable beyond those was one of the Sabre's narrow tires. I began to crawl under the body of the Blenheim, not using the flashlight. I was beneath its further wing, my eyes becoming accustomed to the semidark, when a shadow shifted near the Sabre's wheel. It was the back of a trousered leg. It moved again. I calculated the distance at about seven yards. I crept on, edging around the tail of the next plane, a Sea Fury. The intruder was standing in front of the Sabre's wing. He had his back to me. From his outline he seemed to be in overalls, and he was reaching upward.

I shifted the iron bar into my right hand and continued infinitely slowly, edging only a knee or an elbow forward at a time. Even if he looked around I would still be concealed from his vision by the Sea Fury. I was four yards off when the light went out and I heard Ted shout.

I stood up, relying on memory to dodge three steps around the Sea Fury's wingtip, and flashed the light at the Sabre. The man had spun around. It was Micallef and I had him caught between the Sabre's wing and its fuselage. He dived forward, thrusting a screwdriver at my face. I sidestepped and swung the short bar hard at his head. The bar connected with a thud and he staggered, colliding with me and knocking the light out of my left hand. The glass shattered and it went out. I piled on top of him, trying to get a lock on his neck from behind. But the blow hadn't been enough. He kicked and struggled. He was all muscle, the bastard, and I lost the iron bar. His shoulders strained against my grasp, then I felt a hand grip my right wrist, slowly forcing my fingers open with an irresistibly mounting pressure. Suddenly he gave a great heave like a bear shaking off a dog. I clung with the remaining hand but was flung aside, and the last thing I remembered was falling backward and a stunning blow on the back of my head.

When I came to, it was with the worried voice of the nightwatchman sounding in my ears and a fierce light paining my eyes. I closed them, hoping to ease the throbbing.

"Here, sir, have a sip of this."

I felt the sting of brandy on my lips, felt fractionally better and cautiously opened my eyes again. The light was an ordinary bulb hanging from the ceiling of the watchman's hut. I was lying on a bunk and two faces were gazing down at me in worry—the watchman's and Ted's.

"Take it easy now, sir." The watchman bent down and supported me with one arm. "You had a nasty fall there."

"Must have hit your head against the wing," Ted added. "That's where I found you, once I got the lights on again."

With his help I achieved a sitting position and gently explored my scalp with one hand. To my surprise there was no blood.

"Did you catch them?" I asked slowly.

"Not a hope," Ted said. "Whoever turned off the light got a half-nelson on me, clamped some sort of cloth across my mouth and just held me so close I couldn't move. I heard someone run past, and the next thing I was thrown on the floor and the bloke was away.''

''Were you hurt?'' My brain was starting to function again.

''Scratched, that's all.'' Ted made a gesture of brushing down his jeans. ''No problem. I belted after them but they'd disappeared.''

''Didn't see a soul myself,'' the watchman said. ''Didn't know anything was wrong until Ted here came running and shouting.''

Dimly I remembered a vehicle. ''What about the car we saw?''

''Gone,'' Ted said succinctly. ''They must have cut through the fence somewhere.''

I swung my legs off the bunk and stood up, swaying and quivering like the aspens in *The Lady of Shalott*, but managing to stay upright. ''We must go back to the hangar,'' I ordered, gritting my teeth against an overwhelming nausea.

With Ted's assistance, we did. But even in the full glare of all the lights we could see no sign of interference with the Sabre.

''Doesn't make sense,'' Ted observed. ''Are you sure they weren't mucking about the Sea Fury?''

I supported myself against the leading edge of the Sabre's wing and struggled to think. That might be the best way to leave matters. The last thing I wanted to become involved in was giving details to the fuzz of yet another incident.

''You could be right,'' I agreed. ''We happened to come back at the wrong moment. Why don't you report it to the owner? If he wants to go to the police he can.'' I shook my head muzzily. ''I haven't the time to get involved, not with the record attempts coming up. Besides, I never really saw the man. He threw me aside and that was that. Can you take me back to Cambridge now? There were a few things I wanted to check, but I'll do them tomorrow.''

Fortunately, Ted considered that the most sensible course of action. We left it to the nightwatchman to make a routine report and I spent the night at a hotel, as I had planned.

The next day I still felt slightly fragile, though not enough to abandon returning to Duxford. I had the Sabre taken out of the hangar, ran the engine and tested as many of the systems as one can on the ground. Everything appeared to be functioning normally. I even tried the IFF, bearing in mind the theft from Ottawa, but it was the one item still not operating.

Since I was not feeling well enough to fly the Sabre to Marshalls for further checks, and no other jet pilot was available at Duxford, I had no option but to stick to my original schedule. So I drove back to London, going as slowly and sedately as if I were heading a funeral procession.

In the evening I rang Arain who demanded to know why I had not called on Monday. With my head slightly clearer I remarked that I'd been attacked by a thug, though I had not been seriously hurt. There was nothing to be lost from his knowing his hirelings were incompetent. But he sounded completely unmoved, until I reminded him about the bank transfer, when he asked me sharply to call again tomorrow.

"No," I said. "Thursday. When I know the machinery still works." On principle I wasn't going to let him make the running any more, at least not until the final decision.

Wednesday morning I spent winding up the affairs of Hawker Hall. I paid the bill at the apartment block and packed the few clothes I had kept there, depositing those I didn't want in a case at the Victoria Station left-luggage office. I collected a small package from a firm of industrial chemists in Battersea, returned the rented car and posted one of Hall's checks to American Express sufficient to cover his maximum anticipated spending. I didn't want him leaving any unpaid bills.

After lunch I took a train to Cambridge with the bag I would stow in the Sabre and went to say goodbye to Ted, though it had to be brief, since his lunch hour was short. I told him I was going to beat hell out of the records, even if I had got a plum-sized bruise on the back of my head.

Then I took a taxi down to Duxford and, with some misgivings, flew the Sabre down to Biggin Hill in Kent. She performed as nicely as ever. Biggin was the designated starting point for my London-to-Nice attempt and over the past twenty-four hours I had come to terms with an uncomfortable fact. I would have to set off on the mission without discovering what Micallef had done to the aircraft. I had to hope I could find out in Malta.

A lot of people won't like my saying this, but nowadays point-to-point air-speed records are strictly for self-gratification. There's no distance a civil plane can cover, even Concorde, which some supersonic military jet can't do faster. The Sabre had held a lot of records in its day, but its day was thirty years ago and the only reason Hawker Hall could establish a London-to-Nice record for single-engined jets was that neither the RAF nor the French Armée de l'Air had thought the effort worthwhile. As for publicity, I would have achieved more by pushing a wheelbarrow from Scunthorpe to Skegness: which was just as well, because I didn't want any.

When the moment came, the crowd that cheered my departure from Biggin at midday on Thursday did include a reporter from a flying magazine, because he happened to be down there anyway. The other three people were a mechanic, a customs officer, and the Royal Aero Club's official timekeeper, a portly gentleman of sixty or so in a tweed jacket and deerstalker hat.

The timekeeper's name was Jack and he performed his duties with cheerful seriousness, making notes and carefully attaching lead seals to both the Sabre's airframe and its engine in order to ensure that I arrived in

Nice with the same plane I had taken off in. This was not as laborious as it might have been, since I had arrived early in order to remove all the inspection panels and hunt for evidence of Micallef's handiwork. It had occurred to me that he might have installed some kind of bug that would transmit my position and help the Libyans locate me after the raid. But neither I nor the mechanic helping me found anything unusual. All we did was save Jack a little time.

"There you are, old chap," he said heartily, squeezing the engine seal on to its wire with a pair of pincers that at the same time embossed the lead. "Now let's make sure the basics are correct." He picked up his clipboard from where he had lodged it on the wing and began checking the facts and figures on the certificate he would sign, while the mechanic screwed back the panels.

The calculations that would gain Hawker Hall his place in the Féderation Aéronautique Internationale's list of homologated records, airplanes class C-1-F, depended on the officially recognized distance between the center of London and the center of Nice. The center of London, as entered by Jack on his form, was Latitude 51 degrees, 30 minutes, 15 seconds North, Longitude 00 degrees, 09 minutes, 00 seconds West.

A tourist might have expected this to be either Hyde Park Corner or Piccadilly Circus. In fact it was Charing Cross. But the essential point was that I could start from anywhere within sixty miles of it.

Then—and I have to admit that this was where the average nonmathematician might tend to drop out of the argument—the distance I actually flew would be timed to produce a speed. That speed would be recalculated into the official distance between the centers of the two cities concerned to produce an amended time— the official time over the official distance. I was allowed to improve this somewhat by being timed overhead at the two airfields, as opposed to when taking off and landing: what you might call a flying start.

"Right-ho," Jack confirmed. "So you'll pass over the tower at two thousand feet." He touched the binoculars hanging around his neck. "Don't think I'll need these, eh! No recognition problems with your particular crate." He turned to the customs officer. "All aboard, then, with your permission, sir." He extended his hand and shook mine warmly. "Best of luck, old chap." He was a bit of a caricature, but his heart was in the right place, which was more than could be said of the reporter, an unprepossessing young man, who wore a grubby blue anorak in spite of the muggy August weather, and had a Nikon slung around his neck. He had done his best to give me a hard time already.

I was about to clamber up into the cockpit, when he stopped me.

"Mind another question?" he called out, reaching for the camera at the same time. "You said your one ambition was to race the Sabre. What d'you do for a living?"

"Call it independent means," I said, earning a smile of approval from gentleman Jack, and starting to put on the flying helmet.

"Must have been in the RAF, though," the reporter insisted. He pronounced the initials like a word, "Raff," and promptly clicked off the first photo. But not before the bonedome and my sunglasses between them were hiding most of my head.

This was a moment of serious danger and I had prepared for it. Casual snapshots like Luke's were one thing. Professional mugshots published in a magazine were another. I emphatically did not want friends or colleagues recognizing me, let alone the real Hall. Now I had a sudden fear that the precautions I had taken were not enough: especially when Hawker was going to lose his life in the record attempts, and therefore the pictures would acquire unexpected news value.

An actor once told me that disguise is nothing to do with false beards. It's achieved in two ways: mental attitude and changing some salient characteristic of one's appearance. So from the first of Hawker's appearances three months ago I had greased my hair and brushed it straight back, with a parting on the right, instead of my normal English style of a prominent forelock and a left-side parting. The change had made my forehead seem much broader, and when feasible I wore dark glasses of the kind that adjust their tint according to the strength of the sun, so concealing my eyes and eyebrows. But, as I say, I was suddenly afraid that this might be inadequate, whereas the helmet made all clean-shaven pilots look alike.

"How about a few pics without the bonedome?" the reporter demanded argumentatively.

I glanced at my watch and then at Jack, praying he would respond.

"Sorry, young man," he said, coming up trumps. "We have a schedule to keep."

With that I hoisted myself into the cockpit, gave a wide grin and a thumbs-up for the reporter's last picture, slid the canopy shut and began the start-up procedure. I reckoned I had survived the first photo-call and I wasn't quite so worried about what the local French or Maltese papers might print.

Biggin has a beautiful long main runway and the controller obligingly kept various light aircraft out of the circuit so that I didn't have to hold back in climbing away and coming around over the tower. I was doing 250 knots by the time I glanced down and saw the diminutive figure of Jack standing there. Then I headed southeast over the Weald and became fully occupied with obtaining clearances into the cross-channel airway. One thing was certain, I had to make a show of setting these records in earnest if I wasn't going to arouse suspicion all along the line.

Europe is not a continent for long-distance air racing anymore. Standing on the ground on a nice day you might think there was plenty of room in the European sky. There isn't. It is unbelievably cluttered with air-

ways, control zones, military danger areas, and places
you are forbidden to overfly, like the French nuclear
research complex at Pierrelatte in the Rhône valley.

Accordingly, my London-to-Nice route could not be
direct. I had to follow the civil airways from one radio
beacon to the next, accepting orders from the ground
the whole way, which made my actual flight distance
619 miles. Furthermore the weather over France was
cloudy, with thunderheads forecast up to thirty thousand feet.

However, the controllers allocated me the thirty-five
thousand foot level I wanted, nicely above the storms,
and with no endurance problems I could afford to turn
on the taps. Not that it made so much difference at that
altitude.

One of the things about a jet is that you achieve fuel
economy by flying high, but not at maximum speed.
The absolute fastest speed I could hope for at thirty-five
thousand feet was 610 miles per hour, whereas at sea
level I might hit 690. However, there's not much sense
in going faster if you dry the tanks up halfway. It's all a
matter of striking a balance. Today was easy. On Saturday it would not be.

Yet even today I had damn-all time for complicated
reassessments in the air. The VOR radio beacons were
only minutes apart as I crossed the French coast and
headed past Paris: I was kept busy reporting over Abbe-
ville, Montdidier, Bray, and the others.

South of Paris the workload eased a little. But the
weather worsened. The industrial city of Lyons was in-
visible below thick cloud, and descending toward Nice
during the final leg over the Alpes Maritimes, I hit the
thunderstorms. Unlike an airliner, the Sabre had no
weather radar, and so I had no way of telling where the
storm centers would be. At the worst moment hail was
lashing the windscreen, and I was thrown around so
hard that my bonedome visor hit the bombsight. Nor-

mally I'd have deviated out of the area, but in a record attempt there was nothing for it but to hurtle on, watching the VOR needle guiding me toward Nice and hoping I could make a really fast letdown once I was over the mountains.

Thank God the French are instinctive sportsmen. The Nice controller gave me all the help he could. I broke cloud at five thousand feet, with the Côte d'Azur a hazy line of villas and beaches below, and shot over the airport at an indicated 570 knots, which is around 650 miles per hour, while the tower warned other traffic of what was going on. Then I threw out the anchors in the shape of the airbrakes, slowed to a respectable pace, and joined for a normal approach a couple of miles behind an Air France Airbus. It was the most exhilarating flying I'd done since my Phantom days. I reckoned I had secured Hall his place in the FAI's record books, though whether they would bother with the formalities after he was dead was another question. On balance I guessed they would, since I'd deposited enough cash to cover the fees. I felt unexpectedly exhilarated by the whole flight.

In fact I had enjoyed it so much that I completely forgot Micallef until after I had landed. "Well," I told myself, "whatever he did hasn't affected the way she flies." Anyway, it would have been completely illogical for him to have sabotaged the controls, assuming he was working for Arain.

The French timekeeper had obviously appreciated the drama of my arrival too and, unlike Jack, he encouraged the press. When I reported in to air traffic control he was waiting to introduce himself plus a couple of reporters and a photographer from *Nice Matin*. He was much the same age as me, on the committee of a local aero club, and clearly anxious to be seen as responsible for establishing that a new record had been created.

"I am certain of it, Monsieur 'All," he announced,

more for the reporters' benefit than mine, tactfully ignoring that there was no existing record. "Subject to the verification, naturally."

In no time we were out on the tarmac, with him being photographed shaking my hand by the Sabre. And, *naturellement*, I put on the bonedome and dark glasses for the occasion. It suited me fine that it wasn't my face he wanted in the papers.

Next we adjourned to the airport restaurant and after an enjoyable lunch, which he politely permitted me to pay for, we went and did the requisite check of the seals for the next lap.

Flying south to Malta I could not take a direct route either. The Italian/NATO firing range off the east coast of Sardinia was smack in the way, and there was a NOTAM warning that it was active this week, otherwise I'd have clipped the corner and thirty-five miles off the dogleg.

However, there was no point getting in the firing line before I had to. Navigationally the route was dead simple and the weather forecast was excellent: the summer ridge of high pressure that gives tour operators the sunshine they crave was firmly in place from the Azores via Majorca to Crete. Furthermore, there would be strong upper winds from the west helping me along after Sardinia. All in all the flight should be pure pleasure, and it occurred to me that I had underestimated the value of occasional self-gratification: especially since Malta to Tripoli on Saturday would be nothing but running a gauntlet.

Because of the volume of air traffic and the proximity of the hills, I was being timed from the moment of take off. I eased the Sabre off French tarmac at 3:31 P.M. local time and was given a clearance straight up to thirty-five thousand feet, which again was decent of the controllers. This leg was a trifle longer, 679 statute miles, and consequently closer to the Sabre's endurance limit with only 100-gallon drop tanks as opposed to the 167-gallon ones I had used across the Atlantic. With Saturday in mind, I intended to monitor the fuel consumption closely.

Seventeen minutes later I was over Corsica, its rocky indented coastline clearly visible, despite a lot of haze, and Ajaccio a blur of urban development. I obtained clearance into Italian airspace, the Strait of Bonifacio slipped by beneath and I was over Sardinia, with the haunt of the rich, the Costa Smeralda, off to my left, bringing a pang of memory. I had flown into Olbia once and seen the Aga Khan's Gulfstream three parked there, entirely white except for a gold crest by the door. Whoever flew that had a number I wouldn't mind sharing.

I suppose this sequence of thought lasted about twenty seconds. Twenty seconds too long. When I looked up again I realized I was no longer alone. A U.S. Navy Tomcat fighter was sitting a few yards away on my left. I looked to the right. There was another, just as lean and wicked as its twin. Both two-man crews had their heads turned toward me. I raised my left hand and waved, the front crewman on the left waved back and I turned the VHF to the international distress frequency, which is the recognized channel for conversing with intercepting aircraft.

"This is November Four Sierra," I called, capitalizing on the Sabre's American registration. "Nice to see you around."

"Where in hell d'you get that bird from?" came the reply.

"Chino, California. Keep her in Britain now."

"Holy shit. We thought we must be freaking out. Where you goin'?"

"Malta," I said. "Making a record attempt." Suddenly I had an idea. More than that: an inspiration. "You from the Sixth Fleet?" I asked.

"Sure are."

"Do me a favor. Tell your boys I'll be racing Malta to Crete Saturday. Around midday. Just so they know."

"Sure thing," drawled the pilot. "Well, guess we'd better let you win that race. Be seeing you."

I knew what would happen next. And it did. The two Tomcats surged ahead, obligingly peeling off to either side so the blast from their engines wouldn't shake me out of the sky. Even so, the Sabre rocked in their wash. Seconds later they were together again, streaking toward the horizon. As I said before the military can break records anytime they want.

Cape Carbonara at the southern end of Sardinia was roughly my halfway mark to Malta and the turning point on the dogleg. Off the coast I spotted a few of the ships involved in the live firing exercise, trailing feathery wakes across the blue sea. But there was no sign of the carrier that had to be the home of the Tomcats. It might have been down off Tunisia, where the Sixth Fleet had a facility. Certainly the Americans were not only where the newspaper reports had said. That figured, if they were keeping a serious watch on Libya.

A couple of Italian Air Force fighters buzzed me a moment after I passed Carbonara, though since I was within the airway they didn't interfere with my course, which I was glad of, because the remaining 354 statute miles to Malta were going to be busy ones.

For a start I wanted to call Arain. The fewer conversations I had with him from Malta itself, the better. Stockholm Radio patched me through to Geneva as efficiently as they had done before and, judging from the promptness with which he came on the line, Arain must have been waiting by the phone.

"Glad you called," he answered, with unconvincing bonhomie. "How are things?"

"I'll be there in half an hour," I said. "How's the schedule?"

In case I was being overheard, I added some more to

make it sound like a sales trip. "Have we still got a deal?"

"Sure we have a deal." Arain cottoned-on immediately. But he didn't sound confident. "The signing's due Saturday. Only problem is the location."

"How do you mean?" I didn't like this. If there was one thing I had felt I could count on, even in an Arab country, that thing was a National Day parade being planned in advance. I knew what a kick Qaddafi got out of parades. If it wasn't the anniversary of the Revolution, it was Evacuation of American Forces Day, or of the British bases, or something else anti-Western.

"Our friends feel there should be both a private and public ceremony for the occasion."

"Does that affect things?"

"Could do," Arain said tersely, and there was a world of restraint in the way he spoke. "Guess I ought to send someone down with the details. Where'll you be?"

"I haven't made any booking." I thought for a second. I should have to name a hotel for immigration on arrival. "The Corinthia Palace. If it's not full."

"Expect to see Bob there tonight."

Arain cleared the line, leaving me plenty to consider. Newland had bowed out weeks ago in Ottawa. For the man to reappear must mean a major change in the briefing. That was bad enough. What troubled me more was whether or not to tackle him directly over Micallef's activities. I tried to put it out of my mind. There were more urgent things to be considered, namely the Sabre's precise low-level fuel consumption.

During the brief conversation with Arain I had traveled fifty miles further toward Malta and now had 304 miles to run with 2,200 pounds of fuel in hand, which allowed the customary 500 pounds for a landing and overshoot, and left enough to indulge myself in some high-speed low-level flying over the remaining distance. I called the Italian information region and obtained a

clearance to descend, put the airbrakes out and pushed
the nose forward until she was in a near-vertical dive,
mainly for the hell of it.

Accelerating toward the speed of sound, or Mach 1,
all the things Harragin had warned about began happening, though with no kind of ferocity.

I felt the rudder pedals shiver under my feet and at
Mach 0.95 the port wing dropped abruptly, though it
recovered itself before I had time to react. I took the
Sabre through to 0.98 and the altimeter was soon un-
winding so fast that I had to think about pulling out.
Passing through six thousand feet above sea level I
eased the stick back, careful not to accidentally induce a
high-speed stall that would flick me into a dive again.
The G was forcing my stomach down into the seat despite the pressure suit and my eyes felt as if they were
being dragged out of their sockets. My vision blurred.
Then the plane was racing straight and level, everything
settled back into its normal feel, and I began concentrating on going flat out for the next hundred miles.

At fifty feet above the waves she handled beautifully.
The trial gave me the knowledge I wanted. Going as fast
as she could go in these conditions, the Sabre's consumption was 4,100 pounds of fuel an hour. Without
the drop tanks she carried 2,784 pounds. I didn't have
to be a mathematical genius to work out that my endurance at sea level on Saturday was going to be a fraction over forty minutes. I could extend that a little by
the gambits I was planning, maybe to fifty or fifty-one
minutes. That was all. They were going to be the long-
est minutes of my life, and I was glad to know precisely
how many I would have of them.

When the high-speed run was over I let her ride back
up to ten thousand feet again, expecting to see the coast
of Sicily off to my left. However, there was too much
haze. I established contact with Malta, headed for the
VOR beacon on Gozo's southern cliffs and was given a
straight-in approach to the enormously long runway the

Maltese had constructed for the tourist jumbo jets that now so seldom materialized. It amused me to scrunch down in this great swathe of tarmac. In my squadron days here we had never been allowed to use it in case the British Government was charged part of the construction costs. We always had to land on the older, shorter runway instead.

Following the tower's directions, I taxied to park in an area I knew as well as my own face: the dispersal alongside the former RAF buildings by the older runway. A marshaller with a yellow bat in each hand waved me into position, and it was as though time had rolled away and I had just returned from flying a sortie with the squadron. I killed the engine and slid the hood back and the August heat swamped in along with the memories. I stood up and looked around. A few other private aircraft were parked nearby, and I noticed with relief that the arc lamps that used to illuminate the dispersal were still there, standing like sentinels on their high pylons. At least they would give some security at night.

As I climbed down, a black-and-white car, with flashing lights on the roof and "Pulizija" painted on the sides, rolled to a halt beside the Sabre. A thin, weasel-faced sergeant in khaki uniform got out, a revolver holster swinging from his black leather belt, and saluted half-heartedly. With him was a much more pleasant civilian in a blue blazer and knife-edge-creased white trousers, who advanced and shook hands.

"Welcome to Malta," he said, with almost wooden formality. "Tony Vella. I represent the International Air Rally." He smiled, briefly revealing perfect teeth. "We are sorry you missed our rally in June, but delighted to have you with us now. It will be my pleasure to escort you through immigration and customs. By the way, your unconfirmed timing from Nice was sixty minutes and thirty-five seconds. I believe you have set an unbeatable record. Congratulations."

Altogether, it was an auspicious arrival. Except for one thing. A third man emerged from the car and Vella introduced him.

"Allow me to present Joe, who is one of our best engineers. He will help with any servicing you need."

I gave the man a keen look, felt a hard, calloused palm grip mine, a hand out of character with the fleshy face, and wondered if I was dreaming. The familiar thick hair, round cheeks and thin prissy mouth confronted me.

"I've met Mr. Micallef before," I said.

$\longrightarrow$ TEN $_\longrightarrow$

THE TENSION BETWEEN Micallef and myself must have been noticeable, because Vella quickly intervened.

"How extraordinary!" he exclaimed with exaggerated surprise. "Where did you two meet?"

"In Canada and Britain." I aimed to catch Micallef on the hop and I succeeded, because it showed in his eyes. Nonetheless, he recovered fast.

"That will be my twin brother," he said silkily. "He emigrated to Canada. Like myself, he is an engineer. He goes to UK sometimes."

"You certainly look alike." I took the opportunity of appraising his face. That thick black hair, curling right down the back of his neck and over his ears, would conceal most swellings. But there was something awry with what was visible of his left earlobe. The hell he had a twin brother. Unless they were psychically connected and when you hit one guy the other got scarred too.

"Well, what a coincidence!" Vella echoed, keeping the public relations going. "Shall we deal with the formalities?"

I realized abruptly that we were standing on the hot tarmac, staring at each other like two actors who've forgotten their lines, while the policeman watched and tried to scent the innuendo.

"That would be fine," I said. "I'll get my bag." I climbed back up into the cockpit, hoisted the case out from behind the seat and closed the canopy. Being a military design, the Sabre had no ignition key, while the canopy itself was operated from outside by a small lever and could not be locked. That didn't worry me. I preferred Micallef to be able to check that the wedge was still under the seat, where I had tucked it after landing.

The policeman must have noticed the firmness with which I slid the hood shut because he assured me that airport security would protect the plane. He had clearly been assigned to keep an eye on her.

"Quite a valuable aircraft, a real vintage beauty," Vella remarked enthusiastically. "We haven't had such a well-restored warplane here since someone flew a T-6 down from Duxford for our 1982 rally. That one was in U.S. Air Force colors."

Micallef said nothing and the sergeant glanced at the Sabre obediently, though I could see he was having aesthetic problems. Perhaps he didn't have the collector's instinct. Or tended to see a gun as a gun as a gun, whatever its period. At all events he said nothing until he had driven us around to the main terminal building and through a side door, when he announced, "There is special clearance for private pilots."

I was keeping a weather eye open for the friendly immigration officer number twenty-five, who had grilled me on Saturday, but I did not see him. Nor was there any immigration-stamp problem this time. Hawker Hall was making a perfectly legal entry, insofar as one can on a forged passport.

Once I was through I thanked the cop, who returned to duty, and Vella offered to drive me to the Corinthia Palace, then turned to Micallef.

"Is there anything Joe can do for you immediately?" he asked.

I thought about it. Apart from suggesting a leap off Dingli cliffs, I could not see how to keep him away from the Sabre.

"I could use an oxygen resupply," I volunteered. "If he could make sure that it's available I can explain how the filler valve functions." I paused. I wanted him to feel he had time in hand. "I don't plan to leave for Crete until Saturday, and with no record attempt there's no hurry. How about nine on Saturday morning?"

Micallef looked at me intently. "I will be here," he said.

"Thanks." I shook hands for the sake of assessing him again. He had an extremely strong grip, probably derived from constantly using wrenches, and I could feel the antagonism in it. To my relief, when he walked away he went toward the carpark, though of course he could always drive around and reach the Sabre via the old RAF entrance. Checkmating his activity was going to be a major headache.

Vella interrupted my thoughts. "My wife and I are hoping you can dine with us tonight. It would be an honor."

"Thank you, I . . ." I was about to decline when I saw from his expression how deeply offended he would be and choked back the words, managing to say, "I'd like that very much," instead.

"We dine late. Will eight-thirty be suitable?" Vella smiled as I agreed. "Now, shall we go to your hotel?"

As we drove I reflected how Vella's typically Maltese hospitality was liable to screw up my plans if I wasn't careful. He might insist on taking me sightseeing tomorrow, and tomorrow I had other fish to fry, specifically with Paul, while there was also work to do by myself on the Sabre. My schedule had been tight even before Micallef showed up.

As we drove, I answered Vella's polite inquiries about

the flight from Britain mechanically, my mind occupied by how to contact Paul tonight, though I instinctively glanced aside to look at the old RAF officers' mess as we passed. A sign announced "Airport Hotel," and I glimpsed a group of Arabs in traditional dress walking down the driveway.

"What happened to the old air commander's house?" I asked.

"At San Juan? The Russians occupy it," Vella said disapprovingly. "You know Malta already?"

"I came through once in my air force days," I said, covering up hastily. "Years ago."

"Things have changed. Some for the better, some not."

Mostly not, I decided, if there were Russians and Arabs around the airfield, plus, as I had learned a week ago, Chinese assisting in the dockyard, and North Koreans training the army. The island must be more than ever a hotbed of intrigue—it had been bad enough when there was a NATO headquarters here. I was reflecting on the intelligence reports the Sabre would be generating, when we reached the Corinthia Palace.

I had chosen the Corinthia because it was modern and anonymous while the de luxe category both matched Hall's image and would guarantee that I received messages. It was also relatively close to the airport and far from the Phoenicia. But as Vella stopped the car I realized my enjoyment of its facilities was liable to be short-lived.

Sitting on the terrace near the entrance, apparently enjoying the evening sun, and looking every inch the hick American tourist in blue plaid trousers and a screaming red shirt, was Newland. As we walked past he drew on a fat cigar and puffed out smoke, giving no sign of recognition. He must have been waiting on the island before I spoke to Arain.

The knock on my room door twenty minutes later was unlikely to herald anyone except Newland. Nonetheless

I took precautions, declining to open up until he had identified himself, and then standing well back in case he was not alone. Seeing Micallef had given me a sharp reminder that Malta was not necessarily the safe and friendly place it used to be.

"Anticipating trouble?" Newland asked.

"Not without reason." I closed and locked the door. "Someone had a go at me on Monday." Suddenly I decided to dive in head first. Newland had brought up the subject. He could provide a few answers. "Have you been employing a Maltese mechanic to interfere with the Sabre?" I demanded, facing him, "Because a man called Micallef's been following me around the world like a private eye."

"And you slugged him," Newland said evenly. "Sure he works for us." He glanced around, walked casually to the radio by the bed and flipped it on. Pop music belched out and he quickly lowered the volume a shade. "Helps the privacy," he said, gesturing me to the one easy chair. "Now sit down. We have a few things to straighten out."

"You're damn right we do." I was in no mood to be intimidated, even though he had seized the initiative. "For a start, what has Micallef been doing to my aircraft?"

"Checking what you've been doing to it. And it's our airplane Lloyd, not yours. Registered in a fake name, but all ours. Come Saturday we'll have five hundred thousand dollars and a lot of people's lives riding on how you handle that Sabre, and so far you've kept every damn detail you can secret."

"Because I want to walk away afterward."

"You could be putting survival first, Lloyd." Newland straddled himself across an upright chair, his hairy forearms resting on its back, his deep-set eyes narrowing. "We only have your word you're going to hit Tripoli. You told us those drop tanks are going to carry napalm. What way?"

"You mean Micallef failed to find out?" I asked caustically. I'd had all this before with Arain and I was about as ready to explode as the bombs.

Newland nodded.

"Well," I remarked more coolly, "I take that as a compliment. Before I go, I'll put the jellifying agent in the tanks. It mixes up in flight. The new landing lights are in fact impact fuses. D'you understand now?"

"Neat," Newland admitted. "I should have gotten to figuring that out myself. Then what?"

"I make my own way home."

"Where to?"

"That's my affair. My contract ends when I drop those tanks."

"I guess that's reasonable," he conceded.

"So what are we here for?" I asked.

"I came because we have a problem." He lowered his voice, so that I had to move closer. "Qaddafi's got wind that something may happen. At least, we think he must have."

"The hell he has! How?"

"Instinct, I guess. Or he could have smelled discontent in his air force. There is plenty, for sure. Two more pilots ran out on him to Italy recently. With their MiGs. The ones who were captured in the Chad fighting still haven't been rescued or ransomed. Same time the Russians won't let them near the best planes." He chuckled. "Have to hand it to the Russkies. They know most Libyan pilots aren't the right stuff and they don't mind saying so."

"Which means?" I asked tautly. It was fine for Newland to laugh. He wasn't flying the mission.

"Qaddafi's canceled the airport flypast. Can only be he doesn't trust his air force. There'll be a military parade through Tripoli same as every year, with a flypast there. He's less exposed in the city. Always has his saluting dais against the walls of the old Italian fort on Green Square, and the direction the planes go over would make it mighty hard to hit him there."

"No ceremony at the airport at all?" I was thinking furiously.

"The airport's going to be closed, officially. That's all our guy can find out. We presume the Pakistani Boeing will fly in ahead of the parade with a fighter escort." Newland stopped, successfully reading my thoughts. "Forget about Qaddafi," he said crisply. "Qaddafi's nothing without the bomb. Our aim is to destroy that nuclear weapon, which means before the Boeing's unloaded. Your original idea was to join on the end of the flypast, right?"

"It would be nice to have the Libyan Air Force ahead of me rather than behind." That was putting it lightly. By the time they knew what had happened they would have been miles away in the wrong direction.

"Won't make too much difference," Newland said. "Another reason we know Qaddafi's nervous is that no plane in that flypast will be armed, or have enough fuel to go any place afterward except back to Okba Ben Nafi."

"But the Russian-manned MiGs are there. They'll be armed."

"Sure. All depends how far you plan on going."

"I told you, that's my problem."

"If that's the way you want it," Newland said, obviously concealing annoyance. He heaved himself upright. "Call Mr. Arain early Saturday. He'll give you a time to be ready and I'll be in contact from Rome through the radio when the Boeing takes off. You can figure the rest out for yourself." He gave me a vigorous handshake, as though anxious to dispel any doubts. "Good luck, Lloyd. Don't worry. You'll make it."

"What else did Micallef fix?" I asked, as he opened the door. "The IFF?"

He looked at me, as though I was proving a fraction more intelligent than they'd estimated, and pushed the door shut again.

"Correct," he said. "The Libyans will think you're one of theirs."

At last I did explode. "Why the hell couldn't you have told me that?" I almost shouted.

"We were going to when you took off." He had an expression on his face I had never seen before: a mixture of pride, anger, and concern. "Don't touch the IFF," he said grimly. "Not if you want to fly on Saturday. That code could cost our man in Tripoli his life. You have a way out after this, if you're lucky. He hasn't."

When he had gone I sat down again, mixed a drink and pondered. He had left me a lot to think about, not least how far he had told the truth about Micallef. But I could not believe he wanted me dead, not after the other things he'd said. So who might, apart from Qaddafi? And why had Micallef disconnected the canopy jettison device?

Taking the maps out of my old RAF navigator's canvas flight bag, I began making calculations. The IFF might get me into Libyan airspace. It assuredly would not get me out. On the other hand, if the napalm triggered the bomb there might be no pursuit at all. Using the figures old Moon Watson had given me, I worked out the implications of a ground-zero nuclear explosion again.

Not knowing the explosive potential of the Islamic bomb made accurate calculating close to impossible. A twenty-kiloton weapon—which was very small—would damage houses severely up to a radius of about one and a half miles, a two-megaton weapon up to eight miles. It was unlikely the Pakistanis could have produced anything more powerful than the latter. So the city of Tripoli would at the worst be affected by radioactive fallout and that only if the wind blew from the south. Overall, I reckoned by far the most disabling effect on the Libyans would be psychological. But the Russian pilots wouldn't panic, any more than the blast would affect their airbase. Back in the Soviet Union they train in the expectation of nuclear war.

Eventually I abandoned trying to compute the un-computable. Basically, I would still have to depend on surprise. Remembering that Tony Vella would be coming to collect me before long, I looked up the Saint George's Bar in the directory, found to my relief that it was listed, and then hung on for some minutes while the owner sent a boy to find Paul.

"Tomorrow," I told him. "I'll be down tomorrow at midday."

He seemed relieved and so was I. There were matters to go over that could only be explained in person.

Dinner with Vella and his family passed off very pleasantly. He had a pretty wife and their stone-porticoed villa overlooked the sea. Sure enough, he offered to take me around the island, but I was able to compromise on an evening tour. He also responded willingly to my suggestion that he invite the Canadian consul to inspect the Sabre: I had a fair idea what the consul's reactions would be.

"That reminds me," Vella said. "The local papers were interested too. I hope you don't mind my having told them about your record attempt."

"Delighted," I said. Anything without my photograph suited me fine.

"By the way," I went on, "it was nice of you to provide a mechanic. The engineer who services the plane in England wanted to come, but he couldn't."

Vella smiled. "Joe's a rough diamond in some ways. Strictly speaking he's a radar expert, though he can turn his hand to most things. At heart he's an enthusiast. When he heard about your plane he offered to help at once."

"Very decent of him," I said, and let Vella tell me more. By the time he dropped me back at the Corinthia Palace after dinner he had left me feeling that the key to the puzzle of Newland's actions was probably Micallef, and not the other way around.

I can't say I slept well, but I slept better than I might have after digesting the thought that Newland could yet be the straightforward airline type I had imagined when I first met him light years ago in the Savoy. Arain was different, though. I didn't think I would ever trust Arain.

ON FRIDAY MORNING I was woken by a rustling near the door. I had been half-expecting an intrusion during the night and now I leapt out of bed like the proverbial interrupted lover. Except that I wasn't with anyone else's wife, and the noise had been nothing more sinister than the local newspaper being pushed under the door with the compliments of the management. I reprimanded myself for being on edge, ordered breakfast, picked up the paper and promptly suffered a relapse.

It wasn't the picture of the Sabre on the front page. Vella had warned me to expect that, while the fallacious headline "Canadian Visitor's Record" could only further my ploy with the consul.

No, it was the lead story which set me back. Colonel Muammar Qaddafi was now forecasting the destruction of the Sixth Fleet and the day named was tomorrow, Saturday, September first.

Frankly, you needed to be a connoisseur of political lunacy to understand the Libyan leader. Even Hitler and Mussolini were never in the same league. Qaddafi was constantly throwing his troops into exotic anti-American exercises with codenames like "The Gulf of Sirte or Death," and, without exception, the outcome of these maneuvers was that the Americans were annihilated. Coupled with his vast armory, his self-delusion was a bonus to his enemies. American friends in Dubai had told me that the president could never have got half his Middle Eastern measures through Congress if it hadn't been for Qaddafi's posturing. The more upset he was, the more he huffed annd puffed. I reckoned this latest outburst meant he really had got the wind up, and his fears had to center on the safe arrival of the Pakistani Boeing.

"Any imperialist ship or aircraft found within two hundred miles of the Libyan coast after dawn on the morning of Saturday will be ruthlessly destroyed." Those were the leader's words, as quoted that day.

Unless he seriously believed he could defeat the Sixth Fleet, that meant he would seize the chance to shoot at anyone who could not retaliate. Like myself. I was liable to be in danger a long time before the final run-in, IFF or no IFF.

I was considering this further when the bedside phone buzzed.

"Is that Mr. Hall!" a North American voice asked. "My name's McDermid. I'm the Canadian consul. I understand you have a Canadian aircraft here."

"Not exactly," I temporized, delighted he had risen to the bait so fast. "She's in RCAF colors for historical reasons, but she's American registered."

"May I ask where you are planning to take this airplane next?"

"To Crete. Why do you ask?"

More than a hint of embarrassment came into the consul's voice. "Well, sir, as you may know there's a pretty big NATO exercise taking place right now. Canadian forces are not involved. May I emphasize that, sir. Not involved."

I played dumb deliberately. "My Sabre is civilian registered. She's not military."

"Well, sir. That airplane may not be military but she sure looks it. Is there any way you could change those markings?"

"Mr. McDermid," I said, with regretful firmness. "As a consul you must be aware that an aircraft's paint scheme is recorded in its official documentation. I can't alter it without the FAA certifying the change. Otherwise I'll be in potential trouble wherever I go. I'd need the Maltese authorities' permission to do anything here for a start." I paused a second. "Not that I want to be unhelpful."

I thought that would force the issue. It did.

"May I approach the authorities on your behalf?" he asked.

"No objection at all, Mr. McDermid. I just don't have much time. I could meet you this afternoon, though."

So that was how we left it. I figured he'd have a lot of hassle, but that was what he was paid for. As for eradicating the roundels, I had a brush and two small cans of brown and green cellulose paint stowed in the plane. I just hadn't wanted to arouse suspicion by making the change without a reason.

After breakfast I hired a car and drove to Marsax-lokk, stopping by the roadside en route to alter my hairstyle. I took care to park away from the quayside too, though there was no reason Lloyd should not have changed vehicles. The day was beginning to heat up, the horizon was hazy and the glare off the stone buildings blindingly strong. To be out at sea would be a relief.

Paul was pottering around on the quayside, and welcomed me devotedly.

"I was worrying about you, sir," he said, with real concern. "Nothing has gone wrong, I hope?"

"Not yet," I replied cheerfully. "And I'm sure it won't." The important thing was to bolster the old sailor's confidence. "Did you manage to clean her hull?"

"She is like a new pin, sir. You will see."

We chugged out in the *dghaisa* to where the boat was moored and sure enough all the algae and kelp were gone. After checking that various items of equipment I had left on board were intact, we took *Wanderer* out of the bay to the open sea for a final trial. At full throttle, with the water thumping under her bow and the spray flying, she went three knots faster than before and her cruise performance was proportionately improved too. I

was delighted and showed it by giving Paul a £50 bonus
on the spot, with a promise of more to come.

"A pity your wife is not here," he said, commis-
erating politely. "She enjoyed sailing after all, I think."

"I think she did. It's a pity she had to leave." I had
been too busy lately to miss Susie much, but now being
forcibly reminded of her, I wished she were here. Quite
apart from the emotional side of things, I could use a
reliable ally. There was a limit to what I could expect of
Paul.

Our next exercise was to slow to an idle five knots
while I demonstrated various aspects of the radio that it
was essential for him to understand, making him practice tuning in. I warned him that he ought to obtain at
least an additional fifty gallons of diesel in cans and
stow them in the cabin.

Then we returned to the harbor, had a drink at the
Saint George's Bar, became deliberately involved in a
long discussion with the owner on the possibility of lur-
ing swordfish to bait by day as opposed to night, and
before leaving the bar agreed on a sailing time for early
the next morning. I drove back toward Luqa confident
that my preparations had been as thorough as they
could be. As it happened, they weren't. There was one
possibility I failed to warn Paul about, because it wasn't
so much remote as completely improbable.

In the afternoon I went to Luqa, going in by the old
RAF entrance and being more shocked than I expected
to see the former guardroom converted into a handi-
craft workshop and likewise the departure lounge for
families. The place was now a craft village. However,
further inside I had to show the pass Vella had obtained
for me to be let through a perimeter fence. I parked the
car and walked on through the yellow-washed buildings
of the air traffic control center to the dispersal.

The whole airfield shimmered with heat. Across the
other side of the runway I could see airliners parked outside the main terminal, their outlines seeming to tremble

as if they were part of a desert mirage. Heat beat up at me from the concrete on which the Sabre was parked and the upper surfaces of the plane were too hot to touch. One could literally have fried an egg on them. There was no sign of the ferret-faced sergeant. I imagined he was asleep somewhere in the shade.

I opened the canopy, all but burning my hands in the process, checked that the fuel was properly switched off and climbed down again to attend to the port drop tank. Thank God the flush-fitting filler cap was in the shadow of the wing. I got it off easily, took my packet of chemicals from the battered canvas flight bag and tipped the contents in, glancing around to make sure I was unobserved. Then I unscrewed the cover of a small inspection hole Ted had cut out for me in the supporting pylon, fiddled inside with my fingers, and closed the valve in the fuel line. I didn't want jellified kerosene being drawn into the main system tomorrow. Finally, I removed the landing light from the nose of the tank and substituted the doctored one. I was just replacing the plexiglass when a police car rolled to a halt beside the plane, complete with the sergeant.

"You have problems, sir?" he inquired, saluting limply.

I shook my head, muttered, "Not really," and did not stop work until the cover was back on. Then I stood up, wiped my brow with the back of my hand and grinned at him. "Too bloody hot," I said. "That's the only problem."

He examined the plexiglass suspiciously. "You should have asked for the mechanic."

"Only a faulty lamp," I said. "When you own a plane you tend to do small jobs yourself."

Like fusing your own bombs. Or rather, bomb in the singular. One reason Newland had kept querying my escape route must have been that with both drop tanks converted I would be very short of fuel. Since the Boeing would burn like a torch if it was hit at all, and both

tanks would fall close together, I had decided to con-
secrate the contents of one drop tank to my own future
and use it on the way to Tripoli. I didn't feel that was
cheating Arain. Not when napalm spreads the way it
does.

Happily, at this point we were interrupted by the arrival of the Canadian consul. He was a small, neatly
dressed official, with sandy hair and a reddish, freckled
face. He obviously suffered from sunburn. He was ac-
companied by an airport official and he wasted no time
in coming to the point.

"I spoke to Ottawa an hour ago, Mr. Hall," he announced in a strained voice. "Our defense department is
extremely concerned. I am instructed to do everything in
my power to persuade you to remove those Canadian
colors."

"Did you speak to Colonel Collins?" I asked.

The consul flushed even redder. "As a matter of fact,
I did."

"Well," I said, appearing to capitulate, "I know the
colonel and if that's what he wants, let's get on with it.
Luckily I have some spare paint."

McDermid turned to the official. "Are you prepared
to certify the change?"

The official agreed. I gave him the aircraft documents, and thirty minutes later all trace of the Sabre's
Canadian allegiance had been deleted. As I had anticipated, one coat of paint did not properly hide the white
circles enclosing each red maple leaf, so the roundels
still showed as outlines on the body and wings. I gave
them another coat of green. From a distance they would
resemble the dark circles of the Libyan Air Force's insignia. This evidently did not occur to the witnesses.
They assumed I had botched the job.

"Thank you, Mr. Hall," the consul said, sounding
truly grateful. "I appreciate your spirit of coopera-
tion."

"No sweat," I assured him. The official signed my

documents and they went away. I've seldom known a piece of pure bull to be so successful. Even the police sergeant expressed respect for my willingness to get my hands dirty.

With that the day's work was over, bar the evening sightseeing. The only surprise had been that Micallef had not showed up. I decided it would be prudent to come out in the morning earlier than I had told him, though first I would have to obtain the final go-ahead.

Over the past few months I had spoken to Arain from many places and in many moods. This promised to be the last occasion and I wasn't sorry. All I wanted was to get on with the mission. When everything is set to go you invariably have to wait and the waiting is always the worst time. By comparison the action itself is less strain. "Train hard, fight easy," some Russian general said. I had certainly trained.

Next morning I woke very early and had to hold back from asking the hotel switchboard to get the call until seven. By then the Pakistani Boeing would be in Dubai. I still recalled Dubai with anger and regret. Without some of both I would never have been offered this job, nor taken it on. Money wasn't my entire motive: just ninety-nine per cent of it.

The phone buzzed, the operator said "Through to Geneva, sir," and Arain was on the line.

"How's John?" I asked, "John" being the go-ahead codeword.

"Delayed." Arain sounded curt and uptight. "His flight's late. They don't give reasons out there."

He could say that again. East is East and West is West and I often think it's a miracle that airlines bridge the gap at all. I once flew PIA to Nairobi and after take off they calmly announced we were going to Jeddah. No explanation. That's what they would do to the passengers on this occasion, except the destination would be Rome.

"Is there any estimate of arrival time?" I asked. Arain had the advantage that since the flight was dressed up as a normal schedule he could legitimately make inquiries.

"They say that it will be leaving Dubai shortly."

I did some quick mental calculations. The flight time from Dubai to Rome would be five hours. Say the Boeing reached Rome at midday and took an hour to turn around, it would be at Tripoli between two and three local time.

Three o'clock instead of midday. Out of the blue I remembered Rajni and his predictions. "Up to midday, that period is not to your benefit . . . the actual very good starts at three in afternoon."

Maybe Rajni's guru was right. Maybe the delay was good, though if it got extended much further the rest of my plans would be up the creek. Literally. I couldn't afford too much of Rajni's luck.

"John won't want to miss you," Arain cut in.

"I'll be standing by from midday," I assured him, cursing inwardly at the thought of the heat. The temperature inside the Sabre's cockpit would be well over a hundred, not that I could just sit there cooking like a goose in the oven. Everyone from the police sergeant upward would ask why. "I presume John's funds have been put through."

"I'll be banking them this morning." Arain sounded far from pleased. I imagined he would have preferred to wait until I was airborne, and finally committed. But Swiss banks are not normally open on Saturdays and I had fixed for him to pay the second fifty thousand dollars through the airport bank at Geneva, where my contact went off duty at noon.

"Be seeing you then." I wanted to sound normal for the benefit of the hotel operator.

"I doubt that," he said, and rang off.

I didn't bother with looking for double meanings in the remark, because I had no intention of renewing our acquaintance either, unless something went seriously wrong.

I was out at Luqa by seven-forty, my minimal baggage with me and the Corinthia bill paid. The sun, which when I looked out of the window earlier had been a great yellow orb rising from the horizon's haze, now touched everything with the early warmth that makes the Mediterrean climate so intoxicating. I stood for a minute by the Sabre enjoying it, then got to work on a methodical inspection, firmly dismissing the idea that this might be my last morning anywhere. Fifteen minutes later I knew someone had definitely meant it to be.

Basically a jet fighter is as tightly packaged as a showgirl. The Sabre's sleek body was built around the turbine engine, with the cockpit perched ahead of it and the tailplane behind.

One consequence was that the hydraulic lines to the tailplane controls ran alongside the engine: so close that the pilot's notes warned of the fire hazard if they were damaged.

The fluid in the lines could be observed by means of a small transparent sight gauge, revealed when the airbrakes were open. The airbrakes themselves swung outward from the body and were normally left open to assist the ground crew, as they had been since I landed. I had checked the fluid and was peering further inside when I noticed a dark shape that looked out of place. Using a torch to see better, I reached in and found a small package clipped to the piping. Very gingerly, I detached the clips and eased it out.

The package had a detonator visibly protruding. I laid it gently on the ground and wondered what the hell to do next.

There was no proof that Micallef was responsible though I was certain he must be. He was due to arrive at nine and I didn't want him to know what I had found. I glanced at my watch. Eight-twenty. The normal way to deal with a bomb in a hurry is to put it in a bucket of water. Instead I squatted on the concrete and tried deductive reasoning.

The bomb's purpose was clear: to rupture the hydraulics and blow a hole in the fuselage. When the hydraulics failed the pilot would lose control, at least until
he utilized the emergency override. But by then the
plane would be on fire and he'd have to eject anyway.
End of mission.

Unfortunately, that left the timing unresolved. I
stared at the little package. Somewhere inside there
must be a brain to give orders. Then I noticed that beside the pencil-shaped detonator was a tiny aerial,
scarcely two inches long. It had to belong to a miniaturized radio receiver, probably the kind used in a
remote-controlled model boat or plane. I always carry
one of those razor-sharp Swiss Army knives. I fished it
out and, taking a hell of a risk, began cutting through
the wrapping.

Five minutes later the ingredients lay on the concrete.
A few ounces of plastic explosive, the detonator and a
radio-activated switch. Dead simple. Except that the
switch appeared to be preset to a frequency and there
was no immediate way of telling which one. It could be
one I would use in the course of flight, thus blowing
myself up. Or someone else could make the transmission. The field was wide open. I couldn't even tell if the
bomb was intended to explode on my way to Libya or
on the way back.

Deductive reasoning gave way to self-preservation at
last. I rewrapped the plastic explosive and put it in one
pocket of my flying suit, concealed the detonator in
another and consigned the receiver to my flight bag.
Then I went in urgent search of a power trolley. I
wanted the airbrakes closed, flush with the fuselage,
before Micallef came. An obese Maltese eventually
brought the cart and plugged it in. I climbed aboard and
called the tower for permission to start up. I could have
used the emergency electrical system, but there was
more sense in retracting the brakes if you were doing an
engine run.

Micallef showed up smack on time, wearing overalls and holding a toolbag. I waved, but didn't descend until I had checked all the powered systems were operative.

"Is everything OK?" he asked, a shade too blandly.

"Fine. All I need is fuel, oil, and oxygen."

"What about the daily checks?"

"I've done the hydraulics myself." I handed him the manual. "If you can do the others."

He could hardly argue, though before he started I caught him looking at the fresh paint. I made no comment and he stayed silent. By ten everything was done.

"Thanks a lot," I said. "What do I owe you?" There was no sense in challenging him. Hawker was an innocent and I had to play that game to the end.

He accepted £30, but seemed reluctant to go. In fact, I practically had to hustle him away. When he did leave I noticed he had parked his car just beyond the high fence. It was a Triumph Herald convertible, old yet beautifully kept. They used to assemble them in Malta. He was obviously an enthusiast, as Vella said. Most people have more than one side to them, though I hadn't yet appreciated how many he had.

The next stage was the flight planning and having time to kill I would not have hurried, except that I had to dispose of the plastic explosive. The met forecast was only fair. The sirocco was starting to blow and always brought a haze of sandy dust from the North African desert. From the met office I walked across the short bridge between the two air traffic control buildings and did my bit with the army captain in charge of flight planning, filing for take off at 13.00 GMT, or two o'clock local. He told me I would have to taxi the Sabre across to the Number Eight park to clear customs.

Every pound of fuel being valuable, I argued against this on the basis of the distance to Heraklion and he eventually agreed to ask the customs people to come to me. With that settled, and an assurance that no one would be allowed near the Sabre, I decided the nearest place both to find some coffee and get rid of the explosive was the old RAF officers' mess, alias the Airport Hotel. No longer having a car, I walked, my flying overalls drawing a few curious glances.

You can't reenter the past without paying a price. I had slept, eaten and enjoyed myself in this handsome building. I didn't like finding the honey-colored stone columns at the entrance defaced with Arabic graffiti, and was glad that the carved RAF crest was out of reach. I would have expected that to be the first to go. Inside there was an air of cavernous desolation, yet hardly any change, as though the new owners had no energy for conversion. I ordered coffee in the former bar, still adorned with its old signs. Hell, but we'd had some parties here. Like Duxford, the place was full of ghosts. I choked them down, drank the salty coffee and sauntered off to put my memories to more practical use.

The lavatories were off a passage from the main hall and still had their row of sinks and toilets in cubicles. I chose the far one, stood on the seat and slipped the bag of explosive into the cistern high on the wall. I doubted if anyone would find it in years and the cool water would keep it stable, not that I intended to return. The detonator I kept.

On the way back, passing the huge anteroom where we used to lounge and read the papers, I glanced inside. In the far corner, huddled together with two Arabs in white headdresses, was Micallef. They were in animated conversation. I recoiled quickly before they saw me and left the building, wondering to whom the man actually owed allegiance. There were a lot of ways I would like to have dealt with Micallef, starting by attaching the explosive to his car engine. Unhappily this was not the moment. I was conspicuous in my flying gear and a contract is a contract. I couldn't afford to prejudice the take off time.

At eleven forty-five I reluctantly climbed into the oven that the Sabre's cockpit had become, switched on the HF radio, which could operate on the aircraft battery, and called Geneva via Stockholm. After a short delay my bank contact confirmed that fifty thousand in bills had been credited to my account. I asked him to put the money on deposit, rang off and settled down to wait for Newland, the sweat running down my forehead and back.

Newland came on only a minute late and was so terse that I guessed he must have been in the Rome airport telephone office.

"They made up time," he said. "Now they have a problem off-loading people. John will be on his way around twelve-forty."

"I'll give them half an hour's grace at the other end."

"Too long. Fifteen minutes. Keep time in hand. I'll call again in an hour and you be ready to roll then."

I didn't agree with his arithmetic, but I wasn't going to argue. He had sounded pretty hyped-up and my own adrenalin was starting to flow, like building up power before you let the brakes off. I swung out of the cockpit thankfully and went across to air traffic control to ask for customs and immigration straight away. The captain told me Heraklion had accepted my flight plan, and I mentioned I would like to go fifteen or twenty minutes early.

"That's OK," he assured me. "We are here to help you. Mr. Vella phoned. He is coming to see you off."

Perhaps Newland was right, I thought. You can always fly slower. You can't always go faster, and airport farewells consume time like a rabbit eating lettuce.

However, the departure went smoothly. Newland confirmed the Boeing's take off as 12:48—I imagined him standing at the airport windows watching as it lifted off Fiumicino's runway, trailing unburnt fuel—and that gave me the time of 14:20 to be over Tripoli.

Vella shook hands warmly. "The very best of luck." Those brilliant teeth flashed. "I am delighted to have been an accessory to your triumph."

"Let's hope it continues," I said, noticing Micallef standing by the wire fence and speculating on whether he would be listening on a radio to my transmissions. If so, they would be as dramatic as he could wish, though possibly ahead of his schedule for disaster. Vella, on the other hand, would be genuinely sorry, as might Luke, Ted, and the hotchpotch of other friends Hawker had made in his short career. He stood waving as I taxied the short distance to the end of the runway. I dismissed them all from my mind, went through the take off checks and radioed the tower that I was ready.

The Sabre didn't want to leave mother earth. It was her one bad habit. I had to haul her off the tarmac. But thereafter the coast was slipping past beneath in no time flat and I could see the sweep of Marsaxlokk Bay to my left. I hoped Paul was obeying orders.

"Airborne at five six," the tower informed me. "Contact Approach on one two six decimal one."

I twisted the dial and pressed the transmit button, wondering if this was when the bomb had been intended to go off. Or was there someone on a ship, waiting to blow me up after the raid? I might never know and this was not the moment for idle speculation.

Malta approach rapidly handed me on to Malta control, who cleared me to twenty thousand feet. Six minutes later I was there and almost at the flight information region boundary. It was essential to be outside the FIR before I staged the drama I was planning, otherwise the Malta Rescue Coordination Center would leap into action, and they weren't the people I wanted.

During the couple of minutes remaining I scanned the sea below for ships, but saw none. The horizon was a grayish white blur, thanks to the sirocco, and visibility no better than five miles, despite the clear sky. I was worried about shipping. Merchant seamen don't look around much, which is why they have so many unnecessary collisions, but even they might wake up if a jet howled past at deck level. At four minutes past two local

time I signed off from Malta control, made a quick
cockpit check, eased the power and switched to the international distress frequency. Fate was about to catch
up with Hawker Hall.

"Mayday, mayday, mayday. This is November Four
Sierra." I repeated my callsign the statutory three times,
trying to sound both steady and scared, and launched
into the spiel. "I've lost the hydraulics. Some kind of
explosion." On purpose I left out all the other information Hawker should have given.

A second later an American voice replied, asking with
rocklike calm for what I had omitted. "November Four
Sierra. This is the USS *Independence*. What is your
height, heading and position?"

That was the signal. I cut the power and pushed the
nose forward into a dive.

"My position fifty-five miles east of Malta, heading
one hundred degrees, flight level two zero, descending."
I let Hawker's sangfroid falter. "I have loss of power.
Emergency override not functioning. The fire warning
light just came on."

"We have you identified. Steer one two zero degrees.
I repeat, one two zero degrees."

So that told me the direction of the *Independence* and
her accompanying Sixth Fleet ships: the direction to
avoid.

The Sabre was going down nicely now. Six thousand
feet a minute and passing through sixteen thousand feet.
To the radar operator on the aircraft carrier it would
look about right. Jet fighters, once deprived of their
power, glide like bricks. It was time to develop the
emergency further.

"I'm out of control." I pitched my voice an octave
higher. "She's on fire. November Four Sierra, mayday,
mayday."

I didn't actually say, "Help, help, help, it's me," but
the guy down there on the *Independence* got the mes-

sage. Hawker was panicking.

"Keep your cool, sir. Keep calm. What's your present heading and altitude?"

There was no point in lying. By now a dozen naval craft would have me on their radar, a tiny blob of light falling out of the sky. But I could confuse the issue. I kicked on some right rudder.

"Heading one five zero. Nine thousand feet. She's turning. I can't stop her. The fire's worse."

"Don't panic. We have you identifed. What's your aircraft type?"

"Sabre," I half-screamed. "I've got her level but she's burning."

I stared down at the sea. Estimating one's exact height over water is tricky in any weather. My eventual pullout would have to both bring me down to a few hundred feet and deceive the *Independence*. I eased the nose up, slowing the rate of descent. Hawker's moment had come.

"Ejecting," I shouted. "I'm baling out. Height five thousand feet. Heading one seven zero. Going now."

The Sabre was flying beautifully with three hundred knots on the clock. I imagined Hawker reaching frantically for the rocket seat handles—as I would be doing myself before long, though I hoped not in panic—and went on down.

"We'll be with you," came the *Independence's* final call.

At one thousand feet I leveled out in earnest, giving her enough power to keep at the same speed. Assuming the carrier had an airborne radar plane operating, as in view of Qaddafi's threats the Sixth Fleet would do, they would spot the Sabre's continuing flight. However, it was quite plausible that with its pilot gone and the center of gravity altered the plane could come out straight and level. The same thing had happened on plenty of occasions before. The essential point was that the Sixth

Fleet would be searching for Hall in his liferaft, not worrying about the Sabre's aerial imitation of the Marie Celeste.

I altered my heading toward Tripoli, confident that the Earth's curvature would hide me from Libyan radar until I was thirty miles or so off the coast. The Libyans didn't have any airborne early warning. What they would see was a swarm of rescue and reconnaissance planes rising from the Sixth Fleet well within Qaddafi's self-proclaimed exclusion zone. But they would not know what those planes were doing. I wished them luck. I wouldn't have cared to take on the Sixth Fleet myself.

ELEVEN

THERE WAS NO point in hanging around. At the same
time the Sabre was now theoretically without a pilot,
and if I accelerated suddenly the *Independence* might
send a couple of Tomcats to find out what the hell was
happening.

So I held the speed down to three hundred knots for
some minutes, allowed my altitude to decline slowly as a
pilotless plane's might, and switched on the IFF in case
it would keep the Libyans happy. From the bearings
that the carrier had given I deduced her position as well
north of the Gulf of Sirte, which in turn suggested the
admiral's orders from the Pentagon had been to avoid
unnecessary provocation. If so the Sixth Fleet would
leave me to be dealt with by the Libyans. I held on track
for Tripoli, hoped the bluff worked, and occupied myself with more immediate priorities than worrying.

The first thing was to listen out for the Pakistani Boeing. If the pilot wasn't making his descent by now,
something was badly wrong. I tuned the VHF to the
Tripoli international frequency then, using the Selcal,

called Paul on the HF, praying that he would not be
overwhelmed by nervousness. His normal confident
speech had evaporated when I made him practice using
Wanderer's radio, and in the end I had taken the considerable risk of writing down the frequencies and the
basic operating procedure for the other navigational
gear.

"Paul," I called. "Come in Paul."

Silence. Only a crackle of static.

"Paul, are you there?" It was fruitless using normal
communications phrases. They would only have thrown
him completely.

At last a hesitant reply. "I can hear you." Poor devil,
he must be terrified of making a mistake.

"Did you get there?"

"I am sorry, sir. A ship stopped me. Not a friendly
one, they made me turn back."

I swore silently. A hundred-to-one the unfriendly ship
had been Libyan. Worse, it had scuppered my careful
briefing. Paul was a typical Mediterranean inshore fisherman, who found his way by instinct and experience.
He had told me he could smell land and find his way
back to Malta in any weather. But he could not do the
reverse and navigate to an unmarked position in the
middle of the ocean. To solve the difficulty I had told
him to head due south on the compass at a steady
twenty knots for four hours. Then he should start fishing. Dead simple. Until the formula got interfered with.

"After how long were you stopped?" I asked, switch-
ing the radio compass on to *Wanderer's* frequency and
noting the time.

"Three hours, I think. A little more. Then I go back
for half an hour. Now I am fishing."

The compass needle was swinging around. It settled
on a bearing of eighty-two degrees: *Wanderer's* bearing
from me. I had flown three minutes. One gets used to
doing quick, approximate calculations in the air. Map in
hand, I worked out distances. Assuming he had sailed

due south, and returned due north, he would now be
some sixty miles from Malta. Nothing like as far as I
had wanted.

I was about to reply when the Boeing came on the air,
talking to Tripoli. Paul would have to wait.

The Pakistani pilot spoke in stilted Arabic that I easily understood, having long ago learned the basic aviation phrases. "Descending to flight level two zero."
What was presumably an instruction from Tripoli intervened. I was too low to pick up the ground transmissions yet, but a moment later I knew what they had said,
because the pilot repeated it back and again I noted the
time; 14:12 local.

"Understand I am to make approach fifteen miles
west of city."

That told me a lot. The parade must either be in progress or about to begin. Would Qaddafi delay it until his
Islamic bomb was safety delivered? I guessed his troops'
salutes would be the sweeter if he did.

"Paul?" I called on the other set, the HF.

"I am here." He sounded strained. I could hardly explain to him that in total I was listening out on three frequencies: his own high frequency, the Tripoli VHF and
the Libyan Air Force's ultra high.

"Stay where you are. Put the radio on the other
number. Listen all the time. I will call in three-quarters
of an hour. If I only say one word, come and find me."

"I will, sir." He sounded more resolute, thank
Heaven.

"Goodbye, Paul." I switched off the HF and retuned
the radio compass. The frequency change had been an
elementary security precaution in case the Libyans or
the Sixth Fleet had been eavesdropping. The Americans
kept a very thorough listening watch and would easily
be able to establish *Wanderer's* position. They might
well send a reconnaissance plane to check her out. That
could only be to the good if there were Libyan patrol
craft around. I watched the radio compass. The needle

didn't move. Oh Jesus, had Paul got it wrong? I didn't want to have to swim. Then slowly the indicator shifted a couple of degrees and steadied. We were in business.

Since it stood to reason that the Sixth Fleet would have plotted the source of my transmissions too, I had to assume they would notice a connection with the supposedly abandoned Sabre. But as they hadn't come after me, I assumed they weren't going to now. I was a long way into Qaddafi's exclusion zone. I eased down the last five hundred feet to fly as close to the sea as possible, shifted the stubby throttle lever further forward to give myself five hundred knots and began the countdown in earnest. As always, it was a matter of time and distance.

The time was 14:14. By dead reckoning I had around 185 miles to run and was barreling into thickening haze, made worse by having the sun in my eyes, at nine and a half miles a minute. No point in going faster or I might be in danger of arriving too soon. I had to allow time for the Boeing to land and taxi in.

As if confirming my calculations, the Pakistani began repeating back further instructions from Tripoli.

"Approach over Sobal and Qizar for runway one eight. Understand sandstorms to the south. Now passing through flight-level one five zero. Estimate the field at two seven."

The sandstorms explained the worsening murk. There must be a strong wind for the controller to be directing him on to the southerly runway instead of the long east-west one. He would be landing at 14:27, five minutes before I expected to cross the coast. Ideal. I held the Sabre steady on course, hoping I wouldn't hit any seagulls, and thought of the crew above and ahead of me on the Boeing's flight deck, letting down after what must have been a nerve-wracking flight. I wouldn't like to be carrying that cargo and I wondered if by some quirk of fate the pilot could be Amir, hating the idea of a stop in Libya, with no alcohol and no girlfriends.

A sudden jabber of Arabic came over the air, followed by the Pakistani lapsing into English.

"Tell your friends to speak slowly please." There was a pause, then a message that was more of a command. "I do not want them alongside on the final approach."

The fighter escorts must be overplaying their role. I could imagine them weaving around the Boeing in an excess of excitement. Qaddafi's pride would not have allowed Russians or East Europeans to perform this duty. I felt a surge of sympathy for the Pakistani, who, once he had spoken English, I knew was not Amir. I hoped he would have disembarked from the Boeing before my attack. Napalm doesn't provide a pleasant death. That provoked a more potent thought. If the fire did detonate the Islamic bomb the scenario would be inestimably worse than we had calculated. Even a ground-zero explosion would make the millions of particles in the sandstorm radioactive, and far from the fallout floating away from Tripoli, a southerly wind would deposit it all over the city.

Attacking from the air is a dispassionate business. You usually don't see the target after you've hit it and you certainly feel nothing of the effects, while the debriefing later is a prosaic formula concerning vehicles, tanks, or troops in the open, without blood or guts. But I had enough imagination not to want to be the cause of a million people dying.

A rusty merchant ship loomed up in the murk, I veered and it flashed past, a sailor gazing startled from the deck. That snapped me back into my countdown.

Sixteen minutes to the coast. Too far to pick up any civil navigational beacon and confirm the direction. I was flying in limbo. Nothing save dark-blue water flecked with small waves racing past below and white gray haze ahead. Speed is relative. I only get a kick out of it if I'm close to the ground with all the obstacles land presents. This was exhilarating, yet monotonous. I flicked my eyes down to the fuel gauges. Not bad.

Going even fifty knots slower achieved a major economy as compared with my trial run. The right-hand
drop tank must be empty by now: though there was no
indicator, it replenished the main tanks automatically
and their state suggested I'd have at least 2,500 pounds
remaining when I crossed the coast. If all went well I'd
have enough to reach *Wanderer*, in spite of her being
too far north.

Seven minutes to run. More ships appeared: several
tankers and a bulk carrier. I must be crossing a sealane.
The waves were noticeably larger, their crests plumed by
the wind. Something flashing to the right of the flying
instruments caught my attention. The light on the IFF
panel was pulsing, which meant I was being interrogated
by the Libyan defense radar. I hoped the answer being
given was "Friend." I wouldn't have put it past Micallef to have fixed the opposite. I switched on the UHF
radio to hear what the Libyan flypast was doing.

Voices were immediately audible, giving orders in
Arabic, but too fast for my limited knowledge.

Five minutes. The Pakistani pilot announced he had
the field in sight. At the same moment the needle on my
VOR began swinging, at last receiving the Okba Ben
Nafi beacon. I adjusted the scale quickly, read a bearing
and banked left. The wind had taken me slightly off
course.

Three minutes. The haze was thicker. The Pakistani
Boeing must have landed. Simpler, more comprehensi-
ble Arabic came over the UHF.

"Formation Jalloud leader. Formation Jalloud
leader. Taxi to holding point."

I reckoned I could hear that because Okba Ben Nafi
was a lot closer to the coast than Tripoli International.
Qaddafi was jumping the gun as usual. He or his min-
ions must have initiated the celebration before the Boeing even touched down. When it crossed the coast
probably. And where the hell was the coast?

Two minutes. Still no faint outline of land. I checked

the fuel and rehearsed the single Arabic sentence I had prepared. Fishing boats appeared, frightened faces staring at me. I eased up to five hundred feet. The harbor must be close.

With thirty seconds to go the city came in sight, buildings receding like ghosts into the haze. I screamed into a hard right turn, banking the wings vertical, pressure tightening on my stomach, and rolled level again to fly directly west along the shoreline, noticing palm trees bending in the wind. I pressed the transmit button and spoke with all the high-pitched Arab harshness I could muster.

"One Five from Misratah diverting as ordered."

I figured that by the time they had discovered from the Misratah base, one hundred twenty miles east along the coast, that no aircraft had departed for Okba Ben Nafi, my mission would be over. For a few seconds there was silence. Then as the city proper slipped behind me and I banked left to race inland across the coastal road and the white villas of the more prosperous suburbs, a shrill series of questions erupted over the radio. The ruse had worked. I distinguished a frantic command to clear the area and, to keep them happy a fraction longer, threw back a one-word reply.

"Understood."

From now on until I had completed my attack I was going to be too busy to bother much with the enemy, unless they actually came after me. What mattered was lobbing my napalm splat on the Boeing, like an egg in the pan. I turned up the VHF on the Tripoli ground frequency of 121.9, hoping to catch some confirmation that the Pakistani plane had parked, then switched on the bombsight.

Obediently, the circle of diamond-shaped dots appeared on the reflector glass between my eyes and the windscreen, tracking over the last of the ribbon development west of the city just as cleanly as it had done over the Mojave wilderness. I weaved the Sabre for a second to line up the center dot on a distant pylon and realized with a bump that the sandstorm coming off the desert was a bad one. The bump had been literal: I was flying through severe turbulence and let the speed drop to 420 knots, just in case she started porpoising. The storm itself was only a few miles away to the south, not so much visibly menacing as a gray blurring of land and sky that blotted out the landscape. I remembered how rapidly sandstorms used to close the Gulf airports. But I had no option except to turn toward it, since I was aiming to fly in a high arc to approach the airport from the northwest and see things as the video had shown them. One advantage of not having to follow any flypast was that I could do that.

Nothing came over Tripoli Radio. The Boeing must have parked and switched off. That was good. I hoped the crew had deplaned. My raid was little more than a minute off now. I was a long way west of the city, streaking over countryside, or what passes for it in this section of Allah's acres. The landmarks Newland's video had illustrated began appearing: small sandy fields and stunted olive trees in a brown landscape. The visibility was worsening, down to two miles or less. I scanned the limited horizon, knowing from the VOR that the airport must be ahead and to my left, in what a forward air controller would have called my "ten o'clock." For the last time I ran over in my mind what pattern my attack would follow.

In my book, which was the RAF's, there were two ways of hitting a point target, like a tank or a house. You could go straight in very low all the way, preferably guided by a computer set to the coordinates of the target, and if you had all the electronic gear it would do just about everything including press the button. In fact, with all the black boxes the pilot was damn near redundant. If you didn't have the gear, as I didn't now, you were pretty well in the Stone Age and it was easier to run in on a feature a thousand yards or so to one side

of the target area, pull up into a steep climbing turn to
get a quick overall view and then dive down again to the
attack. In the old days, doing this, we had a pongo on
the ground—the FAC—lying up close enough to see the
enemy and give directions over the air. They did that in
the Falklands War. Not a job I ever envied, given the exposed position he had to be in, but I could have used
an FAC today for directions . . . "I have you visual.
Looking good. Target is in your eleven o'clock, two
miles . . ."

Where the hell was the airfield?

The desert was unrolling ahead of me like the original
Libyan Experience, I had no black boxes, no FAC, the
air currents were throwing me around, and so far as I
could judge I was only just going to miss the edge of the
storm. Already the dust was casting an evening pallor
over everything.

Where was the bloody airfield?

I flipped the landing-light switch, both to arm the
fuse on one tank and illuminate the lamp on the other.
Airliners coming in to land switch on their lights. It
might help confuse the controllers, though basically I
was relying on the Boeing's safe arrival to give their defenses a false sense of security.

In the same instant I caught sight of a white shape in
the distance and a black swathe to its right. I was there.
As the line of the perimeter fence flashed underneath I
pulled up and banked hard to get the crucial bird's-eye
view.

At this kind of speed you need training to appreciate
what you are seeing. As the G dragged at my face muscles, I looked sideways and ahead, mentally checking
off the essential features: the long white terminal
building stood parallel to the runway and about seven
hundred yards from it. There was the round VIP reception, the flagpoles, the high control tower. Parked in
front was a Boeing, the only aircraft there.

That panorama was spread out for a fraction of a

second only. In the next fraction I checked the Boeing's appearance, saw the green livery and the PIA lettering and knew there was no mistake. Target seen.

I rolled out of the turn into a steep dive, my thumb hovering over the firing button on the stick, maneuvering to bring the circle of dots on to the airliner.

Mobile steps stood against the Boeing's nose. Men around them began to scatter and run. A flatbed truck was backing in behind the wing where open cargo doors made a dark gap in the fuselage.

I had the sight centered on the tail, which I thought would compensate for the high wind. My thumb pressed down, I felt the familiar jerk as the tanks fell away and hauled back the stick, aware that I was cutting things very fine.

The control tower reared up to my right. Somewhere beyond was the one hundred fifty-foot pylon. I was going to be lucky to miss the roof of the terminal. The wind had carried me closer to it than I intended, and when you pull out of a dive a plane always carries on horizontally for a moment even though the nose is pointing at the sky. The Sabre juddered and I had to relax the stick pressure as I gave her full throttle. I missed the concrete buildings by feet, shot like a projectile below the level of the control-tower windows, jinked to avoid the pylon—though in reality I was above it— and soared upward. I could imagine the blast my engine had created, sweeping the tarmac with a rush of wind and a roar like the Last Judgment. At three thousand feet I rolled over on to my back, coming out in a steep turn to survey the scene below. Despite the risks, I wasn't leaving until I knew if I had scored.

What a single one-hundred-gallon tank of jellied fuel could achieve was frightening. The airliner was already hidden in a surging sea of flame, with only the wingtips visible. As I looked down an explosion cascaded up, smoke belching. One of the Boeing's tanks must have ignited. The airfield was in total disorder, men running and fire engines starting to move. But nothing could extinguish that inferno. At any moment the airliner's whole structure would melt and the nuclear weapon inside be exposed to the full intensity of the fire. I kept turning, wind buffeting the Sabre as I cut through the edge of the storm, all vision momentarily lost. I gritted my teeth and held on, the G anchoring me into the seat, praying that the engine would not be swamped by the sand and dust. I came out with the airfield below me again and swung out of the turn to head north. I had only just made it in time. In a few more minutes any attack would have been impossible. I established my bearings and began to run for the coast. Not one shot had been fired at me. Then I saw the flypast.

There's a saying about being between the Devil and the deep-blue sea. This was the doubled-up version. The potential big bang was behind, the flypast was in front, and the Mediterranean was beyond. Two devils for the price of one. But why the hell was the long procession of planes making up the parade flying north like me when they ought to be heading west?

The sandstorm must have disrupted their plans. Maybe the formation commander had intended to salute the Pakistani arrival first. Whatever the reason, there was no way I could overtake them, nor go east over Okba Ben Nafi airbase, where the antiaircraft defenses were elaborate. Newland might have been right in believing the planes would be unarmed. On the other hand he might not, and aircraft capable of twice my Sabre's speed would be in that procession, which I was rapidly catching up with. I eased back the throttle and listened to the UHF radio to hear what the leader was saying.

"Formation prepare for turning port. Turning port in ninety seconds. Maintaining fifteen hundred feet and turning port."

He was speaking with extreme simplicity and ninety seconds was an overlong warning. He must have trainee

Libyan pilots taking part and was shepherding them like
a schoolmaster. I made an instant decision. The bomb
on the Boeing was unlikely to detonate unless its casing
melted down. But the furious reaction to my attack
would be immediate. Since I couldn't pass the procession I'd better revert to my old idea and hide in it. I
glanced at the fuel gauges. Over 1,500 pounds remaining. With luck the sandstorm would force the formation
leader to return to base over the sea and I could slip
away with a headstart.

The sun was behind me now and I could see a lot better than during the run-in. Conversely, if the leader did
look back he would be hard put to spot me. I had in-
tuitively altered course to follow behind, and already
had the high-rise apartment blocks along the airport
road in view. I went down to fifteen hundred feet and
prepared to creep in behind the last aircraft some three
miles ahead.

"Creep in" may sound an absurd phrase, but it was
what I had to do. In the air you can't race up to join
someone, then slam on the brakes. I could not risk over-
shooting and giving myself away. I edged closer while
the formation was making its gentle turn, trusting to
Allah that anyone on the ground who noticed would
take me for a straggler.

Furthermore, Newland had been right in at least one
respect. The old MiGs were bringing up the rear. Unfortunately, the last four were in a V, with the box position filled, so I stationed myself fifty feet behind, as if I
was a singleton completing the parade.

As we streamed sedately over the city at two hundred
knots the hullabaloo started. An outside voice cut in
with a near-hysterical cry that the airport had been attacked and was on fire. Hostile aircraft were in the
vicinity. The rest was beyond me. But the formation
commander didn't panic.

"Flypast will continue," he ordered. "Passing overhead Green Square in forty seconds."

The wide expanse of Green Square came into view, three columns of tanks rolling across it. On the right were the stone-battlemented walls of the old fort, palm trees sprouting along the walls. I glimpsed a line of green flags, the awnings over stands and a tiny figure that might have been Qaddafi, arm raised in salute. Then we were gone.

The commander didn't hang around. There was an authoritative snap in his tone and he allowed no warning time as he announced an immediate return to base just as we overflew the landmark of old King Idris' palace, now the property of the people.

"Formation will turn starboard, turning, turning, now."

That told me another thing. Newland's intelligence had been accurate again. If any of the flypast aircraft had been armed they would have been told to break away, climb to altitude and await orders. My advantage was intact: and as quickly compromised. Although the leader turned toward the sea, as I had hoped, he came around so tightly that he was heading back barely a mile out long before the tail-end planes began to bank for their turn. He was one hundred percent certain to glance across at the formation following him around, and unless he was a lot less competent than he sounded, the moment he saw an extra aircraft he would start calling out the reserves.

I held on as long as I dared, not wanting to draw attention to myself unnecessarily, then as the leader came level in the opposite direction I dived straight ahead, piling on the power, to skim the rooftops for a few seconds before swinging north over the sea. As I did so, the commander lost his cool.

I couldn't understand most of the tumultuous Arabic which followed. But I did get one word loud and clear. "Traitor."

So with luck the Libyan defense radar would now be searching for two rogue aircraft, and so far as I could gather from the jabber as I streaked north clipping the waves, they were completely foxed at not having located the first. Furthermore, it had not occurred to them to shift to another frequency, or channel. So I could still listen to their orders, albeit that my pursuers were likely to be the best-equipped Libya possessed: the Russian pilots of the supersonic MiG-25s, each with air-to-air missiles and computerized interception systems. Everything depended on how much of a start I had gained. I switched off the IFF, not wanting to help them unnecessarily.

When I spoke to Paul earlier I had marked his approximate position on the map and now I headed for it unyieldingly, occasionally easing up to pass over ships, otherwise keeping close to the water, relying for protection on the reflections that radar picks up off the waves and that technicians call "clutter." The further away I was, the harder it would be for land-based radar to pick me up. In three or four minutes it would be impossible. But could I reach *Wanderer* on the fuel available?

The 1,500 pounds had dwindled to 1,300 when I quit the formation. I was flying flat now, the airspeed indicator flickering around 570 knots and the flowmeter, a large, round, easy instrument to read, steady at 4,100 pounds an hour. That gave me nineteen minutes flying or one hundred eighty nautical miles. If I was right about Paul's position, I had thirty miles to spare. If I navigated correctly. If I was not intercepted. Again I began a countdown, this time in reverse.

With fourteen minutes' fuel left I was past the shipping lanes, visibility was improving slightly and the UHF radio was silent. Suddenly I noticed that the IFF light was still blinking. I checked the switch was off. But the thing stayed obstinately on. Micallef must have fixed that deliberately, damn him. So now the Libyans had me identified.

Twelve minutes. Seventy miles out from the Libyan coast, almost halfway to *Wanderer*. I felt a surge of

confidence and bit it back the way I would have tried to
subdue fear. Mustn't count one's chickens. I turned the
radio compass to the boat's frequency and got no reaction. A seagull flashed past, flailing ludicrously to
avoid me. All I needed was a birdstrike cracking the
windscreen, obscuring my vision with blood and
feathers. My right hand, gripping the stick, felt stiff and
cramped. I tried to relax and could not.

Suddenly a voice sounded on the UHF. Not loud, but
distinct. And not speaking Arabic. Another voice
answered. With a nasty feeling in my gut I guessed the
language: Russian. A pair of Foxbats were somewhere
behind me, higher too or I wouldn't have received them.
Eleven minutes left. How long would it have taken them
to scramble into action. Two minutes? Three? More
calculations. Going at twice my own speed they'd cover
eighty miles in four minutes. Add a small margin. Allow
for the Libyan radar losing contact and their having to
track me on their own. Conclusion: they ought to be
here any moment.

The voices were conversing in short, sharp sentences.
But I could hear uncertainty. Were they worried about
running into the Sixth Fleet? If only I had some kind of
countermeasures. Modern combat aircraft had a detec-
tor that indicates which direction a pursuing missile is
coming from. The pilot can throw out decoy flares to
mislead a heat-seeking missile or chaff to disorient a
radar-guided one. I had nothing. The MiG-25s missiles
would be fired at a range of four or five miles and travel
the distance in sixteen seconds. The first thing I would
know would be the explosion. And the last. Instinctively
I adjusted the Sabre's rear-view mirror to scan above
and behind, aware the action was futile. My pursuers
would be coming out of the sun. It would be a miracle if
I spotted them.

Nine minutes' fuel. Sixty miles to the boat. Surviving
this long was a bonus. The radio-compass indicator was
revolving sluggishly, as unsure of itself as a drunk, but

at least reacting, which was another plus, given the low power of *Wanderer's* HF set. However, the situation wasn't unclouded. The voices in my earphones had become clearer and more decisive. Abruptly a brief interchange culminated in a single word of obvious command, which could only be "attack" or "fire." I banked into a left turn, high-tailed on for a few seconds, swerved right, then left again, keeping so low the spray from a wave speckled the canopy. Conceivably the miniaturized guidance system in the missile would be confused by the clutter. Conceivably.

What followed was as nightmarish as it was unexpected. A fountain of water erupted a few hundred yards ahead. I maneuvered violently to avoid it, realizing in the same instant that a missile must have overtaken me and detonated.

I was wondering where its inevitable companion had gone when I saw a ship. Long and lean-hulled. Painted gray. A destroyer or frigate. I didn't give a damn whose. I headed for its stern, hoping to fly around the back, knowing the massive radar signal the ship would return to any missile would keep me safe for a mile or two more. Then I realized that the flashes flickering on the ship's superstructure were weapons being fired. At me.

There was still only one formula for escape: to hug the sea and keep my profile as thin as possible. If I banked out of the way I might as well rip the Sabre's belly open myself. I altered course a fraction to show I was not trying to do a kamikaze act. The Sabre jolted as something banged into the fuselage. I hung on, glimpsed the white-painted insignia "D 27" on the stern and the Stars and Stripes hanging from a pole above, and then was past.

Whether the destroyer's firing ceased or the Sabre merely wasn't struck again I could not tell. I just kept going, rising fifty feet above the water for safety while I scanned the instruments. Whatever had hit me must have caused damage. My eyes flicked across the top row of instruments and were caught by the hydraulic pressure gauge. Normally it showed three thousand pounds per square inch. It was down to 2,000 and falling. The alternate system for powering the flying controls should have engaged automatically, illuminating a warning light. The light was not on. No time to wonder why. I felt with my left hand for the manual changeover, failed to find it, had to glance down to locate the switch, flipped it across and when I looked up was skimming the waves. I pulled the stick back hastily, found the response sluggish and began to realize that things were still going wrong. I managed to level out at five hundred feet, acutely conscious of being a sitting duck, though that was better than flying into the sea. Then I heard the first Russian's voice.

The cry over the radio was one of horror more than fear. I looked up. Several thousand feet above was the unmistakable swept-back silhouette of a MiG-25, climbing fast and trailing smoke. The next moment the image disintegrated into flames and pieces of metal fell from the sky. The pilot did not eject.

Of the number two MiG there was no sign. The destroyer must have loosed off missiles at both as they followed me. Perhaps one of theirs had hit the ship, not that it would have done much damage. There was no way of telling. What was extremely clear was that an element of the Sixth Fleet considered it had been attacked and mine was the sole "Libyan" aircraft left in the vicinity. I reckoned some American planes would be along to finish me off very shortly. The irony of their succeeding where Micallef had failed would have been more acute if I'd had more fuel remaining. As things were I had all of seven minutes left. I told myself a lot could change in seven minutes. It damn well had to if I was to get close enough to *Wanderer* for Paul to locate me. Miraculously it did.

The hydraulic pressure recovered on the alternate system and the controls began responding. Nonetheless I

could not tell how badly the fuselage had been damaged
and had to assume the slipstream at high speed would
aggravate matters. I eased the speed further, down to
three hundred knots, and climbed to three thousand
feet, giving myself a little more room for maneuver in
emergency. I also needed height to obtain an accurate
bearing to *Wanderer*. Slowly the compass indicator settled on 350 degrees. I altered course accordingly and
pressed the transmit button.

"Paul."

A pause. Then, audibly terse, "I am here."

"Stand by. Don't answer." The less chance anyone
had of locating his position the better. Mine they must
already know.

I flew on, hoping the slowness and altitude would persuade the Sixth Fleet pilots that I was not hostile. The
fuel would last longer too. The gauge showed 450
pounds. For the final time I recalculated, as the ocean
slipped placidly by beneath, the flight deceptively calm
after the wave-top chase. The figures I came up with
showed that instead of six I had eight and a half minutes' fuel left and that the boat was roughly five minutes
away. Five endless minutes of being an unmissable target. So this was what it felt like to be a coconut on a
fairground stall.

You have to keep a sense of humor, but mine was as
cramped as my muscles. I began rehearsing the actions
for ejecting, touching the handles and lowering the seat.
Ditching was not advisable. The Sabre's great air-intake
would suck in water like a drain and she'd go straight
down. That was what the notes said and I wasn't interested in proving them wrong. Besides, the aircraft
still had a role after I'd left her. If we survived to play it.

With twelve miles to *Wanderer* the radio compass was
steady. I peered into the haze hanging over the sea, saw
not a single ship, and automatically scanned the sky.

High ahead white vapor trails curved in the blue. A
pair of them, each pluming back behind a tiny arrow-

head. These contrails continued to circle until they were
coming my way, then petered out. I knew what that
meant. The arrows were jet fighters and the tell-tale
condensation had ceased because they were descending
fast. It made little difference whether they were MiGs or
Tomcats. If their pilots were doing as I would have done
they'd be lined up to shoot me down long before I
reached the boat. Paul was just going to have to find me
instead of my finding him.

Without altering the power setting I pushed the nose
gently forward, letting down to one thousand feet, leveled the Sabre again and methodically adjusted the trim
so she would fly hands-off. While she settled I trans-
mitted a final call.

"Now, Paul. Start looking."

I checked the time and grasped the handgrips in the
front of the seat armrests, hesitating deliberately. The
Sabre was continuing straight and level without any help
from me. I was low enough not to be dangling on the
parachute when my pursuers came by. I counted on
their not noticing a khaki parachute in the sea when
their attention was concentrated on pursuing a plane.
Now came the moment Micallef had tried to sabotage. I
took a deep breath, lowered my head and firmly pulled
up the right handgrip. If it failed to function my left
hand was clutching a second chance. It did not fail.

The canopy blew off, opening the cockpit to a whirl-
wind of slipstream and noise. The harness yanked tight,
locking me upright in the seat. I tucked in my chin,
hooked my heels back into the footrests and squeezed
the trigger in the handgrip. The world exploded under
me. Then I must have blacked out because the next
thing I knew I was still in the seat and falling toward the
sea at an alarming rate.

I kicked away, thrusting violently with my arms, and
pitched forward out of the seat. A moment later I felt a
tugging at my shoulders, there was a cracking noise as
the parachute opened and I found myself swinging

below it like a puppet. I looked up to make sure the lines weren't tangled, then glanced around. The Sabre was gently climbing away in the distance, wings still level. I looked down, realized I couldn't estimate my height above the water and felt for the catches to unclip the survival pack strapped to my backside. It detached and hung below me on its lanyard, hitting the sea a second before I splashed in myself, having completely misjudged when to bang open the release box of the harness. Inevitably the parachute subsided on top of me.

In a water jump the parachute that has saved a man can almost as easily drown him afterward. I tore off my oxygen mask, took a deep breath of what air there was beneath the smothering nylon, managed to turn the harness release and force it against my stomach so that it opened, and floundered clear, feeling pretty stupid. But at least I hadn't lost the bright orange survival pack, which was bobbing a wave away, and I hauled it toward me by the lanyard, giving a strong tug to open it. The liferaft inside would inflate automatically.

As the raft ballooned into shape, a wail like a banshee split the air and a pair of Tomcats thundered overhead, one slightly behind the other. A gout of flame belched behind the leader's wing. For a fraction of a second the missile he had fired was visible, dropping slightly before it accelerated ahead of the plane. Then both aircraft vanished over my limited horizon, leaving a swooshing roar in my ears. With an effort I twisted my wrist and checked the time. I had started baling out at 14:55. It was now 14:57. I could scarcely believe so much had happened in two minutes, then I realized the shock of ejection had knocked half the sense out of me. What the hell was I doing floating in my Mae West, sodden, already feeling chilled, when I could be in the dinghy?

A couple more minutes and I was squatting in its confined, but welcome space, feeling the warmth of the sun and making sure the device that would guide Paul to this pinpoint in the ocean was working.

The "Search and Rescue Beacon," or SARBE, was part of the survival gear. It bleated out a signal on 243 MHz UHF, which Paul could pick up with the homing receiver I had given him, assuming he was not more than twenty miles away. I was certain that by hanging on in the Sabre I had come within five or six miles. Provided he hadn't seen the plane shot down by the Tomcat's missile, and assumed I was beyond saving, he ought to be here in a quarter of an hour. All he had to do was steer *Wanderer* so that the two needles on the dial, one indicating "left" and the other "right," were aligned. Equally, all anyone else equipped with SARBE had to do was the same, whether it was a helicopter from the Sixth Fleet, or one of Qaddafi's patrol craft, if they were searching, that was. I hoped to God that Paul reached me first.

The dinghy rocked on the waves, the sun beat down and my flying suit began to dry. The silence seemed intense. With difficulty I rolled the parachute into a tight bundle and threw it overboard, followed by the bonedome, remembering that I should have chucked the helmet into the water as I descended on the chute to help judge my height over the sea. No matter. I was here. I had no regrets for the bonedome either, though I was sorry to lose my old RAF flight bag, with its worn leather straps, which I had left in the plane, stuffed with Hawker's passport and other papers and the aircraft documents. The bag he always used had to be available, just in case anyone took the trouble to search five hundred meters below on the sea bed for the Sabre's wreckage. "Jesus," I thought, "I've succeeded." The mission was over, bar the shouting, and the Islamic bomb hadn't blown up either Tripoli or me, though it would certainly be unusable after the fire. Suddenly the relief of tension and the motion of the dinghy combined and I found myself retching uncontrollably over the side.

The distant throbbing of diesel engines sounded somewhere out of sight to the north. I sat as upright as the squashiness of the liferaft permitted, shaded my eyes and scanned the wavetops. I doubted if I could see half a mile. The noise increased. I thought the boat was passing to the west until a shape appeared, the outline of a superstructure. For a few seconds panic seized me. It was the bridge of a patrol craft. Then I began to laugh, semihysterically. My low-down perspective was distorting the steering shelter of the *Wanderer*, as well as her size. She approached. I waved when I could distinguish Paul's face in the cabin. The engines churned water as she slowed. I prepared to stand up and make a grab for the rail as her stern slid by: and found myself staring up at Susie.

Everybody experiences moments that freeze in the memory as immutably as photographic images. This was one. Susie was standing in the stern, in a spray-splashed pink shirt and jeans, her hair blowing in the breeze, her left hand resting on the rail. But she didn't reach out to help me and in her right hand she had a gun.

→ TWELVE

"WHAT THE HELL . . ." I began, coming out of the sea-sick daze with a jolt. Why was Susie here and why with a gun?

"Did you do it?" She looked down at me, tense and inquiring. "Did you do the job?" I could only just hear her above the rumble of the diesels. Presumably she didn't want Paul listening.

The raft lurched in the swell, then rubbed up against *Wanderer's* side just as I began to realize what Susie meant. I clutched at the coping, gaining a fingerhold, straining to keep alongside so that I could make a jump for it.

"Help me up, damn you."

"Get back." The gun was pointed straight at me and there was a determination in her face such as I had never seen before. "Did you make the attack? I have to know."

The raft was caught by a wave, I lost my grip and fell back.

"Yes," I yelled, trying to stand up again. "Not that

267

it's your bloody business." But I knew that it must be,
and to a serious extent. "My bomb went off, theirs
didn't." This was no place or time for scientific explanations. I wasn't even one hundred percent sure she
would have heard a nuclear explosion at this distance.
"The Boeing's destroyed," I shouted at her. "Now for
Christ's sake let me on board. Or are you waiting for the
Libyans to arrive?"

She hesitated, then called to Paul, whose head I could
just see through the steering-shelter window.

Paul emerged like lightning, and his sorrowful expression told me everything. All he had known was that I
was paying him to rescue me if a flight I was making
went wrong. She must have told him she knew he was
picking me up: conned him completely. He produced a
short stepladder, hooked it in place over the stern and I
scrambled aboard, keeping a firm hold on the liferaft's
lanyard. The way things were going I might not have
finished with it yet. As for Susie, she stood back and
watched, clearly reserving her position. Whatever her
reasons, and I was making some rapid guesses, she intended to stay in control, though she wasn't going to
find it easy in this confined space, not least because a
sizeable swordfish was already occupying half the cockpit.

"Let's go, Paul," I ordered, deliberately challenging
her, and hauling the raft up over the side.

"Leave that," Susie countered sharply.

"I don't know what this is about, sweetheart," I said
crisply, feeling on more level terms now that I was
aboard. "Or what the popgun's for. But ditching the
raft is a bloody stupid idea. Some busybody upstairs
will spot it and wonder who rescued the occupant." I
began letting the gas out, gathering the fabric in my
arms to speed the process, and prepared to take it forward.

The way *Wanderer* was constructed divided the hull
into four parts. There was the cockpit with its fighting

chair, then the solid steering shelter with a couple of other seats and, more important, the helmsman's station to the left of the low doorway through to the main cabin, beyond which again there was a small bunk area in the bow.

The helmsman's high, black leather upholstered chair was duplicated by another on the right of the companionway. This was where Susie retreated to. So she had Paul covered as he sat holding the steering wheel and manipulating the pair of polished chrome throttle handles, though it would be difficult for her to see what was going on forward without giving him a chance to seize her. Not that he seemed inclined to. He was as mesmerized as a rabbit by a stoat.

"You can take us back," Susie conceded, and he gratefully thrust the two levers to full ahead. *Wanderer* surged up in the water, spray flying.

"I'm going forward," I announced, clasping the rolled-up liferaft in front of me and moving to stoop through the doorway.

Susie held herself back and she didn't try to stop me. I had a feeling that now she had let me on board if the gun did go off, it would be by accident. However, the most pressing need was to get out of my flying gear. There may be parts of the world where sporting fishermen wear G-suits, but I suspected the Mediterranean wasn't one of them.

My own clothes were in a grip in one of the cabin lockers. I stripped off completely, dried myself, dressed in a check shirt, slacks and canvas shoes, rolled up Hall's clothes round a lead weight and tied them with string. The detonator and the miniaturized radio receiver I kept, consigning them to the bag. Even more than before, those two items must hold the clue to what the devil was going on. Then I stuffed the liferaft in the locker and prepared to dispose of the last earthly possessions of Hawker Hall.

"I'm coming through," I called out, maintaining a

pretense of calm and walking past her to the stern.

"Stop!" she demanded, the gun steady in her hand.
"What is that?"

"A present for Neptune. Flying clothes." I lobbed
them overboard, challenging her to fire. She didn't. I
asked, "Would you want those to be found if we were
stopped?"

She looked at me, almost as if I were a stranger.
"No," she said, after a pause.

I sat down. I was immensely tired. Yet a new surge of
energy swept through me as the realization sank in that I
had bloody well done it: fulfilled the mission, earned the
money, dumped Hawker Hall forever and been safely
picked up. All I had to do now was catch the package-
tour flight back to London, Tom Lloyd returning from
his vacation, trundling in the line with the others. I did
not intend to let Susie get in the way. Nor anyone else.

"When did you catch the fish?" I asked to change the
subject, noticing with approval that the tackle was all
set up, one rod in a holder and line suspended from an
outrigger.

"Paul got it," Susie said, not lowering the gun.

"Thanks, Paul," I called out. I had to restore his
loyalty. During the whole episode so far he had not said
a word, simply held *Wanderer* steady by the compass
mounted in front of him as we charged through the
water.

"I was lucky, sir," he said, without looking around.
"One of the night boats brought the fish in and I bought
it."

"Great stuff. You deserve a drink." I wanted reasons
for moving around too.

"No thank you, sir."

"Well, I could use a beer. Anything for you, sweetheart?" I deliberately used the word to annoy her, but it
had no visible effect.

"I'll have a Coke," she said stolidly. "You may fetch
it."

I brought the drinks and settled myself on a seat. "Tell me," I asked, "did Arain think I would fail to honor the contract?"

She gave me a sideways glance. "It would have been less dangerous to take the money and run."

"Except that I'm not that kind."

She said nothing and I gulped down a mouthful of the cold beer gratefully, then sipped more slowly as I digested what she had effectively admitted. I thought back to May and how she had rung out of the blue about Arain's advertisement. Then when at her urging I accepted the "job," she had reentered my life. I allowed the conclusion to jump to itself.

"Why recommend me to Arain if you didn't trust me?"

"I knew you were a good pilot and spoke enough Arabic."

"And don't like Arabs much?"

"And needed money."

I felt myself flush with anger. The bitch had encouraged me to fall in love with her a second time, after breaking it all off earlier. Up to fifteen minutes ago I had wanted to marry her, had planned to ask her the moment we were both back in London. I felt completely betrayed. Worse still, if she turned on the warm tap now I'd probably be hooked again. She had that effect. She probably always would.

"Do you recommend all your boyfriends as mercenaries?" I asked, and then the inevitable jealous question burst out. "What the hell's your relationship with Arain anyway?"

A curiously secretive smile flickered over her face, withdrawn and inward-looking, yet self-confident. "I used to work for him once. He got in touch and asked if I knew anyone suitable. He knew I'd been with Gulf Air."

"And then he asked you to see the project through?"

The last four months suddenly made sense: the way

she used to turn up unannounced, then disappear again, her getting leave to come on the Malta holiday. Throughout she had angled me into making the suggestions. If I had been less bitter I might have appreciated the irony of having tried to conceal what I was doing from her, when in fact she had been my minder.

"I like you, Tom," she said, reading my thoughts, not that it would have been difficult. "Very much. But other things matter more."

"Like letting Micallef burgle the flat?"

"That was a mistake," she said tightly.

"I'm surprised you didn't bring him along today. We could have had a party."

I meant it as a jibe, but the way her jaw set I guessed I might have accidentally hit the truth.

"I suppose he failed to turn up." The implications were chilling. Micallef would have shot me in the raft, dumped Paul overboard and a day later the boat would have been found drifting. Yet I could not believe Susie would have gone along with that. She might be good bait for oversexed aircrew, but she was no kind of professional killer. Somewhere along the line Arain's plan had gone wrong, at least if he had wanted me dead after the mission.

"You bloody well did make a mistake with Micallef," I said, taunting her further. "He was at the airfield to see me off this morning." I deliberately didn't mention the bomb planted in the Sabre.

"I can manage," she snapped, glaring at me. "Joe will be there when we get back. He wasn't meant to come on the boat."

I was just revising my estimate of her capabilities when Paul interrupted us.

"Sir." He pointed excitedly to his left. "Another ship."

I moved up to stand beside him in the steering shelter, noticing Susie's gun follow me around. Some three miles off, a dark outline was going like the clappers and heading to cut across our path. I looked over Paul's shoulder. We were making twenty-eight knots ourselves.

"Keep going," I told him. "Stay on course. It may not mean anything." I turned to Susie, possibilities crystallizing in my mind. "If we are stopped, you'd better put that toy away."

"When I'm ready."

"You'd look more convincing sunbathing in the stern."

She huddled herself stubbornly against the window, but there was deep apprehension in her eyes. This was the moment when, in more normal circumstances, a man would start making soothing noises of the "it's all right, darling" kind: in practice it was time to put on the pressure. I took Paul's old and treasured binoculars and studied the other ship, which was rapidly overhauling us.

The ship had a sharply raked bow, a long gray hull and a relatively small, high superstructure with a round-topped gun-turret in front. I watched until a number painted on the superstructure became readable, "4" and above it a name, written in Arabic, which I could not yet decipher. The number was enough. I'd done my homework for this mission during lonely evenings in motels and the Sloane Avenue apartment. This was one of the Combattante fast-missile craft built for Qaddafi by the French.

"Was the first one that stopped you number four?" I asked Paul.

"I'm sorry, sir. Yes." To his credit he was completely steady.

"Listen, sweetheart," I said with deliberate savagery. "How would you like a few years as Qaddafi's guest? Shall I introduce you?"

She paled, but did not move, though she must have known she would have to. Tight-fitting jeans are no place to hide a gun.

"I'm throwing the homer overboard," I announced. The SARBE was still perched in front of Paul, alongside the compass. Perhaps foolishly, I had hoped to return it to its owner. Disregarding Susie, I picked it up and pitched it over the side away from the Libyans.

As I returned a fountain of water erupted ahead and the crump of a shell exploding deafened us. A ribbon of smoke was trailing from the patrol craft's gun.

"Get in the cabin, you idiot," I yelled at Susie.

For a second she remained defiant, then realized she was losing her options. She stood up and began descending the short stairway backward, keeping the gun pointed at my guts. I had to admire her refusal to panic, though she had left retreat too late.

At last Paul took the initiative. Not that he had much choice either, given the warning shot. He yanked the throttles closed. Deprived of power, *Wanderer* slumped in the water pitching violently. Susie lost her balance, and as she tried to save herself I slammed a fist into her stomach. She slumped through the opening, striking her head on the top, and I piled after her. It wasn't gentlemanly, but it was effective.

"It's for your own good, sweetheart," I muttered, taking the gun and lifting her onto a bunk. Then I straightened up and looked through the porthole. The Libyan missile boat was very close.

"Paul," I shouted. "Talk to them."

Susie was moaning and clasping her hands to her stomach, though I doubted if she was anything worse than winded.

"Stay ill," I ordered. "Stay ill until they've gone."

"You're a bastard," she managed to say, not looking at me, still half doubled up.

"Too many people have been trying to get rid of me," I said, picking up a couple of cushions. "Here," I stuffed them beneath her head. "Now listen. If you want a trip to Libya, get up and start talking. If you don't, leave things to me."

She obeyed, which was something, and I began to think seriously about hiding the gun. Since she was conscious, the cabin was a nonstarter. So was the forward compartment. Hurt or not, the moment I was aft she would be in there like a hooker after folding money.

I glanced through a porthole. The patrol craft was much closer now. I darted up to the steering shelter. It was too late to throw anything overboard. Anyway I might have use for a weapon if Micallef was waiting on shore. I looked around. There was no safe hiding place, except maybe under the seat cushions, and to hide the gun there would be like playing grandmother's footsteps with a wolf, if the Libyans made any kind of search at all.

The fish lying in the stern caught my eye, its long-bladed bill wicked even in death, and beneath that bill the equally vicious teeth in its great mouth were just visible.

Officers and gentlemen always carry handkerchiefs. A plastic bag would have been better, but a handkerchief would serve. Twenty seconds later the gun, wrapped in a square foot of patterned linen, was resident inside the fish. I cut the back of my hand slightly on the teeth and I had to hope our visitors wouldn't throw the monster overboard for being in the way. I lugged it as close to the side as possible. When I straightened up the ship was less than fifty yards off.

You could acquire a serious inferiority complex gazing up at a warship from a cabin cruiser. Technically the *Waheeg*, whose name I now recognized, might be a patrol boat. Physically she was the size of a corvette, all of one hundred fifty feet long, and her steel side rose like a wall above *Wanderer*. An Arab officer in white uniform and peaked hat gazed arrogantly down at us from the deck, raising a megaphone to be heard above the rumble of his own engines.

"What are you doing here?" he demanded. "You were ordered to leave this area."

In his own terms this was approximately correct. Since turning back in the morning Paul had gone north for thirty minutes, hung around, come south again for a quarter of an hour to pick me up and then sailed north again for twenty minutes. So *Wanderer* was still roughly fifty miles from home, even though she was definitely not in Libyan waters and there was no shred of justification for firing a shot across our bows.

"Going to Malta," Paul shouted.

"I am searching your boat," the officer announced. He motioned to some crew members, a rope ladder was let down and a couple of minutes later he was standing in the stern, while three Libyan sailors with submachine-guns kept us covered.

Sharing the cockpit with the dead swordfish cut the officer down to size a little. He might be arrogant, but he was no taller than Paul and several inches shorter than me. I decided to lay into him verbally and hoped he wouldn't take it out on the fish.

"We are in international waters," I said coldly. "You have fired on us without provocation. You are in breach of all international law. We shall report this to the Malta government."

He spat on the deck, murmured "Maltese scum" in Arabic, and disregarded what I had said.

"Tell your men to clean that up," I stormed at him. "What kind of officer are you?"

Usually people who behave like that are cowards and I had a trick up my sleeve, which I was tolerably certain would work, or ought to on an Arab employed by a leader with Qaddafi's religious regard for purity.

"You were not on this boat before," he said accusingly.

"When you illegally stopped us? I was asleep forward." I nudged the fish with my toe. "This one fought like hell. I decided to rest."

"Where?"

I pointed through the main cabin and prepared to

play the trick. "There is a bunk in the bow."

The officer felt for his revolver, pulled it from its holster, and moved toward the doorway beyond which Susie lay.

"Stop!" I ordered. "My wife is in there. She is sick."

He swung around, uncertainty on his dark face.

"If you disturb my wife in her quarters," I said, spelling out the bluff very slowly and distinctly, "my friends in the Malta government will personally inform your leader." I turned to Paul and said loudly, "He has already called the Maltese 'scum.' You are the witness to this."

"You understand Arabic?" There was apprehension in the query.

"I have also read the Koran. That is why I respect the Prophet's guidance concerning women."

He grunted agreement. As a good Muslim he had no alternative, and by definition he must be a good Muslim or he'd be out of a job in Libya. The Koran states that women are fields into which men should go as they please, but the corollary is that wives are entitled to protection and honor, especially in illness, which was why I had preferred to have Susie feigning sick rather than on her feet and provoking the sort of lascivious thoughts the Prophet emphatically condemned. The illness of a wife had to be respected.

The officer began getting himself off the hook by examining the radar. "Why do you have this?"

"Our coast is rocky and dangerous," Paul said unexpectedly. "Many fishing boats have such equipment." The intervention was unnecessary. The officer wasted a few more minutes scrutinizing *Wanderer's* fittings, then turned to Paul.

"You may continue to Malta." He shot a glance at me. "Have you seen aircraft today?"

I pretended to consider. "We heard some about an hour ago. We didn't see any, did we Paul?"

Paul shook his head. "People should leave our sea in

peace," he remarked, making it clear to whom he was referring.

After that exchange the officer left us, the missile craft thundered off, and we continued toward Marsax-lokk.

"How's the fuel, Paul?" I asked, reverting as always to worries about time and distance, and recovering the gun from its smelly hiding place.

"I put the extra in, sir."

So we had range to play with. Had we time?

By now, if the mission had not been delayed, we would have been back in Malta. As it was, we could not dock before six. The tour bus, collecting passengers for the airport, was due at the hotel at ten. The hire car was in Gozo. Some aspect of my plan would have to be scrapped: especially if Susie's threat about Micallef was correct. She had certainly screwed things up.

There was no point recriminating with Paul. I could imagine how easily she had duped him. I touched his shoulder.

"It's not your fault, old man," I said kindly. "Blame me. But if necessary, we'll have to dump her."

"Yes, sir." The mournful tone in which he agreed suggested that in the future he would stay with inshore fishing, and not for mermaids either. Women always have spelt trouble for mariners. Possibly he would brighten up when he got his bonus.

I went through into the cabin and checked on the cause of our discomfiture. Susie sat up and rubbed the back of her head gingerly.

"Still alive?" I asked, knowing how she felt and feeling little sympathy. If you employ thugs to knock other people around you can hardly complain when the game reaches home base.

"You're even more of a bastard than I thought," she said very slowly, as if she couldn't believe the fact.

"Have a wash," I suggested. "You'll feel better."

I opened the toilet door, ran a generous amount of

Wanderer's fresh water supply into the sink, then helped her across. She flinched at first, but accepted the assistance.

"Leave the door open," I ordered. I didn't want any damn fool tricks until she had done some explaining.

She splashed her face and demanded her bag. Suddenly it occurred to me that she might have a second weapon in it. Susie's bags were large and one hundred percent for carrying junk. I picked it up and ferreted inside, then handed her the makeup wallet. She scowled, but took it. After a few minutes she was, if not her usual self, at least presentable and comparatively composed.

"Where did the Libyans go?" she asked.

"Away." The question was no longer relevant.

"I suppose I should thank you for that." She sounded about as grateful as a scab being let through a picket line. Some people take a lot for granted.

"Why bother?" I said. "I don't like Libyans either. Now, how about a few explanations?"

"They're out of stock, Tom. I'm sorry." She sat down firmly on the bunk, giving every indication of intending to remain silent.

As a way of provoking her I went through the rest of her bag's contents and found her passport, a scarf, various papers, and a small black VHF radio transceiver of the kind police forces use, which I noticed was of a high-powered variety.

She stayed silent as I fiddled with the set, two and two adding up in my mind with disturbing speed.

"Paul," I called out, moving to show him the transceiver. "Did she use this at any time?"

He twisted around in the high seat to look. "Yes. She took it in the stern, but I cannot hear what she was saying."

"When? On the way out?"

His sunburnt forehead furrowed. "No," he said. "Much later. Before we start to look for you."

"How long before?" I found myself trembling, almost preferring not to pursue this investigation if it was going to lead where I feared.

"Five, ten minutes, sir. About the time you tell me to stand by."

To my mind that was conclusive. I took a grip on myself and prepared for an experiment that ought to jolt the truth out of Susie. I went back into the cabin and fetched the miniaturized radio receiver that had been part of the bomb, recovered the detonator from my grip and carefully reattached the wires that had joined them together before. Then I took the assembled device out to the cockpit and positioned it on the decking alongside the fish, filled a canvas bucket from the sea against emergencies, and returned to Susie.

"You called me on this, didn't you?" I said, holding her own radio in front of her. "Don't deny it."

"I wanted to know what you were doing." She glanced apprehensively toward Paul. "That you had carried it through, I mean." Her composure wasn't lasting well.

"Come off it, sweetheart. Why didn't you use *Wanderer's* radio?" My anger was beginning to show.

"I was told you wouldn't be able to hear that one. Mine was set on a frequency you'd be listening to all the time."

"Then come and see what was intended to happen when you used it." If my hunch was wrong, I was going to look a fool, but that would be a small price to pay. I took Susie by the arm and propelled her up the step into the steering shelter.

"Now," I ordered. "Send a message on your radio."

As she pressed the transmit, before she could even speak, the whole device lying in the cockpit jumped in the air, a puff of smoke billowed up and the sharp crack of the detonator firing sounded in our ears.

Paul swung around from the controls in alarm.

"Nothing to worry about," I assured him, and turned on Susie. "I wasn't meant to survive, was I?"

"That's not true, Tom," she protested. "No. No. No!"

I pushed her through into the cabin again and let fly. "You knew damn well you'd be blowing up my plane."

"No!" She was swaying slightly, though whether from shock or from *Wanderer's* hammering through the water I couldn't be sure.

"Where did you get the radio?"

"Joe Micallef gave it to me." She stifled what sounded like a sob, but I didn't believe in it.

"And the gun?"

"He gave me that too, for self-defense."

If all this was true it meant Micallef had definitely planted the bomb on the Sabre, presumably because he had discovered the wedge was missing at Duxford. I was beginning to think Susie wasn't lying, because there were real tears in her eyes.

"Listen," I said, taking her by the shoulders. "Was it Micallef or Arain who told you to come out on the boat?"

"Arain did. The trouble was he no longer trusted you."

"Which was why you were waiting with a gun?" The hell it had been for self-defense.

"I was to force you back to Malta if you had tricked us. You could have gone to Sicily easily." She blinked, wiped her eyes with the back of her hand and said more calmly. "If you must know, they didn't expect you to survive unless you welshed on us."

As a conversation stopper that was near perfect. She might just as well have directed me over a cliff in the dark on our honeymoon. I lapsed into speculation about how Micallef really fitted into the puzzle, not that I was in any doubt about part of his job having been to dispose of me.

"I thought you'd make it," she said suddenly. "I thought you were a good enough pilot to succeed. If you did get shot down, at least you'd known the risks beforehand. I can still hardly believe Arain wanted you dead."

"You've been had, sweetheart. Arain intended me to succeed and be killed. The bomb in my plane wasn't the first piece of sabotage."

"What do you mean?"

I told her about the wedge and how the ejector seat and canopy jettison device had been sabotaged and she seemed genuinely mystified.

"I'm certain Newland didn't do that," she replied at last. "It must have been Joe Micallef."

"Or his twin brother," I suggested sardonically.

"He never had a twin."

"You think he'll be waiting at Marsaxlokk when we get back?"

"I'm not so sure now," she admitted. "He said he would be."

"Does he know my real name?" If he did not, then settling my personal score with him was a secondary consideration, in fact not a consideration at all. My aim was to leave Malta as smoothly and as inconspicuously as I had entered. Nothing more. Revenge can be expensive, and anyway I've never had much taste for it.

"He might know."

"From breaking into the Fulham apartment?"

She shook her head. "Neither Arain nor Newland would have let him know more than he had to. He thought this boat was hired in Hall's name. But he did see me with you in the rented car in Valletta last week, quite by chance." She smiled fractionally. "As for the apartment, he was never there. Your coming back that day caught me by surprise and I gave the first description that came into my head."

"Stupid of me," I remarked caustically, though it shook me to realize she had been the thief. Quite a convincing piece of acting that had been. "I suppose you passed my post office box key to Arain?"

She refused to reply, and since this dialogue could

hardly last much longer I decided to probe Arain's real motives.

"Tell me," I asked. "What will Arain do now?"

"Nothing. Nothing at all. Once he has confirmation that you actually destroyed the Boeing, he'll leave you alone. He may be hard, but he's straight. The trouble was that he ceased trusting you."

There was no mistaking the sincerity in her voice, but for myself I was convinced Arain was about as straight as the proverbial corkscrew. The question was whether he would now be satisfied. I tried to sum up the situation from CONOIL's point of view.

Even if the Islamic bomb had not exploded, the heat of the fire would have damaged it enough for it to be highly dangerous to handle. Its career as a weapon was over. Nor could the Pakistanis simply make another: their resources of weapons-grade plutonium were too small.

So the company had gained itself a breathing space of a year or two. If the figures Arain had originally quoted were anything like correct, that alone was worth hundreds of millions of dollars. He ought to be satisfied. I didn't believe for a second that he was concerned about peace in the Middle East for its own sake. His interest was in the bottom line. Like mine. And I was content. My cash was in the bank: if I could get home to enjoy it. The fly in the ointment was Micallef. He had been ordered to put me out of the way and he would be a danger until Arain called him off, which was unlikely to happen today.

As for Susie's role, I could hardly believe why I had not seen the connections before. Pakistan, Sandspit weekends, her unnamed pilot boyfriend: all the fragments of the scenario that had emerged over lunch at Xlendi only a week ago, though it seemed like a year. She had been embarrassed. With reason.

When Susie, as Arain's associate, went to Pakistan, it could only have been to figure out which PIA plane was taking the Islamic bomb to Tripoli, and what better way than by having an affair with a PIA pilot. Air hostesses are always traveling, both on and off duty. She could have flown in any time without arousing suspicion. Did British Caledonian really operate charters to Pakistan? How else could Susie return to Malta unless she had in fact taken a complete two weeks leave?

I was so mind-blown by this line of reasoning that I sat for several minutes, my elbows on my knees, simply staring at her, while she stayed silent. The strange thing was that, though I had been forced to manhandle her, she still aroused me. I stifled the feeling and checked on our progress with the radar.

At a quarter to five a segment of the Maltese coast showed on the radar screen, between the twelve- and sixteen-mile circles.

"Paul," I asked quietly, "could you take me to Xlendi instead?" The last ferry from Gozo sailed at 7:20 P.M. I could just about make it, bring the car back, and avoid Marsaxlokk.

"Where do you want to go exactly, sir?"

To prevent Susie overhearing, I took the map and pointed at the outskirts of Sannat village where the car was at the Ta Cenc Hotel.

"There is a better place to land, sir." He indicated an even smaller creek. "From there you can walk in half an hour and will be there sooner."

"You can take her to Marsaxlokk?" I indicated Susie. "There could be delays with customs when you arrive if she's difficult."

Paul smiled. I reckoned he had as much desire to get his own back on her as I had. "Don't worry, sir."

"And then you could find her a taxi?"

"It will not be easy." He winked.

"Fine. Keep her at the harbor until nine."

Having wet my pants over the woman once too often, I was going to make damn certain she left Malta at my discretion, and that only if she cooperated.

I went down into the cabin, sat facing Susie, and gave the gun a careful examination. The short black stock bore the three arrows trademark of P. Beretta. I slipped the magazine out and counted fifteen rounds of 9 mm Parabellum ammunition, practiced arming and firing it, then slid the magazine back into place.

"What are you doing?" she challenged suddenly, as though coming out of a reverie.

"Securing our future." Covering her with the Beretta, I picked up her tote bag where I had deposited it on the floor by the toilet, extracted her passport and held it up. "You can have this back at the airport. If you play ball." I put it in my own bag, took out the package I had prepared for Paul, and moved toward the companionway. To my surprise, Susie blocked my path.

"What exactly do you mean by 'our future' and 'playing ball'?" she demanded.

"The next six hours. I want to get off the island and I imagine you do too. Unless you're keen to meet Micallef again?"

"So?" She was as wary as a cat.

"All you have to do is cope with him at Marsaxlokk. If he's there." I would bet a fortune that he would not be.

"Give me back the gun." She held out her hand. She certainly had a nerve.

I shook my head. "You're the sweet-talk specialist. Sweet talk him. Paul will make sure there are other people around and find you a taxi. Now get out of the way."

She retreated reluctantly and I gave Paul the package. It contained £500 Maltese in notes: a decent sum for a Maltese fisherman even in those days.

"Look after yourself," I told him. "If she gives you any trouble stay at sea until sunset and then take her back to Gozo. She'll have missed the last ferry by then." And she could make her own explanations about her lost passport to the British consul next day.

"Damn you!" Susie shouted.

I smiled at her. She always did look beautiful when she was annoyed. "Count your blessings," I said.

The inlet was guarded by yet another of the Knights of Malta's stone watchtowers, and as we slowed down to pass the headland I glimpsed the bulky white shape of the ferry passing Comino in the distance. It was ten minutes to six.

The beat of the diesels reverberated off the rock as we glided into quiet water. The inlet proved to be a cleft between two hills barely more than a quarter-mile long and was already mainly in shadow. At its extremity was a dilapidated quay, from which an earth road ran up a steep valley.

"You will find another track, to the left. It leads to Ta Cenc." Paul shook hands, clapped me on the shoulder in a totally unexpected avuncular gesture, and I jumped ashore. Susie remained sullen in the stern. I waved cheerfully. God knows what I had to be cheerful about, except having got this far. I was still racing against time: and possibly Micallef. Once he suspected I was alive he would be searching for me, not Susie.

The road twisted and I lost sight of *Wanderer* long before the echoing thump of the engines died away down the creek. A few hundred yards further on I appreciated what Paul had meant. A much better road was separated from this public track by a barrier. I swung my legs across the bar and set foot on the Ta Cenc private estate, dimly recalling plans for hundreds of villas here. Stopping and gazing toward the sea I noticed a couple of distant roofs. For all the magnificent view toward Malta, the development had evidently not progressed. The barren, treeless slopes were as primitive as they had been countless thousands of years ago when Neolithic man gouged out the cart tracks and built the burial mounds that the map indicated. As for present-day man, of him there was happily no sign.

I walked on, passing a large boundary stone on which

he initials "RTO" were daubed in white paint. Like the
Italians, the Maltese—and equally the Gozitans—were
crazy about shooting. Every field and hillside had its
hunting rights, marked by the abbreviation of the Italian word "*Risservato.*" Equally, anything that flew was
considered fair game, from a hawk to a sparrow. Maltese sportsmen exacted a bloody tribute from birds mi-
grating south in the autumn.

I had only gone another few yards when the bang of a
shotgun underlined the memory. I stopped. Another
discharge followed. Someone was hunting between me
and the hotel.

Ten minutes later I saw the man, gun over his shoulder, outlined against the western sky. He was absorbed
and took no notice of me. I continued until the low profile of the hotel came into sight. Ta Cenc had been designed not to intrude on the ancient landscape, though
trees had been planted around, and I had to halt to get
my bearings. When I had parked the car, well away
from the main building, I had noticed an old stone
windmill tower nearby. I searched for its stumpy shape,
realized the road I was on must sweep in a half-circle
around it to reach the hotel itself, and fifty yards away
recognized the low wall of the carpark. Sitting on the
wall with his back to me was a man in a white shirt: a
stocky, broad-shouldered man with thick hair.

I left the road and dropped flat beside a large rock.
The hunter's shotgun crashed out, much closer, and the
man turned his head. The profile confirmed the identity. It was Micallef. He must have tracked down my
car. The keys were with the hotel's hall porter. I could
visualize a way of reaching the building without being
seen, by working my way around by the swimming pool.
But how to reach the car unobserved after that?

The second barrel of the shotgun fired. A bird flew
squawking into the air. Micallef stood up, restively. He
must be bored with waiting. I felt for the Beretta. I had
never killed a man before and told myself there has to be

a first time. I assessed the distance. Micallef was way out of range. Could he be lured away from the carpark?

Beside me lay a sizeable stone. I cradled it in my hand, knelt and lobbed it toward Micallef. It fell a couple of yards short. He spun around, crossed the wall and came a few paces nearer. I lobbed another, then as he scanned the area, called his name softly, ''Joe.''

He stood stock still, searching, the dying sun catching his cheek.

''Joe,'' I repeated, staying close to my rock, the Beretta now in my right hand.

''Who is there?'' he called. A worried voice. He came nearer, his head and shoulders skylined, and what appeared to be a knife in his hand. Soon he must notice my crouching shape beside the rock and he was still twenty yards off. I knew that that was long range for a 9 mm pistol.

He advanced another few feet, very cautiously. The hunter's shotgun blasted and in the same instant I fired myself. He gasped and fell. I doubled across the stony ground and crouched again by his body. The hunter's second barrel echoed and I knew the sharper crack of my shot had been successfully lost.

Micallef lay on his back, his whole body writhing as he clasped his neck, blood spurting from between his fingers. He saw me and tried to speak, but only a gurgle emerged. Wishing to God I was a better shot I clubbed him with the pistol butt and his body went limp.

I looked around and listened. No footsteps sounded on the rocky soil. Water splashed distantly in the hotel pool. Only the figure of the hunter was moving further down the slope, intent on his sport.

My position was acutely dangerous, close to the hotel and within sight of the road. Micallef had to be finished off, though it meant I would never discover if he knew my name. All at once the whole meaning of killing had been brought home to me. I should have held the gun at his head, but that was so much like an execution that I couldn't do it. Instead I leveled the short barrel at his chest, where the shirt was already caked with blood, and waited for the hunter to fire again.

The delay seemed endless. A car ground slowly up a hill and I could not tell if it was on this road or the other. When the shot came I was so on edge that my hand jerked and I pressed the Beretta's trigger late. Micallef's body arched upward in a last spasm of life and then collapsed. I wiped the pistol all over with my shirt-tail, then using that grasped the gun, barrel first, and pressed the stock into his right hand, curling his fore-finger through the trigger. The deception would not have taken in a trained detective for thirty seconds, but it might throw a village-educated Gozitan policeman off the scent for a few hours.

I picked up the bag and Micallef's knife, walked as calmly as I could to the road and continued around toward the hotel. The car passed shortly afterward and as I stepped aside to avoid the dust I saw the figure of the hunter still progressing toward the sea, shotgun on his shoulder. I hid the knife beneath a rock and went on.

The entrance to Ta Cenc was as understated as the whole design, and scarcely indicated the luxury within. I paused in the driveway to make sure I was unmarked by dirt or blood, brushed dust off my trouser legs and went into the marble-floored reception area. The porter I had tipped for keeping an eye on the car was behind the counter.

"Come for your keys, sir," he said smoothly. "I hope you had a pleasant cruise."

"I did indeed. Any problems with the car?" Since I had not been a guest at the hotel, he was performing a favor.

"None at all." He beamed, and accepted the note I offered with an inclination of the head.

I thanked him politely and left.

Outside the day was fading. Micallef's body might not be found until tomorrow. The car itself was standing where I had parked it. I risked the time involved in checking the underside for booby traps, examined the engine compartment briefly and still felt a butterfly in my stomach as I turned the ignition key.

However, there was no explosion. Micallef must have intended to settle matters in person. I drove to the harbor by a side road through Xewkija, where the strings of lights that delineate the shape of the church's enormous dome were already illuminated, and reached the ferry with minutes to spare.

It was dark when I parked the car in the driveway to the Phoenicia's stately entrance, praying I did not appear as totally shattered as I felt. Worse, a fear that some part of my clothing must be spotted with blood obsessed me. During the uneventful drive through the dusk I had gone over what I had done many times and come to no very satisfactory conclusion, save that Micallef had not been waiting at Ta Cenc to offer his congratulations, and once the Libyans worked things out he would have been a dead duck anyway for having failed.

Whatever I looked like, the receptionist greeted me as blandly as ever. "I hope you enjoyed your stay in our other island, sir." He reached up to the pigeonhole for the room key and extracted a letter as well. "This came while you were away, sir. May I suggest we bring your bags down immediately. The tour bus is arriving early."

I paid for the car rental and tore open the envelope in the lift. To my astonishment the letter inside was from Susie. It was dated August twenty-seventh, last Monday, and posted in London.

"Sweetheart," it read, in her rounded writing, "please don't ring when you get back. The vacation was beautiful, but we just aren't made for each other. So please don't." She had added her usual scrawling signature, a single kiss in a circle, and the words "Take care."

It was the pay-off I had half-expected a week ago:

presumably sent before Arain had ordered a change in her plans.

I folded the letter in my shirt pocket and walked briskly from the elevator to my room, half-expecting her to be there. She was not.

The room appeared to be as I had left it. I checked the suitcase lock. No one had tampered with that. I washed hastily, discovering the trousers I had on were not as dirty as they might have been, and changed into gray flannels and a blazer. Then I repacked and carried the case downstairs myself.

The bus arrived at nine-thirty, the tour leader fussing in exactly the same upstage way as before.

"Your wife did not return, Mr. Lloyd? What a pity. You missed so many nice excursions."

"She is here, but just now she's visiting some friends," I managed to cut in. "She should join us at the airport."

The woman gave me a look that plainly expressed her disapproval of this freebooting attitude, and we climbed on to the yellow bus to be greeted by a chorus of ribald comments.

I grinned, waved and settled into my seat. My fellow tourists had evidently fortified themselves in advance for the flight. If they were half bombed at the airport, so much the better, they could attract as much attention as they liked at my expense: all I needed was to be one of them until they disembarked, bleary-eyed and staggering, in the early hours of tomorrow morning.

The charter flight had one other colossal advantage: it would not be overbooked. I allowed myself to be overtaken in the check-in line and hung around the end, waiting.

Susie eventually debouched from a battered Volkswagen when only half a dozen other passengers separated me from the desk. She launched into a magnificent display of excited feminine concern.

"Darling," she exclaimed, kissing me quickly. "I'm

so sorry I'm late. I simply couldn't find a taxi. Have you got the tickets?'' She tugged at my arm. "Where are they?''

"No need to worry, sweetheart. They're all with the courier.''

They were too. The woman had scooped both them and our passports off everybody in the bus, probably concluding that some of her charges were too drunk not to lose them, and we were being marshalled through as a group.

"But my passport, I must have my passport.''

"Don't worry,'' I reiterated, speculating on why she was so anxious. "We'll get the passports back when we're through.''

She gave me one of those looks that proverbially turn people to stone, or worse, then made a despairing gesture toward the driver of the VW, who was still waiting. He drove away. Whatever she had cooked up since Paul put her ashore was off the menu, but I couldn't help wondering if she would have a final trick to play when we reached London.

During the flight the more rowdy passengers sang songs, we ate a plastic-tasting snack, and Susie barely spoke a word. She seemed entirely preoccupied, or more likely what she wanted to say was unfit for public consumption. However, approaching the final hurdle of immigration control at Gatwick, she clung to me as devotedly as any lover, and I did not discourage her. We were, after all, still each other's alibis.

The young blue-uniformed officer glanced at my passport and smiled in a friendly way: quite an achievement at four on a Sunday morning.

"Busman's holiday?'' he remarked.

"You could call it that.'' I grinned back, feeling a moment of real elation as he let us through.

The elation didn't last. Susie's warmth evaporated noticeably the moment we were through customs, and tiredness began to overwhelm me.

"D'you want to stick with the tour to the end?" I asked. There was a bus organized into London.

"Not unless we have to." She shrugged her shoulders. "You take the bus if you like."

By a miracle I found a taxi. As we settled into it the driver turned around.

"Like a paper, guv?" He passed it through and switched on the interior light. The newspaper was the early edition of a Sunday tabloid and it brought me around faster than any pick-me-up

"QADDAFI BATTLES SIXTH FLEET" was the front-page headline, and I spread it out for Susie to read as well. Altogether seven Libyan planes had been shot down, Qaddafi himself claiming to have sunk an American destroyer and accusing the Americans of a suicide raid on Tripoli, not to mention that agents of U.S. imperialism had tried yet again to assassinate him.

At the bottom was a five-line item headed "BRITISH PILOT MISSING."

"Record-breaking British ace James 'Hawker' Hall was reported in distress over the Mediterranean yesterday afternoon as conflict raged between Libya and the Sixth Fleet. An American spokesman said efforts to search for his ditched jet were hampered by Libyan attacks. Hall, thirty-four, is unmarried and comes from Duxford, Cambs."

"Satisfied?" I asked.

Susie glanced at me. "I still had things to do in Malta." The yellow motorway lighting gave her complexion a ghoulish pallor. She looked resentful.

"Like settling with Micallef?" I suggested. "That's been done."

"What do you mean?"

"I happened to meet him."

She seemed to relax. "You're a surprising man, Tom."

"You think I ought to tell Arain?" I put the question more out of curiosity than serious intent, but she did not reply.

When the cab reached London my resolution faltered and I asked where she was going. There would never be anyone else like Susie. In spite of everything I did not want to lose her.

"Drop me at South Ken," she said in her everyday, competent voice.

However, when the cab stopped outside the underground station she leaned across and kissed me quite tenderly.

"Goodbye, sweetheart," she said. "I have a soft spot for you too. And don't waste your money ringing Arain. He won't be there."

"What do you mean?"

"He left his apartment. Newland won't be around either. No one will." She began to get out of the cab.

"Hey!" I caught her arm, suddenly aware of what she was saying. "But CONOIL . . ."

"They have no connection with CONOIL. They never did." She gently pried away my fingers. "That's why they always met you away from an office. Anyway, 'Arain's' not his name. We call him 'Aaron' and even that's a cover."

"Susie!" I tried to pursue her out of the cab, no longer giving a damn for my self-respect. "Will you be at Gatwick?"

She stood on the pavement, the first light of dawn challenging the streetlamps. "I left British Caledonian two weeks ago. Anyway, I'm not Susie. My real name might have been unacceptable in the Gulf. I'm sorry, sweetheart, you were the only one in the whole operation who really existed."

She blew me a kiss and walked away. I didn't see much point in following.